Mood Reader

A Genre Sampler Anthology

Stories submitted to Hale Patton Publishing, edited by Persephone Jayne, Amanda Fernandes, B.A. McRae, Carmilla Voiez, Elizabeth Willsea, and Sonya Lawson.

With an introduction by Persephone Jayne of Hale Patton Publishing.

ISBN: 9781950460182 (eBook)
ISBN: 9781950460199 (paperback)

For all our fellow Mood Readers:
We understood the assignment.

love you C.

xoxo

M.W.

Contents

Introduction By Persephone Jayne

Amidst the 2nd year of a global panini... I turned 42. Yes! That cosmic age where all the secrets of the Universe are revealed. I got this wild idea of producing an anthology of 42 stories, see what I did there? But the catch was I'd only accept works from my tiktok author family. Because, I had found my book family and they were amazing!

I was off and running. I posted about my idea and started accepting submissions.

Then someone pointed out that it might be hard to market a book with no clear genre linking us all together. Well, much how we fight the algorithm and don't let TikTok niche us, I said, Universally speaking, you can't pigeon hole me!

So I leaned into it and our Genre Sampler Anthology fell into place as if we had planned it that way all along. Of course we had ;)

The authors in these pages have helped in EVERY aspect of this production. Without them, well, Mood Reader would never have seen the light of day.

It is this "group project" vibe, this collaboration of the minds, that keeps our book affordable. I'm not producing this to "get rich" or make money off my friends hard work.

I'm producing this book to celebrate the amazing writers I have met in my 42nd trip around the sun.

Thanks to them Mood Reader is a real thing.

And thanks to you, dear mood reader, for picking up our anthology and giving it a try.

mood reader

Sci-fi / Fantasy

The Human Files

By Jiya Kaye *(CONTENT WARNING: blood, fighting, violence)*

> *Cyrox, The Human Files,*
> Interaction with a Human, Rule 3
> Humans are a warrior race. They abide by the policy of "Shoot first, ask questions later". They are known to fight anything and everything – even themselves. For interaction with this race, it is recommended to lift both your hands. It is said that this gesture shows that we, the Ammoths, are unthreatening. However, since the humans perceive everything other than themselves a threat, it is highly recommended that every Ammoth interacting with the Human race engage with the utmost caution.

Ondith looked up from the copy of *The Human Files* on his tab. He saw the humans: Kiara Varma, Arno Kanumba, Vasya Pavlovich, and Ammoth Hiran sitting at his table. Human Pablo Hernandez was in the medical bay tending to the injured from their last mission.

He had to remind himself that their names did not need to add the "human" in front of it.

Ondith was from Amon. His people shared their star with the Ta'als. So, to specify that they came from different planets in the same star system, it became customary to introduce themselves as the Ammoth Ondith, or Ta'al Zengren. He just had to remind himself that the people of other star systems didn't do that.

Ondith looked down to his tab. He read Rule 3 again before looking at the humans sitting in front of him.

Kiara made a little triangular paper. She was aiming it at Vasya as she tried to flick it. Vasya had his index fingers linked, looking at Kiara in anticipation. Kiara told him that it was like a goal post. Some sort of game they played back on Earth.

The Humans looked peaceful enough, Ondith thought. There hadn't been many problems with the humans in his crew or any crew he knew of. Where had these observations originated?

Did these observations need an update? Ondith thought again. *They had been updated only a few days ago.*

Ondith shook his head. He froze when he felt something brush against his feet. In his shock, he   flinched and raised his leg.

He looked down to see a small robot. The robot picked up crumbs of food.

"That's a Roomba," the human cook told him. "There's so many of you to feed; I'm always cooking. He helps me clean."

"Him?" Ondith asked. "Is this an alien species that helps you with your chores? I have not read of them." Ondith was about to greet the Roomba when he heard Oza, their cook, laugh.

"It's a robot, my friend! It's not another alien! It's a machine."

That confused Ondith. Why would humans speak with their machines? But that wasn't the last of his confusion.

Kiara stuck moving eyeballs on the Roomba a few days after she arrived on the spaceship. She called them googly eyes. The eyes seemed to move every which way the Roomba moved. She also said that she still had to name the Roomba.

Humans seemed to have an affinity for animating inanimate objects. Ondith didn't understand. Mostly because what he saw and what he read about them were two completely different things. Ondith wanted to see a human fight. What was so special about a human in war that almost all the books he'd read mentioned it?

Ondith was the last person to join the crew. This would be their first mission after he'd arrived. Their mission was to monitor any Tra'Khal activity in their area. Maybe he'd get to see humans in action then?

His attention shifted to Kiara when he heard her scream.

"Yes! And that's how you win!" she boasted as she got up and moved close to Vasya. She turned to Ondith next. "Do you want to play?" Her eyebrows shot up, hopeful Ondith would agree.

Before he could answer, an alarm blared across the spaceship. Red light blinked in time with the wail. Ondith looked back at Kiara. Her once smiling face morphed into an expression of serious concentration.

"Grab your weapons. We meet in the crew cabins," Vasya, the Captain, ordered. He rushed out of the commons without turning to check his orders were followed.

Arno sprinted behind the captain.

"Let's go," Kiara shouted at Ondith before heading in the opposite direction   .

Before Ondith could move, the red lights   were replaced with blinding white light which seemed to grow ever brighter.

A jolt ran through their spaceship knocking Ondith over. He grunted as he rubbed the area that hit the table as he fell.

"Ow!" He heard Kiara yell as she hit the side of the chair.

Before Kiara and Ondith could get up, another jolt shook the spaceship. This one was stronger than before. The alarm had stopped long ago. The only sounds that permeated the air were the shouts and screams of injured crew members.

The white light engulfed every one of them. It hurt Ondith to open his eyes. A high-pitched noise pierced his brain. Screams increased as all the crew members covered their ears, trying their best to shield themselves from the noise.

Within minutes, the crew members of SE New Hope fell unconscious, defenseless to the Tra'Khal invasion.

Cyrox, The Human Files.

Interaction with a Human, Rule 9

Humans are greedy. In any situation, individual self-preservation and self-interest outweighs that of their race as a whole. This has caused unwanted troubles and several wars in Human's past. Common phrase used by humans in this case would be, "What's in it for me?" Suggestions for peaceful agreement with Humans in this case would be to provide them something they value before asking for help or consultation.

Ondith rubbed his eyes as he got up. His tight muscles ached as he struggled to stretch. The dull throb at the front of his head circled around to the back.

"Good! You're up." He heard a voice beside him whisper. It sounded like the Ammoth Hiran. "Get Human Kiara."

Why is he whispering? Ondith thought. He tried to remember what happened. Images flashed into his mind making him clutch his head.

He remembered.

He remembered the bright white light that surrounded them.

He remembered the piercing noise in his brain.

He remembered watching Kiara hit herself on a chair as she fell.

Opening his eyes, Ondith looked to his side, to where Kiara had fallen. He was alarmed when he didn't see her. He frantically turned around and let out a breath when he saw that the Human Ki – Kiara – opposite him.

Ammoth Hiran must have moved her, he thought.

Kiara stirred as she woke up. She moaned slightly as she rubbed her eyes and forehead.

"Where are we?" she asked. Her voice was husky.

"Tra'Khal ship," Ammoth Hiran whispered.

With Kiara awake, Ondith looked around his surroundings. They were in a rectangular cage of sorts. So far, it had only been him, Kiara, and Hiran in one corner. Had they been the last ones to wake?

Vasya, Arno, and a few other Ammoths stood around the cage. They were discussing among themselves.

"Where's everyone else?" Kiara asked. "Pablo, Oza, Udon, Yava. Where are they?"

"The Tra'Khal killed them. We are all that is remaining." A hint of sadness tinged Hiran's voice.

Ondith looked around. Only eight remained from their twenty-member team.

Five Ammoths and Three humans.

Ondith followed Kiara as she approached the group. It seemed that none of the crew members had the chance to send out an SOS. If they were to get out of this one, they would have to go at it alone.

The Tra'Khal had already killed more than half of them. It was only a matter of time before more of them were killed. Ondith didn't know why, but he kept focusing on Kiara.

Gone were her jovial laughs and smiles. She had a serious expression that he hadn't seen before. She seemed relaxed, and her face was blank, but it was almost as if he could feel her shaky breath.

Ondith itched to grab his weapon but found nothing. The Tra'Khal must have taken their weapons. Just as he was about to ask what the escape plan was, the door opened.

All eight of them turned toward the door. A being with scaly skin emerged. The chromatic shimmer would have been mesmerizing were it not for the yellowish snake eyes that gazed across at the eight of them, or the rows of yellow teeth revealed when it snarled at the prisoners. Moving to the side, it allowed more Tra'Khal to enter the room.

Holding up a weapon, a Tra'Khal opened the door to their cage. Each Human and Ammoth had their hands tied at their front before they were escorted out. The Tra'Khal held a weapon to the backs of each Human and Ammoth.

Ondith walked beside Kiara, watching the Tra'Khal holding her carefully. He wasn't particularly violent, but if the Tra'Khal did anything to Kiara, Ondith didn't think he'd be very pleased.

The group of eight were guided to the cabin. A sharp pain on his calf made him fall to his knees. Ondith looked around. It seemed that his crewmates were in the same position. His jaw tightened as he saw one Tra'Khal walk up to them.

It stood in front of Ammoth Vron. Drawing in close until the Tra'Khal's nose almost touched Vron's ears.

"Ammoth." The Tra'Khal sneered as Vron flinched back.

That was the only word Ondith understood. The translation device attached to their ears should translate almost a thousand languages around the galaxy. Ondith rubbed his ear against his shoulder. Something must have happened to his device during the attack. All he could hear was a gargled noise every time someone other than an Ammoth talked.

He tried to get some clues as to what was going on by analyzing the situation.

Things became more tense by the minute. The look of disgust in the Tra'Khal's face morphed into unbridled rage as he shouted at Vron and Vasya. This rage burst as he brought his hand up and slashed Vasya, cutting him deep from chest to face. The Tra'Khal then turned to Vron. His hands dripped with Vasya's blood as he brought them up to Vron's neck. He squeezed, sneering as life drained from Vron's face.

And with a snap of Vron's neck, the Tra'Khal threw Vron's body down as if it was nothing. For him, it probably was. Vasya held onto his sides and grew paler by the minute as blood oozed from the wound.

The Tra'Khal finally turned to his men and gestured for them to take the remaining Humans and Ammoths away.

Whispers were hissed between his crewmates as Ondith marched behind them. His back straight as ever. Something about a ransom and getting the Federation to do what the Tra'Khal wanted. He figured that killing the crew was one way to send the Federation a message: the Tra'Khal were serious.

Ondith looked around. If this were to continue, there would be none of them left. The Tra'Khal could come for anyone next: Arno, Hiran, or Kiara. Or even himself. They needed to get out of here if they were to survive.

A plan started to form. This was a Tra'Khal scout ship. He'd studied these ships extensively when he was a kid. There would be safety pods near the cargo bay. Ondith wanted to say something, but he groaned when he remembered   his translation device was destroyed.

"What is it?" Kiara whispered as she walked beside him.

Ondith learnt a few words and phrases during his short time with the Humans. Most of them were not good but some of them came in handy now.

"Distraction," he whispered back, hoping Kiara would understand what he wanted to do.

Kiara looked up at him, searching his eyes. He didn't know what she saw, but she gave him a grave nod.

Ondith brought his hands up. With an immense force, he punched the Tra'Khal behind him. His Tra'Khal staggered back. Ondith grabbed the laser from the guard's belt hoop and killed the monster. He turned to Kiara, shooting at the Tra'Khal holding her. Ondith turned to the Tra'Khal on the ground, and with a sneer, shot him.

Moving closer to Kiara, he helped her out of her bindings. When Kiara returned the favor, Ondith checked to see how his other crewmates were faring. Several of them used the distraction as an opportunity. They kicked and punched the Tra'Khal holding them. The only one not fighting was Vasya.

A Tra'Khal guard grabbed Vasya's neck and lifted him, pointing his laser at Vasya's abdomen. Vasya had almost no fight left in him. He was losing a lot of blood. His feeble punches had no effect of the monster.

Ondith rushed towards Vasya as Hiran shot the Tra'Khal. Vasya's labored breath frightened Ondith. He had already lost too many crewmates.

No.

Not crewmates.

Ondith had lost so many friends within such a short time. He wasn't going to let Vasya die as well.

He carried Vasya, careful not to hurt the man any further. Ondith realized he hadn't seen Kiara in a while. He looked back to see where she was.

His mouth opened wide at the sight before him. He was sure it would be etched in his mind from that moment on.

For, in that moment, he understood Rule 3 of *The Human Files.*

It seemed that hearing the commotion, a swarm of Tra'Khal came rushing. However, none of the six Humans or Ammoth even felt the oncoming Tra'Khal.

Because amid the carnage of the oncoming swarm, was Kiara.

One woman against an army of Tra'Khal.

Her lasers blared as she shot Tra'Khal after Tra'Khal. Not stopping for a moment to consider her injuries. Ondith saw a gash in her thigh and her upper arm.

Every time her laser lost its charge, she dropped the gun, bent down and picked up another from the fallen Tra'Khal and shot again.

The number of Tra'Khal descending upon her only increased. Kiara stopped for a moment and turned around.

"Go!" she shouted at them.

Someone tugged Ondith's arm. Before he turned to leave, he saw Kiara pick up another laser and what seemed to be a hammer. She swung the hammer and bashed the ones near her, while shooting the ones farther away   . She was a force to reckon with.

And Ondith understood.

Humans were a warrior race. They might have other attributes, but nothing could beat them in brutality. Nothing could stop them. And Ondith feared for any poor soul that made the Humans their enemy.

Cyrox, The Human Files.

Interaction with a Human, Rule 1

Humans are one of the apex predators of   Planet Earth. Considering all the other animals of Earth, this was not our initial assumption. Humans have no evolutionary advantage, whatsoever. They have no claws, night vision, or any advantage that awards them the title of 'Apex Predator'. However, this disadvantage can be overlooked.

Humans have a unique capacity for endurance and intelligence that puts them in a category of both a 'Persistence Hunter' and an 'Ambush Hunter". Meaning, if a Human targets you, it does not matter if you hide at the edges of the galaxy, they can and will, somehow, find you. It is only a matter of time.

Do not make a Human your enemy.

Ondith carried Vasya as he and his crewmates ran across the Tra'Khal ship, searching for the safety pods to escape. Ondith kept glancing back to see if Kiara would follow.

But it was just empty.

He trailed his crewmates as they weaved around the spaceship. All breathed a sigh of relief when they reached the cargo bay.

All of them, except Ondith.

He had yet to see Kiara. He knew she was still alive. She was the only one stopping the Tra'Khal from following. If the Tra'Khal hadn't found them, it was because she was still holding them back.

Ondith didn't know how much longer she could hold on. She was already injured.

From The Human Files, Ondith knew Humans could recover from anything save a direct headshot – sometimes even surviving that.

However, he didn't know if Humans could survive being torn apart by Tra'Khal. And he didn't want Kiara testing that theory.

They were about to turn right into another corridor when Ammoth Zeka started shooting. Ondith looked forward quickly to see a Tra'Khal standing in front of them.

The Tra'Khal that had held Vron as the other killed him.

Ondith cursed, still holding onto Vasya. All of them hid behind pillars and carts, trying to avoid the Tra'Khal's laser fire.

Ondith heard a groan from one of his crew members. Ammoth Shah'sun had been hit. Dark blue blood oozed from the wound in his side, turning his shirt black.

Shots from the Tra'Khal did not stop. Ondith covered his head as Vasya lay beside him. Arno signaled to him, moving his mouth, but Ondith couldn't hear anything in the laser fire. Even if he could hear, Ondith wouldn't understand Arno. His translation device had been broken. Ondith tapped his ear and shook his head making Arno sigh in exasperation.

Arno gestured to Ondith and everyone else to go to the cargo bay while he distracted the Tra'Khal. Although concerned, Ondith nodded. Hiran, Shah'sun, and Zeka tried to move discretely. Ondith tried his best to carry Vasya and made sure no one else was following them.

~~~

When the Tra'Khal lost the laser power, he threw the gun away. Arno took this opportunity to charge at the Tra'Khal. Holding his dagger in one hand and his laser in the other. he fired at the Tra'Khal's chest.

Although, the Tra'Khal's vest seemed to deflect the laser. It disorientated the Tra'Khal. Arno took this opportunity to slash the Tra'Khal's face.

The Tra'Khal snarled in pain as it staggered back. Slashing at the Tra'Khal's arm, Arno brought the laser up to the Tra'Khal's neck.

"This is for Vron." Arno shot the laser into the Tra'Khal's neck. Green blood splattered across the ceiling and onto Arno's face.

He tried to wipe it away, but only smeared it across his face. Breathing heavily, Arno staggered a couple steps back.

"That was nasty," Kiara said from behind him.

Startled at the voice, Arno turned and raised his laser. Kiara gave him a bored expression.

"You're one to talk," Arno said, catching his breath and lowering his gun.

She looked terrible. Blood seeped from the wounds on her thigh and arm. She gripped her side as she tried to breathe. A broken lip and several gashes marked her body.

"Let's get to the pod before more Tra'Khal arrive," Arno said. He walked over to Kiara. Perhaps she could not lift her arms up to his shoulder, because she rested her hands on his torso and leaned into him.

When they reached the cargo bay, they saw the other Ammoths boarding the safety pod. Ondith stood guard as Shah'sun and Zeka tried to get Vasya into the safety pod.

"There are still a lot more of Tra'Khal that will be here if we don't move soon," Arno said.

Footsteps could be heard in the distance. The Tra'Khal were searching for them. They didn't have long.

Shah'sun left Vasya in Zeka's arms. Shah'sun entered the safety pod. He fiddled with the controls, trying to turn the pod on.

Vasya pushed on Zeka. He patted Zeka's shoulder, urging him to go into the pod. Once he was able to shakily stand on his own, Vasya mumbled something. Ondith looked at him confused, making Vasya shake his head.

"How many more?" Vasya's weak voice came out. In the silence of the bay, Vasya's voice was loud.

"I don't know. But we only got a small portion of them," Arno said.

Behind them, Shah'sun still struggled with the controls. The Tra'Khal's stomps and snarls were closer. However, it seemed that Zeka and Shah'sun were no closer to getting the pod to work.

"I have a plan," Vasya's voice was still weak, but his tone was urgent. "I'll buy you some time. Just figure out how to get out of here."

It took all of them a moment to understand what Vasya was saying, before their faces revealed their dread. Ondith noticed the shift in mood in everyone around him. But he didn't understand why. Vasya had spoken too fast for Ondith to understand.

"You can't do that!" Kiara said, limping forward.

The sounds were closer to them. A loud snarl alerted them that the Tra'Khal leader was leading the swarm. Everyone looked to the door of the cargo bay and then back at Vasya.

"I am already dying. I will not be able to make it through the entire journey. It'll just be a burden for you." He looked at them earnestly. "At least here, I'll be of more help. So, go."

The snarls were louder now. Any minute, they would be found.

"Go!" Vasya growled, pushing those beside him.

Ondith still didn't understand what was going on. He just relied on the expressions of those around him. Except they gave him no clue as to what was going on.

Arno walked up to Vasya, standing beside him. "I'm not letting you do this alone."

"Well, count me in," Kiara added, standing beside them. "Let's show them hell."

A second later, Kiara looked to Hiran. She told him and the other Ammoths to leave. Hiran looked as if he would argue. But the determined glares   from all three humans stopped him short.

Giving them a short nod, Hiran entered the pod.

~~~

Ondith didn't need anyone to explain what was happening. Kiara, Vasya, and Arno were staying behind. Giving the Ammoths a chance to fly away.

A heavy feeling settled in the pit of Ondith's stomach. He tried to gulp but couldn't. He was just starting to warm up to the humans. Especially Kiara. With a heavy heart and a nod, Ondith gave Kiara his gun and entered the pod.

Closing the pod door behind him, he kept looking outside at Kiara.

"What's wrong?" Hiran shouted at Shah'sun and Zeka.

They kept working at the controls. However, nothing seemed to work.

"The main interface of the pod is damaged." Shah'sun looked back as he tried to fix the wirings.

"What do you need?" Hiran asked.

Hiran rushed around in the pod trying to help Shah'sun and Zeka. Ondith stared outside one last time.

Kiara stood beside Vasya. Arno was nowhere to be seen. When Kiara turned around to look at the pod, her eyes connected with Ondith.

He sensed her fear.

No, her terror.

The dread knocked him off his feet making him want to gag.

Just as Ondith looked to the cargo bay doors, a Tra'Khal entered. Kiara turned around and shot it at the same time Vasya did. Her attention was back to the oncoming Tra'Khal.

Now the Tra'Khal came in droves. Ondith's heart quickened as he looked out. He shook his head.

The commotion inside the pod grew louder as the other three Ammoths continued to find a cause for the issue. Clearing his mind of Kiara's face, Ondith walked over to help them.

He lifted the panels as Zeka worked on them. When Zeka couldn't understand what was going on, Zeka and Ondith changed positions. Ondith moved beneath the panels. The shouts and screams from Vasya and Kiara outside spurred him on even more. He had to do this for them.

The Humans' sacrifice had to mean something. A blood curdling scream came from the outside, making all the Ammoths flinch. It sounded like Vasya. Tears blurred Ondith's vision. The memory of Kiara's terrified expression was the only thing that kept him going.

"We got it!" Zeka shouted as the control panel whirred back to life. The safety pod lit up, alerting the Tra'Khal. Ondith returned to his seat and looked outside the window.

Vasya's dead body lay to the side. Torn and bloodied. The Tra'Khal surrounded Kiara. She struggled to hold her own. He saw the slashes all over her body as the pod lifted. She was getting weaker by the minute as the Tra'Khals inched towards her. Ondith closed his eyes as a tear slid down his cheek when one Tra'Khal slashed Kiara across her back.

She had no chance now.

Several Tra'Khal slammed against the pod as Zeka and Shah'sun tried to maneuver it. Finally, being able to completely control the pod, the Ammoths blasted through the Tra'Khal ship letting the Tra'Khal freeze and die in the cold of space.

<u>*Cyrox, The Human Files,*</u>

Interaction with a Human, Rule 53

Ignore Rules 1 – 52 if this happens. Humans are generally guarded, and their trust is only given to a select few. Their loyalty, to even fewer. However, on the rare occasion that a Human trusts you completely, and you have earned the loyalty of the Human, cherish your Human; it is your job to protect your Human. Ensure no harm will come to them. For they will do the same, if not more, for you.

Humans have been known to endanger themselves by walking through severely irradiated areas, or dangerous environmental conditions to ensure the safety of their team. Several Humans were lost in such battles.

Handle your human with care. For they are not as strong as they look. They are just immensely brave bordering stupidity (See phrase: Hold my beer) with enormous hearts for those dear to them.

"A recommendation to edit *The Human Files*?" Commander Volak asked.

Ondith had just submitted his report on the Humans. It didn't take him long to write. It took Volak even less time to read it.

"And you added Rule 53 to the book?" Volak said, more to himself. "Are you absolutely sure about this? Our experience with the Humans agrees with the first 52 rules."

Ondith paused for a moment before answering. "Almost all our previous interactions with Humans had been with their leaders. We, of all species, should know that the leaders do not always represent the people they rule."

Ondith stopped walking, making Volak pause mid-step. "What is it?" Volak asked.

"I have seen firsthand the greatness of these Humans. I've seen

Humans lay down their lives just so we could survive." Flashes of Kiara swirled through his mind. The terror on her face. That was not something he could forget anytime soon. Or ever. "I have seen Captain Arno blow up the Tra'Khal ship just to make sure the other Tra'Khal could not hurt anyone else."

"Couldn't these Humans just be an exception?" Volak asked.

"No, I don't think so. I've read of other Humans who have done the same feats. Some had suffered even worse fates." Ondith shook his head. "These Humans. They're still a young race. We need to give them a chance."

Volak looked down thoughtfully.

"If my assumption is right, the Humans would be the best of us. And also, the worst of us."

At last, Volak nodded, and a sigh of relief passed Ondith.

"Monitor them closely. If your Rule 53 is correct, then I believe we need to make another handbook about Human safety." Volak shook his head. "Monitor them like we look after our children, please? I'd rather them not die again, if we can help it."

Ondith let out a small smile – which for him meant that he was jumping for joy.

This is for you, Kiara. He thought. His smile faded as sadness dulled his eyes again. Volak patted Ondith's shoulder before leaving.

A new day of the Human-Ammoth relations had begun.

And Ondith would make sure that no other died like Humans that protected him.

On The Beach of Broken Shells

By Shanti Leonard

Down on the beach of broken shells, tucked back into the rocks where it looked like there might have been a few caves, a small boy held a small thing. The boy's rain boots were tan and wet on the outside, covered in blue Paddington Bears holding umbrellas. But the insides were dry and warm, filled with feet and thick wool socks to keep the cold out. With him was the writer.

The writer was dressed in black, with dark shades, and leather shoes. They could have passed for dress shoes, but the bottoms were rubber, and suited for not slipping on sea rocks, since he had been here before.

The small boy looked at the rocks that surrounded them. They were green and gray and red and brown, chewed up, with a million marks and facets. They pushed out of the caves and stretched into the clouded sky. Maybe they would reach it one day.

The caves behind the boy were not usually noticed. Sometimes somebody would see them from afar and say, "Hey, look! Caves! You want to check them out?" or "Race you to those caves!" But no matter what they said they would always forget about them. Sometimes they would get in a fight with their fellow adventurer, or turn their ankle in the sand, or they might just get distracted by the sky and how the clouds filled it. If they actually made it to the caves, up close, they would simply lose interest, or they wouldn't see them anymore. Maybe it was a trick of the sunlight bouncing off the ocean mixed with the strange way the rocks grew, maybe it was just how people's minds worked there, but almost every time when somebody would get up close enough to peer into the dark, they would see nothing instead. "Huh," they might say. "I guess they aren't caves-- oooh look a shell!" Which was a particularly silly thing to say on a beach filled with broken shells. "So," the small boy said to the writer, "this is where you get all your ideas, Daddy?" The boy held the thing in both hands, feeling a particular feeling that was almost exclusively reserved for children, *disappointed wonder*. "This one seems so small."

"Ah, yes," said the father, still peering from behind his dark glasses. They might have helped him find this place originally, back before the small boy had even been an idea himself, and they may be helping him see it now. Not to mention they helped a good deal with the glare. In any event, best not to take them off. "There is a secret though."

The boy looked up into the black lenses of his father, probably seeing himself in the reflections, interested enough in the promise of a secret to pull his gaze away from the tiny idea. "The secret is..." the father said, leaning slightly forward, speaking slightly softer, and holding the secret in his mouth until the boy leaned into the words. "They are *all* like this in the beginning." The boy looked back into the idea.

"When they find them, many people still miss them, disregard them, starve them, let them go, or try to pawn them off on others, or even try to force adoption on somebody already filled with ideas themselves... and as any living thing does, when its needs are neglected, they die." The small boy let out a small gasp, still studying the idea. "But if you spend time with them, feed them, live with them, give them drink, let them nest, and let them be what *they* want...they will grow." A spark lit in the boy's eye. His right one. That eye was the one that seemed to see things a bit better. "Many people ask writers where they get their ideas, and many suspect we have secrets about the matter that we do not tell. But they will never know they are right. And you must promise to never tell them about the Beach of Broken Shells where we get them all."

The boy looked up at his father until the idea pulled his eyes back again.

"Is it a good one?" the writer asked.

"It is," said the boy, his smallness seeming to leech away into his hands.

"Do you have your Idea Box?"

The boy's face dropped. He closed the idea tight in his left fist, that one could squeeze harder, and fumbled in the kangaroo pouch of his sky-gray hoodie with his right hand. "Here it is, Daddy!"

"Good." The father looked at the box for the first time. It was a good box. Simple, and not quite a square, but it was charming. Red...The father would not have gone with red...but all the better, it was not *his* box. "Do you have the bits?"

"Yes!" the boy said and began to open the box, but then stopped himself. The father smiled. "Turn away," the small boy commanded. Not a harsh command, but his will was in it. The father straightened his face dutifully and did as he was told.

The boy opened the box and gently laid the idea in among the bits.

"What's it doing?" asked the father with his back still to the small boy. He didn't peak...not at the box or the idea anyway...maybe once at the boy's face.

The boy stared into the Idea Box. "Playing with the bits," The boy said. And then his eyes widened. "...and it's eating them up!"

The father faced the rocks. "Anything else happening?"

The boy stood silent for what seemed to be a long time until he said, "Something is appearing on it." The boy had just learned the word *appearing* and was taking to it. He had used it three times today. Strange, he had known *disappearing* for a long time.

"Are they little squiggly lines, almost like the colors of an oil slick?"

"Sort of...but darker."

"Ah, yes..." The father felt his throat get a little sore. "Those are its wings."

"Wings?"

"Of course, didn't you know? The really good ones fly."

What The Catching Wood Caught

Erin Slegaitis-Smith (*CONTENT WARNING: violence*)

The wind was whispering, and then that was never a good sign. Enialis tucked a wind-pulled strand of red hair behind his pale, pointed ear. He was only half-listening to the human Magistrate who relayed details about the rundown two-story shack before them. It was always hard to focus on a low gravelly voice like that man's when there were so many competing noises.

Enialis glanced over to Sage, a diminutive human girl tugging at her kinky hair. Her pine- brown skin was hidden under a bluish-gray hue, confirming that her gesture was from nerves. Sage was, after all, one that changed color due to mood. She had appeared at his home in Vynsyrfeil three days before the human Magistrate's letter and hadn't left his side since.

Enialis focused on the Magistrate's voice. "You can see why we would request the help of someone of your reputation."

"My reputation?" Heat burned in Enialis' cheeks. "I have barely done anything notable."

The Magistrate clicked his tongue. "You sell your achievements short, sir. You have solved at least eight great mysteries, and as reclusive as we are, there must surely be many more."

Enialis's throat tightened.

Sage tugged his hand. "It's okay. It's good for people to know that you can help them."

Enialis quickly pulled his fingers from her, pretending to tuck another strand of hair behind his ear, hoping that his human company hadn't noticed that Sage had moved his hand.

"How many disappearances did you say again?" Enialis asked.

"Five families who took residence, four neighbors who investigated, and three investigators sent by the town. Eight men, eight women, and fifteen children."

"What makes you certain it is the house? It might be a murderer or some other phenomenon? This home is remote enough that, Shaleig forbid, a murderer could have had their way without immediately raising suspicion."

"Siris," the Magistrate beckoned a scrawny young man forward. "Tell him what you saw."

Siris flushed. "I was sent with my master to investigate the house. He went in before me. Then, from the door – I saw him vanish, sir."

"Vanish? How?" Enialis tilted his head.

"I don't know, sir," Siris said.

"No, not what made him vanish. In what way did he vanish? Did he suddenly snap out of view or fade like a fog in the morning sun?"

"Fade, sir. He looked like he turned to speak to me, and though his lips moved, I heard nothing. He seemed so afraid, sir, and I had never seen a glimpse of fear in him before."

"Could a spirit have eaten him?" the Magistrate asked.

Enialis suppressed a chuckle. "No, what you call spirits do not behave that way. I suppose the more pertinent question is, what do you expect me to do? Am I not to fade away just because I'm an elf?"

The humans looked at each other guiltily.

The Magistrate quickly bent in a low bow. "I assure you we do not weigh our request to you lightly. Of course, we have no guarantee of safety, but we do need your help. If you succeed, we will pay you with whatever you may want."

"What do you suppose that might be?"

"Wealth, land, an estate, whatever compensates *your risks* to give *us* answers."

"Please," Sage said. "My parents went missing in there. You can help. I know it." She turned a red-orange as Enialis ignored her.

"What I want is nothing so trivial that it could be bought," Enialis sighed, tightening his jaw. "I will do what I may."

"Thank you!" The Magistrate and the others bowed multiple times.

Enialis slung his bag off of one shoulder and extracted a couple of candles and a tinderbox. Pulling out the flint and steel, Enialis pushed the candles into the soft earth and lit them.

"What are you doing?" The Magistrate asked.

"It is a tradition of my people." Enialis picked up the first candle of red and gold wax. "The red candle is an homage from a stranger, entering a stranger's home." He slowly waved the candle before the shack's door and then blew it out, wafting the smoke over himself. "It is to purify the guest of any ill intention or bad omen they may have acquired on their journey." Enialis then picked up the second candle of blue and silver wax and repeated the motion. "This candle is to appease the dead, any forgotten remnant, in the home and to give due respect to any ancestor of the family who remains to protect the family."

Sage's body shimmered silver a moment as she drew close to his side.

Enialis tucked the candles and the tinderbox back into his bag. "You shouldn't come with me."

He couldn't hear the Magistrate over Sage's response. "I need to. I need to know what happened. Please let me come."

Enialis sighed and nodded discreetly.

He reached out and opened the door. From outside, the shack looked abandoned. Dust clung to every surface. Everyday items were left out as if the occupants had expected to return. There was a dry washbasin by the door, a table set for an unprepared meal, and a fireplace filled with wood yet to be lit. Enialis stepped inside.

He took a deep breath of the stale air, cautiously checking the room for anything out of place or any sudden change. He looked back to the Magistrate. "Can you still see and hear me?"

"Yes," the Magistrate replied.

Enialis walked further in and turned about, taking in the living space.

Sage scurried up to him, back to her anxious blue-gray. "It looks so - normal."

Enialis nodded and slid his pack to the floor. "I expected it to feel different," Enialis whispered. "Heavy or thick like something bad lurking in the air."

Enialis strode around the edges of the room, inspecting every inch. He climbed the ladder to the shack's loft, and Sage followed. The roof was low enough that Enialis could only stand at the center. Sleeping mats lay on the floor for the last family who lived there. A round window on the far wall let in some meager light. Enialis stooped down to pick up a straw doll.

"That was mine," Sage turned a deep blue as she ran a finger over the doll's head.

"Your parents kept it for you." Enialis handed her the doll, and Sage nodded. "Is there anything here or downstairs that didn't belong to your family?" Sage looked around. "No, I don't think so. But it is strange. My family only went missing a couple of weeks ago. How is everything so untidy, so dusty, already? It looks more like they've been gone for months, right?"

Yes." Enialis stood. "We need a better look. Let's go back to my pack."

"Why did you ignore me outside?" Sage hugged the doll. "I thought you had changed your mind about helping me."

"I'm sorry." Enialis put his hands on her shoulders. "But you have to understand; I'm the only one who can see you, love."

He started back to the ladder. "If I had responded, the villagers would not have known who I was talking to. Any attention I draw to myself, even if it looks positive at first, could put me under dangerous scrutiny. Being aware of you, being able to speak with you – it's not normal."

"But you're an elf."

"Even for elves." Enialis descended and went to his pack. He glanced out of the door and saw the villagers' faces light up upon his reappearance. He opened the bag and rummaged through his traveling gear.

"What are you looking for?" Sage asked.

"Tools," Enialis pulled out another candle of purple wax, the tinderbox, a bound journal, and some wool.

Sage wrinkled her nose. "What is all of that for?"

"For seeing what I cannot." Enialis laid the items on the table. "Each of these helps reveal the history of a place. You'll see." Enialis lifted the journal's cover, and the pages turned themselves, leaving the book open to a set of notes.

"Magic!" Sage chimed.

"Yes, we can use these things to see what kind of creatures have been here." Enialis retrieved a stone mortar from the nearby counter. He placed wool inside and used the flint and steel to light it.

Sage watched wide-eyed as it burned. "What does burning the wool do?"

"There are two major classifications of creatures. Mundane and non-mundane. First, the wool shows us roughly how many of each type have been here, and then the book narrows it down further."

"How does the wool tell you what has been here?"

"Well, if I set wool on fire, what would you expect to happen?"

"It would burn?" Sage turned the bright pink of curiosity.

"Right, so because it is burning, we know a good many mundane creatures have been here. That's not surprising considering it is a human dwelling, and humans are mundane creatures." When the flames went out, Enialis lifted the charred wool. It dripped water. "And that means non-mundane creatures have been here as well."

"Because burning wool doesn't make water."

"That's right." Enialis smiled, and Sage smiled back triumphantly. "And with this amount of water, either there have been many non-mundane creatures here, or one visits frequently." Enialis dripped some of the water on the page of the journal, and the pages flipped again. Sage leaned around Enialis's arm.

"What are Kyst-sahth-mo-mi-mul?" She stumbled over the word.

"Kyastahmamyul are a category of non-mundane that derive their power from or feed off of mundane creatures." Enialis flipped through the pages quickly, and images of strange, horrible creatures flashed before their eyes.

Sage clutched her doll, tears spilling onto her cheeks. "My family is dead - aren't they?"

Enialis looked back out the door at the villagers.

"Come here," Enialis pulled Sage out of the line of sight from the door. She had shifted into a deep blue, tears raining from her eyes. Enialis wrapped her in a hug. "Those creatures can be awful, but only a handful actually kill. Don't give up hope when you may still have it. I need to keep looking. I will find your family."

Sage nodded, wiping her tears. Enialis squeezed Sage's shoulder and returned to the table. He picked up the candle made out of purple and red wax. He lit it and began walking around the home, wafting the smoke towards the walls.

"What does that do?" Sage sniffed.

"The smoke clings to anything that doesn't belong here - a trace of the creature." The smoke dissipated against the wall as he walked around the room. When he made it to the door, the smoke stuck to the door frame and shone silver.

"What does that mean?" Sage asked as a sudden heaviness filled the air.

"A trap," Enialis's eyes widened. "Get out, quick!"

Enialis grabbed Sage by the wrist, flinging her towards the doorway, but before she made it through, it was like the ground fell out from under them. They were lost in a cloud of grey, falling.

Enialis pulled Sage into his chest, and she clung desperately to his tunic, screaming. The wind huffed out of Enialis' lungs as he hit the ground. Enialis coughed, heaving to get his breath back.

Sage scrambled off of him. "Are you all right?" Sage turned a near-translucent white.

"I'm - okay," Enialis pulled himself to his feet. "What about you?"

"I'm fine." They took in their new surroundings in broad sweeps. "What is this place?"

The sky was a hazy green-gray with no sun or moon visible to explain the meager lighting. They were in a clearing of pale green grass amidst a vast dark forest.

"A pocket dimension of some kind – or another plane entirely. This is likely where all the people were taken. So, on the bright side, we are a step closer to finding your family."

"But if we're in a trap, how are we going to get out?"

"One step at a time, love. First, we need to find your family while avoiding whatever brought us here. We had best start moving." Enialis drew a blade from his belt and took Sage's hand with the other, leading her into the dense woods.

The forest was composed of deciduous trees with dark bark and near-black leaves. Only the occasional break in the forest canopy allowed spotlights of murky light to guide their way. Sage clung tightly to Enialis's sleeve, sticking as close as she could.

The heaviness in the air intensified, and Enialis heaved under the pressure. Sage glanced up at him nervously as he struggled to catch his breath.

"We need to stop for a moment." Enialis sunk to the foot of a tree and leaned his head back, pinching his eyes closed.

"Are you all right?" Sage knelt in front of him.

"I will be. It's just – all elves are sensitive to magic. I'm particularly sensitive, which is why I can see ghosts, or spirits, or things between the world we know and another. The magic is so thick in this place - it weighs on me. It's like everything is becoming too much - sights, sounds, and feelings. I need a moment to ground myself. Otherwise, I'll get lost in it."

"Can I help?"

"Thank you, but no. Just keep your eyes and ears open for me for a minute." Enialis took in controlled, deep breaths, and Sage waited patiently. After a couple of long minutes, Enialis opened his eyes, refocusing in the dark. Sage still knelt before him, a greenish color, quietly picking the grass. Then, looking over her shoulder, he stiffened.

The trees around them all bore faces. Low limbs protruded from the bark in the shapes of human arms and legs. One particular form captured Enialis' attention.

"Are you better?" Sage asked, scootching closer.

"I'm better," Enialis smiled at her and stood. "Remind me, how long were you dead before your parents disappeared?"

Sage rubbed grass off her translucent palms and pouted. "I don't know. A year or so."

"I'm sorry to ask. I'm still just trying to piece together this mystery. Now that we're in this place, I'm getting a hunch. So anything you can tell me from before your parents disappeared could help the final pieces click."

Sage nodded. "I understand."

"When did you notice they disappeared?"

"About a month ago, they stopped visiting my grave, and so I went looking for them thinking they forgot me."

"I see, and how did you find me?"

"I don't see how that helps," Sage folded her arms.

"It might, answer, please."

"In the in-between, you are well-known. You've helped so many. I had to try. There's no one else like you that I know of. You're unique." Sage tracked Enialis's gaze over her shoulder and turned a deep purple. In a tree behind her was a frozen face that resembled her own. "Wh- what's that?"

"I would assume - that's Sage. Which makes me wonder who you are?"

"No, I am me. I don't know what that is." Sage turned a peachy orange.

"Sorry, no, love. These trees tell me exactly what kind of trap this is. It's a catching wood. Creatures are trapped in trees for other creatures to feed on or to use later. For your face to be in the tree, you'd have to be in the tree. The girl in that tree is alive, just waiting for whatever caught her to decide it wants her. So, who or what are you?"

"I should have expected you to know that. How inconvenient." Sage sighed. Enialis's grip on his blade tightened. "No point in lying anymore. You're here. That is what matters. Who I am, does not make a difference. What I am, is bait. Now, be a good elf and get in your tree." Sage's form began to ripple, and she turned a deep red.

"No, thank you."

Sage chuckled. "It's not a choice. It just is a matter of whether you want to enter your tree in one piece or multiple. So, long as you're alive when you go in, Dhara doesn't care." Sage's form morphed into a large centipede-like creature, and Enialis raised his blade.

"Is Dhara your master? The Kyastahmomyul?"

"We're done talking, elf." The creature's voice was now a low rumble instead of the voice of a little girl.

"We don't have to be," Enialis said.

"The only thing that matters to me is that you take your place in this catching wood."

"Then I guess we are done talking," Enialis said.

The creature lunged at him, and Enialis ducked beneath its pincers, slicing upward with his blade and drawing another shortsword. His first blade caught the beast in its tough hide. It used one of its many legs to smack him aside.

Enialis tumbled across the forest floor, landing hard against a tree. He regained his feet in time to avoid another swipe from the creature's forelegs. Enialis charged and leaped towards the beast, slicing down with both blades and ripping the centipede's forwardmost shoulder. It hissed and whipped around, catching Enialis in its pinchers. The serrated edge cut through Enialis' tunic and into his waist. Enialis pushed against the thick mandibles trying to break free as they crushed the air out of his lungs.

He stabbed his blades into the soft flesh around the creature's maw, and it dropped him screeching. Enialis rushed the centipede slicing down its belly, and a thick, dark ooze splattered across him. The centipede bore down with several of its legs, cutting his shoulders and chest before he could raise his blades. He jumped back to put some distance between them, but the creature pressed forward until his back was against one of the thick trees. The centipede thrashed at him with multiple legs and bit down at him with its mandibles. Enialis couldn't block enough of the blows, and the beast sliced his sides, arms, and forehead. Enialis pushed forward, sinking his blades into the creature's underbelly and slicing down, deepening and widening the gash he had already created. Thick, putrid liquid burbled from the wound. The centipede reeled back, wavering in the air until it finally collapsed.

Enialis panted, wiping blood, sweat, and goo from his brow. The creature dissolved in smoke that burned Enialis' lungs. When his vision cleared, he was back in the shack. He gripped the doorframe and heard the villagers gasp. The missing suddenly stumbled out from the walls of the house. Enialis caught his breath, let out a sigh, and collected his things.

As he crossed the threshold a burning pain snapped up his left arm.

He noticed a copper ring on his middle finger that had not been there before. An ancient script was engraved on the surface that transfigured before his eyes into his native tongue. The writing was one word: "mine."

"Master elf!" The Magistrate grabbed his hand and shook it vigorously. "You did it! I don't rightly know what you did, but my people are returned. I cannot thank you enough."

"Burn it."

"Excuse me?"

"The house. I defeated the creature holding your villagers, but it wasn't the one truly responsible for them going missing."

"What do you mean?"

"The creature responsible for this was a Kyastahmomyul. What I fought was a Cepeurd. A lower-level monster in the thrall of something far more powerful." Enialis ran his thumb over the ring now on his finger. "If you let the house stand, the real monster will just find another minion."

"O-of course. In the meantime, let me escort you to my home. We'll get your wounds taken care of and get you cleaned up, and then we'll discuss your payment."

Enialis noted the captives' hands as a magistrate let him away, none wore the strange ring. His eyes lingered for a moment on a family with a young girl with pine bark brown skin, kinky curls, and a newfound smile that sparkled like the free sunlight he was no longer sure he shared.

Illuminating Manuscript

By Sonya Lawson

T he snake looped and circled her leg, shimmying up her calf and back down again, where it bit into an apple right on her ankle joint. That part of the tattoo had been painful as hell, but the end result – a riot of green-gold scales circling her right leg, reminding her of Eve and Milton – was well worth the pang of the needle into flesh and bone. Now, the snake's body peaked out in bits and pieces on the short expanse of skin exposed where her black capris stopped, and her bright yellow running shoes began. Well, supposedly bright yellow. Now they were caked in mud and grime from the trek through empty late-summer fields.

She was close to finishing up her MLS with an emphasis in seventeenth- and eighteenth-century manuscript preservation and was working her summer away in the Special Collections at The Ohio State University when a call about this book came down the line. A farmer in the middle of nowhere found an old text in some field. The head of SC hemmed and hawed, trying to get the farmer to bring it to Columbus, but after a brief discussion of some of the markings and printing information, her boss got a greedy gleam in his eyes and said they would send someone over in the next few days. Enter her. She was the perfect choice for errands. As a graduate student, she already served as a glorified gofer in the library system. Her expertise in what seemed to be the era of the text also helped. "This is all a bit unusual, I know," the supervisor told her, "However, discoveries in our field come in the strangest ways. It's best we find out if this is something special, a feather for the cap of our collection." Still, he wasn't the one traipsing through the July muck of a field alongside some new organic farmer who wore his dirty hair up in a manbun and felt the need to fill the void of silence between them while she tried to focus on her breathing. It was a much longer trip from car to book than she expected.

"Never saw myself as a farmer, but the land calls to me. So many vibrant smells and colors here outside the city, you know?" He turned slightly, an expectant look in his eyes. He wanted conversation, but she ignored his signal and simply nodded her head. She needed answers to her own questions to get all this over with, not small talk about the idyllic nature of Ohio farmland.

"Why, exactly, did you leave the book where you found it?" she asked as she trudged on, looking straight ahead at the massive tree in the center of a large, unplanted field acres away from any structure.

"Oh, yeah. I thought it was like archeology. You or someone else wanting to study the thing needed the scene preserved."

She scoffed a bit. She wasn't a detective looking to catch a serial killer or Indiana Jones. The temperature-controlled environment of Special Collections was her normal home, and she resented having to come out to the fields of Ohio and paw through the dirt. Though, if this book was what Manbun described it as, it would be a boon for her and the library. An eighteenth-century almanac untouched for who knew how long, lying buried in a field where some early colonial American farmer landed back when this part of North America was still terra incognita – a vast, unmapped, unknown wilderness for encroaching settlers? It could be great, for her and her program. Or it could be an exaggeration and some book left sitting in the field in the 1980s.

As they got closer to the tree, she could tell it was not just gnarled, but old. Like, really old, in the way trees can be, having seen centuries pass around them. Unlike the trees marking the edges of the field, this tree was bare. There were no summer leaves growing there. It was a birch, or maybe an alder. One of those trees where the white bark looked like peeling skin, stripped down in spots like brown-black wounds exposing the wood beneath it. It was huge, though. Those trees were usually tall and thin, almost spindly. Not this one. It towered above her and Manbun, at least thirty feet in the air, with a sturdy trunk her arms would go halfway around if she tried to give it a hug. Large shafts of limbs shot into the sky and tendrils of finger-like branches shifted around in the humid July breeze. The tree swaying rhythmically, heaving to and fro, even though the slight wind shouldn't have the power to move such a sturdy trunk. It looked like it was dancing or heaving with deep breathes in and out. She shook her head and focused on the ground. Large knots of roots poked through the soil, forcing her to step gingerly around so she didn't fall flat on her face.

"Welp, here it is," Manbun said with a crooked grin he probably thought was charming. She studied it from full height for a moment, then dropped to a crouch. She looked up and around for a moment, then back at Manbun. "Why were you digging here?" What she saw made little sense. A nearly laser-cut rectangle of dirt, about three feet by four feet, was dug into the earth about four feet from the trunk of the old tree. The roots in the hole weren't disturbed. Manbun couldn't have done this with a regular shovel, it required a long, slow, and deliberate process.

"Needed to see if the tree roots were healthy, and if I could somehow get this old girl out of here, give myself a bit more open space in the field."

"Okay. Fine. But why like this? It's an odd way to do it."

Manbun gave a shrug. "The old farmer I bought the land from suggested it, so I first brought a big shovel to dig down quickly, but once I got here, I felt it needed more care. Went back for a garden trowel. Took a long time, but it did the trick." He trailed off then, looking confused by his own actions. All of it was weird, she stopped her train of thought. She needed to focus on her own expertise. Why and how some dude wants to dig in and around a tree was not her concern. What did concern her was the old iron box resting at the bottom of the neat hole. The box should have been covered with tree roots, not nestled within them like it was. They curved and bent and weaved around, cradling the box inside. She stopped short before sticking her hand in the hole. She felt an odd pulse in her fingers, the sensation enough to make her shake her hand a little and pull back. This hesitation lasted only a moment. Diving in, she lifted a rusty latch at the front of the box and opened the lid.

A single book sat neatly in the center of the box. No wrapping, no protection, no other trinkets or belongings encroached on the space. Just the book. Even without context clues or artifacts to confirm it, even before she touched the thing, she knew it was real. At least she knew it was very, very old. The smell of old books – a hint of musty paper mixed with the metallic tang of aged ink – hit her hard. This was definitely a find of some kind, and she pulled her hand back to put on vinyl gloves.

She lifted the book from the box and felt its odd heft. Books have a weight, and it was something she often found comforting. This book was deceptively heavy. Small enough for her to comfortably clutch in one hand, it felt like it should be much bigger based on its weight. It was more akin to the old seventeenth-century Bibles she'd worked with before; giant tomes meant to house knowledge and intimidate with it in equal measure. Leaning back, she went to her butt, unconcerned as wetness seeped into her pants and the roots prodded her. Her sole focus was the thing she gently turned in her hands.

Carefully, she examined the outside of the book. It was leather, strong and sturdy, but thicker than most bindings. This likely meant the leather itself covered a different material. Something hid under this cover, to protect it, for one reason or another. The spine and front cover featured embossed lettering, something slightly degraded with time. The words were still clear. "Almanac" was plain to see and read, both on the spine and the cover. Under it, on the front, was a series of symbols she did not recognize. They weren't images in the usual sense. They were pictograms of some sort. She didn't know what the old angles and lines and curves were supposed to tell her. They did fascinate her, and she caught herself staring long and hard before continuing her initial evaluation.

She cracked the book open and let out a soft hiss of air. It was perfectly preserved. There were no stains or blotches or signs of mold she could see. The binding held true, flipping the pages with ease. There were no cracks or groans, no dog-ears or creased pages. It was a perfectly pristine specimen. She turned to the frontispiece and title page, looking for any identifying information to help verify authenticity. The image was pure eighteenth-century pastoral, which would be standard in an almanac printed then. The publisher information showed it was printed in Massachusetts, which tracked. Although it was produced in Innsmouth, not Boston, an odd but exciting detail. She'd never heard of Innsmouth, never came across a reference to an early American printer there. The more unique the book, the more important the find. There was no author listed, but not unheard of in early American publishing. The full, lengthy title – also a trait of its time – was "An Almanac, for the Wilds of the American Frontier, Presented to the Reader, as a Nightly Instrument of Sight and Instruction for the Year Proceeding 25th of December 1758." She saw all she needed for now. This was the real deal. A great find, likely to catapult her career if her boss let her have partial credit for the discovery and gave her research time alone with the thing.

She got to her knees, still ignoring the soil and roots around her, and pulled out a large plastic bag she'd stuffed in her tiny pocket. She sealed the book inside, eyeing it hungrily and thinking about all it could do for her, what she could do with it, and how she would crack it open and learn all of its secrets in her little cubby hole in Special Collections. She turned towards Manbun, who was now standing off to the side with his hands in his pockets and wiped the eagerness from her face. "So, what did the Head of Special Collections tell you about our process?"

"Oh, like, what you'll be doing with it? Yeah. He said it would have to be evaluated in the department before it can be authenticated or valued."

"Yes. It is yours. I have paperwork you and I can sign to establish you as the owner. However, I will be taking it back with me so we can study it and determine the nature and value of the volume. You, of course, can refuse. You do not have to let us take it to study. You could find a private book dealer to do it for you, but there's no guarantee someone will come out here or take it off your hands or help you find a proper place for it. They would also charge you, even if they find the book isn't valuable. Our study will be free to you." She wanted to be honest with him. She was, at heart, an honest person. She also wanted him to sign those damn papers so she could rush back to the school and start looking through her discovery, so she put a certain spin on these words. They weren't lies, but they didn't give a clear picture of how much he could get from a private auction and how quickly he'd likely get it.

"Nope. I'm an OSU alum. Go Bucks, or whatever. I want your department to take it to study before anyone else gets it."

"Excellent" she chirped, finally rising to her full height and spinning herself away from the tree. She felt a pull back, did a brief stutter step. She pushed past the feeling, walking quickly while Manbun chattered behind her. He talked and she daydreamed about all she could accomplish with the weighty book she gripped in her left hand.

~~~

They tried everything they could. She knew that. Didn't make her any happier. She slammed her car door savagely after pulling her backpack out of the back seat. Nothing for it, though. Her car wouldn't start. The battery turned over, everything worked as it should, but there was no spark, no fire, no mini explosion of the modern combustion engine to make her little red coupe leave this farmhouse and head back down I70 toward the bright lights of Columbus. She and Manbun were apparently useless when it came to anything beyond the most basic vehicle repair, and it was a Sunday evening. There was no one to even call to look over it until the morning. She was definitely kicking herself for letting her roadside assistance lapse. Grad students survived through frugality, and AAA seemed like an expense no one needed until the day a person actually needed it.

"I'm sorry this happened. It's a real bitch, I know. I can take you into town. There's a roadside motel there, but it seems a little shady." Manbun then elaborated, "Likely a lot of oxy and meth." Yeah, very likely in this part of Ohio. "You're free to stay here. I have an extra room. You'll be totally safe. Cross my heart." He did the hand-gesture across his chest, and she nearly laughed with hysterical annoyance. She didn't trust him, didn't want to stay here, but also wanted to be with her car and ready to go as soon as possible, so she took him up on his offer of a guest room. He was kind enough to offer her some dinner as well, and she even managed to give him a small amount of polite conversation while at his table. It was the least she could do. He opened his home and fridge to her, and she wasn't a complete savage. She did, however, make it clear she was too tired to hang out after eating and politely hinted she wanted to be left alone in whatever room was hers for the night. Manbun, to his credit, complied graciously. He led her to a small room in the back of his house. A single twin-sized mattress, with mismatched sheets and no frame, was on the floor. "Sorry I can't offer more, but I just moved in and ..."

"No, no, no. You've done a lot. I do appreciate it. Thanks." She reassured while also using her body to block him from most of the room. It wasn't exactly rude of her. It wasn't friendly either. She wanted to be clear he was not welcome in this small space with her while she occupied it. She also wanted time alone with the book if she was stuck out on this farm.

"Yeah. Okay. I'll call a guy I know a few towns over. He won't come out tonight because he refuses to work Sundays, but he'll come early in the morning. If it can be fixed, he can do it or tow it where it can be repaired. No problems."

"Great. Thanks. Gotta get back to work tomorrow."

Manbun muttered his goodnights and left her alone. Maybe she could have been kinder, more open to spending time with the guy, but she didn't want to give her host any ideas. She also felt a pull from the book, an almost physical need to flip through some of those pages and see what else she could find. She crawled onto the small mattress, sat up crossed-legged, and pulled the weighty volume from its protective plastic wrapping. She let her fingers drift across the leather cover, feeling the inlaid dips and raises of the words. "Almanac" was in a fairly archaic font — not at all abnormal. The coloring, though, was a bit odd. It glistened in the low light with a metallic sheen, but it clearly wasn't made from the usual materials such as gold leaf or mercury or silver. It was more bronze in tone with a hint of red. Mesmerized, she found herself staring at the word, those letters, the old font in the shimmering ink stamped into leather, her brain turning over the color and shape and empty space, tracing with her eye, again and again, the contours of curves and angles. She remained unaware she stared for long minutes, entranced in a hazy way, at the cover, until a door slammed somewhere in the house, the bang drawing her from her study.

With a shake of the head, she opened to a random page. It was an entry for February 19th. There was small, unobtrusive scroll work along the borders of the page depicting intertwined winter branches, ice clinging to spindly offshoots in random ways around the page. The subject matter didn't seem out of place. Like any almanac of the era, it gave weather possibilities, planting advice, scriptural quotes offset in bold. However, the scripture quoted wasn't from the Christian Bible. It also wasn't in English, but in an alphabet she did not recognize. The words appeared on the page in the exact same way a Biblical quote would have, given its publication date and region. At least it wasn't easily recognizable as a particular chapter and verse because of the language.

She studied the words there more closely then jerked back her head. Blinking her eyes, she looked down again. The words were static, but for a second, she could have sworn she saw them shiver, literally ripple as if chilled. The branches seemed to sway, like they were blown by a wind sweeping across the page. She shut the book with one hand and brought her other up to her face, rubbing her eyes with her thumb and middle finger for a minute. It had been a long day, filled with excitement and annoyances. She was exhausted. Nothing else.

She sighed and looked down at the closed book. Again, she opened to a random page: June 21st - the summer solstice. Because it was the solstice, the entry was a little longer, a little more detailed. There were more elaborate hand-drawn borders with muted colors slightly dulled with age. A tree, full and lush with leaves, sat at the top right of the page, taking up a good chunk of room. The top of the page was the scenery around the tree: grass meadows, specs of birds, small puffs of clouds. The sun, with penetrating rays, shone down from the upper left edges of the page. The sides and bottom displayed an intricate root system, dark and web-like, caging the words on the page. It was very similar to how the roots in the tree hemmed in the iron box and this book itself, encircling and tightly containing but not fully encroaching. More like engulfing. She brought up a finger and tried to trace a root line through its loops and curves around the page, quickly getting lost in the design, staring wide-eyed at the protective mass of roots.

She again shook off her study and reached for her phone. The display told her she'd been studying the book for an hour. There was no way. Couldn't be. She'd spent no more than ten minutes on the first page. She couldn't have stared at this root print for fifty minutes. It was impossible, yet her head thudded a bit and her shoulders felt tight – a sensation she experienced only when she hunched over a text without moving for long stretches of time. She set the book away, looking at it from the corner of her eye, seeing how even closed and no longer in motion, the ink on the cover still glistened in the light. Shaking her hands out, she decided to leave the book where it was for the evening. Best to let it alone for now. She needed sleep or else she'd keep zoning out.

~~~

Her dream was filled with color. She knew it was a dream, being both passive and active in a world real and exaggerated or imagined. This was obvious for her because she was in space, and it was all colors. Wasn't space supposed to be dark, a blank vacuum void of anything? This space mimicked the same golden green shades as her tattoo, streaked with bold and pulsing pinks like old neon signs leaked vivid color and formed shifting clouds. There were bright blotches of yellow, purples so dark they sat right on the edge of nothingness, blues swirled with whites then bled into soft gray tones. All faded in and out as if the chaos of color occurred inside a kaleidoscope. She didn't simply view the colorful space. She was in it. She imagined the touch and feel of the colors, but the physical forms receded every time she got a little too close. Blink, blackness, blink, color, blink, white void – blinks back and forth in a dizzying array that made comprehension impossible beyond basic, vague impressions. The colors dominated, but she also saw silhouettes of branches. Fruit fresh then molded. The sway of leaves hitting dry dirt. There was soil, too. So dark and rich and teeming with roots she practically smelled it even after the visual flash dissipated.

She blinked awake and felt dirt crumbling between her toes. She smelled the soil, tilled and ripe. Her mind staggered in the jump from dream to reality. The old tree where the book was buried loomed in front of her. She stood frozen, still dazed and mesmerized by her odd dream. Worried about how she found herself out to this field, far from her room. She realized she gripped the book in her hands and dropped it, backing away like it was a snake poised to strike. It thudded to the ground and the world shook for a moment, shimmering around the edges of her sight. The tree branches stretched and unfurled, alive with movement and knowing.

She wanted to run. None of what she saw made sense. She should be in the twin bed, not out in a field far from the house. It had to be another dream. Must also be why she couldn't move, why she felt truly rooted to the spot. Then, the colors returned, flashing overhead across the night sky like trailing beacons. They originated somewhere behind her in the darkness, purples and greens and blues and pinks, all rushing toward the gnarled old tree. The colors faded and disappeared somewhere beyond its branches, past her line of sight.

She couldn't help it. She unstuck, walked like still in a dream, reached out to a tree with a soft glow in a spectrum of violent colors. It pulsed with its own internal beat, calling her to dance. She slid up, rubbed a hand along the bark, which gave way. Her hand melted into the trunk, her arm followed, and soon, her whole body. She felt the colors then, and the things that slithered in their wake, as they took hold of her and pulled her deeper into the bright space where enormous, lighting-like branches stretched across the horizon. Other beings stumbled there – too large to be people, too oddly shaped to be any animal she recognized.

Roots shot up from the hard ground, twining around her, planting her firmly. She looked behind her, frantic, thinking of escape. An odd rip in the atmosphere showed where she entered, the Ohio field in the dead of night. Faintly, she saw Manbun pick up the book and place it back inside the iron box. He looked her way, eyes devoid of consciousness but filled with wild colors. She screamed but roots cut her off, creeping higher and tightening around her neck. The rip knitted itself closed. The last vision she saw of her world was a book buried once again in the protective embrace of iron, roots, and soil.

Equals Until Eternity

By Elizabeth Willsea (*CONTENT WARNING: attempted suicide & suicide*)

I slammed my fist into his shoulder.

"No!"

The snot and blood dripping from my nose over my cracked lips and scabbed chin was nothing. It didn't matter how I looked on the rooftop in the full gaze of the sun and happily rolling clouds. "You don't dare give up!" I screamed in his face. His brown curls fell over his distant eyes clouded with pain.

"I can't," He whispered. The sob in his throat was choked by my own scream.

"You have too!" I shook him by the shoulders. "You don't get to give up! You can't give me first place so easily!"

"You think it's so great?" He gripped my shirt front and pulled my face to his. Our noses were inches apart, and the discoloration around his eye nearly made me sick, but he deserved it. It was better than his neck being broken and his brain splattered across the pavement. The mental image would have made me gag if it wasn't for the heat of his breath keeping me present. "You think it's so great?" He sobbed and tossed me aside. "Then you can have it."

"No," I said. "Not like this."

Being number one was an honor I was going to win. I would deserve it. I would earn it, because I was better than him. Not because he gave up.

"Try again," I begged.

He turned away from me, and that familiar fire spurred my feet forward. My arms locked around him, and my face smashed between his shoulder blades. If we did come out of this alive, his mother would hand us both our asses for the stains she'd have to clean up. "Try again!" I screamed.

"Please," he begged.

"You jump, I jump." Everything in him stilled. "We're equals, dammit. Don't you understand? Maybe you've got a hair's width ahead of me, but we're equals in everything."

I was so distraught it was a minute before I noticed he had turned and was holding me against him. His hand gripped the back of my neck. His lips pressed to my temple. "Equals?" It was like he spoke of salvation. I nodded my head.

"Of course."

~~~

That hair's width between us widened. Five inches. He was valedictorian, and all I had was a special seat behind him while he gave his flowered speech. A foot. His internship was with the most loved hero, while I was still doing grunt work for the local police station. A mile. He stood in front of cameras. I stood with citizen control. That's how it seemed life was going to continue until now.

"Oh my god! That was thrilling!" He swung his arm over my shoulder.

"Only for you," I said, a bit miffed at the turn of the situation.

It was a domestic problem. Would have been worse if we had arrived any later, but it wouldn't have happened at all if the rest of the family had the resources to protect themselves. Government, Heroes especially, were pushing that citizens rely a hundred percent on the appearance of Heroes for any and every situation. Self-defense was now labeled as intent to harm, and it was the dumbest thing I had ever heard. It wasn't national law yet, but some communities were already enforcing it. Communities like this one.

"Are you mad?" He looked at me.

"That could have gone a lot worse if we were any later." I gently removed his arm from my shoulder.

The mother of the family had pushed her husband off of her and managed to grab a lamp to knock over his head. That bought us the time we needed to arrive and help, but it still resulted in her receiving a severe warning from the local authorities.

I shook my head. "A mother should never be warned against protecting her children."

"Yeah, but she could have killed him, which would have been a worse crime than what he committed."

"Worse?" I stopped and looked at him, my jaw dropped. I knew he agreed with the law, but listening to him now felt like I had entered an alternate reality. "He was going to kill all of them. I think one life is better than three."

He shrugged his shoulders. "But with us, no lives are lost. Period."

"Unless we're late."

"I'm never late. You...." He looked me up and down. "Good thing we're a team."

"Since when?" I stopped walking. I watched my toes wiggle in my shoes that were a half size too small because I couldn't afford better.

When was the last time we were a team? The rooftop maybe, but that was so long ago it didn't matter. With his super strength and speed, he didn't really need me anymore. I might have a remarkable mind that any company would pay their last dollar for, but it wasn't a flashy ability to show off or to use to save a life. No matter how much I trained, I would never equal the power he was born with.

"Hey, come on. I wasn't trying to be harsh."

"No." I stepped back. "You were. It's fine. I'm done. You can support taking away the freedom of the people, but I'm going to try and give it back to them." I wiped my nose before shoving my hands in my pocket and turning my head away from him. I still couldn't meet his eyes. "I'm going to show that those who might appear to be weak have their own strength, and *we* don't need you anymore."

"What?"

"See ya on the other end." And I walked away.

~~~

That seemed like ages ago. The two most important days that determined who I was, the day I begged him to stay, and the day he let me leave, were branded in my memory, so I could never forget.

I dangled my feet from the edge of the roof. I could tempt death, the fall, the end of things, all night. He would never come. He's been number one for so long, and I've only been steadily slipping down the ranks since the beginning; him forgetting me was inevitable. That hair's width stretched and became miles between us. I've never been prouder of him though. He used to be so scared, and now he was all strength, strong will, and pride. He stood for something.

I was proud of myself too. I stood for something I believed in, and for once that wasn't him.

Using the edge of my knuckle, I wiped the corner of my eyes before I could betray myself and let a tear fall.

I wonder how he'd feel knowing what I've become, because it became easier believing other, darker, morals. Freedom wasn't heroism. Freedom was individual control. That's what I fought for from the bottom of the barrel.

I found the lost and forgotten victims of Villains and government abuse and trained them, gave them power, helped them to be faster and stronger. There were too many people Heroes didn't get to in time, too many survivors of late Heroes. Too many people the Heroes didn't know about or chose to forget. It wasn't right, and I made sure the people knew.

Vigilantism wasn't heroism, but to the people who it helped, there wasn't a difference.

The giant billboard in front of me told me he believed the opposite. What control did he have? What control did he give? I shook my head in cold dismay.

The heat I used to feel for him was barely embers now, ashes I let get cold. It was dangerous loving him.

"Maybe, it was dangerous loving me," I whispered to the blowout of his face lit by a million LED lights.

A piece of old brick chipped from the wall where I kicked my heels. I watched it, mesmerized by it's seemingly slow descent to the busy street below. The honking cars and choked traffic was white noise to the cacophony of blaring sounds in my head. They were sounds he used to silence with a touch of his hand, when he grazed my ear, smoothed down my bed head, or pressed his lips to the corners of mine.

Lost in memory, the calloused pads of my fingers crossed over my lips.

Catching myself, I slammed a fist into the cement beside me.

I cast a finger at the image of him, "You lost me!" Why was I upset? I chose to walk away. He let me leave. He never begged me like I begged him.

It was supposed to be us to the end. All those times he held my hand and pulled me across the finish line with him, I could feel his pulse pumping. He would pull my head to his chest when he pumped his fist in the air, and I can remember the erratic beat of his heart, full of life and screaming for more. The passion he felt. The passion he shared with me.

When did he let me go? When did my fingers slip away from his?

Did it matter?

I stood up on the ledge and spread my arms like the wings of a bird. A draft of air blew up against me, encouraging me, calling me to join it, to slip between its folds and be carried off with it.

"This is what we've come to? Saving each other at their end?"

I slowly turned and found him leaning against the door to the stairwell. How ironic that he was here. "Save each other?" I asked.

"You saved me, and now—"

"You condemned me."

He shook his head. "I've never left you behind. You quit trying. You quit holding on. You gave up." He uncrossed his arms and waved a hand for me to get off. "Come off the edge," he said. "We can talk about this."

"I'm not sure we can." My voice was barely there, already gone, already decided on the final outcome. The wind was aware, blowing harder, blowing my voice away from him.

I looked at him then. He was still where he was, filled with expectation and demand, but no freedom. The pride filling of his chest and the neatly styled curls, told me enough.

"It was to the end."

"We haven't made it to the end!" I could see him then, in high school, enraged by dogma and status quo. "Us! Do you remember! It was us to the end! But where were you when I needed you? You pulled away and I—" He clenched his fist and turned his head away from me. "We were supposed to be equals."

"That was never possible, I think," I said. "You'll always be better, and I'll always be in opposition. The people need freedom and that's what I've given them." I closed my eyes and spread my arms. "That's what I've given myself."

The rush in my ears was euphoric. It was faster than I thought, but it took all of eternity to fall. There was a moment when I loved the feeling, and the next an extreme panic because I heard my name reaching for me. His arms were around me, the familiar pulse of a heart in my ear, and the comforting pressure of his lips against my temple. He whispered something I couldn't hear, but I knew the shape of that word like I knew the shape of him.

"Equals."

And then eternity ended.

Julia

By Kai Mathis (*CONTENT WARNING: death and dying*)

Julia woke up and immediately knew it had happened again. Shaking her head to dislodge the last of the sleep, she slowly looked around her surroundings. The room was sterile, white walls, white floor, white sheets, white everything. There were no knick-knacks, nothing personal at all, but the room didn't feel abandoned either. To the left of the bed was a closet with white long-sleeve shirts and white pants. There was a pair of white shoes on the floor of the closet. A small dresser was next to the bed on that same side. There was nothing on the top and it only had two drawers. Across from the bed was a doorway, the tiled floor (again with the white) made her assume it was a bathroom. To the right of the bed was a closed door. There was nothing else in the room and no windows. She swung her feet off the bed, clutching the sheet to her chest, and fought the despair that wanted to wash over her. It was always the same yet so different. She didn't know how long she had been doing this, how many different worlds she had drifted into. All she knew was that it wasn't home, it was never home. She wiped the few tears she had let fall off her cheeks and settled her determination around her like a shawl.

"Get it together Julia. Clothes first, at least I get clothes this time."

She slid out of bed and opened the top drawer. Inside were socks and tank tops. The bottom drawer was empty. She grabbed what was offered and headed toward what she assumed was the bathroom. Inside she found exactly what she expected, toilet, sink, and a shower. There were a couple white towels hanging on the shower. She quickly took care of business and got dressed. Now came the fun part, figuring out if she was locked in or not. It was always a tossup. Testing the only other door in the room, she crossed her fingers and turned the knob. She grinned when it opened for her. It always went better when she could leave the room.

"Now to find out where the hell I am this time."

The hallway she walked into was just as white as the room she had just left. It dawned on her that she could see but couldn't tell where the light was coming from. That was a new one. Looking right and left they both looked identical, so she slipped out and headed right. The hallway looked like it went on forever in either direction. There were no breaks in the blank white walls on either side of the door to the room she had come out of. She walked cautiously, keeping close to the wall, and trying to look both behind and in front. Eventually she came to a door on the right. Taking a deep breath, she jerked it open. She let the breath she had been holding out and looked around the room. It looked identical to the room she had left. Everything was in the same place even. It was also empty of life. She stuck her head into the bathroom just to be sure. Shaking her head in annoyance, she headed back out into the hallway.

She left the door open behind her so she could have some frame of reference in the never-ending white. She headed to her right again, continuing her exploration. The faint illumination was still there, enough to see the hallway ahead of her. The temperature was just right for the shirt and pants she was wearing. There was no sound, not the hum of an AC or a lightbulb, no voices in the distance, not even the sound of her footsteps in the carpeted hallway. The only sound was her breathing as she slowly walked down the hall, praying for something besides unrelieved white.

Time had no meaning to her as she crept on. It could have been minutes or hours when she came upon another door. This one was on the left side of the hallway. Taking a breath she tried the door, unsurprised when it turned under her hand. This time the room she entered was all black. It was almost identical to the white rooms, but there was an extra door across the room. Again, the room was empty of sentient life, as was the attached bathroom. Steeling herself she crossed to the other door and yanked it open. She was faced with another hallway, this one black, like the room behind her.

Now she had to decide if she continued exploring the white corridor behind her or this black one ahead. "Six of one, half dozen of the other" she softly muttered. The black hallway had the same faint illumination as the white hallway. They both felt the same to her and both seemed to be endless. Basing her choice on the fact that black was her favorite color, she headed into the new hallway. She left the door open behind her and once again headed to her right. The monotony and repetitiveness were something she had become accustomed to. She let her mind drift to other places, some like this, some with challenges to face, but all of them wrong. There were never any people. She couldn't remember the last time she had talked to a real person. Getting up at each new place was getting harder and harder. Sighing she once again focused on the here and now and tried to hold onto the last little bit of hope that she would one day get home.

The silence and the lack of color were getting to her. Her inability to mark the passage of time was also maddening. She didn't think she had been exploring for that long because she wasn't tired, or hungry, or thirsty. Unless of course that was a condition of this place and she would never have to worry about those things. She decided humming some of her favorite songs would help. Three badly hummed songs later she came upon a door on her right. Thinking she knew what she would be looking at, she checked anyway to make sure. Her assumption was correct, another black room with a door on the opposite side, that when she opened it, once again showed the white hallway. She closed that door and kept walking. She passed three more closed doors on her right before she came upon the open one. So, the hallways weren't straight, the curve was just so faint as to be indistinguishable. They curved into a circle. Circle within a circle, since the white hallway probably did the same thing around the outside of the black rooms. There was only one way out of the white room against the far side, so that must be as far out as the circles went.

"So, left-hand doors it is" she grouched as she headed back into the black hallway. She passed through purple, blue, green, yellow, orange, and finally red. They were all identical except for the color. The lack of people was disconcerting and the monochromatic hallways felt like they would never end. It was all so bland and boring. Time had no meaning in these hallways. It could have been minutes, it could have been hours, or days. Julia had no way to tell. The lack of any noise other than ones she deliberately made was maddening. Trying to find the light source became her goal for a while, but each circular hallway was the same. She had stopped going all the way around by the time she hit blue. All in all, it really fucked with Julia's head. She was an anxious, sweating mess by the time she found the left-hand door in the red hallway. She swung the door open expecting more of the same. Bright white lights blinded her, burning through her retinas, and setting off a kaleidoscope of colors on her eyelids as she quickly closed her eyes. The after images lingered as her eyes watered and pain stabbed her eyes. Sounds slammed into her eardrums, louder than she could have imagined. The loud music was mostly bass that echoed in her skull, it was accompanied by the sound of sirens, and a high-pitched whine that felt like nails being driven into her head. Through the cacophony, she heard a steady beeping and the low drone of voices. She couldn't see and everything was too bright and loud. Overwhelmed with all the stimulus, she slammed the door and rested her back against it. It was all too much. She slid down the door and pulled her knees to her chest. It was always the same, the first part was easy, boring even, but crazy-making in the lack of stimuli. Then, just when she knew it would last forever she was blasted with sound and lights and pain. So much pain. She felt like she had been traveling these worlds forever. She would think it was a dream, but she had never slept in a dream before and the pain was too real. If it was a dream, it was a nightmare. One she prayed daily she would wake from. She never did. Just kept waking up in new places that were similar, but never exactly the same. Always trying to escape, but never knowing how. Getting blasted in the end, by something she hadn't been able to overcome. Knowing what would happen if she gave in to the exhaustion that was pulling at her, she fell over, curled into a protective ball, and cried herself to sleep.

~~~

"Kelly, did you see that?! I swear she almost had her eyes open." He looked so excited, I didn't want to bring him down, but reality was reality. "I'm sorry Jax, I didn't notice. It's been 8 years now. She is probably never coming out of this." Jax glared at me, and then turned back to the bed. I started to walk out of the room, visiting hours were almost over and I had to get home to the kids. The years had taken a toll on all of us and I knew we would have to make some hard decisions soon. Jax had his head in the clouds and still believed that love conquered all. I knew better. My sister was gone and Jax needed to face the facts and move on with his life. We all did. She wouldn't have wanted to linger like this. Soon, we would have to let her go. I would give Jax a little more time, and then say goodbye. Julia deserved better.

What Lies Within

By Erica Jackson

T he day had been an absolute drag. Working at a dead end, part-time job for a handsy forty-year-old man who knew less about the fashion industry than I did, tended to suck the fun out of most of my waking hours. I only took the stupid job because I liked the clothes in the boutique, and the extra money kept my bookstore from going under. Business in the bookstore had always been pretty slow, but the pandemic made my cozy shop a ghost town. COVID-19 killed more than people these days.

I sighed under my face mask.

"Well grandma, we made it through another day," I said, looking up into the night sky as I walked down the block to my little safe haven.

A chill ran up my spine. It felt like someone was watching me. My feet sped up on their own. I could see the bookstore's iron sign a few yards away. I strained to hear footsteps behind me, but only heard the echoes of my own.

Something screamed inside me to run. I took off as fast as I could, frantically searching the inside of my purse for my keys. Another strange sensation hit me that I couldn't place, like I was being pulled in the opposite direction. My body felt heavier and my movements began to slow despite how hard I pushed myself.

Panic took hold of me. The store was so close. I could almost reach out and touch it. Beads of sweat started to run down my back. I could feel something gaining on me.

Whoosh!

A massive gust of wind blew past me, stinging my cheeks with its chill. I held up my arms to guard my face. The invisible lasso holding me back was released. Keys in hand, I bolted to the front door, raced inside, and slid the various locks into place. Out of breath and shaking, I dragged a table in front of the door from the little cafe in the corner for extra security and flipped on the overhead lights.

Looking through the windows I could see the world was still again, but I wasn't taking any chances. I walked behind the main counter of the bookstore and grabbed the metal bat I kept in case of emergencies.

A few silent moments later, I decided to head upstairs. "Looks like I'm paying extra on the light bill this month," I thought as I trudged my way to the spiral iron staircase near the back of the store, the metallic clang of each step echoing louder than the quiet of the shop. The dark didn't sit well with me at the best of times, but if an invisible stalker didn't constitute a need for all the lights on, I didn't know what did.

Halfway up the stairs a wave of peace washed over me. That same strange voice inside that raised the red flag earlier was telling me everything was alright. As odd as it may seem, I was comforted enough to drop my guard and take a much needed shower. The bat, however, stayed with me wherever I went.

Cleansed, fed, and ready for sleep, I finally made my way to my room. My little twin sized bed never looked so welcoming. But sleep would have to wait.

My eyes connected with the beat up blue and white Fender Strat leaning against the corner of the wall across from my bed. She needed new strings, and the paint was beginning to chip around her edges, but she still sang like an angel on the dark side of the moon. Her and I had grown quite the following over the last few years playing improvised songs and popular covers. I couldn't bring myself to replace her.

I picked her up and positioned myself on the edge of my bed. I needed to practice a new song I'd been working on to debut on my weekly live stream. If all went well, I was planning on using it in a compilation album I'd created for my followers on Spotify.

Like every time before, the music consumed me the moment I plucked the first string. It flowed out of me from somewhere deep inside that I couldn't quite place. Notes would come to me from some cosmic source as if I were a conduit for the voice of the universe. It was an overwhelming surge of human emotions in their purest forms aching to be released or crush me under their weight. The intensity scared me as a child, with its raw passion and strange ability to draw people in, but I learned to embrace the emotions as I got older. Fighting the call to harness my odd musical gift was more painful than facing what I couldn't understand.

Tonight I played a haunting tune. It was a sad lullaby that

penetrated my soul. I'd heard the song in my dreams for the better part of a year, and there were strange moments during the day when it would faintly float back to me, like someone was whispering to me in acoustic chords. It was so overwhelming I had to get it out of me.

Tears dripped down my face by the end of the song. No matter how hard I tried I always cried when it was over. I needed to get a handle on that before I streamed Friday.

Slow clapping near my door jolted me off my bed.

"Well done, Ms. Clifton. Very impressive."

A slender man with bright eyes and a Cheshire Cat smile was leaning against my bedroom door frame. His voice was as languid as his movements as he straightened himself and walked toward me.

"Of course, I wouldn't have expected anything less."

I clenched the neck of the guitar, finally able to find my voice again, "Who are you?! What do you think you're doing in my house?!"

The man stopped with a chuckle. My voice came out less menacing than I hoped it would, cracking a bit at the end.

"You don't have to be afraid, Maria. I'd harm myself before I'd ever even think of hurting you."

That was it! I lifted my poor Fender over my head like a bat, hoping she would forgive me for ending our relationship like this. The man's eyes went wide and he threw his hands up in defense.

"Wait! Wait, wait, wait!"

The guitar sliced through the air with all the force I could muster. The man narrowly dodged the blow with a mischievous laugh.

"Woah, you're quick!"

"Ugh," I grunted as I swung the guitar in the opposite direction.

He caught it with one hand, blocking it from connecting with his jaw. I released it and dashed for the door. I didn't look behind me. I was downstairs and at the back door in seconds. I flung the door open and screamed.

The man was standing in the doorway with his arms crossed and a smug grin on his face. "You can't out run me, Maria. Although, you're welcome to try again."

I slammed the door in his face, locking it. I fled to the phone near the counter register and started dialing. By the time my finger pressed the second number, the phone was yanked from my hand. I gasped as I frantically backed away from the counter.

The unnervingly handsome man looked more serious now. He hung the phone up and avoided my terrified gaze.

"I'm afraid calling the police is out of the question. Getting them involved will only make things harder than they need to be."

His voice was strangely calm and remorseful. Mine came out quivering.

"What do you want? Why are you doing this?"

His eyes met mine and I suddenly noticed something I hadn't before. They were garnet. I thought they were a brown shade, but the bright lights of the store almost made them crimson. He must have read the new fear on my face, because his expression softened even more.

He tried to walk slowly toward me with his hands reaching out like he was trying to sooth a frightened animal. "Maria, please try to calm down. Just let me explain."

My breaths quickened. The closer he got, the more I noticed. His short hair wasn't black but a deep blue. His ears were slightly pointed, and every so often, when he moved a certain way, the light glinted off something large sticking out of both sides of his back.

"Don't come any closer," I cried out, bumping into a book cart as I retreated.

"Please..."he pleaded.

"No! Stay back!"

My foot caught on the edge of a bookshelf and I tumbled backward. My head bounced off the floor and darkness overtook me. I heard the stranger yell out my name before slipping into unconsciousness.

~~~

Time had no form. Sounds were erased by a void I couldn't climb out of or explain. Everything was going numb.

A small prick of light appeared. With it was a faint, almost unintelligible sound. The spot grew bigger, or rather, the light was getting closer. Fragmented notes floated into the nothingness that surrounded me. I began to recognize the melody. Feeling returned, and my heart beat faster as the light that penetrated the darkness consumed me with its warmth and filled the endless expanse with my beloved dream song.

My haunting melody brought happiness that I didn't know was possible. Then a voice filtered in, a whispering echo of my name.

My eyes fluttered open. A groan escaped my lips. I heard the soothing voice from the void again.

"Oh, thank goodness. You had me worried."

Still a little disoriented, it took me a moment to realize what my eyes were seeing. I was back in my room. The lights were dimmed and my comforter was pulled up to my chin. I scanned the room, slowly remembering what led up to my black out.

A man came into view, sitting in my computer chair with his legs crossed and his worried, unnatural eyes fixed on me.

I shot up in bed.

"You shouldn't move so quickly," He insisted. "Just take it slow. You knocked your head pretty hard."

Despite my throbbing skull, I remained upright and prepared to defend myself.

He read my expression and rolled his eyes. He let out an exasperated sigh. "Come now. Do you really think I would go through the trouble of helping you if I wanted to do you harm?"

I said nothing but thought it over carefully. He had a point, but I wasn't convinced.

"Maria...what is it going to take to win you over?"

"You can start by telling me how you know my name and why you're in my apartment," I said, crossing my arms and pursing my lips.

He searched my face for a second. Holding my ground under his penetrating gaze was more of a challenge than I thought it would be, but I refused to back down. I didn't like the uneasy expression he was trying to mask.

"I've known your name for a very long time. Just as I knew your grandmother's."

"My grandmother's?! What does my grandmother have to do with -"

He held up a hand to stop me. "Please, Maria. This will go a lot more smoothly if you let me explain without interruptions."

I raised my brows at him in disapproval.

It made the corners of his mouth twitch upward. "I've been assigned as your guardian. Your grandmother was my first charge. To put it simply, you inherited me from her."

A thought struck me then. It was so absurd I tried to dismiss it. But the idea nagged at me the more the man spoke.

"I was in your apartment because you called out to me."

"What?! No I didn't. I don't even know who you are." I looked him over. "Or...what you are."

That Cheshire Cat grin showed up again. If I wasn't so freaked out, I might have thought it made him look even more handsome than he already was. I internally shook the thought away.

"Verbally, you didn't. But your soul...now that's a different story. Guardian Fairies tend to have that ability given the right circumstances."

I looked at him like he was the village idiot. "F-fairies? You're telling me that you're a fairy?"

"Guardian Fairy," he corrected proudly.

I squinted my eyes at him. "Prove it."

This time he looked at me like I was the idiot. He gestured to himself, letting his nearly invisible wings flutter a little behind him.

I inhaled sharply. Either I was losing it, or this was real.

"Breathe, Maria. You have to breathe."

I finally exhaled. Denial and panic started to set in.

"This isn't real. You aren't really here. I'm...having a nervous breakdown because of all the stress. Or better yet, you're just a hallucination brought on by a COVID induced fever." I shook my head up and down at him to coerce him to agree.

He shook his head no. My head involuntarily mimicked his movement.

There was a pause. Images of the strange sprint to the bookstore earlier in the night flashed through my mind. That must have been him helping me...from...what exactly? I stopped the thought. I needed to take this one step at a time.

"So ... you're telling me ... that I inherited a fairy godmother from my grandmother?"

He made a face. "Guardian Fairy. Calling us all fairy godmothers is actually extremely offensive where I come from. That ditz Cinderella spread that stupid rumor to get back at her Guardian Fairy for only giving her 'til midnight to dance at the ball. Ungrateful child still got her happy ending."

"Um...how is that getting back at her Guardian?"

"Because Guardian Fairies are only male."

"Oh ..." I said absently, struggling to stay focused on the tangent.

I fell back on my pillow with a sigh. The nagging thought from earlier came back with a vengeance. My grandmother always stressed how important the bookstore was. I thought it was because it was full of memories for her, like a family legacy or something; everything in me was screaming that it had to do with this man instead.

I caved, staring up at the ceiling at no spot in particular.

"Okay. I give. You're really here and you knew my grandmother." I turned my head to face him.

"What do you mean by my soul cried out for you?"

A lighthearted grin brightened his face. "That's where the fun part comes in."

"I shudder to know," I mumbled sarcastically.

"As it turns out, you're my soulmate, Ms. Maria Clifton."

I popped back up with wide eyes.

"Excuse me?!"

He pouted a little. "Oh come on. I'm not that bad."

"You are ridiculous."

He shrugged before crossing his arms. "I don't know what to tell ya. I don't make the rules. God chose us to be together, and who am I to argue?"

I shook my head at him. "How romantic of you - being with me purely out of duty."

He laughed. "Ah ... but God writes the best love stories. Why not go along with it?" His garnet eyes were full of mischief, and I hated that I liked his crooked smile.

I silently told God He had a twisted sense of humor.

"Now, don't you want to know your lover's name," he teased.

"Ugh...don't call yourself that."

He smiled. "My name's Taeyon. Taeyon Valor.

I looked him up and down before reluctantly sticking my hand out to him. He leaned over and shook my hand gently. His touch made my stomach fill with butterflies, which irritated me beyond measure.

"Are you going to tell me why my family needs a mythical bodyguard?"

The mood in the room shifted, and Taeyon's face fell. He let out a sigh as he leaned back in the chair. His tone was edged with irritation. "Not all of my people are as fond of your kind as I am."

My brows furrowed. "What does that -"

Something burst through the window beside my bed. I screamed as someone slammed Taeyon against the far wall. The two struggled to land blows on each other, crashing into furniture and knocking pictures from the wall. My eyes searched for a weapon. The cloaked intruder headbutted Taeyon, disorienting him. I yanked my metal bat off the floor as the intruder pulled a dagger from the depths of his cloak.

"Duck," I yelled.

Taeyon dropped out of the way just before the bat smashed into the surprised attacker's face. It only managed to knock the intruder off balance.

Taeyon grabbed my wrist and careened out the door. He waved a hand behind us less than a second before the cloaked man followed suit. A pink hued barrier appeared, causing the man to bounce backward and tumble to the floor.

We rounded a corner that led to the spiral staircase. I kept glancing behind us to see if the man got free.

"That barrier won't last long," Taeyon called. "We have got to get you to safety."

The two of us rushed down the stairs.

"Why is that man after me?!"

Another window exploded, followed by another in the bookstore as we stepped on the first floor.

"These people want to steal your voice. You're becoming powerful enough to stop them."

"Ah!" I heard myself scream as we barely dodged a fireball. Taeyon guided us to the storage room in the very back, right next to the back door.

"Where are we going? The exit's that way."

"Not the exit we're looking for," he answered.

He waved his hand again and the door slammed shut behind us. We raced past the stacks of boxes and old bookshelves, heading straight for a brick wall.

"Taeyon! What are you doing?!"

"Just hang on!"

He swung me into his arms and launched us into the wall.

I screamed and wrapped my arms tightly around his neck, squeezing my eyes shut.

I began to feel wind on my face. I gasped as I took in the world around us. Taeyon was flying over a vibrant, sunny landscape that should have been impossible. Giant mushrooms and floating crystals hovered over multicolored trees and creatures that were only real in fairy tales. Birds, or at least I assumed they were birds, glided past us with golden feathers, long tails, and iridescent eyes. A purple ocean transfixed my gaze in the distance.

"Where are we," I asked in awe.

"It has many names. For now we'll call it Home."

I actually liked the sound of that.

A fireball shot passed us like a rocket, hitting one of the

mesmerizing birds.

Taeyon growled. "These witches won't give it a rest."

"Witches?! I'm being stalked by witches?!"

Taeyon banked to the left. A giant ball of ice missed us this time.

"Witches crave power. They run most of this world and manipulate the rulers of yours. Whenever they find someone with a powerful voice, they seek to steal that person's gift. If they can't, they eliminate the potential threat."

I looked over Taeyon's shoulder and gasped. "Right!"

The fairy swerved out of the way of a massive rock. "This isn't working." He squeezed me tighter and nose dived.

We pierced through the sky like a bullet. I didn't even have time to scream. Trees started to whizz around us. All at once, Taeyon skid us to a stop on the forest floor. He raced behind a giant boulder with me still in his arms.

"Don't even breathe," he whispered as he set me down.

The witches weren't far behind. Four cloaked men came into the tiny opening a few feet away from the boulder. They flew in on black, rune covered stones that closely resembled surf boards.

Taeyon was gone in the blink of an eye. He reappeared in front of the unsuspecting men, kicking and punching like a master martial artist. His movements were almost impossible to see. Fear began to replace the witches' menacing gazes. Taeyon flipped backwards, displayed his wings, and thrust his arms in front of him. A whirlwind of hurricane force sent the witches and their stone boards flying into the forest's depths.

My guardian turned as he tried to catch his breath. When his fierce eyes locked on mine, they were glowing. A strange melody flowed into my mind. It was new and alluring. His feral expression softened, and he walked toward me. The closer he got, the louder the consuming song became.

"What is that," I asked in a hushed tone.

He smiled gently, reaching up to tuck a loose curl behind my ear. I was hyper aware of the mere inches that were between us.

"That's my soul. It's calling out to yours."

I swallowed hard, unable at first to break from his burning stare. I finally willed myself to turn away.

"So," I struggled to get out as I stepped around him, "how come they were called witches? They were male."

He chuckled softly with a knowing grin spreading across his face.

My maneuver to change the subject wasn't that subtle after all. "You can't believe everything the storybooks tell you. Men who aren't very powerful at magic are known as witches. Female witches are the only truly fearsome practitioners to look out for."

"I don't think I'm ever going to get used to all of this. This is insane."

Taeyon held out his hand to me. "Insanity or not, we better keep moving. I'm sure there will be more coming to finish what the others couldn't."

I sighed and took his hand.

"I don't understand what's so great about my voice. I'm not much of a singer. Instrumental music is more of my thing."

Taeyon guided us through the ethereal foliage as he spoke. "A voice takes many forms. Someone can have a powerful voice without ever saying a single word."

My heart nearly stopped when his hands grabbed my waist and he lifted me over a spiked log blocking our path.

"How is that possible," I asked shakily.

"Hehe. Did I surprise you?" His smug expression made me want to hit him.

"Just answer the question."

He smirked. "Creative expression speaks volumes. God given gifts are blessings meant to be shared with the world. People's talents can influence the hearts and minds of so many, both for great good or great evil."

"You definitely knew my grandmother. She used to say things like that."

"She was a wise woman."

We fell silent for a moment, fondly remembering my warm hearted grandmother.

"Are there others who have supernatural powers...or gifts...or whatever you want to call it?"

"Yes. There are others. Everyone has varying degrees of gifts. Some people just have bigger roles to play than others."

We both jumped over a small stream.

"I'm guessing I have a bigger role to play then."

"It would appear so," he said warmly.

I thought for a long moment about how heavy that responsibility really might be; how easily I take my musical gift for granted; how there is a deeper purpose behind the creative talents people are endowed with. It was humbling. Knowing that my voice was needed to make a change made me want to give all I had to ensure the world around me would be left in a better state than it was when I was born into it.

I looked up at my Guardian Fairy. He was still as mysterious to me as the duties I'd been entrusted with. I didn't know where we were going or if my heart would truly come to love him as a soulmate should. But what I did know was that this power, this voice, was meant for greater things than myself.

No matter the cost, I decided, I would become a voice of light for great good.

Mystery

Prepare

By Lucas Barnes (CONTENT WARNING: *missing person, murder*)

Detective Leibowitz knocks on the front door for the fourth time and still no reply. He takes a step back slowly taking in the scenery. The mailbox hanging to the left of the door is overflowing with mail. He knocks one last time then tries to catch a peek through one of the windows near the door. "Damn it, blinds," he growls in frustration. Maybe there is a better view through another window, so the detective makes his way around the house.

While he walks around, he thinks about the details of the missing person's report. The last time she had been seen was with a former partner of her's who, apparently, she had a falling out with. Aside from that there is no other information; it is as if she never existed. Earlier in the week Detective Leibowitz spoke to an informant of his that said her partner's last known location was at this house. The detective has a gut feeling that something is going on here but alas he cannot get a warrant based on feelings, so he is investigating the lead on his own. Heaven forbid the captain knows what he is doing, then again this isn't his first rodeo.

"Jackpot!" the detective exclaims as he spies through a window without a blind. It was a little high up, so he moved a trash can to the house and climbed up to peer inside. His first impression from the street was this house was vacant; however, one look inside proves otherwise. The room appears to be an office or study with a huge desk in the middle of the room. Leaning against the wall to the side of the desk on the floor appears to be a cork board with 4 polaroid's pinned in a row. The first picture Leibowitz cannot make out because it is crossed out, but the other three looked like children with the eyes removed from the pictures. There seem to be more pictures as well as papers pinned to the board, but he cannot see it from this angle. There are boxes and papers scattered everywhere, but is it because of a struggle or is it another sad story of a hoarder? As the detective climbs down a ray of light glints off something that catches his eye from the corner of the room. On a filing cabinet there is a golden statue of a cat. Egyptian maybe? Whatever it is, it appears to have dried blood at its base. Leibowitz climbs down from the trash can and continues further along the house when he comes to another window. This window has a broken blind in it, maybe he can see inside. Once again, he uses the trash can to reach the window. Is he looking at a bedroom? He really can't tell, but it does look like there is a headboard against a wall with the letter R mounted at its peak.

Leibowitz hops down off the trash can and is suddenly overwhelmed with a horrible feeling in his stomach. He knows he should call for backup but what can he say? "Hey, Cap, I am searching a house without a warrant, because my internal crime alarm was sounding off." Yeah, that wouldn't work at all.

Leibowitz draws his pistol as he reaches a gate to a privacy fence boarding the house's backyard. To his surprise the latch is not locked. He slowly opens the door and steps into the back yard to a site that stops him dead in his tracks. The scent is so strong it nearly knocked him off his feet. There is red everywhere and he hears a voice inside him that screams *run you fool!* Never in his life had he seen a garden with such beauty. It looked as if Alice had come through painting every rose. Roses are everywhere. Secured to the privacy fence surrounding the whole perimeter is a lattice that is covered in crawling rose plants. Red, white, and pink roses saturate the garden from the walls to the rows upon rows of bushes. Every bush is placed precisely in a position that mirrors the opposite side of the garden, and centered in the garden is an immaculate white marble bench with an arched trellis over the top. The trellis is covered in exquisite green moss that provides shade. Carved into the trellis are multiple unknown symbols that look vaguely familiar. Leibowitz never cared for the feng shui of his own house, but it is apparent that whoever lived here did. A bead of sweat trickles down the side of Leibowitz's face as he holsters his gun before sitting on the bench to get out of the sun. Looking around the garden he can tell that oddly enough not all the soil matches. Some soil looks very dry and packed into the earth like it has been there for years. Then there are a couple of places where the soil is dark and wet and seems very loose. He can see from the bench some common garden tools as well as a couple of half-emptied bags of mulch and soil leaning against a tool shed next to the back of the house. This makes no sense that the house looks so vacant, yet this back yard is some sort of utopia that has obviously been cared for possibly even recently.

Something is still off, so he picks up his phone to call the captain. Surely, they can think of something creative to get a warrant to search the house. He taps the number on his phone, and as he is about to hit send, something catches his eye. A lone pink hair lay near his feet as a ray of sunlight bounces off of it igniting the hair like a glow stick. He pulls a pen from his pocket and picks it up to examine it further. Doesn't the missing person have pink hair? His eyes widen with excitement and alarm as he looks at his phone briefly before catching the reflection of a flash of gold before he collapses to the earth. A pool of blood slowly grows bigger under Leibowitz's head until the silence is finally broken by the sound of a phone ringing.

"Hello Christy's Greenhouse, thank you for calling, how can I help you today?"

"Hey Christy, it's your favorite customer. I'm looking for... something new."

"Hi James! I have been waiting for you to call, I just got in some new yellow island rose bushes. I don't think you have bought yellow before. Can I put you down for one?"

James looks down at the detective's lifeless body while casually flipping a golden blood-soaked statue in his other hand. A smile slowly crept across his lips. "Better make it double."

Just Desserts

By Christina E. Patrick (*CONTENT WARNING: death, child abuse*)

Dread, a word one did not normally associate with simple things. A word more commonly paired with things like monsters, scary movies, or that seven-page paper you've been putting off and is due tomorrow.

For Anna though, dread was an all too familiar emotion, one that tended to pop up at the most unfortunate times. Though one would never guess it just by looking at her.

Anna, a short, well built woman whose curves were the work of many years sampling her own work with pastries was never seen without a smile. Her smiles, just like the deserts she carefully crafted was hard to resist.

Just looking at her, one might think she was one of the happiest women on the planet. They would be wrong.

Anna Brown was at one time of the brightest and happiest girls that lived in Seven Rivers, a sleepy little town about an hour away from any big city. Not hard to do when one lived in the more rural parts of Arkansas.

She was the kind of girl who as a child, would go from house to house with her mother's homemade jams, jellies, and fresh bread, taking them to those who didn't leave their houses much. Her bright green eyes and radiant smile were always welcome, especially to the older women who longed for lively conversation.

Never once had an adult complimented her to her mother without saying how sweet her smile was, and how good a little girl she had grown up to be.

Her mother of course would exclaim how grateful she was, and pat her on the head. Proclaiming for all who could hear how grateful she was to have such a wonderful daughter.

For a few happy moments, Anna would be filled with joy, believing she had made her mother happy. That she had done well to be praised so.

Once their guests had left, and her mother began closing the blinds, however, she would feel it rise once again. Dread.

Like a snake coiled around her stomach, she felt it rise up to her throat. Fear clutching, clawing, grasping; her mind screaming at her to run, but her feet were nailed to the spot in fear.

The vision shattered as Anna shook her head to block out the unpleasant memory. She hated when those memories clawed their way back into her mind.

Slowly returning to the present, Anna watched as her childhood kitchen faded from sight as simple pale wooden cabinets were replaced with darker woods and marble countertops, and she once again stood alone.

Now an adult of twenty-five, Anna lived alone in her city apartment far from Seven Rivers. Not that she minded, of course, she preferred to live alone. It was easier that way.

Not that she didn't have offers of course. Close friends had offered to be her roommate, but she just wanted to live alone.

It made things easier this way. This way, she didn't have any explanations to give or arguments with those who didn't understand. Here, she could be at peace.

"Fuck!" she exclaimed as she caught sight of the clock above the archway. The time was four-fifteen. She should have been halfway there by now.

"Stella is going to kill me."

Shoving the last lid closed, Anna piled up all of the boxes into her arms and grabbed her purse. Maybe if luck was on her side, then traffic would be in her favor. It wasn't likely, but she could hope.

If there was one thing she didn't want, it was to be late to her best friend's surprise proposal. Too much work had gone into making today perfect for her to mess it up now.

Stella was her best friend Grim's fiance, and the two of them had been working on this surprise for far too long for it to fall through because she was late.

Nearly juggling the boxes in her arms, Anna shut the door with her foot, and with a kind of grace that even surprised her.

"Alright" she huffed nearly out of breath as she went down the flight of steps towards the front door. "If it's too close to rush hour. If I take the main road, I'll be late for sure." Going over routes in her head, she finally decided on one. "I'll have to take Statham road."

Dread fluttered up in her chest again, but she pushed it down. She could do this for Grim, she had to be there.

Nearly running into someone as they came in through the front doors, Anna paused only long enough to apologize and move towards her car which thankfully was parked right by the front today.

"Mrs.?" the voice of the man she had passed called out to her.

"Sorry, I can't talk, I'm in a rush." she called back, not even bothering to turn to see who it was. She secured the boxes in the trunk of her can and hopped into the driver's seat.

"Mrs. Brown, I really need to speak with..." but his words were lost on her as she backed out of the parking lot and drove away. Whoever he was, and whatever he wanted could wait. She was already pushing it on being late.

Leaving the apartment parking lot, Anna drove off as fast as she could without drawing attention. Instead of going towards the main road, which usually would be faster, she turned left towards Statham road.

The moment her car turned, she could feel the cold twist of fear in her stomach. She hadn't been on Statham road since the incident and knew now that she wasn't ready.

Once again, she felt the cold rush of memories, except this time she wasn't a helpless little girl. This time, she was a young adult, barely nineteen.

There she was, sitting in the passenger side of a beat-up silver Toyota, and listening to Brittney Spears as loudly as the speakers could take it. Beside her, driving the car was one of the most beautiful women Anna had ever seen. She had thick curly black hair that fell on her shoulders like clouds, and skin that glistened like obsidian in the rain.

Reani sang along with her, though her singing was half laughter as she kept looking over at Anna and cracking up over the overly dramatic faces she was making.

Reani had been Anna's reason for living, her everything. The one that she had wanted to spend the rest of her life with. They thought that they had it all. Happiness, love, a bright future together.

The ring on her finger, a promise that one day when they had enough money, they would make things official.

It would never be though. One day was all it took. One rainy day and a driver too tired to see the road took that all away from her.

The flash of light was their only warning as Reani and Anna went from laughing and listening to music to screaming as their car was hit by another.

Tears streamed down Anna's face as the memories flooded back into her mind. She tried to shut them out, to push them away, but they kept coming back.

To try and drown them out, she turned on the radio, on anything that wasn't a pop station, trying to drown them out. It took a while, but eventually, the echoes of her past faded. For now at least. They always came back though.

Hoping some of her makeup survived, Anna wiped away at her tear-stained cheeks. Her now red-rimmed eyes staring blankly at the road ahead of her. If she could just make it through this part of the trip, she could make it through the evening. She owed it to herself and to Stella.

Barely aware of the rest of the drive, Anna finally came back to herself as she arrived at Greenhill Park.

Driving around a bit, she searched for the familiar dark green jeep. Finding it, she could feel dread well up inside of her once more. She chalked it up to her worries about being late, however. What else could it be?

Parking, she pulled into the lot right next to Stella's Jeep. From the looks of it, they were already in the park, and Anna knew that she had to hurry.

Running around the back of her car, she flung open the trunk and began pulling out boxes of pastries. Going a bit too fast, she nearly dropped the smallest one onto the ground.

Just barely catching it with her knees as she dropped into a squat, she let out a gasp from the sudden, almost disaster.

Her whole body froze in place as dread filled her at the idea of nearly messing it all up. Too much. Too much time had gone into this to ruin it now. Not when she was so close.

After taking a few deep breaths, she calmed herself enough to pick up the box and stand back up.

"Now" she turned and began walking towards the little secluded part of the park. "Let's go find them."

Making her way through the park, she passed the area full of kids. Loud noises, laughing children, and screams of children being chased.

Screams of Anna as she was chased through the dark house. Dread filling her body, making her run faster, making her breath come in sharp gasps.

Behind her in the dark, the monster followed, its body falling and crashing into objects that she had thrown in its path. Hoping against hope that she would trip it up enough to get away.

"No no no nooo" she cried, her throat sore from crying and screaming as she ran. There was nowhere to hide, there was never anywhere that she could hide, that she could be safe.

The monster's voice yelled for her to stop, screamed at her to come back, but she couldn't. Not this time. So many times, this monster had come for her, but she could take it no longer.

Anna gripped her right arm, which she was sure had broken when she escaped, and continued to run. Nothing would stop her this time. Nothing.

"Anna!" the monster's voice called to her, but... it wasn't her monster.

"Anna" Stella stood about ten feet away waving at her from a small grove of trees.

Shaking off the memory, Anna smiled at Stella. "Hey girly, Grim here yet?" she asked as the feeling of dread slowly simmered in her stomach.

"Hmm? Oh yeah, he just went to use the bathroom real quick. He'll be here soon."

Walking over to her, Stella helped her set all the boxes out onto the table. Making sure to hide the effects of her most recent visions behind her sturdy mask of a smile. Thankful in the moment that Stella likely wouldn't catch any slips in her own excitement.

"Good, I'd hate to be late for this." Anna said as she began setting up the table. hummed to herself as the two of them set up the table.

"Oh you know I would have waited for you." Stella laughed, and helped her friend make everything look perfect.

Once the plates had been set, Stella pulled Anna into a tight hug. Not noticing the slight flinch from her best friend before she hugged her back. "I couldn't imagine doing this without you."

Anna patted Stella on the back, and pulled away, smiling brightly and pulling her hands into hers.

"I'm so excited for this. I can't tell you how long I've been waiting for this day."

"Me too" Stella's face lit up. "Though I have to say I'm a bit nervous. What if he says no?"

"Don't worry." Anna grinned. Letting go of her hands, she went to the cooler beside the table and opened up a drink for the both of them. "Things will go perfectly today."

Taking a deep drink from the cold soda, she smiled off into the thick Grove of trees surrounding them. "You deserve it after all."

"I don't know about deserve" Stella chuckles, not noticing the look in her friends eyes in her own excitement.

Then, noticing someone coming out of the trees towards them, she straightened up and waved them over.

"There you are, Hunny. Look who dropped by? And with pastries no less."

Anna turned and waved as well to the tall, well-built man who was walking towards them. Grim had always been one of her best friends. He had even been the one to introduce her to Reani.

The flood of emotions in her stomach began to roil again when she saw him walk over and pull Stella into an affectionate hug. For a split second though, while watching them, she swore she saw herself and Reani in their place.

"Happy to have you with us Anna Banana." The two girls chuckled politely at his joke, Anna breaking free of her brief vision. "What's the occasion?"

"Hmm?" Anna just smiled. "What? A girl can't just bring her friends treats?" She winked at Stella making the woman blush and grow visibly nervous.

"Besides," she turned back to him. "I brought your favorites."

Waving over to the table, she drew his attention to the plates filled with sweets of all different kinds. His eyes were immediately drawn by the plate of eclairs.

Always easily won over by sweets, Grim said no more on the subject, just happy to indulge in treats.

Sitting back, Anna watched the well-practiced scene unfold before her. All she had to do now was wait for the perfect moment.

Stella, who had been planning to propose to Grim for months, now asked Anna to help her. The two had set up a simple plan of getting together where the two had had their first date.

Anna even made sure to make both of their favorite sweets for the occasion. Taking special care with the ingredients for Stella to cater to their allergies.

Her stomach twisted as she watched the two happily profess their love for each other. Again, for just a moment, one brief agonizing moment, she saw Reani's face over Grim's and it tore at her heart.

Through the haze of her tormented emotions, she watched as the two opened the last pastry boxes which were decorated like little wedding cakes in their favorite colors.

She watched the play of emotions across their faces as Grim realized what was going on, and Stella got down on one knee.

She watched as he pulled her into a deep passionate kiss, and from his own pocket pulled out a ring he had been keeping for the right moment.

Her neutral smile slipped into an eager grin as the Happy pair, still smiling, laughing and kissing, began to eat their special little desserts.

The moment Grim's pastry touched his lips, Anna's grin widened. Her face no longer hidden behind her carefully crafted mask of happiness revealed something darker. Her smile was no longer that of an eager friend. Her smile was that of a monster who had finally caught its prey.

"Grim? Grim!" Stella screamed as suddenly, Grim began coughing and gasping for breath, his throat swelling under his finger tips. Dropping to his knees, he seemed to be trying to find his bag, but in his panic couldn't seem to find it.

While Stella tried furiously to help, Anna walked casually over to his bag, the place she knew that he kept his epi-pens for just this occasion.

Noticing what she had found, Stella called out to her "Anna! Hurry, please!" Stella, fear and urgency in her voice held out her hand for the life-saving device.

Instead of giving it to her though, Anna turned her manic smile to Stella who on instinct nearly scrambled away on the ground. The woman before her could never be mistaken for the kind and happy woman that had become her friend. The light in her eyes had dimmed, leaving them looking dead, and her smile? The twisted sneer of a smile curled across her face like a woman possessed.

"Now why would I do that Stella dear?" Anna's voice held a deadly calm to it, completely at odds with the look on her face. "You are finally getting what you deserve." With that, she threw the epi-pen to the ground and stomped on it hard enough that she heard it break under her foot.

Stella just stared at the spot the pen lay broken, in shock. Grim, still gasping though, stared at Anna, betrayal clear in his eyes. Something that might normally break her heart coming from him. As she was now however, she felt nothing but vindication.

"I am truly sorry Grim." Anna's voice softened as if speaking to a child. "If you had only listened to me, then you wouldn't be involved in this. You could still be living your life, blissful and happy."

"What did he do to you to deserve this?" Stella stood on wobbly legs as she glared at Anna, her voice broken by sobs as Grim lay still now on the ground.

"Him?" Anna laughed, slowly stalking closer to the couple on the ground. Her lifeless eyes never leaving Stella's "Oh, he is not the one at fault here."

"Then why?!" Stella wailed, her fist beating on the side of the table sending pastries falling to the ground. Anger mixing in with the terror as she tried to hold her ground.

"Why?" Anna laughed, a dark malicious laugh. A monster's laugh.

"Because you needed to learn what it means to have your love and your life taken from you. Just like you took mine."

The park vanished, and all around her there was only chaos. Sounds of screeching, of metal on metal, of Brittany Spears still playing on the radio. The pain blocked out most everything else, but she could just see out of the vehicle in her dazed state as a woman jumped out of the other car and looked at them.

Her face was blazed into Anna's mind, something she would never forget as she got back into her car and drove away, leaving the two of them alone.

Anna smiled at Stella in front of her. "I may not get my Reani back, but you" she pointed her now shaking finger at Stella. "Will never get your happily ever after either. I'll make sure of that."

As Anna walked closer, Stella scrambled backward, terrified. "I'll be the monster in your shadow, the demon in your mirror. No matter where you look, where you turn, I will be there."

Leaning in close, she reached out a hand, sliding her fingers across the terrified Stella's face to emphasize her point. "You'll have nowhere to hide"

With that said, Anna stood and smiled brightly. The transformation from monster to carefully crafted happy woman was nearly instantaneous. Brushing herself off, she walked away, back towards her car.

All Stella could do was watch as the monster in human form walked away from her and the now dead body of her fiance, as cool as could be. No one in the park would think such a sweet woman capable of such atrocious things as she walked past everyone. To be sure, Stella and Grim had not.

Today they had both learned a lesson little Anna had learned early on from her mother.

Monsters are not always demons or creatures of the night. Sometimes monsters are those closest to us. People who profess to love and care for us.

Sometimes though, we create our own monsters with our own monstrous acts. We warp the good in others and create new monsters where once there were none.

Both kinds are always there, always watching. Waiting for a moment of weakness, a moment to strike. So you have to ask yourself. In those moments, what are you?

Are you a monster? Or are you Prey?

Imaginary

By Stephanie Houseal (*CONTENT WARNING: death*)

There was no white light. There was no tunnel leading to it. I didn't expect there to be anything past death. I'd told myself for years that when I died there would be nothing. I would forever cease to exist. No reincarnation. No Heaven. No Hell. Nothing.

What I didn't expect was becoming something more ... other. I found myself in a yard that seemed vaguely familiar. I was approached by an adorable little girl dressed in a sparkling green princess gown. She asked me to have tea with her and her stuffed animal friends. I was utterly speechless.

What the ever-loving hell was going on?

"Come on, Mariah!" her small voice called to me.

I blinked slowly, registering. *Oh no*, I thought bitterly. *That* can't *be my name*. I'd considered correcting her, but then I couldn't. My brows furrowed as I tried to remember what my name really was. I couldn't recall, but I knew I didn't care for Mariah.

I glanced around, taking in everything. The backyard had large trees, the sun's rays filtering between the emerald leaves and piercing the shade like spotlights on a stage; a chain link fence outlined the perimeter of the property; and on the back patio was the little girl at a table, hosting a tea party with her toys. A brick house was attached to it all. I could tell this was a basic cookie-cutter type neighborhood. Most homes looked alike, most neighbors knew each other, and the area was fairly safe.

Living the dream, I mused, shaking my head.

Speaking of living, I noticed the girl's big hazel eyes and wide smile. Her dark hair was pulled up, a tiara sat at an angle on her head. She motioned with her hand for me to come over but I could only stay in place. I was extremely confused. I had a million questions running through my head.

The most prominent one was how I arrived here in the first place.

How did I come to be in this location? I remembered dying. The truck carrying fuel, rolling over my car and exploding in flames was very vivid imagery. The memory was so raw. I could almost feel my lungs burning like rice paper again. Yeah. That was how it went. It was traumatic. Those were the only details I could conjure, though.

It was that and then I was here. Pain, and then calm. Maybe reincarnation was real. But then...

Perhaps I hadn't died. I could be dreaming. Or really just living a nightmare. It occurred to me to ask the girl a few simple questions. Clearly not talking to strangers hadn't been instilled in her yet. I chose to take advantage.

I made my way over to her, kneeling a couple of feet from her and resting my hands on my knees. I didn't say anything as she was busy pouring the "tea" for her guests. There were some crackers on a plate which she was kind enough to place on everyone's plate. I tried to remember being her age and playing pretend, but nothing came to mind.

Without looking at me, she kindly said, "You can sit in one of the chairs."

I saw the tiny foldable chair across the table. It was next to the one she occupied. I laughed a little. "Thank you," I replied, "but I don't think I'll be able to stay." That made her look at me.

She frowned and tilted her head slightly. "Why?"

"Good question." She raised her brows at my flippant response. I didn't realize I'd said that out loud. I brought a fist to my mouth, giving a fake cough to clear my throat. "What I mean is, I need to go back home." She didn't care for that and shook her head.

"You live with me, though."

It was my turn to frown. What an odd thing to say. "Sweetie, I can't live with you. Your parents wouldn't like that." The moment I said that, I checked the back door and windows worriedly. One or both of them might see me and freak out. Justifiably so.

When she giggled I brought my attention to her, confused. "What's so funny?" But that only made her laugh harder. I then added, "Besides, I'm sure they wouldn't like you talking to strangers." She stopped her laughter after a few more seconds and patted my hand as if *I* was the child.

"They can't see you, silly. You're invisible."

I raised a brow at her simple yet ridiculous explanation and heaved a sigh. I resolved to accept her previous offer to sit in the chair. She watched as I moved around her and sat down in the uncomfortably too-small seat. I didn't consider that maybe it would buckle beneath my weight. No matter.

I wasn't sure how to continue our conversation without admitting a very seemingly real truth about myself. Kids were perceptive, though, so she might understand. I started with the basics.

"What's your name?"

She let out a long breath and rolled her eyes as if we'd been over this many times before. "I've already told you," she chastised. "My name is Queen Firelight." She began to pour the tea again. "D o n ' t   y o u remember?"

"No, actually," I said. "I don't think we've ever met." She stared at me in what I could only assume was disappointment. I raised my hands in defense, giving as disarming a smile as I could. "I know it seems impossible, but I don't." I lowered my hands and folded them together on the table. "And I can't be invisible. No one is. That's why I should probably go."

She stood up suddenly and stomped her foot, crossing her arms over her chest defiantly. She was really too cute. "No!" she snapped. "You can't go anywhere. You live *here*!" With a curt nod, she thought her word the final one and sat down, the skirt of her gown poofed around her with the force. There would be no more questions I guessed.

I leaned back and pondered the little girl's words for a moment. Technically if I was dead, then I wasn't invisible. I was a ghost. But didn't ghosts typically haunt where they'd died? It turned out, I didn't know shit about anything afterlife related. I scrubbed my face with my hands a couple of times then turned my gaze upward. Clouds were now dotting the sky. I imagined plucking an answer from one.

This was wholly absurd.

I returned back to Queen Firelight only to find that she was gone. As were her toys and tea set. Panic settled in and I looked around for her. I caught the screen door to the house shutting. My shoulders slumped at the thought that I may have hurt her feelings. However, that vanished when she came back outside and stood before me, grinning.

"We have to go inside now, Mariah." I grimaced at the name, but she ignored me. "Daddy's made lunch. It's our favorite!" Her chipper tone made me a bit nervous. Before I could protest, she grabbed my hand and pulled tightly. I decided it wouldn't hurt to follow her instructions.

I am a ghost, I thought. *So maybe it won't be too bad.*

It was worse. Her parents had set out an extra plate for me at the dining table. Queen Firelight - seriously, what was her real name? - skipped over to her chair which was next to mine. I could hear some light humming coming from the kitchen to my right. It was her dad and he was stirring something on the stove.

It hit me then that I couldn't smell anything. I had no idea what was in that pot. It could be soup. It could be dirty underwear. I mentally reprimanded myself for that. Who boils underwear on the stove? Ever?

A thought struck me. "Good afternoon, sir," I said politely. He didn't acknowledge me. This whole situation seemed surreal. "Hi!" I said this more loudly. Nope. He continued with his humming and now moved on to getting cups from the cabinet.

"He can't hear or see you," my little friend stated. I gave her a droll stare. She just smiled and kicked her feet under the table. She was definitely excited for lunch.

"Are you talking to Mariah again?"

My eyes widened at the sound of my horribly given name. So Queenie really had told her parents about me. Her mother came in from the hall, with a small basket of laundry on her hip. She gave a sweet smile to her daughter. It was perplexing watching Queen Firelight bob her head eagerly.

"Uh-huh," she said. "But she forgot where she is and who I am." She glared at me and I shrugged. How could I respond to that? I was still processing my new name.

"That's too bad, isn't it?" her dad asked. He placed the pot of what I could now see was spaghetti on the table. Huh. It was my favorite dish. He gave her a reassuring pat on the shoulder. "I'm sure you'll remind her who she is."

"Emmy! You forgot to put your toys where they need to go!" her mother called from the other end of the house.

Aha! So, that's her name! I was relieved for some reason.

Emmy gasped and quickly got up, sprinting toward her room. "I'm coming, Mommy. Mariah told me to just put them down."

"What!" I cried. I put my hands on my hips and looked to her father in disbelief. "I did no such thing." My hands dropped. I could have kicked myself.

He can't hear or see you.

Emmy's words rang hollow. The realization that this was possibly my life now crept along the corners of my mind. I didn't want this to be true. A little girl's ghost friend? Maybe Hell did exist.

I resigned myself to current circumstances for the moment and walked over to the table. It was cute and oval shaped. Large enough to fit eight, but only four places were set. There was a small vase of daisies and a light blue tablecloth beneath everything. A large hutch was against the far wall with stacks of fine china within. Upon looking in the glass, I found I also had no reflection.

"Well duh, stupid," I chided. "Ghosts don't have reflections." I reconsidered that. "Vampires don't, I think." I held up a hand and waved, thinking maybe I could catch a glimpse of some part of me that was connected to this world. I was disappointed again.

"You're invisible."

This time Emmy's voice sang the phrase and I was starting to get annoyed. I took a deep breath and let it out slowly, then turned to her. She was seated and patted the chair next to her for me to do the same. The irritation I felt melted away as I took in her playful expression. Why not, then?

As I sat, her mom began to serve the food. There was now a salad, dressing, and rolls added to the table. I thought perhaps I would be hungry, but apparently I was void of that discomfort. Interesting.

"Don't forget, Mariah," Emmy reminded her mother.

Her mom chuckled a bit and scooped a tiny portion of spaghetti onto the plate before me. I gave her a disgruntled glare. "Am I a joke to you?"

Emmy laughed out loud. "Mariah says she wants more than that."

"Well," her mother said, sitting, "When she eats all that and she's still hungry, she can have more."

Emmy and I looked at each other and she shrugged. "You have to eat it all," she mimicked.

"I can't have any of this," I replied, trying to keep the frustration out of my voice. Being dead sucked. "Ghosts can't eat." I at least figured that was true.

Emmy took a bite of her roll. When she replied, it sounded like, "Er noh uh ghoss."

"Don't talk with your mouth full," I said at the same time her mom reminded her to chew her food.

She gave a low growl, trying to finish her roll. When she was satisfied she could speak more clearly, she said, "You're not a ghost. You're invisible."

"Does Mariah think she's a ghost now?" her dad asked.

Even though I knew they couldn't hear me, I responded

incredulously, "You really want to encourage your daughter's talking to a dead person?"

"Not dead, *invisible*," she corrected.

"Emmy," her mother chided softly. "I don't think you need to be talking to your friend at the table right now. You need to finish your food." She corrected herself at that moment to include, "Both of you."

"Oh, c'mon." Emmy's father smirked and took a sip from his water before continuing. "Let her have some fun with her imagination." He winked at Emmy and she giggled. "I had an imaginary friend, too, once."

"Imaginary!" I shouted, slamming my fists on the table. Emmy yelped in surprise at my tone. "I'm right here! I'm a ghost! I'm dead! Emmy should *NOT* be talking to me!"

"What's wrong, sweetie?"

At her mother's concern, I settled down. I knew she wasn't talking to me. I glanced at the innocent little girl next to me and saw the fresh tears in her eyes.

"You're not dead," she whimpered. "I made you up. You're my friend."

I slowly, gingerly sat back down. I felt horrible. I shouldn't have yelled. I let out a heavy breath, realizing I truly had hurt her feelings this time by disregarding what she believed to be an imaginary friend and not a ghost.

"Emmy, honey, come here," her mother urged softly. "If your friend is hurting your feelings, she probably needs to apologize or leave."

These parents were saints. I couldn't believe they were still playing along. I thought they would have told her to stop imagining dead people, but that was not how they viewed it. They loved Emmy as she was. It was all too evident.

My bad attitude deflated tremendously then. If she wanted an imaginary friend, who was I to deny that? Would my life be so miserable if a child wanted to play dress up and have tea parties with me? It didn't seem that horrible. She could call me Mariah. Who cared?

Emmy went over to her mom, and the woman picked her up and placed her on her lap. She took a napkin and gently wiped Emmy's tears away and kissed her forehead. Her dad took her hand and held it for a while. When her tears were gone, Emmy gave a half smile to her parents.

"I'm okay now," she told them. "Mariah didn't mean to scare me." She gave me a pointed look. "Did you?"

My jaw dropped. The girl was going places. Those leadership skills, though. I wasn't about to disagree with her again, so I shook my head. "No, I didn't. I'm just having a bad day."

That's the understatement of the year, I thought miserably.

She hopped down from her mother's lap and came to my side. She wrapped her little arms around my neck in a hug. What did this even look like to everyone else? A little girl hugging air? Like...how did this work?

I briefly returned the hug and she let go. "Everyone has a bad day, sometimes." She went back to her seat and began to eat again, happily chewing her food.

I waited until lunch was over, watching as the family went about their life. Her father went outside to clean the eaves of the house and do some yard work. Her mother vacuumed and played a board game with Emmy for a few rounds. They all had dinner before settling in for a movie. Emmy included me in almost everything throughout the day.

"Don't forget Mariah" was a main theme for her and it felt nice to hear. I followed her around as she flitted from place to place like a hummingbird. She talked constantly, and was very inquisitive. She mostly asked her parents the question, because I really didn't know a lot of the answers.

That gave me pause. Why would I not know the answer to most of the questions she asked? Was this part of my condition? To learn everything all over again? Something was more off than ever.

At bedtime her parents tucked her in, her mom reading a story to her. I was sitting on the floor, my back against the foot of Emmy's bed. I was unable to concentrate on what she was even saying as I grew tired. I couldn't understand how hunger didn't affect me yet sleep did. That was something I would explore tomorrow. Maybe. I wasn't really sure anymore.

I didn't know when I'd fallen asleep, but I was suddenly awake with Emmy whispering to me. I yawned, turning a tired gaze to her. "What did you say?"

"I can't sleep," she replied. "Can we play for a little bit? But we have to be really quiet."

I stretched and nodded. "Okay. What do you want to do?"

Her eyes lit up and she hurriedly got out of her bed. She went to her door, making sure to shut it as quietly as she could. She came over to me and gave a few small jumps of excitement. I moved to stand, Emmy grabbing my hand to lead me over to her closet.

"Let's get in here," she whispered playfully. "We can pretend we're hiding from pirates who want to take our gold."

I gave a slight chuckle and nodded, crawling in after her. We sat there in silence. I liked her. I was certain I used to do this when I was her age. She put a finger to her lips and I remained as still as possible. She peered cautiously through the slats of her closet door.

"I think I can hear them coming."

I took a deep breath in and sighed softly. I decided that being a Debbie Downer would only worsen my situation. So I crouched to her level and looked with her.

"What the fu..."

"Sshhh!" Emmy hissed. "They'll hear you!"

I couldn't even speak. I had no idea what was going on. Her room was gone and in its place was a vast beach, a tropical jungle lining it. The waves lapped at the shore as seagulls flew about. There, in the deep, was a massive ship. Flying proudly above the billowing sails was the Jolly Roger.

I snapped out of my stupor when I felt Emmy shaking my shoulder. "We have to fight," she stated bravely. "They can't have our treasure!"

I couldn't find my voice. How was any of this happening?

Emmy stood, pulling her cutlass from its scabbard. *When did she get that?* As I took in her appearance, she was wearing a canvas doublet and leather breeches with a satin sash tied at her waist. Her boots came up to her calf and she wore a tricorn hat with an adorning feather.

"Emmy, what is going on?" I finally asked, though my voice sounded hoarse. I cleared my throat and took in another view of the off-putting scene before me.

I shrunk at her devil-may-care grin. Oh, no. I couldn't believe it. I watched as she opened the closet door and marched out to confront some burly pirate, whose own weapon was drawn. It was a dagger and he was using it like a toothpick.

I wanted to pass out.

I made you up. You're my friend.

I was trembling. What do I do now? I didn't know if I should close my eyes and pretend it wasn't happening or join Emmy in her battle against a terrifying pirate captain and his crew. If I was brutally honest with myself, becoming the role of Imaginary Friend was pretty scary. It was letting go of who I was and forced to be this until I would be nothing as she would get older. She would forget me, wouldn't she? Wasn't that how this Imaginary Game worked?

Or ... would I move on to the next child? The pirates Emmy was trading silly insults with, were they part of her fantastic little world already, or did they just show up like me? Had they been brought to life through another child's creation, cast away, and then ended up here? Were we a snowglobe of souls, shaken from life and randomly landing in scattered piles between this fake world and oblivion? I wanted the answers so badly to understand what I was doing here at all.

I shut my eyes tightly and bowed my head, bringing my hands to rest on my temple and grabbing fistfuls of my hair. What was wrong with me? I let my hands slide down my face as I raised my head, stopping with my fingers just below my eyes and covering half of my face. I looked out at the beach, watching as Emmy and the pirate began a duel. It was amusing how she dodged and moved just out of reach of his sloppy swings and jabs.

Of course I knew she would be the victor. Why would she ever lose in her own fantasy? She could go to a million destinations with only the worry of her parents catching her out of bed at a late hour. Even then, she knew they would tuck her back in and remind her that she needed sleep, and she could play again tomorrow. And *oh*! I knew there would be something amazing planned as she would build and create new journeys to travel. How exciting it would be to take part in it!

It was then that I found what I was searching for. I was a little girl's imaginary friend. If I couldn't bring to mind what my life was like before my death, then maybe I hadn't truly been living. Perhaps my time *was* limited, or maybe I would move on. But for now, as long as I was part of Emmy's fantastical creations I could at least make the most of my time while I had it.

As I rose from my spot, I laughed and unsheathed my sword. I set my pace at a run to join my young friend in her fight.

This was Heaven.

...Meta...

The Great Journey

By Monroe A. Wildrose

We are given life by our mother's breath, and she stands tall and reaches toward the sun. Her body is strong and grasps deep beneath the earth gathering nutrients. She is healthy and has borne many children. She mocks the barren bodies of others that stand around her and laughs at their misfortune. Most of them twist away in shame and wither from insult. None can compare to our mother as she is selfless and mature, and she cares only for us. She feeds and nourishes us with her own body. We all cling to her taking in what she has to offer. My brothers and sisters spread out all around; we sleep and eat and wait.

I am alone, growing on one of mother's many fingertips. Taking in the sun and the water I get riper and richer every day. A patch of my once green skin touches the sun during the hottest part of the season. My skin is golden and warm now; like the color of the clouds when the day sinks to the tips of the hills before nightfall. I am large and plump, and my skin is taught with tiny ridges. I know that I am almost ready to be separated from my mother.

She tells us stories of what the world is like beyond the family that we have now. She is stationary but she hears much from the wind and the birds that land amongst the branches. The twittering of the small, feathered creatures hold so many promises. They speak of what others like us have done. I cannot understand what they say, but my mother can, and she tells us stories of the world beyond. This is the world we will journey to. The world which will give us a purpose.

Sometimes there are whisperings of this great journey. We know not what ours will be but sometimes we whisper to each other and dream of what it could be. We speak through the veins of my mother at night after the sun has gone down, we wake up from our sun-drenched comas and fantasize about what the journey will be like. What will it be like when we leave our mother? What will it be like to fulfill our purpose?

I am ready for the future and my travels beyond. Some of my siblings are scared and even my mother shows a little sadness at the prospect. I refuse to be scared or sad. I am ready to be rid of the hand that holds me and go off into the world to do great things. To sit upon the table of a king perhaps. Shall I go into my future and be the adornment of a fine meal? Perhaps I will be cut and served on a tray of many colors.

I sleep in the sun and dream of everything that could be.

It is not long before the trucks come. I have heard of the trucks before and the men that operate them. I have seen them come to harvest other families. It had been their turn, and now it is mine. This will be the start of my journey.

The loud hissing and bumbling noises of the machines cease as the giant men get out of the car. Their faces are already sun-kissed and sweat glistens on their brows. They wipe away the perspiration with cloths that they keep in their pockets. Their large hats protect them from the sun that has cared for my family and me so dearly. They drink the water that has nourished my family, letting drops of it fall into the parched ground. It seems we both need similar things to prosper. I feel like we are brothers in that way.

They work hard and fast and more sweat gathers around the front of their shirts and makes moon patterns along their backs. They smell like dirt and salt and tiredness. They don't talk to each other much as my siblings are knocked down from our mother's nurturing hands and onto the hard dirt floor. The men gather them up and stuff them into large green boxes that are laid into the back of the trucks. They are rough and careless with our delicate flesh. I am worried that I will be bruised in the fall.

The last of us whisper our goodbyes to our mother before our time together runs out.. She weeps inside of herself not answering our departure calls, but the men rattle the tree and pay no attention to her cries. The swaying back and forth and all the shaking is confusing but I don't let go. I want to say goodbye to my mother. I scream out to her, but she can't hear me, and my voice is lost in the chorus of so many others.

Suddenly, I am gripped firmly by a strong and sweaty calloused hand. A man has climbed up and is pulling us off and dropping us to the ground. Those of us who did not go easily or as willingly as some. The man tugs and I break free without much of a fight and the snap of my freedom is a crisp, and glorious sound. He turns me over in his hand and contemplates my skin as I beam proudly. I have no time to mourn the fact that I did not say goodbye to my family. I am basking in the glow of this man's attention. I am the best of my family. Surely this man can see that. The crisp orange color of my dimpled rind glistens as the man turns me repeatedly examining my whole form. He is wearing a large hat that has been knocked onto his back revealing ebony hair speckled with white. It shines amidst the black, speaking tales of strength. He nods twice solemnly and doesn't drop me to the ground with the rest but sticks me instead back up in my mother's fingers.

I feel abandon as he picks my brothers and sisters and drops them to the floor to be picked up and I sit wedged between two fingers. Fingers that used to hold me. I can't hear my mother anymore; her cries have gone cold and so have I. I have been cut off from my family and I am here alone, alone and abandoned by the man. I feel worthless and any pride I had about being the best has been shattered.

He grabs me as he climbs down, and I am renewed with hope again. The truck is full of bulbous mounds of bright fresh orange mounds. I wish to join them.

We descend and I am breathless to begin my future, but I am disappointed again as I am shoved deep in the end of a rough sack. I am slammed into something hard. I cannot feel the light of the sun. I cannot see anything. I am clouded by a total and complete darkness. The thick and suffocating feel of the sack surrounding me is unbearable compared to the freedom of the air I grew up in. The darkness is different than the darkness of the nights spent prattling with all the others. This darkness is empty and lonely, and I wish to return to my home. Muffled sounds of the trucks start again, and I roll being tossed aside like trash. I can hear the men chatter away. I cannot understand them and have no great desire to. I am cold cut off from the life of my mother and I feel alone. Is this my purpose?

The darkness consumes me for a time until thankfully it doesn't. I am taken out of the sack by the same man that picked me from the tree. I am surrounded by a small dark space that drips in heat. Even as the sun goes down the small room is hotter than the sun itself. A blast of cool air hits the room and caresses my skin. It sweeps across and ruffles loose things that are strewn about. It blows the smell of sweat and dust around and around. It does little to deter the heat and only as it passes by do I feel reprieve.

I am outraged that I have been brought here. That I was not allowed to join my other siblings on the great journey. I have been cheated out of my purpose by the man with the storytelling hair. The man that was supposed to deliver me to greatness has brought me to where he resides. In a dusky damp room that could serve no great purpose. I have become obsolete, and I know I will never transform into anything truly important. I can never do anything worthwhile in this tiny place inhabited by a man who doesn't matter. Oh, how I hate him.

The man's eyes shine deep and dark as he picks me up and shows me to a woman like a trophy. Her face is also bronzed and tired. Her eyes shine like the wings of a crow in the sunlight. The tired wrinkles that surround her eyes are labor and sadness, but still, she smiles. Her hands reach out and gingerly grasp me. The touch reminds me of my mother. Her fingers are so much softer than the man's as she caresses my skin and brings me close to her mouth. She presses me against her face and inhales my sweet aroma, and I can feel her teeth against my skin as she smiles.

She holds me in one hand as she grabs the man's hand in her other. They walk to a small bench inside the hot room. Both sit and sink as deep into it as they can, adjusting so they are as close as possible. For a minute I am cradled in the woman's lap as they sit in silence holding each other's hands. They say nothing yet I feel as if they are communicating just as I did with my mother and brothers and sisters. They talk without words, and they understand without hearing. They are family.

Sitting in the woman's lap as her finger slides over my sweated skin I feel like I can understand them too. I feel like family, and I no longer hate the man that brought me here.

The woman lets go of the man's hand and digs her nails into my peel. The feeling is sensational, as life is being pulled from me and my soul is exposed to the world. My family did not warn me about this. But the woman is being so gentle that I feel no pain. Her fingers rip me open to my center and the smell of my oil is everywhere. It surrounds me and sprays from my pores.

The woman pulls my skin off and now it is my soul that she holds. I am bare and naked before her. She pulls me in half and hands part of me to the man sitting next to her. This is my journey I know, both holding my soul within their hands. The man and woman clasp hands again and raise me to their mouths. The sun is completely gone from the sky and the room is cool now.

And in good faith, we do not speak.

Good News

By Carmilla Voiez

I flicked through the oversized pages of the morning newspaper from force of habit, barely registering the articles, while my Bialetti espresso pot perched silently on the hob in a glowing nest.

Outside, skeletal branches waltzed with the north wind but inside, protected by triple glazing and central heating, my silk pyjamas and satin dressing-gown were concessions to modesty rather than comfort. You never knew which neighbours might have their binoculars trained on your window. I rudely discovered that I was the subject of intense study a month ago when someone, presumably the passive aggressive wife of my admirer, left a box on my doorstep. Inside was a single cupcake, spoiled only by the word whore, daubed on the top in red icing. She'd probably baked it herself. Unfortunately, the ennui of my neighbours' empty, provincial lives had started to infect me as well. I was so bored I even considered visiting my mother. I rustled paper until I found the holiday listings. Time for a change of scene.

The doorbell dragged my gaze from the page and my feet to the hallway.

A smiling stranger greeted me. "Have you heard the good news?"

One of the buttons was missing from his cheap grey suit and, between the front panels of his jacket, I glimpsed infinite darkness. Beyond him, the world was engulfed by freezing fog so dense that the wind seemed unable to disperse it.

I shivered. "It's a bad time." The comforting scent of coffee warming on my stove filled the hallway. It would burn if I didn't cut this short.

He flipped open the tattered khaki of his courier's bag. I anticipated a pamphlet covered in smiling faces and sunshine; instead, a goldfish bowl containing a tiny octopus balanced on his wrinkled hand.

Forty-two eyes fixed their combined gaze on me, and a plaintive voice wriggled inside my mind. *"Save me and save yourself."*

I splayed my fingers to support the weight evenly when he transferred the fishbowl.

The stranger nodded, "I knew this was the right place." He stepped away from the door.

The muscles in my right arm shook. I wanted to grab him, pull him back and refuse his strange gift, but the bowl was too bulky for me to hold in a single hand. "Wait. What am I supposed to do with this? Who sent it?"

The man faded into the mist, leaving my questions unanswered. I couldn't even draw my flimsy robe around myself for warmth. I growled at the veiled street then took my burden to the kitchen.

I set the bowl gently on the kitchen table, switched off the hob and stared at my new—pet didn't seem like the right word.

"Who are you?" I asked.

"Good News, and I'm here to put your life back on track."

My bills were all paid; I'd been promoted at work, and my handsome boyfriend, Trent, was attentive, sometimes nauseatingly so. As I considered my situation, how comfortable and lucky I was, a desire for change grew inside my chest. Even ten years earlier, I could not have imagined that being an adult would make a person feel so empty. Financial security, a lover, and an unlimited supply of coffee were all well and good, but were they really all I should expect from my life?

"That's why I'm here." The voice sounded like melting chocolate. *"We can save each other."*

"What do you need?" My higher brain was repulsed. *Look around. Everything you could ever desire is here. You're living a better life than you have any right to expect. Following the advice of a voice in your head is madness,* but my yearning was stronger than logic.

"Take me to the beach." The plea was delivered with such urgency that I felt I must obey without delay and pulled my cashmere coat over my pyjamas then grabbed my car keys.

~~~

A vast world stretched away in three directions, but the only sign of humanity was a fishing boat tumbling on distant waves. I couldn't watch the vessel without my empty stomach churning in sympathy with the broiling water, so I gazed up at soot-coloured clouds before reverting my attention to my aquatic companion.

"*Mother's close,*" it said. "*She'll put everything in perspective. You'll see.*"

Wind stabbed through my coat, finding no resistance when it encountered my nightclothes. "Aren't you cold?" I asked.

"*It won't matter soon. Move closer to the sea.*"

Salt and musk hung in the air despite the bulldozer wind.

"What's she like, your mother?" I saw her moonlike body rise, iridescent. A thousand eyes glared above colossal jaws that contained an army of dagger-teeth. I tried to blink the vision away.

"I don't want this," I pleaded, letting my rational mind take the wheel. Within the chasm of her mouth, I glimpsed the same infinite darkness that had yawned through the gap in the stranger's jacket. I dropped the bowl and turned my back on the ocean.

My car was hidden by the sea wall, but its warmth and flimsy metal shield called to me. I managed a single step forward before the shifting sand dragged me down, sucking my foot into its jealous embrace until I fell forward. Shards scratched my chin and clogged my mouth with salt. Using my nails as anchors, I fought for every inch of progress while muscles strained, tendons snapped, and my eyes streamed hot brine.

"Please, let me leave."

"*Are you sure?*" the octopus asked.

I nodded emphatically. "I'm not the one."

"*Then, you must choose another.*"

Who? My mother would be too weak from her arthritis to hold the bowl, although whatever waited beneath the water might provide relief from her pain. Would Trent leap at a chance to save me and fulfil some heroic fantasy? A stranger would be easier—less guilt, and I could pretend they deserved it while letting the tiny octopus work his magic on their weak mind rather than mine.

"Okay," I said. "Come with me."

~~~

I leaned across my kitchen table, staring at the cute little monster. What now? I could keep it as a pet but how big would it grow?

I searched for the number for the local aquarium. "Hi, do you take donations?"

"Pardon me?" the female voice answered.

"I have a baby octopus."

A click and silence. Did she think I was a prank caller?

The creature in the bowl lifted an arm and waved. I laughed. If the creature was a curse, I should pass it to the creepiest person I could find. No better place to find creeps than on Tinder. A few swipes left, and I found a match.

~~~

He answered his door in a blue shirt and jeans. A flinty glint in his watery eyes belied his shy smile. I passed a bulging carrier bag across the threshold.

The man peered into the bag then looked at me. "Are you coming in?"

"I'll return tomorrow," I lied.

"That's that," I told myself as I marched away. *I hope so,* my higher brain replied.

I drove to the end of the street and parked at the crossroads, not knowing what to do. I couldn't stop thinking about the helpless creature trapped inside glass. He needed his mother. I remembered my childhood, tucked tight in bed while my mother sowed stories in the warm air before planting a kiss on my forehead.

Dont! My mind flailed in protest as I touched the steering wheel. *Please,* it begged as I made a U-turn and headed towards the man's house.

I watched him place the goldfish bowl on the passenger seat of an Audi, and I reached for my mobile phone, but who would I call?

When the man pulled away, I followed him. The Audi turned right towards the beach. I turned left and found myself pulling up outside Mother's bungalow. Her eyes sparkled when she saw me at her door, and she seemed young again, vibrant, and pain-free. She pulled me into a strong embrace and her curled fingers felt like claws against my spine.

"What's wrong?" she asked.

Of course, she knew. Mother had always been able to read my emotions, perhaps seeing in my face a mirror of her own fear and emptiness.

"Nothing's wrong," I promised her, and it wasn't a lie, not really. As I stood on her doorstep, embraced by her self-sacrificing love, I knew without doubt that my mother would protect me, keep me safe, even from the end of the world. I felt unequal to that love, unworthy, and promised myself, that if the world wasn't about to end, I would visit her more often.

Something blocked the sun. The darkness was thick and humid, like a quilt under which I might hide from night-time monsters.

"Come inside," Mother said, ushering me into the sitting room, where we sat on antique chairs too large for her modern bungalow.

Rain pounded the window, shaken from the shoulders of the rising horror, if my imagination could be believed. Mother cupped my chin and pulled my gaze from the storm to kiss me on the forehead. I hoped that Good News's reunion was as poignant as my own, and that his mother would be similarly completed by his presence. Maybe her devotion would prevent her from unleashing madness and destruction on humankind. It was a slender hope, but enough for me to accept my mother's offer of tea and cake and endure her questions about my love life.

The truth made her sad but gave me the impetus to break things off with Trent, realizing that I used him like I used my dressing-gown, for appearances rather than love. My higher brain did not object to this decision, only suggesting that a change of career should be considered while I was cleaning house. The rain had eased by the time I left mother, ready to start a new life.

I Am One With The Universe

By Rethley Gil Chiru

I know better than to check the news first thing in the morning but I can't help myself.

Star-U Times: *A new record broken today by a Mr. Howard Cook from Manchester, UK who received his first and only message from the Universe before his passing early this morning as confirmed by doctors and family.*

"He was an accomplished man who lived a long life and got to meet his great grandchildren," said his granddaughter. "But he always talked about how he felt like he was missing something. I'm just happy he got to have the closure he's always needed in this life before he died."

First Contact is usually initiated within the dates of one's star sign. If it happens exactly on your birthday you are dubbed "Whole". Statistics have shown the age upon receiving your first message from the Universe between thirteen and nineteen years old. Although rare, there are individuals who make contact much earlier with the standing record by Márcia Scovino da Rosa, a three year old from Maravilha, a municipality in the state of Alagoas, Brazil back in 1973.

Recent studies have shown the rise in people who have spoken to the Universe in their fifties and even as early as their mid thirties all thanks to Étoile, a stimulant developed at Asterisque Laboratoires.

"In the past two decades we have seen a very steep decline in those who can speak to The Universe after the age of twenty," stated Asterisque Laboratoires's CEO Marcel Cortazar. "By that age the odds are halved and continue to be cut in half with every year after. It's a frustrating situation. We hope the work we are doing will help those who have given up hope of becoming Whole—

I resist the urge to toss my phone. After groaning into my pillow I roll over to face the blank ceiling. Is taking the stimulant really going to raise my odds of speaking to The Universe? How could I be certain it's not some drug induced hallucination? What was the point of talking to The Universe if it's not accomplished naturally? In the pit of my stomach butterflies stir, fluttering up and clogging my throat. No amount of deep breathing or counting back from ten would cull the thrumming within my chest. My body craved movement. It's time to run.

It's still dark when I step out of my apartment but even without the sun it's still hot. I'm immediately covered in a thick layer of moisture from the heavy humid haze which is a summer morning here. I pull up my running playlist on my phone, set it to shuffle, and match my stride to the music.When I round back to the apartment complex I fall forward and steady myself with hands on my knees and gasping like a fish out of water. Music blares from my earbuds but I can't make heads or tails of what is being sung with my heartbeat pounding in my ears. As my heart finally settles I pause the music and turn my face to the sky as sunlight creeps over star light.

"I am one with The Universe."

Along with running, the mantra is part of a new routine guaranteed to open communications with The Universe. Something about healthy habits being what It favored in people It spoke to.

"I am one with the Universe."

A woodpecker pecks loudly somewhere close and the steady flow of traffic from the highway fills my ears. The same old noises. Nothing extraordinary. Until I turn away from the sky and catch a sound I've never heard before. It's brief and then drowned out by a car backfiring. I strain my ears but it doesn't sound off again. What if that was the chance I've been waiting for my entire life and it was thwarted by someone who needs to get their car checked?

"I am one with the Universe."

It comes out more like a question than a statement.

My body gets heavy, my shoulders sag, and I drag my feet up the steps back into the apartment to shower and get ready for the day.

I usually don't work morning shifts but someone called out last night and I took the shift. It's not a big deal. I work more hours, I get more money. Everything works out.

My work uniform is a pair of khakis that are too snug around the crotch and a polo with a collar constantly rubbing the back of my neck. My stomach growls and I have a few minutes left to squeeze in a breakfast of whatever I can find in the kitchen. All that's left in the fridge is a few slices of cheese, some fruit, and celery. I search the cupboard for oatmeal and find it's also running out. I make a list of things I need to pick up after work including what I need for dinner tonight. Part of the routine to get The Universe to speak to you is to have at least ONE home cooked meal a week. The more I think about it the more I feel like I'm being scammed out of my time. But I don't have anything else to lose now, do I?

With the list in hand and my teeth brushed, I grab my bike from it's spot in the hallway and make my way to work.

I follow the same route alongside the steady flow of morning rush hour. The bike lane is a new installment across town but some drivers still disregard it. As I turn into the parking lot, a car turns and hugs the curve, almost taking me out. They honk the horn and all I can do is scowl after them. I chain up my bike to the rack and make my way inside to the relief of cool air.

"Morning," I say to the only person in the break room.

"Morning Scout." The manager calls everyone Scout because she can't remember names too well. She takes one look at me and makes a face. "You look terrible."

"Gee thanks."

"Have you been getting enough sleep?"

"Sleep is hard to come by these days."

"You shouldn't be here," she says. "You should be at home resting on your day off."

"I'll sleep the rest of the weekend off, how's that?"

I know it's not enough for her but she knows me well enough to leave it.

I spend most of the shift restocking shelves. I take my time with everything because if I finish too early there would be nothing left to do and I'd be put on the register. The idea of talking to people makes me anxious.

As I place each item in its designated area, I can't help but wonder why I couldn't be born as a bag of chips. Their use is short but purposeful before being dumped in a landfill to poison the earth just like humans tend to do. Is it wrong to think of my species in such a way? It's not like I chose to be human. I laugh at myself for yearning a life as a plastic bag.

A sparkling shimmer caught my eye and when I turn to face it, a glint momentarily blinds me. A hand thrusts into my vision but before I could react to it something is placed into my palm.

"Here you go," says a musical voice and I can't help but accept. The touch sends a spark up my arm and branches out through the rest of my body and fills with me warmth. "It's for a free consultation, please come visit soon."

I try to meet their eyes but looking into their face is like trying to stare into the sun. They breeze past me and that's when I see they are dressed from head to toe in iridescent fabrics. I need to tell them they aren't allowed to hand things out in the store but the words are knocked out of my mouth. I watch this strange person in bright clothing strut down the aisle and continue on with their handouts. When they turn the corner my words jump back into my mouth.

"Excuse me," I call out, rounding the same corner and into the other aisle. They aren't there. I go to the next aisle and they aren't there either. I'm sure they went this way but just in case I round back and search the aisle on the other side. The person dressed in iridescent fabrics is nowhere to be seen. There is no way they could have gotten away so fast.

A man passes by me and I notice a ticket in his hand. I open my palm to find the same ticket with nothing on it. I almost want to ask the man if his ticket is blank too but he's already slipped it into his back pocket and is now looking at cans of baked beans.

Either I'm going crazy or I really do need more sleep. Imagination or not, standing around isn't going to finish restocking for me. I slip the ticket into my shirt pocket and promptly put it out of my mind.

When my shift ends, I gather all the things I need on my shopping list and the manager rings me up. I place the bags of groceries into the rear basket and walk my bike up the small hill to the parking lot entrance before hopping on. The need to deviate from my usual route is immeasurable and instead of turning left, I go right which leads to everything but a shortcut.

The thoughts protesting this change are shoved to the back of my mind by a pressing force I've never encountered before. It's the same force which keeps my legs pedaling and my hands gripping the handle bars so tight my knuckles turn white.

I bike past the entire length of the shopping plaza and across the bridge and into the main part of town. Past gas stations, coffee shops, a bookstore, restaurants, and a bar. A police station, the post office, neighborhoods, and then past a small field with cows and a barn in the distance. My calves are on fire and my breathing is labored but I can't bring myself to stop. The sun beats down on me and I'm covered in a puddle's worth of sweat. How much farther must I go on?

Just as the question echoes in my mind, I finally find myself at a full stop on the road leading into the park.

Anger boils inside me but I'm so tired it quickly simmers to muted irritation. Why the hell did I do this? How do I expect to bike all the way back now? I have food that can spoil in this heat. Why am I so stupid?

There's a pinch on the bridge of my nose and a misting sensation bursts across my cheeks. I take a deep breath and my vision blurs with hot tears. I look to my feet to hide my shame even though there is no one else around to see me. A few tears fall before I pull on my sleeve and wipe the rest away. That's enough crying, it's time to go home.

A tug on my shirt stops me but before I can react something slips out from my shirt pocket and is carried off into the sky. I reach for it but it slips through my fingers. Aw well, it's not like it had anything on it anyways. I put my foot on the pedal but then stop short again to watch the ticket floating through the air into the park without a gust of wind to be felt.

Curiosity gets the best of me and I turn my bike onto the one lane road and start pedaling.

The ticket guides me to the very back of the park where it snags on the bark of a pine tree. I pull up to the tree and I stare for a while expecting something extraordinary to happen. After a beat, I lower the kickstand to my bike and hop off. There is something on the ticket that I didn't notice before and once I grab it, I spot a big bold number. Forty two.

The force from before is back but now a fully formed presence breathing down my neck, poking my temple, and tugging on my hands, beckoning me to step into the woods.

What about my stuff?

Leave it, it says and I step into the line of trees.

The ground is at first covered in a thin layer of dry pine straw, bark, and broken branches but after a while it all transforms into lush greenery. Even in spring I've never witnessed so much green. The sunlight filtering through the thick canopy flashes like a chlorophyll light show. Moss covered boulders breach the surface of a sea of ferns with insects of all kinds swimming from frond to frond. Deer, birds, and squirrels skirt all around me and they are green too, blending in and out of the environment. Farther and farther I go into the green, wading in the ferns and petting a deer if they draw near, its body the texture of fur and moss and something else I have no word for.

Before long I am running alongside the deer and my lungs fill not with air but butterflies. It's different from usual. These butterflies flutter through my veins and leave behind something I haven't felt in a long time.

I stop running when I reach a clearing. The deer don't stop and continue on their way, melting into the green surrounding the open space.

After all that running I should be breathing heavily but I'm not. I turn slowly to take in the scene and realize the forest is making a noise. It's not a noise you hear with your ears but rather feel it on the soles of your feet or the tips of your fingers. I kneel down and place a cheek on the bed of moss to hear the earth speak. I don't understand what it says because it's ancient and deep.

I could yell out in happiness if it wasn't for the child standing before me.

"You came, hooray," this child exclaimed. "Took you long enough."

I recognize the voice but I don't know where it's from. My shock is delayed and doesn't fully form so all I do is sit up as the child approaches and plops down in front of me. I hold out the ticket which they snatch and pocket away.

"Go ahead, ask your questions," the child says. "We don't have to worry about time."

"Time?"

"Irrelevant," they reply with a twinkle in their eye.

I throw away the concept of time and ask my second question. "Where are we?"

"In a forest."

"Why?"

"Because you wanted to meet me."

"Why would I want to meet you?"

"You really don't ask interesting questions."

"I guess not," I say and the child laughs at that.

My thoughts are slow and harder to grasp.

"Here, this should help." They offer their hands with their palms facing up and I know to place mine on top. Contact is warm, friendly, too much. It sends a jolt up my arm and branches out though the rest of my body like a thunderbolt. Suddenly I am suspended above the trees, weightless; soaring through the atmosphere, beyond the earth's orbit, past the dark side of the moon, and into infinite possibilities.

Consciousness slams into me and when I notice the child again they are no longer a child but a teenager. It hurts to look at them but not only because they are brightly burning but because they are everything I could never be again. Jealousy fuels me, envy ignites within me, and sadness takes me by the throat.

The teenager pulls their hands away and the overwhelming feeling ceases. I blink and the person ages again. Now an older adult who looks like an older version of me. They see the recognition in my eyes and take the moment to help me back onto my feet.

"Who are you?"

"You know who I am."

"Where have you been all this time?"

"I've always been here."

We are walking now, wading through the sea of ferns dancing under the chlorophyll lightshow. I know what's happening and I can feel the panic rising in me. But the other version of me is keeping it subdued somehow.

"Do I have to go back?"

"Yes."

"Can I stay a little longer?"

"You can stay for as long as you like but you have to go back eventually."

"Why?"

"You won't find what you need here."

"Do you tell everyone that?"

"More or less."

"And they all leave willingly."

"Most do."

"What about the ones who don't?"

The Universe doesn't answer me in words but I can feel the reply. If you don't leave, you waste away, get swallowed up by a black hole and spit out somewhere else with no guarantee you'll end up where you want to be. What if somewhere else is better than where I was before? What if I was willing to risk what I already know for a chance at something different? My questions are back to back and The Universe's answers are arbitrary and trite but I don't care. It's nice to have someone to talk to.

The Universe leads us to the edge of the woods and back to my bike. We place our hands on the handlebars and look into each other.

Will we remember this conversation for the rest of our lives? If we leave, will we stay together? If we stay, will we be happier?

I turn around to ask my new questions but find myself looking at a wall of trees. I don't have to check the date to know it's a different day from when I first stepped in. My phone starts buzzing in my back pocket with delayed texts, phone calls, and notifications. I'm back to a reality of clear blue skies and a single bright star directly above.

"I am one with the Universe."

The words cascade from my lips and pool out around me like fresh spring water. It pulls me further out from where I've been until I have one out and one foot in. I'm suddenly terrified to move. Terrified of what will happen after taking another step into either extremes of the unknown. Both equally as mysterious, exhausting, and full of the ineffable.

"I am one with the Universe."

A woodpecker pecks from somewhere close, traffic sounds off in the distance, and something else, something different, fills my ears. I realize It has been trying to speak to me all along.

I step into the unknown but it's different than it has ever been before. This time it's my choice. This time I have control.

"I am one with the Universe."

Finally I am whole.

One Minute Of Death

By Jeni Lee *(CONTENT WARNING: stroke & stroke symptoms)*

22:34:00

The smell of honeysuckle floating through the evening air on a perfect summer's night. A little girl's laughter as she is pushed higher on her tire swing. *My lips are numb.* Dipping my hot french fries into my cold vanilla milkshake. A school bell ringing and the crunch of gravel under my feet as I run to line up for class.

22:34:01

Skinned my knee on Monica's front walk playing hopscotch. Stealing a Thin Mint from the freezer. Dipping my toe into hot bathwater and pulling it out as I realize it is too hot. Chewing ice cubes. The smell of chlorine at the pool. Neon orange shirt with bright red tights. My first haircut.

22:34:02

Scrounging in the trash for a lightswitch to add to the secret hideout I have built under the forsythia bush. Delivering my dog's puppies in the back of a closet. The smell of the baby powder my daughter kicked over as I changed her. Holding my first flute for the first time. *Tingly.*

22:34:03

Being at church camp and sitting on the edge of the decorative well while the cute boy carves my name in the spindle and feeling the rough stone beneath my fingers. Falling on a hurdle that was set up incorrectly and twisting my knee so badly; I never ran track again.

22:34:04

Fried chicken picnic lunch at the base of Monk's Mound in the freezing rain with my dad. Watching the KKK walk down the street in full regalia on Halloween while I had to stay home with tonsillitis. Brut by Fabergé in the green, long-necked bottle on my dad's dresser.

22:34:05

My grandpa jumping into the pool fully clothed because he thought I was drowning and laughing the whole time. The first baby bird born to my cockatiels, yellow and fuzzy and cheeping for dinner. Disneyland in California and the seemingly unending strawberry fields on the way. *Numb now.*

22:34:06

Bashing my brother in the head with a plastic birdhouse and crying as I carried him, bleeding and screaming, into the house. My bike with the pretty red and white checked seat was stolen off the front porch while I watched Sesame Street. *Muscle spasm in my cheek.*

22:34:07

Lightning hitting that tree in the backyard and splintered it into a million pieces and we had to pick them up all over the neighborhood. Standing in the road trying to stop a rock fight and getting hit in the eyebrow. The Catalina Mountain range lit in oranges and reds at sunset.

22:34:08

A two-headed albino rattlesnake. Sitting on a milk crate in my cousin's rusted out car as he did donuts in the dirt driveway laughing and coughing at the dust. Digging for diamonds in Arkansas. Visiting Old Tucson, the movie set my grandpa built.

22:34:09

Preservation Hall in New Orleans. Feeding Mike the Alligator in Houma. Diving into a pool and smashing my finger on Kirsten's head. Cutting my bangs and hiding it under a leather visor for two weeks until Mom caught on and threw the visor on top of the fridge.

22:34:10

Finding "alien poop" in the woods behind our home and being disappointed they were just walnuts. Light as a Feather; Stiff as a Board. Our rotary phone was beige; Grandma's was green. The wallpaper in our basement bathroom says "Masochists, you are only hurting yourselves."

22:34:11

My dad's pinky rings on my right ring finger since he died; one silver and one silver inlaid with turquoise. I gave private music lessons for twenty-five years. *My eye is twitching.* Mom and Dad debated for weeks over VHS or BetaMax.

22:34:12

We got our first microwave when I was in middle school. My neighbor's first, middle, and last names were the same, and he lived in a huge house that had white rugs. *Turn off the TV.* I had a tricycle Daddy painted beige. I used to ride on the porch when it rained. My favorite color is purple.

22:34:13

I still have the book called "The Pink House" and the main character is named Jenny. We had "unbirthdays" with our family friends once a year. Grandma's candy recipe has the words "stir until it clicks" in the directions. Can you tell me how to get to Sesame Street?

22:34:14

The basement smelled musty and creepy and scary. The bookmobile smelled wonderful. *Remote is very heavy.* There was a groundhog under Grandma's mobile home that was huge. Chocolate peanut butter ice cream. How many licks does it take to get to the center of a Tootsie Pop?

22:34:15

I found a rug for my secret palace under the forsythia bush. War and Peace took four days to read in eighth grade. Failed Algebra; aced Geometry. I love pizza. I have two best friends I love like sisters. Nutter Butters. Camping at Woodland Hills in an old army tent that flooded in the rain.

22:34:16

Lady, Pepper, Brandy, Rocky--good dogs. I loved that silly book about space but got in trouble for reading it in front of kids who couldn't. Hooked on Phonics. *Stand up.* Why does a cursive Q look like a big 2? If I tell two friends, they'll tell two friends, and so on, and so on.

22:34:17

My first boy/girl party, we watched Star Wars on Laser Disc and put our empty cans on the stairs to warn us when Mom was coming, and then watched the movie. I miss my Quaker parrot, Boogie--I thought she was an Oscar, but she loved me best. I miss horseback riding.

22:34:18

I miss my Daddy every day. The second Alien movie was the best. *My head hurts.* Marple, Poirot, Tommy and Tuppence, in that order. Sense and Sensibility by far. What happened to my old Nintendo? James Alexander Malcolm MacKenzie Fraser.

22:34:19

I need to hide my accent so the kids won't make fun of me. "Can You Read My Mind?" Playing Mozart's Horn Concerto No. 3 in E-flat on my new French Horn at the audition for a scholarship. Candy cigarettes for 10 cents at the local mini-market. "I am a leaf on the wind. Watch how I soar."

22:34:20

Walking in a blizzard to get Grandma's medicine at the store. I used to be fluent in German. Mom used to call liver "kaboodle" so we would eat it and I loved it. What happened to Po' Folks restaurants? Sneaking down the stairs and seeing a scary movie with a dismembered hand.

22:34:21

Hugh O'Brien kissed me on the cheek. Hosing down the eucalyptus trees around the mobile home park during the Santa Ana winds to protect against fire. I've never seen the Grand Canyon as an adult. *I can't stand up.* The football game where the piccolo froze to my lip. I like hockey.

22:34:22

I wish I could live in New Zealand. Run, Forrest! Run! Woolworth's had a picture window with a birdcage filled with parakeets. Peanut butter milkshakes. My mom's cat loves me. I used to think that Thanksgiving was a two-day event.

22:34:23

Jill used to get trash bags filled with Halloween candy because her mom took her to the "rich" neighborhood to trick-or-treat. I was the best at hopscotch. I hated dodgeball. How far away is the sun? I wonder where Voyager I is now? I wish I lived on Mars. Electric cars should be cheaper.

22:34:24

I am so hungry for deviled eggs. *My arm is heavy.* Arsenic and Old Lace. I wish people wore hats again. Why Didn't They Ask Evans? Our first remote control had four buttons. I loved my ABBA albums. Why has Art Deco fallen out of style? I prefer paper plates.

22:34:25

I wonder what really happened to Jack the Ripper? I should have been an anthropologist. Chocolate milk made with Nestle Quick. Rhonda used to eat the wax bottle after she drank the juice inside. I sold the most cookies when I was in fourth grade. Gloria Vanderbilt perfume.

22:34:26

What stories do the stones of the earth have to tell? *Really heavy.* Time travel should be a thing by now. High heels hurt my feet. I wish I had learned to dance. I don't like beer. My brother took apart the Commodore 64. Worlds of Fun. How far away is France?

22:34:27

I used to get pushed into my locker at school. YYZ. Everyone should have cake for breakfast the day after their birthday. Building a teepee with my junior class at church camp and choosing spirit animals. The smell of barbeque ribs. Our neighbor had a Husky with bright blue eyes.

22:34:28

I once stole a big bag of M&Ms from a store but took them back and confessed. Cream of Wheat with butter and milk. I'm afraid of drowning. The wallpaper asked me if peace had a chance. Elephants are so adorable and smart! *My head hurts really, really bad.* Pickles.

22:34:29

I used to like rainy days. Outlander. I used to tell my brother that Sugar Smacks were really cockroaches in a box so I could have more of them. Always take a banana to a party. I love crossword puzzles. I had my first kiss in 9th grade. "You go your way, Dolly Levi, and I'll go mine."

22:34:30

Sea salt caramels are the best. Making Bible story scrolls in Sunday School. Peach picking in the summer. The first time up in the Gateway Arch was frightening and thrilling. I lost a tooth in a popcorn ball once. *Why can't I lift my right arm?* I have three sets of china and never use them. What do lizards think of?

22:34:31

My back never hurt when I was pregnant. Corps style marching in marching band. I like Kirk better than Picard but Janeway is best. Driving in a convertible in the winter with top down and heat blaring. The stained glass window casting a rainbow on the water in the baptismal font in Independence.

22:34:32

Daddy had cancer surgery the day before my daughter was born in a different hospital. Gardenias. My brother being scared of the actor in the Frankenstein costume at Disneyland. My biology teacher was so cool. Someone stole my blue sweater that my grandma knitted for me.

22:34:33

Learning to sew. The smell of pot roast filling the house after church on Sunday. Helping Grandma after her double knee replacement surgery. The riverboat at the waterfront that was a McDonald's. I wanted to be a bacteriologist in third grade. I like pie more than cake.

22:34:34

I think I am drooling. We are climbing Jacob's Ladder. My daughter used to name all her dolls Penny. Buttered popcorn. Dawn is the moment when all things are possible. I miss Walter Bishop. I don't understand the point of pouty duck lips in photos.

22:34:35

Found a dead rat under a couch once--boy, did he stink! Visited Independence and joined in at the Native American Conference at the Auditorium and watched a real Sun Dance. Teaching people to read music is so rewarding. I once had an 80-year old oboe student.

22:34:36

My first pair of high tops were Kangaroos. Delivering Pantera's pizza using a fold-up map. There used to be a house down by the river at our church campgrounds, but I don't know what happened to it after it was flooded. Baby Groot. More scared of AI than aliens.

22:34:37

Taking my daughter to ballet and tap class. My son watching Bananas in Pajamas. My youngest explaining why unicorns are real. Painting my first kitchen blue. Our car was stolen out of our driveway once. My first novel was written on a word processor, was a romance, and took place in 1832 St. Louis.

22:34:38

My french horn teacher in college was a stuffy, snooty man who lived in a house decorated like *Wuthering Heights*. Purple jelly beans are the best. *I should call someone.* I remember my Aunt Rose's long, long black hair.

22:34:39

My cousin used to kick me in the shin and laugh and run away when he was three. I've only truly loved two people in my life that weren't my children. Helping a friend study for his HVAC exams by opening up our furnace and letting him show me the answers as I quizzed him.

22:34:40

Baskin Robbins Bubble Gum Ice Cream. Finding a refrigerator box and making it into a lemonade and cookie stand and trying to sell "ice cold" lemonade in the Arizona sun. I used to write my stories in a spiral notebook that had black paper in it and I wrote with a pink gel pen.

22:34:41

The look of pure joy on my daughter's face when we got Oreos. Clan of the Cave Bear. Starting to teach myself to read lips when I realized I was losing my hearing. My dad always chewed peppermints. Grandma used to clean house before her maid would come in to clean house.

22:34:42

My friend and I used to pass notes in school writing in Viking runes so nobody would be able to read them.I haven't had beef since 2001 because I can't digest it and I miss it terribly. I love the variety of people on this planet. Sunday, Monday, Happy Days.

22:34:43

It's exciting to learn something new. *Something is very wrong and I need help.* I had a funny little closet in my room in West Virginia that I pretended was a doorway to Narnia. Monsters outside my window on stormy nights. "I am Groot." I love oranges, but not grapefruit.

22:34:44

Crawled under a stack of boxes to help our dog deliver her puppies because she wouldn't let anyone else come close to her. Moving to the basement bedroom made me feel so grown up and independent. I would love an omelette right now.

22:34:45

The day I realized I was finally taller than my mom, Daddy took a Polaroid picture of me standing next to her. Tiramisu. There really is a point where everything clicks for a student and you can see the light come on behind their eyes.

22:34:46

Still bite my nails. The tattoo on my neck is the first five notes of Close Encounters theme. I wish I had a piano. I love tech gadgets. "Leeloo Dallas, Multipass." I collect Nativity sets. My favorite fruit is a mango. I love popcorn. Aliens must be real; we can't be alone.

22:34:47

Standing on the earthquake simulation platform at the Science Center as it shook. Programming my Commodore 64. Waiting happily in line to see Star Wars: A New Hope for three-and-a-half hours in the blistering sun. Chipping my front tooth on the dining room table.

22:34:48

My dad was an artist and I still have a lot of his paintings and my favorite is the one of the quails in the flowers. I always wanted to have blue eyes. I'm so proud of my kids. I learned to type on a manual typewriter. Pop Rocks and Coke.

22:34:49

Dropping a weighted drawer onto my right big toe and dislocating it in three places. Why do people keep rats as pets? Number 10 is my favorite Doctor, but I'm still a Browncoat. I got Barbie stuff and my brother got Star Wars stuff for Christmas one year.

22:34:50

Marching band; that tenor saxophone is heavy! Dad used to eat potatoes raw with a sprinkle of salt. Making whirlpools with friends in their above ground pool. Played Baritone Saxophone in Jazz Band in college.

22:34:51

Rainbows are pretty. I really don't like the texture of oatmeal. I've never been to Florida. My third grade math teacher used her hole-filled paddle often and on me. Grandma taught me to cook. I lost two of my fingernails in third grade and carried them in a box for months.

22:34:52

I like being alone. Grape jelly, not jam. I have always hated my feet. When did I last read Harry Potter? *Where's the phone?* I like dogs more than cats, but don't tell the cats. I used to have a brown suede coat that was lined with fleece.

22:34:53

We had a collie we named Tippy and a beagle next door loved her a lot. What happened to her? Playing leap frog in the living room and slamming my forehead into the radiator. My brother burying his little cars under the trees in the front yard then forgetting where he put them.

22:34:54

Found it. Hunting Easter eggs in the snow. Dr. Pepper. I used to pretend to be a fur trapper and the dog house was my cabin. I accidentally set fire to the dry grass in my backyard when I was "stranded on a desert isle". I used to dream in German with English subtitles.

22:34:55

I only went to three school dances in High School. Coffee with sweetener and lots of cream. Tea with no sugar, but sometimes milk. I wish I was British. I love movie special effects. Learning the bassoon was so much fun; I can't play on a drum set, though. Area 51.

22:34:56

Marvel, then DC. I think I liked Middle School best. I'm terrified of drowning, *but this is frightening me now.* "Just keep swimming." No amount of lotion has ever fixed the rough patch on my left pinky knuckle. I forgot my solo at the talent show and I still get embarrassed thinking about it.

22:34:57

I can't dial with my left very well. I'm not allergic to poison ivy, but my kids are. I wonder how long it would take to travel to the Oort Cloud? 9. Cap'n Crunch Peanut Butter Cereal. Grandma used to scrub my knees raw trying to clean them, but they were just brown in the summer.

22:34:58

Birds are so fun to watch; they're so busy. I like office supplies. Green Fluff Ambrosia was my mom's favorite dessert. Lists are so nice for organizing our thoughts. 1. Never did win the lottery like I dreamed about. Traveling the world would be so exciting.

22:34:59

I broke two toes climbing out of bed because they got tangled in the sheets and I fell on them awkwardly. 1. Louis Armstrong. Where in the World is Carmen Sandiego? Are there "B" batteries? I want to see Wizarding World of Harry Potter.

22:35:00

Push talk button. "I think I'm having a stroke." *F. Facial Drooping, check. A. Arm Weakness, check. S. Slurred Speech, check. T. Time. I hear sirens now. Have I made it in time?*

Denouement

By B.A. McRae (CONTENT WARNING: *death*)

I have found that recently my life doesn't seem to feel like my own. Perhaps it's the feeling of the winter air caressing my bones I've never been able to outgrow, but in the tone of my reality, I feel alone. I wear sunshine on my sleeve, but the night took up rent in my soul a long time ago. It has gotten quite dark in here and I can't stand this feeling of being lost in my own mind; absent amongst color, a constant moving shadow. This morning could have been better, along with this weather, if I'm late for work one more time I'll be fired. I'm young, I know, but I've recently acquired an overwhelming desire to retire; I guess I'm just tired. The morning's population has its own vibe of habitation; by the afternoon the populations are mending together, it's a different world by the sunset. This morning is still, there's a snowman on the corner who's missing a button on his invisible jacket. The words I heard and said today I can't stop replaying. After a while of arguing I couldn't even remember why I was yelling. I think we'll be just fine, we can get through anything. At least that's what I think of when I look at this ring. I think in the reflection of his eyes I saw right through my own disguise; I finally saw what my mind blinded me to see. I saw a frightened little girl who was given a completely different picture of the world and is now feeling highly unprepared. All I ever wanted to do was find the right words to make her not feel so scared. Far too early I suppressed a depression I didn't know was in need of a confession. I thought; everyone gets sad and mine would leave upon my requests. From an early age I learned life is a confusing process and nevertheless I profess at the loss of my compass I have been a mess.

As I drive under the bridge, in the rearview mirror I saw a kid run across. All I can hope is they're okay; it's too cold to be lost. I hope their mother finds them and holds them tight. I hope despite our fight me and him will be alright, since my change of appetite and my clothes not fitting right things have been a delight but a little uptight; maybe we'll feel a kick tonight. At times I don't think I can handle this, and the future obstacles life will bring. At times I have that overwhelming urge caught in my throat to run to my mom and tell her everything. The hands of my internal clock weigh on me and no one can see. I just want to feel a piece of humanity touch me. I wanted to feel like someone's miracle then maybe I wouldn't be so miserable. But I believe it's critical to have the right ingredients for a recipe of such significance; to think I'm vital is the first sign of denial. How he hasn't left me yet I do not know. Why, I wish I could have left myself long ago. He tells me I am a good person and I'm nothing less than kind. But how good can I be if all there appears to be are bad thoughts in my mind? As careless as the bitter wind outside, the thoughts inside make me freeze in its selfish hold. They whisper the things I fear, they make it clear, no one would notice if I wasn't here; I'm not crying I'm just sniffling, I have a cold. I've tried to find ways to drown them out. Their echoes always find their way about. The louder my music is the less I can hear their noise in my head. They scream 'can you hear me now' and I don't know how to answer them; it's harder to ignore them when I'm in bed. And it's hard to not sound crazy in your own thoughts as you speak out loud of these horrid voices hoarding in your mind to someone who can't hear them at all. Describing them isn't an easy task and I am getting bad at wearing this mask; and so they win again, I didn't think it was possible to feel even smaller. I have tried to do things to occupy myself so maybe then I wouldn't hear the dark and it wouldn't be able to get my attention. Hobbies came and went, still the dark was sending in its rent, but one stuck with me and for awhile released some tension.

   I love to paint, But life seemed to have its own set of complaints. The colors that gave me life couldn't be my life sponsor. Though each time I pick up a brush I feel an exciting rush, I know this much; though this I feel is what I was made to do that doesn't stop bills from becoming overdue, since then things have gotten darker. He loved- he loves, my paintings and wishes I'd paint more. I can't find the point in my mind, it doesn't come to me anymore when I watch the paint pour. I've sat in the audience of the same empty canvas that mocks my eyes; I can see what I want to create but when my fingers meet the brush it's too late. The images rush away from my grip, my eternally freezing fingertips; if the images make it out into the world the darkness will be evicted, and so they insisted to keep their stolen estate, and so again I shall continue this wait I hate. Waiting for the day my eyes will feel wider and life will feel extraordinary once again. And he will notice the pleasant change of my smile and hold me in his healing embrace for awhile and ask me where I've been. He is the good person; he is the good in the world I see. Maybe I am a miracle to him, even after our stupid tossed words this morning he reminded me before I had to get going that he will never stop loving me. Can't the dark see this, how can it want to tamper with such a thing? I already can hardly see what use to fill so much happiness in me, how much more dark can it bring? Though he can't see the chaos in my thoughts he believes me. He refuses to leave, he will not flee; he reminds me I deserve to be free. The dark doesn't care for caring things that make me feel like I'll be okay. I try to remind myself everyday that I just need to make it through the day. The days pile up, they get heavy; in my mind I am sitting in a chair as the dark sits across from me. Just the scared little girl in the company of all the things her parents warned her about, these bad thoughts attached and won't get out; maybe that's why she constantly says sorry.

The drive seems longer this morning, maybe it's the cold, but I will say I enjoy driving through the empty city. To see the unoccupied sidewalks and unaccompanied shops, the street lamps are still awake, it's like taking a small break from within reality. I need to replace this ratted jacket of mine; a lot of things are in need of replacing. Maybe soon I won't have to go to work once I get farther along, but the farther along I get the more I find myself worrying. What if I'm not cutout for this and one day I wake up completely numb? What if the dark finds a way to leak inside of them? I can't bear the thought of me being held down by the dark and witnessing it take over. Once dark marks its way it tends to stay and its welcome feels like forever. I'm too afraid to open up about this; I'm scared it'll drive him away. Even though I know he's going to stay. My thoughts turn back to the chairs, I wish my mind had a set of escape stairs. I want to stand up to the darkness, to shout in its emptiness that I can and am more than its created mess. I know I can and maybe someday I will, I hate feeling hopeless. A few more blocks then it's time to clock in. It's snowing pretty hard, I guess it could have been for awhile, I've got too much on my mind so I'm not sure when. At least there isn't much traffic, I hate driving in these conditions. People can make poor decisions. My windshield looks like my blank canvas at home; my wipers aren't much help as much as they try. I need to just concentrate on driving, and like the wipers I am trying; when it's quiet these thoughts just amplify. A shock takes over it all with a slam of my breaks. A little girl has run into the street, and before our paths were to violently meet I swerved; I've spun, I see snowflakes. Maybe the girl is lost; now I've lost where exactly I am. My head is throbbing and I think I'm crying; my body hurts from the slam. The hands of my clock and winding down, they scrape to escape my throat as I start coughing. I look down to see I'm bleeding, and one of my buttons is missing. I don't want this, this isn't fair. But the world around me doesn't seem to care. I want to tell him he's the last thing I'm thinking of besides to keep on breathing. I can't stop thinking of his last words just as much as this body can't stop bleeding. I didn't say the goodbye I wanted to, I don't want to leave; this has to be a nightmare. Dark has finally let me go; my new company seems to be the ruined snow, as it drifts away, leaving two unattended chairs.

Children & Parenting

Tired

By A.M.Brown

They say I look "tired,"
I tell them, "no shit.
I'm working this job
That I simply can't quit.

Now I can't remember
When I slept through the night...
Was it two years, December?
For sure that's not right...

Some days we get lucky,
And they sleep in past five,
But most days I just function -
I'm barely alive.

So, when I look "tired,"
I hope you won't say.
Just hug me and tell me
It will all be ok.

First Passengers On A Hot Air Balloon
By Zain Patton

T rue Story: The first passengers on a hot air balloon were a sheep, a duck, and a rooster, and this is their story ...

Duck

I was sitting quietly when Rooster came over clucking nonsense "Duck Duck Duck!!!!!" He said.
"Yes?" I replied slightly annoyed
"Did ya 'ear tha news?" He said excitedly
"No" I answered, getting more irritated
"Farmer John is workin on a .... " He trailed off.
" A what?" I asked frustratedly,
"I don't know but it's somethin!!" I rolled my eyes. Rooster always got excited over nothing. Rooster finally left after clucking at the cows nearby.
Sheep sauntered over to me.
"Ya know" He said nonchalantly,
"I saw this project Roosters been clucking about ... "
"Oh really?" I said only slightly intrigued, Sheep was prone to spreading rumors.
"Yeah he's been having other people over to look at it; Farmer Larry and his greyhound Sathie were here just a minute ago." He said smoothly.
"And how do you know?" I asked suspiciously
"I have my ways," Sheep said. I narrowed my eyes
"Ok," I said mainly to get him off my back. He sauntered off to bother someone else thankfully.

Sheep

After I was done talking with Duck I walked over to Mrs. Cat and her kittens.

"Mr. Tomcat around?" I asked, slightly hopeful.

"No I apologize" replied Mrs. Cat with a slight hint of venom in her voice. Gosh, I thought while walking away, she really doesn't like me.

I headed in the direction of Farmer John's work area. Maybe, I thought as I walked, Maybe I can see for myself ... I got to Farmer John's work area and he wasn't there. Perfect I quietly slipped in and looked at what seemed to be a large, and I mean large, wood woven basket and an assortment of cloths. Huh, strange, not like any project I've seen. Then again I hadn't seen many; usually my informants did these types of things, I continued to look around hoping for something more informational.

But to no avail, the only other things I found were a journal, a sewing kit, and a cloth pattern. I left disappointed and headed over to the chicken coop to see Rooster.

At the chicken coop, I found Rooster clucking up Mrs. Hen and her son Hen Jr. but he calls himself Jr. I wouldn't blame him with a name like Hen,

"Hey Rooster, can I talk with you for a minute?"

" Yeah o'course" He said cheerfully; he excused himself from Mrs. Hen and her son with something that sounded like,

"Talk later Mizez 'en' " and came over his normal walk now an exaggerated strut as he does when he's trying to impress. "

'Ey Sheep 'ows it goin?" Rooster said.

" Good good good," said Sheep

"'Ery good, thahs 'ery good indeed!" he said exaggerating his 'slang' as he called it to sound cool.

" So," I started "Heard you been down in Farmer John's work area" Rooster puffed up slightly

"Ya 'eard true, I been in sneakin 'n pokin, spyin that kina stuff"

" Ah," I said

"I see, cool very cool see anything of interest?" Hopefully he has and I had missed it, I thought

"Notin but a big pile 'o blankets" He laughed in an extremely chicken way a sort of halfway cluck screech "An a big, and I mean big, woven basket!" He said, finishing with what he probably thought was a mysterious stare, it looked like he had just stepped into bright light and was confused.

"Cool so nothing… out of the ordinary?" I asked

"Nope!"

"Not even a bit?"

"None"

"Zero?"

"Yup!"

"Zip?"

"Uhu!"

"Zelch?"

"Wazzat mean?"

I sighed a long sigh and left. Well that was a waste of time, I thought, as I walked to my favorite spot to nap.

Rooster

Sheep walked away leaving me behind. I was quite disappointed when he left without saying 'Bye!' or 'Thanks for all the help!' I sighed and started heading to my nest but then I thought, I need to go back and see what else I can find. so I headed out of the coop and toward Farmer John's work area hoping to find something.

I got there and it was locked. "Dang it" I muttered trying to think of another way in. Sheep needs the info, I reasoned as I searched for a window. Where where where, ugh if I was a window where would I b- "Aha!" I exclaimed when I saw the open window, then I realized it was seven feet off the ground, and then I realized I couldn't fly up to it. Darn my useless chicken wings, I thought. I stared at the window, and then an idea came to me: Maybe Duck can fly me up!

"Duck! Duck! Duck!" I yelled as I ran over to him.

"What do you want from me?" Duck said exasperatedly

"Can you fly me up to a window!?" I asked hopefully,

Duck stared at me dumbfounded for a moment before finally saying "Absolutely not"

"Oh c'mooooon" I pleaded,

"No" Duck said.

"What can I do? Please I need you to at least try!!"

"Well," Duck said "If you leave me alone for the rest of the month I will"

"Ok!" I said cheerfully "Besides I have plenty more animals to bug!"

Duck

I don't like flying, I thought as I walked with Rooster to the window he was so excited about. Once we got there I said "Hey wait a minute,"

"What?"

"Isn't this Farmer John's workshop?"

"It in fact is"

"Ok," I said suspiciously

"We gonna go?" asked Rooster.

"Yeah Yeah I'm working on it," I said as I flipped my wings. "Hop on." Rooster jumped on my back and I unsteadily made it to the window, Rooster jumped through and I heard a thud.

"Rooster?"

"Yup! I'm fine!"

I sighed "Ok can I go?"

"No I need to get down" Oooooooof course, I thought as I squeezed through the window and into the small shack, I didn't even bother looking around. I just wanted to get out. Rooster hopped on my back and I flew him back up and then squeezed out myself. Finally done, yeesh, that took forever! I thought as I waddled back to my pond.

Sheep

I was eating when Rooster ran up to me yelling something about new info.

"What's up Rooster?" I asked,

"I saw in the shed a ... a ...." He said through gulps of air

"A what!?" I asked

"Tanks, huge cans of fuel"

"Huh strange". Something caught my eye. A bunch of animals were gathering around ... around something. I walked over to the assembled animals and pushed myself to the front, there I saw Farmer John assembling the different parts in his shed into …? Huh, I thought, the thing Farmer John constructed looked so strange; the basket had the tanks in them and it was connected to the fabric. I was studying it when Farmer John started calling names. First, he called Rooster and I could see his excitement as he walked up the second name was Duck. He walked up looking nervous for some reason when he walked up. The third and final name that called was mine! What??? I thought as I walked up. Farmer John lifted us into the basket, Rooster was practically vibrating with excitement and then after we were placed a fire flickered above and as the cloth filled with air we lifted up off the ground.

Duck

"AAAAAAAAAAAAAAAAAAAAAAAAAAAAAAAAAAAAAAA AAAAAAAAAAAAAAHHHHHHHHHHHHHHHHHHHHHH"
"AAAAAAAAAAHHHHHH"
"AAAAAAAAAAAAHHHHHH" I screamed panicking
Rooster looked at me like I was mad.
"You good?" He asked above my screaming
"WAY. TO. HIGH. AAAAAAAAAAAHHHHHHHHHHHHHHHH"

Rooster

Duck was screaming his head off.
"What- How is it too high??? You fly for crying out loud!!" Aaaaaaand he continued screaming. After five minutes Duck finally calmed down and said,
"Sorry about that."
"Duck you FLY!!!" Sheep exclaimed.
"Yeah what was that about??" I asked. Duck stayed suspiciously silent, we had only been four feet above the ground but now we were at least ten feet up when … the cloth popped and we fell!
"AAAAAAAAAAAAAAAAAAAAAAAAAHHHHHHHHHHHHHHHH HHHHHHHHHHHHHHHHHHHHHHH" this time Duck wasn't the

only one screaming. It wasn't a long drop but the landing still hurt. After Farmer John collected us from under the torn tarp we hurried off to share our experience.

The End!

Make A Grown Up Read This
By Javier Garay

O nce upon a time, there was
A book I found for you,
(Yes, you!)
I heard you like to laugh a lot,
So tell me, is that true?

This is the story of a boy
With a fantastic secret.
But I can only share it if
You promise you can keep it.

The boy's name is Mateo, and
He has a superpower.
He can't quite fly like Superman,
Or breathe a lick of fire.

As soon as I explain it,
Well, the reader may just cringe.
(Wait a minute, that's me.)
It's truly unbelievable,
So where shall I begin?

With his imagination, see,
Mateo there can make
A grown-up say and do the most
Insane of things, awake.

(I don't like the sound of this.)

Javier Garay

Let me prove Mateo's skill
Can drive a grown-up mad.
What you now see before you are
Arms flapping *(this is bad . . .)*

(What is happening?)

Would you now like to see what else
Mateo can do, maybe?
That sound you hear is an adult
Who's crying like a baby.
(WAAAA – WAAAA – WAAAA)

It's obvious Mateo finds
All of this very funny.
*(I'm craving pickle ice cream, it's
Delicious and so yummy!*

Wait, no I'm not. Mateo made me say that.)

If you don't believe me that
Mateo's skill is real,
See him order this adult
To act just like a seal.
(ARF – ARF – ARF – ARF)

(He really does have superpowers.)

If that cracked you up, just wait,
And watch so you don't miss . . .
Mateo's used his power and
Oh no, I'm stuck like this.

(Why are my lips pursed?)

I see you think it's funny,
Well, if you thought *that* was strange
This book keeps getting better,
And this grown-up, more deranged.

Another thing Mateo loves
Is watching people dance.
Is that why I am shaking like
There are ants in my pants?

Mateo has the most intense
And strong imagination.
That must be why I am barking
Like a spotted, big Dalmatian!
(Woof – Woof – Woof)

What Mateo next will make me do
Remains a silly puzzle . . .
I've never even heard of words
Like *taradiddle or bumfuzzle.*
(Are those even real words?)

Will Mateo ever tire of this
Ridiculous old nonsense?
I guess he won't because he's got
Me saying *WOCKA-FLARTNESS.*
(Now that is definitely NOT a real word.)

It should be clear by now that he
Does have a special power,
Otherwise, would I be here,
Acting out a shower?

(Next time YOU are reading this book.)

This is getting way too hard
To read this way forever . . .
Unless Mateo makes us do
These silly things together.

Let's hop around on just one foot,
And now, let's touch a nose.
Let's wave our arms, and stretch them out,
And wiggle all our toes.

Javier Garay

(Are you wiggling your toes?)

Let's spin around three times, then sit,
And stay here for a while.
Let's fill our hearts with happy thoughts,
The kind that makes us smile.

Before this story ends, there's one
Last thing he wants to do.
I guess I'll give my kid a hug,
And whisper, *"I love you."*

Leap Day

By Persephone Jayne (CONTENT WARNING: *infant near death*)

After countless days, months, years? in this darkness, a light appeared. It blinked into existence and has pulsed with a regularity both familiar and foreign. The light grows brighter, breaking the pulses that whirl around me. And she screams.

The voice that is not as constant as the beats that pump through me, she screams now as the light squeezes me again. And again. And again.

I wonder.

Is this my new constant? The new way in which I exist? The pulsing interrupted by the screaming and punctured by the light squeezing me.

The light squeezes me and I move toward the scream.

The scream gets louder.

"Three A-M."

The light blinds and releases me simultaneously and my constant pulsing is no more. The bright light comes from within me now, not from without. I turn toward it.

Dead? Sounds bad.

Pushing and pumping from the outside pulls me from the bright light within.

"She's back! She's with us."

"A Leap day miracle. Have you picked out a name?"

Unknown Caller

By Juniper Lea

I dipped my teabag in and out of the water steaming from my mug. I breathed the smell of mint and julep deep into my lungs letting it fill me with cool warmth. The buzzing sound from our bedroom interrupted my calm.

Ignore it. Leave it for Doug. It's probably his phone anyway.

THUD. A muffled buzzing followed. I imagined the phone sitting on the carpet after Doug knocked it off the nightstand. Knowing he was flailing after it, trying to make it stop, made me smile. One had to find the little pleasures in life. And enjoy them whenever the universe presented them. If I couldn't sleep, why did he get to? Since quitting my job, 4 months ago, I had yet to sleep in. One of the things I had most wanted to do.

Stumbling into the light of the kitchen, Doug held out the phone for me to take. I took the phone with a sympathetic smile. Not Dougs after all.

"Work calling," he said, through hoarse grunts, then stumbled back to the dark cover of our bedroom.

Work? How? I changed my number after two months of them pestering me to return. Shouldn't be surprised. Figured they'd find me, eventually. Just thought I'd be on a faraway island, unable to answer. Or out of range, hiking jungles. But no. Just sitting in the early light of dawn, sipping tea and wondering what I'll do with another day.

I flipped the phone over in my hand and stared at the number. It wasn't even labeled and Doug recognized it. A sure sign of trouble, right? I sipped a few more times before sliding the phone unlocked, sipped again as I contemplated hitting the delete button instead of the call back button. It rang. I didn't jump. Nothing made me jump now. It rang again.

"Hello," I said firmly.

"We need you again," the familiar voice said. I said nothing.

"It's an emergency," they continued, pleading tones creeping into their voice.

I sighed, "Only cause it's an emergency."

The caller hung up before I could reconsider. I was pretty sure they breathed a smile as they did. Can one hear a smile through a hang up? Yeah. I think so.

I stood at the kitchen counter, slowly and deliberately sipping my tea until the mug was empty. I made no attempts to move, get dressed, brush my hair, nothing. I made sure to enjoy every last drop of the tea in my mug. I knew the day wouldn't allow for another. Not for a long while anyway. I was going in. Heading back into the fray and time seems to stand still there. It could be one day, it could just as easily be a week before I got out again. If I'm being honest, part of me thrilled at the idea. I shoved it down with a granola bar to finish off my breakfast.

"You're wearing that?" Doug asked as he finally came into the kitchen for breakfast.

"Yup."

"Really?" he asked, unsure if I was brilliant or crazy. I nodded at him and walked to the closet. "No. You don't need those ... " he said, almost a whisper.

"If I'm going back, I need to be prepared for any and everything that may happen today. You remember my last day?"

He did. The blood was hard to get out after it had sat for hours and congealed. He dropped his head in futility.

I knelt, reconsidering, "I'll only take the necessities."

"I'll leave all the Big Guns here," I offered with a smile.

"I never know what you'll be when you come back," he said, taking my hand and pulling me in for a kiss. I let him, kissed him back, fiercely, then walked straight to the closet. Doug hadn't been with me long, but over a year is enough to see the daily toll. I disliked it. Doug hated it. He called it ludicrous, said it wasn't natural and went against all his understanding of the human psyche. He's really quite dramatic. I loved him for it. His drama and complete bafflement at my job had helped me admit that I didn't like it either.

Admitting was the first step. It wasn't long after that I had quit.

But today? Dressed in my pajamas, armed with three cases of tools and tricks. I would walk up to the front door and greet those preschoolers with a smile.

The Magpie

By Carmilla Vioez

Mum knelt before a flowerbed. Wrist-deep in dirt with a trowel in her hand, she dug a hole. Her wide-brimmed sunhat cast shadows across her shoulders, and a dirge filled the garden, originating from a battered CD player that squatted on a rusting table in need of a fresh coat of paint. Pinned beneath the stereo was an envelope; its exposed corner fluttered in the breeze. A jug of green liquid, full of shredded mint leaves and drowning flies, sat beside an empty glass.

A flash of black and white attracted my attention. A magpie landed on the upper branches of an old apple tree that no longer bore fruit. Mum might not have noticed my arrival, but the bird did. It blinked enviously at the sparkling rock on my left hand. Rotating my wrist, I meditated on a myriad of rainbows painted across my fingers by the refracted sunlight - traditional symbols of hope and second chances. I removed the ring and hid it in the pocket of my jeans before speaking.

"Hi, Mum!"

She spun round on her bare feet. Her painted lips widened as she attempted to rub soil off her fingers.

"Lily! Home already? Would you like some lime juice?"

I recoiled.

"No, thank you."

Mum's smile dropped. "How was your day?"

I avoided the question, unable to offer any amusing anecdotes. I worked in a clearing bank, counting out their money. Was she worried I might follow in my father's footsteps and put my hand in the till?

"What are you planting?" I nodded towards a cardboard crate full of bulbs.

"Lilies."

I focused, beyond her, on the thorns of climbing roses encroached upon by ropes of ivy. The small courtyard garden with its barren tree was Mum's sanctuary. The music, which grated my nerves, gave Mum a sense of tranquillity that I found hard to comprehend.

Love's umbilical cord tugged me out of the doorway. The makeshift breezeblock step, pitted and ugly, shifted under my weight. I made a mental note to replace it, imagining my future daughter or son scraping knees and shedding blood on its rough surface as they crawled. *Children? Dare I?* The diamond ring filled my pocket: a life sentence.

The magpie rose from the tree. It soared overhead and settled on the low wall beside the freshly dug hole, looking for insects probably, but it felt like an omen.

Mum poured herself a drink, seemingly unaware of the dead things tumbling into her glass. Repulsed, I watched the magpie pull a wriggling beetle from the disturbed earth. Registering the noise of the music system being moved, I glanced back and saw Mum straightening her shirt. The envelope was gone. Had she stuffed it in her bra, beside her heart?

I imagined *him*, simultaneously beside the garden table and on a filthy mattress in his prison cell, scribbling a love letter. His black hair was white at one temple. Older than Mum, but handsome. His eyes held no warmth, and his smile was cunning. It had taken years to recover from the chaos he created. We stayed, Mum and I, after our house was emptied by police. Mum created a home inside the shell, working double shifts so I could stay at school then college, while quelling her rage with antidepressants to keep her compliant enough to hold down a job. When I protested, haunted by the dark shadows of exhaustion beneath her dull eyes, I would hear the same response.

"I'll be damned before I let your father ruin both our futures."

I knew the letter was from him. What I didn't know was why Mum hadn't torn it to shreds and made compost with his lies. The only thing that kept me going after his betrayal was knowing he was out of our lives. It was why I didn't know how to tell Mum about my engagement. Men couldn't be trusted. I could tell her that Tom was a good guy, that I could rely on him, and maybe Mum would believe me if she didn't stare into my eyes and see the doubt I harboured there.

"Who is the letter from?"

Mum licked her lips. Her fingers twitched, still rubbing at the soil. The glass of lime and insects was back on the table. Had she noticed the menace or taken a sip and swallowed the corruption?

"Is it from Stefan?" I asked, offering a lifeline.

She nodded. Colour bloomed beneath Mum's pale foundation. Her kohl-rimmed eyes stared at the chipped flagstones, avoiding my gaze.

"Your father's getting out next month. He doesn't have anywhere to stay."

"Well, he can't stay here!" I ground my teeth. A vein pulsed in my temple. My hands became fists that twitched to strike Mum's gullible face. "Do you still love him?"

"It's complicated."

"I'd say it's pretty simple. He took *everything* from us."

"He gave me you, and he's not a bad man."

"He gets to leave his prison, but I'm trapped forever. I can't trust anyone."

"You can trust me," she said.

"Not if you think you can invite him to live with us."

I reached into my pocket and pulled out the engagement ring. I waved it in front of Mum's downcast face. "Tom asked me to marry him."

I'd expected Mum's response to be tainted with worry, but her face glowed and her wide smile seemed to make two halves of her head.

"Congratulations, darling. That's wonderful news."

I grunted, not willing to surrender my anger.

"Yeah, and we won't share a bank account; I won't give up work, and I can't sign for a joint mortgage. We'll have to rent."

All these things, which had once served as protective amulets, became cause for complaint, ammunition I hurled at my mother.

She didn't return my volley. Tears smudged her make-up. I peered at the breezeblock step and doubted I would ever have children who might scrape their knees on its surface. Even as I pushed the ring onto my left hand, I imagined pulling it off again to throw in Tom's face, enraged at the slightest provocation and running, running, and never stopping.

Mum's eyes met mine.

My skull tightened like a brace around my thoughts. "You can't trust him. You can't be that naive."

"He's my weakness. Your father can charm the birds from the trees."

"So can worms."

Periwinkle

By B.A. McRae

My head was tipped over the bathroom sink, opening my eyes to see the water running clear now. I lifted myself up to the mirror to witness my newly dyed hair. Green, forest green, her favorite color.

Tonight wasn't anything particularly special, so I wanted to make it special because I found her so extraordinary. My hair dried into the natural wavy mess that she always makes a point to compliment, usually while she was twirling it. And with a few lit candles and our favorite album playing softly, I set the table for a surprise mac n cheese night.

As she came through the door an aura of somber carried her in. Normally, I wouldn't have tilted my head in any curiosity, she's typically soaked in some kind of melancholy that's just a part of her. But this appeared to be different; she didn't kiss me on the cheek like she normally does.

Taking in the scenery I had intricately put together, she looked burdened rather than surprised. Finally, well after 30 seconds of standing at the door, she entered. With puzzlement and not much room for patience, she gestured to my hair.

"I dyed it your favorite color," I smiled.

"Goodness gracious," She sighed. Waiting for her to laugh or for affectionate easement out of this confusion, she apparently decided to cut straight to the chase. "I'm moving to California."

Instantly I felt droplets of excitement drip to cool down the heated worry that had festered quickly in my chest; this is fantastic news!

"Wow!" I exclaimed, a little too hastily; it's already out of my character to express myself this colorfully. But I wanted to show her my support, and I truly did feel excited about this. "California sounds incredible, you've always wanted to go there, and I bet there's a really cool music scene we could get into there and-"

"Holland" She put her hand up. But not to reach for mine in shared plans, it was to halt any of my rambled possibilities from coming into existence.

Not only did I get the clue that her next words would most likely stun me, but she used my full name. She didn't like my full name, she called me Holly. She disassociated my full name from me for so long, 4 years total, it seemed that to recall it back was on purpose. As if she wanted to speak to me from a stranger's standpoint.

Then, over about two minutes, she disclosed to me that she would be going alone. I asked her why; she didn't like the feeling of being alone. To which she said "You're right, I don't. I'm meeting someone in California, I would like to be with them."

Finding myself calmly confused, I began to think out loud how her leaving would make our anniversary plans next month quite difficult if she was going to be in California. We had already bought tickets to a show. Her tone became elevated as she told me, almost reluctantly, that this was a reason why she was driven to someone else.

Seemed a bit unfair, and unclear.

But I was slightly impressed, it took her a whole of five minutes to dismount and alter the very course of my life.

What a powerful gothic woman I love.

I say that in the present tense because I imagine it will take my heart some time to fall out of love with her. I've never been immensely in tune with my feelings and sorting them, but that much I can say with certainty.

Watching her pack her belongings, label her boxes, take pauses to answer text messages with a bit of a smile, and leave in a car I had never seen was like watching the last two seasons of *The Office*. Most wouldn't have watched, they would have turned away or taken off, but I stayed and watched in the company of both familiarity and agony because I'm a fan.

I guess I live by myself now, this is my first time.

I lived with my parents until I was 18, and then I lived with a roommate in a cold, hippie decorated, dorm until I was 20.

After that, I had always lived with her.

When she met me, I was untangling Christmas lights in the hallway of my residence hall. She was on her way to watch some friends play *Magic: The Gathering* a few rooms down from mine. But something intrigued her to grab the other end of the tangled mess and help me.

I didn't say anything to her when she did this, I simply pressed on with my mission. My roommate promised to leave for the weekend if I untangled those lights; I had my heart set on binging some fascinating cult documentaries.

Once the stringed lights were untangled, utilizing the hallway outlet, I plugged them in to see if they worked. As the prongs met the socket, I looked over the small sea of multicolor to see her eyes sparkling at me.

No one had ever given me the time of day as she had in just those few minutes. And I had never loved anyone apart from my parents and brother, but something in me knew that I would one day utter the words while looking into her thickly eyeliner eyes.

Almost every person I've encountered, in proximity, has either indirectly or harshly told me that I am not easy to be around. I am aware of this; it is harder for me to pick up on matters that are entangled with emotions. I always mean well though. I never thought she'd join that demographic.

I once told her, during a night of glasses half-filled with wine and half-filled with vulnerability, that I knew why I was like this.

My brother and I loved playing pretend, mainly as wizards. We flew around and cast spells on trees or had epic battles with greedy goblins. But one intensely exaggerated time, we imagined ourselves in this crazy realm.

We were lost and trying to get back to our own timeline. As I recalled, we concluded that we would never make it back home and we didn't want to 'die of sadness'. My brother cast a spell that took away almost all my emotion, only logic left, and once it was done I was to do the same for him. But once under the enchantment, as a logically emotionless wizard, I saw no point in wasting my magic to do such a thing. We took pretend time quite seriously; we grew up in a video game-free home.

This is not a factual reason. In all reality, this is just the way I seem to be wired. But sometimes it's relieving to believe in a small fantasy.

~~~

I do think she would have liked the show, from an observer's perspective. People watching was one of our pastimes, and I liked that it wasn't more her thing than it was mine. Although now it just reminds me of her. But maybe eventually, it won't.

I've been able to use some of my savings to cover the other half of the rent she used to pay, but I'm thinking I'll have to get a roommate soon, or temporarily move back in with my parents. My job doesn't pay enough to keep afloat on my own; maybe I can get some more hours at work.

There's a radio station nearby that has a podcasting wing; a few booths are dedicated to local podcasters. I'm a co-producer, of sorts, just a fancy way of saying I edit the audio. My manager said the podcasters like to work with me because I'm detail-oriented and get the work done without any 'dillydally.' I guess podcasters are now the small pool of people who don't find me completely intolerable.

During a break between sessions, my manager asked me how I've been lately. I think this is one of the best things about humans. That we ask each other how we are doing, like a check-in, I think there's something neat about that. It's wholesome if you think about it.

I informed him that I am newly single and learning to live without her. It is extremely odd to have something present for 4 years and then reprogram all the details of your life.

I no longer see her when I roll over in the morning.

She's not going to text me during the day to make sure I ate something.

No more random relatable funny memes.

I told him with a shrug that I was just relearning, I guess.

"Doc," My manager said with determination. I have no idea why he calls me this, he's never explained. "There's a friend of mine who's also single, and I think you guys would click. I can set you up for coffee or something if you'd like? No hard feelings if you don't."

I gave his sentence some serious thought, approximately 15 seconds, and without asking for many details besides where I would be meeting this mystery person, I gave my manager a confident "Sure."

I was to meet the stranger later tonight at a dueling pianos coffee bar. I winced inside that my first thought was that she would've loved to go here together, with the mission of pretending to be characters in a movie. For some reason I always ended up playing a robot, that was my fallback. Looking back, the last time we did that she didn't laugh like the other times when I pretended to be a robot.

It started to feel weird, analyzing that she had let go long before the disastrous mac n cheese night, so I ordered a shot of espresso. Nothing like caffeinated anxiety. As the tiny cup met my hand, I was greeted by my company for the evening.

"Holland?" I looked over to the voice, and they reacted with an inviting smile. "Hello, thought that might by you, I was told to look for the cool chick with green hair," The stranger extended his hand. A firm handshake, a social cue that makes sense to me, and that I'm good at. "Nice grip, that's some hand strength even the burly men in public office don't have; and I mean that as a sincere compliment."

To be quite honest I wasn't going to take it as an insult, by appearance I do not look strong, so having it acknowledged was nice.

"Whattaya say we grab a table, looks like there's an open one kind of by the stage." With an easy-going nod, I followed him through the sea of brimmed hats, unused tobacco pipes, and I genuinely believe I saw a rather large orange cat peeking out of someone's jacket.

I also noticed he was carrying a briefcase. Which is immediately linked, in the remaining adolescents in my mind, to a secret agent.

We sat at a rounded table across from one another, accompanied by the loud but talented pianists.

"So, green hair huh?" He tossed my way after a while of observing the ivory duel. His phone was on the table. I simply gave him a nod, which was also bobbing unconsciously to the music. "Might I ask why?"

Drawing out a breath I started to zone out, because sometimes I do that rather than looking at someone when answering something I don't particularly want to answer, "I dyed it for my ex-girlfriend while we were still together, it's her favorite color." Just as my words cut off, there was a slam on the table.

Looking up in reaction, he apparently, and frankly thankfully, didn't hear my answer. He was staring at his phone in disbelief, the briefcase on the table.

"Those BASTARDS!" Furiously he began typing out a message on his phone, and then quickly, but impressively still politely, he talked to me. "This is highly embarrassing, and I am usually not like this at all, but I must ask you an *enormous* favor. I have an emergency; did you drive here? Could you please take me somewhere? An Uber would take too long."

I had always thought it would be cool to chug a drink and exit a bar, so I took the opportunity and we hopped in my car.

As he was giving me directions he simultaneously apologized, asked me my favorite food, and if I had any plans for the remainder of the night.

To which I answered "It's alright. I enjoy buttered toast. I have no plans."

Pulling up to the destination, he had a completely different manner. He looked at me, with his briefcase held close to his chest and exhaled. "You're free to follow me in if you please." With that, he briskly and dramatically got out of the car.

And I spontaneously and surprisingly decided to follow him into city hall.

~~~

Clearly, this was like a second home to him, he knew exactly where he was marching. I noticed the few people we passed, four to be exact, tried very hard not to make eye contact with him.

We approached a large set of wooden doors, closed for a meeting that was currently in session. But he had no regard. With a burst of the doors, the crowded room of seated people turned to see the interruption and I could practically hear the eye-rolls like a giant marble rolling down the hardwood floor to our feet.

Confidently he made his way to a podium that was up in the front, about 10 feet away from important-looking people, and I searched for an open seat.

"You know for a FACT this is an OUTRAGE" He angrily directed at the important-looking people, with poise. Being politely aggravated is one of his talents.

There was a seat open next to an old lady who was embroidering; I would have preferred to sit alone, but at least I could nonchalantly watch her embroider.

As I took my seat it broke her out of her stringed trance. She looked to see what was going on up front. In response, she scoffed under her breath "This fricken guy." There was something in her rugged hush that made me smirk.

I was intrigued to stay as he started rapidly riddling off fact after fact, one of the important people desperately tried to intervene.

"Young man, if I've told you once I have told you a thousand times, an immediate filibuster is *not* necessary!"

The old lady chuckled; I was pleased to know I wasn't the only one finding entertainment here.

"Has he done this before?" I asked the embroideress in a whisper.

She gave me a glance and then returned to her small hoop "Oh yea, almost every month. The city won't shut down a petting zoo on the other end of town whose exhibits are horrid. The little cockalorum won't quit until the animals are freed. I agree with his cause, but his voice is annoying as hell."

I pondered a moment, "Hmm, then why come back if you know he's coming?"

She gave me a cunning grin "It's also entertaining as hell." Just then, her statement was proven with hard-hitting evidence as my previous company pulled out his own battery-operated microphone. "You know that fella?"

Pulled away from the entertainment, the old lady brought me back to reality. "Not really, we were sort of on a blind date. But he needed me to bring him here; I didn't mind."

"Sounds like you didn't really want to be on a date."

"Why do you say that?"

"Why is your hair green?"

I didn't make eye contact with her. "It's her favorite color, I dyed it for her. She broke up with me."

"Because you dyed your hair?"

"Because she wanted to be with someone else, in California."

"Interesting." The needleworker bluntly stated and continued her stitching of what appeared to be an alpaca who's also sewing.

Now I looked at the old lady, "No, not interesting, it hurts."

And the old lady looked at me. "Why? Why continue to let it hurt? You seem like a thoughtful nice person; you dyed your hair someone's favorite color to obviously make them happy, and you drove this obnoxious stranger to fricken city hall out of selflessness. Why let someone have control over how you feel when they're not even around? You can provide your own happiness, do it, it's liberating. Comfort yourself, it's life's best tip. Feel the tough emotion when it comes, understand why you're feeling it, let it dance, then shove that shit out. You'll be just fine, that's the real secret you don't hear, you're always going to be okay." The old lady returned to her stitching, and I returned to my inner thoughts with a whole new perspective.

After a few seconds, 30 to be precise, I stood up. I walked to the center of the room and called out a word of attention to the stranger. He turned around to me, and I waved goodbye.

With a nod of farewell, he spoke "Godspeed" into his microphone.

Walking out, the old lady gave me a wink, and something in that small gesture and conversation awakened a truth in me I needed to hear.

My whole life emotions seemed foreign to me, I thought I would never truly be loved because of my inability to '*act normal*'. But that sly hag gave me the unapologetic truth.

I was completely capable of feeling, I always have been, I just feel and process them in my own way and that's okay.

I can be my own comfort.

My own source of happiness.

I am a pleasantly kind person.

I will be okay.

I can be my own favorite color.

Holy Ransom Demands!

By Veronique Manfredini (*CONTENT WARNING: threats of violence*)

Dear God, who art in Heaven. I have Your son. This might sound surprising since I'm only 8, but I've done my research. I know You're a good Dad up there wherever You are, but I don't understand why You insist on sending Your Son to Earth. He is incredibly aloof and is so easy to capture. Also, He ate all the hot pockets we had at home and gave my mom a great fright.

Anyway, this is my list of demands for His safe return. Otherwise You will find Him nailed to a cross.

Again.

(No I will not do it myself, I'm obviously too short to reach; I know someone who will though).

But this time we'll make sure He's dead, dead. Like dead. Really dead. Super dead. Extra dead. Like really, super, extra dead. As mommy says all the time "Deader than a doornail," even though I really don't get it.

First, Dear Lord, I'd appreciate world peace, but if that can't be done, may You grant me a pony. But not just any pony, it has to be Janice's pony. I hate her. She stepped on my new shoes and then called me lizard girl because of my pants the other day. And then she encouraged the others to do the same.

Anyway, Lord, please grant me this pony so she may be jealous until her hair falls out and she becomes uglier than a lizard, so they'll stop calling me that.

Second, I'd like to have a baby brother. But maybe don't put him in mommy's tummy because then God, I'd have to wait too long for him to come out. Just send him over with my favorite pie and new toys to play with, that'd be awesome.

Third, I'd also like to have my daddy back if You don't mind too much, Lord. He's been up there a long time and I feel like You're being very selfish. I hear mommy cry herself to sleep every night since he's left and I miss him too. She doesn't know I hear her, but that's why I sleep with her so often. It would be nice to have him home again.

Those are all of my demands for Your Son's safe return to wherever You needed him to be right now. Be hasty because He's demanding more hot pockets and I don't want to share.

Amen.

TikTok Angel

By Melanie S. Wolfe (CONTENT WARNING: *funeral, grief, regret*)

Wearing all black, the Lawrence siblings stood in the very kitchen their mother used to bake cookies. They stared in silence at the sea of food dishes on the kitchen island. The last guest had left, along with their spouses and kids. It was the first time the siblings had been alone together since the dreaded call.

Jennifer, the oldest, took a sip from her wine glass and then said, "I should have called her more. It had been six months. Can you believe that?"

Jennifer's taller but younger brother, Mike, stared out the 1880's breakfast room window at an old friend's Coastal New England home, and said, "Come on, Jen. Don't beat yourself up. You own a business, you and Angie have teens, life's busy." He gulped his wine feeling every bit of the bitterness as it went down his throat and leaked into his heart. He went on, "Mom knew that."

Jennifer nodded and buried her face into Reed's chest. "Hey, she's better off," Reed, Jennifer's other brother, comforted her. "No more lonely nights, no more drinking herself to sleep."

Clover sat in one of the chairs at the island and fiddled with a fork. "No more mid-night calls just to talk about her guilt. God, I wish she would have gone to a priest or counselor instead of me," she mumbled, then paused, considering her words. "Mom and dad are back together—that's all that matters."

"How do you know they're back together? Mike asked. "Dad might be up there, like, screw you, you broke my heart."

Jennifer smacked his harm. "Really, Mike, wow. And remind me, why are you getting a divorce?"

"That's low, Jen." Mike folded his arms. "My relationship with Kenzie didn't start until Amy and I were separated."

"He's not wrong, Jen." Clover downed a shot of vodka. "Mom broke dad's heart, and we still don't know if that's why he did it."

Jennifer pointed at Clover. "Don't you dare imply that it wasn't an accident. It was *ruled* an accident. That's proof enough, Clover."

"This is so typical." Clover downed another shot. "Look the other way, there is nothing to see here, folks. Just the Lawerence family refusing to deal with reality. "

The room fell silent

"Well, here's some reality." Reed huffed, "It took me a year of therapy to figure out all my female problems were due to her. The irony of it all, she returns to her love in heaven but because of her I get to spend the rest of my life jumping from one relationship to another."

Jennifer's voice deepened, "Victim much? Don't blame her for your commitment issues."

Luke, Clover's twin, walked in their mom's nautical themed kitchen as the screen door slammed shut behind him, his cheeks red and rubbed raw. "Guys, you need to see this!" He held up his phone and pushed the TikTok icon.

Maxine Lawrence's tired, worn out but sweet face was crystal clear on the screen. "Mom," Jennifer whispered as she put her hand over her mouth.

Reed pulled the phone closer to get a better look. "No way. She could barely check her email. How'd she—"

Sadness seized Mike's heart as he realized she was gone. His mother; the woman that had prepared him for life wasn't here anymore.

"She had a TikTok account?" Clover interrupted, curious.

Jennifer leaned in and said, "Wow, she has more followers than me!"

"Oh, just wait, you guys." Luke tapped the screen.

"Is this recording?" their mother said to someone next to her and a young male voice whispered, "Yes, see the red dot turned to a square? When it's a square you're recording and that blue bar at the top, shows you how much time you have."

Luke swiped the screen with his finger and Maxine proceeded, "Hello TikTack," she yelled.

"No, TikTok," the masculine voice said. "And you don't have to talk so loud. They can hear you."

"Oh, oh, sorry." She giggled and smiled at the screen. "TikTok. Um, hello, I am Maxine Lawrence, and I am making this video for my children: Jennifer, Mike, Reed, Clover and Luke. I hope you find this video because I can't get a hold of any of you, and I have some things to say." She paused and spoke like it was the last time she would talk to her children. "I didn't tell you about the cancer because I didn't want to worry you. I thought I could beat it. But now," she took off a beautiful wig, displaying her bald, vulnerable head. "I have been given a year or less." She sighed. "I just don't think you need to know right now...for many reasons, really. Maybe you see that as selfish, but I see it more like I'm saving you from a long season of sorrow as you watch me struggle. Telling you here and now seems best for me. This way I am not disrupting anyone's lives, you can grieve for a little bit and then move on. Simple as that."

Luke scrolled to another video. "Taylor, my neighbor's son, told me about this TikTack thing, and I thought it would be the perfect place to leave you messages. You know how your generation is so active on this social media stuff."

Jennifer ran out of the room and returned with her laptop. She sat it on the island and typed in the TikTok address then clicked on the next video. Maxine proceeded. "Parenting is a beautiful symbiotic relationship of give and take–but in our case, mother gives a little too much and in return the children take a little too much, and to be honest, for some reason that doesn't bother me."

"She thought *we* took a lot? Really!" Clover huffed. "Why are Boomers so self-absorbed?"

"Shhh," Jennifer hushed Clover and Maxine's voice played on. "I am fully aware of my blind spots. You know if anyone else treated me like you do I wouldn't tolerate it." Maxine laughed. "But for some reason, I guess because I love you to the core of my being, I've allowed you to take more than you give." She paused with a big smile and said, "I'm like your very own Dobby, I'm your house-elf." She smiled. "Luke will get that."

Luke laughed and wiped a tear that escaped when he recalled the time she visited him while he was doing his residency at Boston Children's Hospital and they watched Harry Potter together. They ordered pizza and ate her famous caramel chocolate popcorn balls for dessert. His childhood favorite.

In the next video, Maxine sat on the beach and held a hat from blowing off her head. "I had an affair. It's none of anyone's business, really. But, you kids seem to hold a lot of resentment over it. So for your own closure, I'll explain. All you left for college, and your father was still working long hours. I was very lonely. I had been taking care of you five for the last thirty years of my life and suddenly my role in the world changed. I had no one to take care of and I didn't know how to deal with that.

"I was lost and vulnerable, and David was there when no one else was. Our friendship simply grew into something more. I loved him, but I loved your father more. When your dad..." she paused for a moment. "Died. I ended my relationship with David for good. And as part of my penitence, I chose celibacy for the rest of my life. I paid the price for my actions, and I sure didn't need any of you adding to my punishment by pushing me away. Trust me, I punished myself for years."

Another video began and Maxine spoke into the camera from her sunroom. "You kids did give me some good lessons." She looked at a plant and pruned it as she spoke. "I taught you the basics of being human and in return you challenged me to become a better person." She paused and looked at the camera. "All five of you came into my life and turned it upside down. You taught me how to love unconditionally, and how to be patient.

"You challenged me with worthy debates on genders and cultural traditions and most of all you taught me not to take life so seriously, and for that, I thank you. I am so proud of the people you have become and are becoming. And I say this with all sincerity..." Her eyes filled and became glassy. "It was my greatest honor to be your mother. Have you ever heard of that quote, *we're all just walking each home*? That's what we were doing. In our time together we were learning and teaching each other. And sometimes they were really hard lessons."

Maxine's children stood silently and stared at her paused face on the screen. Tears rolled and heaviness filled their hearts. Reed began to doubt himself, maybe his perception of his mom was wrong? He never looked at things through her perspective.

"Go to the next one," Clover urged and Mike clicked the video.

Maxine spoke into the phone propped up on the kitchen window sill. "Now that I know how to make these videos." She washed a dish, seeming more comfortable with the technology. "I'm going to record a video every day just for you. When you lose your way, and I am no longer here for you to run home to, come to this channel. I am making this not only as a memorial but also because I can't stand the thought of you needing me and me not being here. I want this channel to be a place for you to find your way home if you get lost. I also want you to get to know me outside of the role of mom. There's so much more to me that you don't know. So this is my parting gift to you. I will always be here as long as TikTack is here." The video ended.

The five siblings took the laptop, a bottle of their mother's favorite local Maine wine, the tissues, plates, forks and a blueberry pie and sat together in the living room to watch every single video, all 315 days' worth, together.

As the videos progressed and Maxine's following increased she began making all sorts of videos; from comical to giving life advice. The younger generations, especially those who lacked a caring mom, saw the value in Maxine's wisdom but most of all they loved her gentle spirit and words of encouragement. They nicknamed her GranMax, and Maxine loved it. She found a redemptive aspect in being there for the younger generations as if it was making up for all that she did wrong with her own children.

As the videos became more recent, Maxine's impending death showed in her face. Her voice and movements grew weaker and it was hard to watch. After the last video, Clover cleared her throat and set her plate down on the coffee table, "That was really hard to watch."

"She seemed happy, like she really enjoyed making these videos." Luke looked down at his phone with her account still pulled up and read the comments under one of the videos.

"You're the coolest mom anyone could have."
"GranMax, your kids are stupid for not hanging with you."
"Your TT family is going to miss you."
"Will you be my mom?"

Luke sighed. "We are so selfish. We failed to be there when she needed us the most."

For Mike, this other side of his mother was too foreign and he wasn't sure he was ready to forgive. "But in all fairness, these kids who think she's all sweet and all weren't there when dad took his life. They didn't see the shame she put on Jen when she came out, or how obsessed she was with making us good Catholic kids growing up. We saw that."

Clover nodded. "But, people do change. Mike, we can't punish her forever. We all make mistakes. She ended up coming around for Jen even though it was against her religion—imagine changing all your beliefs for someone else, that can't be easy. And obviously, she felt horrible about the affair—she was never with anyone since. Give her a break, we all left for college and went our separate ways and then dad died and all. That must have been hard on her; we abandoned her. She lost everyone in such a short time. And I was completely oblivious to what she was going through."

"Me too," Jennifer said. "I was focused on starting my own family. Plus, I was really hurt. She said some mean things at my wedding." Jen wiped her cheek. "I guess we're all a little beat up but like she said, we're all just walking each other home, and might I add, we're walking each other home from a fight. She was hurt; I was hurt; we were all hurt."

Reed nodded. "She had to have been lonely but if I'm being honest, it was hard to come back with dad gone. I just felt this hole with each visit, and all mom and I did was argue, that's why I stopped. It was too sad to come back."

"Same here." Mike patted Reed on the shoulder.

Luke stared into his wine glass. "But, mom did a lot for us. Despite her flaws, she gave and gave and never expected anything back—sure she was religious and a little controlling but her intentions were good. She was always there for us." He chuckled, swirling the wine around the bottom of the glass. "She really was a house-elf." He stopped, and wiped his cheek. "She walked us home and we never once said thank you."

Everyone silently agreed.

Reed, humbled, put his wine glass up in the air and said, "To Mom, the best friend, and guardian angel we never knew we had."

Jennifer's glass joined the others. "To our TikTok angel."

A Pair of Cokes and a Cream Soda

By Francis Alex Cooke *(CONTENT WARNING: language)*

Now before I get into it, we were far better off than church mice, so my clothes were left intact and the gas tank was always full. Any other likeness to real persons or events is purely coincidental or daringly deliberate. The places are real. Ask me how I know. While we're at it, any likeness to a grammatical or spelling error was deliberate or I'm not as educated or well-read as I pretend to be. Make up your own mind on both points. Now go on and enjoy this literary disaster.

Even back in my early school days, I was desperate to be one of the kids with a strip of As down my report card. I always felt like I was hanging off my mother's neck and choking her out, so I wanted to make her proud of something. One morning when I was six, I was sitting in one of only two classrooms in the rural school I went to back in the early eighties. To me, that doesn't seem so long ago but my age and my gray hair tell me different. Anyway, I was one desk from the front and I almost couldn't see a lick of what the teacher was writing on that board. I leaned and I squinted and I opened my eyes wider but little worked. Squinting did the best job, I guessed - I could focus on little bits of writing at a time - but I missed nearly half the work. Makes the smartest kid feel stupid when he's still frantically writing the last thing he could remember reading before the eraser came out and the chalk scratched out a whole new boardfull. I looked over at Preston, another lefty, but who had the most ridiculous spiral contortion going on with his hand as he wrote. Preston was also peculiar in that he had just gotten glasses. In a school of twenty students and only one teacher for three grades, he was the only one with a set of specs. Glasses were supposed to be for old people, but there he was happily scrawling along without missing a beat because, you know, he could see the damned words.

A week or two passed and I approached my mother about this issue that was only getting worse. She made an appointment with the optometrist only a ten-minute drive away across the bridge to New Waterford, the coal town she grew up in. I'd seen a lot of pictures of the place even by six and it had already been drained of much of the charm my mother had grown up knowing and basking in. People leaving and shops closing or shelves left half-empty; it was a town that would spend thirty years or more dying or maybe even killing itself. I didn't really understand my mother's love of the place but I guess I was just too young to get nostalgia; now I may be too old to let go of it myself.

Doctor Falsmouth was an early middle-aged man and a bit of a rude arrogant prick. He didn't know how to handle kids, so I figured he either didn't have any and didn't like the thought of it or his household was a fifties stereotype where he went to his job and his wife stayed home and did all the real work to keep his life moving along. From the second I sat in that chair he was almost yelling at me. For the sake of context, I'll tell you I'm a pale ginger and I squint on a sunny day. My eyes water if I don't. On top of that, I'm soft. For the love of all that is holy, don't go spreading that around. But a strong enough word from the right angle is going to bring a little saline. So some dingbat quack of an eye doctor shining a bright light directly into the peepers and demanding loudly that I stop the damned squinting is not going to help. Faucets on to a drip. He did a little more testing. I barely made it through and I know I didn't read that 20/20 line.

Falsmouth asked my mother if anyone in my class had recently gotten glasses. She told him about Preston.

"I see the problem," he said. "A little case of monkey see, monkey do." He went on to tell her that this happens all the time. I just wanted glasses because another kid got glasses. After all, what child wouldn't want to be tied to a pair of fragile, awkward, dirty, insult-inducing goggles for the rest of their life? Clearly Doctor Falsmouth did not have an unrealistic view of his place in the world. Master of the eye and fashion expert of six-year-olds everywhere. When mom questioned once more about the vision complaints, he stated snarkily, "he's just having trouble focusing."

His explanation would ring in both my ears and my mother's years later when he finally diagnosed my farsightedness. After all, if I'm having trouble focusing, isn't that exactly the reason why I...ugh, never mind. You get it. And just to be clear, if caught early enough, farsightedness can sometimes be improved or even completely corrected. In my case, by the time Falsmouth got it right, my glasses should probably have come with a zoom function. Still, it was from that near-useless swindler that my mother bought my first pair. Word to those wiser than me: If you want better quality, just skip his office, go straight to the candy store, down a couple actual Cokes, and hold 'em up. They last longer, you'll see better, and you won't look any worse.

~~~

Nearing the end of grade seven, I was almost thirteen and two years into wearing glasses. My mother had changed eye doctors to one with a little more gray matter between the earlobes and a lot more manners. She had also purchased a new pair of glasses that would, if still ugly as sin, at least last past the evening news. By then, along with Coke bottles, the creative minds of the other 12s, 13s, and basically the rest of the fellow pupils of my new school came up with such masterpieces as four-eyes, nerd, loser, and bookworm. Buncha unoriginal cro magnons. But I admit, between the glasses, the good grades, the small stature, and the strict curfew, I made it all too easy. I may as well have held up a five-foot target and offered up bean bags with insults involving slightly bigger words than they were capable of understanding written on them. I wasn't innocent though. I was saucy. I threw back after I had enough. And luckily for me, I was at least agile enough to get away when I bit off more than I could chew, although I never flinched from that first punch.

Not that I ever thought that a hard shot to this mug ever mattered. Ginger hair and pasty skin, the whole look of the British Isles was pulled together with heavy blotchy speckles from cheek to cheek, down each skinny arm, and across my back. I hated the freckles on my face most of all, so a puck to the bullhorn wasn't going to make me any uglier. My parents also didn't have much money. My father's carpentry business went bust during the recession; you can't live on your own goodwill and trust, even in family, so he was spending half of each year out west to make just enough to survive. They couldn't afford the umbrella for the 'Pennies From Heaven', so haircuts were infrequent and clothes weren't replaced before they looked like they'd been blessed by the Pope himself. And while he was gone, my mother could rarely fill a tank, so I fast wore holes in my shoes walking two miles along the tracks to Dominion every day or so with a little bag on my back, carrying a thermos of water, a journal and a pencil or two in hopes of finding some like-minded soul. Things did not go well and I generally walked home worse for wear.

On the last "teaching" day before school was out, class was an absolute crime scene. Lloyd Price was appropriately howling out the story of a pair of lowdown gamblers in my head. The teacher was at the front reading the newspaper. The popular kids were talking and pointing out the kids they disapproved of. The bullies were in the back shooting spitballs or digging treasure from the far reaches of their nasal passages. Just as Stagger Lee took out that poor Billy, I was hit with a few of the spitballs, as were the other undesirables. Looking back, I still hope it was just the spitballs. The thought just turns my stomach. Just like every other day that school year though, there was one good reason for me to be there. There was this one girl planted at the right, skinny and taller than the rest, quiet as could be, always reading to herself or writing down her work. It seemed like nobody paid any mind to her and, aside from the teacher, I doubted she ever paid any mind to anyone in turn. But almost every morning, I walked into that classroom and glanced sidelong in her direction to see if she noticed me. As far as I could tell, she never did and I just slid to the front left of the class and settled into my seat. I thought she was polaroid ready but I was sure she didn't even know my name. Nonetheless, her name rings like a bell to six courses: Amy Kathryn.

That Friday morning was grading day and it thankfully came and went with little to-do. With all the parents around there was only one, "see ya in grade 8, Coke bottles," and a quick shot to the shoulder blade as I made my way up the hill and away from the school to my waiting mother. Amy, the one person I would have liked to see, was like a ghost; I thought I could sense her, but I was sure these four eyes didn't lie. Probably for the best; I couldn't rub two words together around her anyway. My sister had been in and out already. She was waiting impatiently in the back seat, sitting in a frilly pink dress and white leggings and kicking my mother's seat with her matching white shoes.

"Hurry up," my mother said with a smile. She heard one of the cows at the farm was calving and asked if we wanted to see. We were both exclamatory in our agreements. Upon our arrival, we parked ourselves on the fence to watch. Much to my 8-year-old sister's surprise and eventual horror, however, the scene quickly took an unexpected turn. The farmer brought out a big shovel and some rope. As he bound the calf's two protruding legs and his brother fastened the other end to the shovel, he explained that the process had been going on far too long and the lives of both mother and baby were at risk. Then the two big men gave a massive tug and in one fell swoop, the miracle of life left such a scar on my sister that she remains childless to this day.

We went straight home after that. My mother had a present waiting that I had known of and talked about to all two people who would listen for a month. Sitting in the yard, perched on its kickstand was a brand new black 10-speed mountain bike.

I ran to it but just before I kicked that stand up, my mother yelled, "Francis Alex" (pronounced Elik, if you please)! "Eat and change."

I marched in, ate the lunch she already had waiting for me, and tripped my way into my room to get out of the only good set of clothes I owned and back into the usual striped t-shirt and ragged denim shorts. I practically ran into my holey shoes and nearly crashed right through the glass pane in the door to get to that bike. I rode off to the hills less than a quarter-mile from the house. Short-lived, I made one pass around and hit a big ol' rock dead center on the path. I bent the rim and flattened the tire. Grading day celebrations officially over and the gift broken all before noon. That has to be a talent.

~~~

By early afternoon, I was done hearing about the bike. I grabbed my bag, filled my thermos, and threw in a couple extra books for good measure; Robert Service and Lord Tennyson would keep me company on the bleachers in town when I inevitably landed there after another few failed attempts at socializing. After all, who wouldn't want to be reading Service's verses (not poetry, Robbie himself insisted) of Yukon gold and guns or Tennyson's long complicated nonsense I was too young to understand? The answer was actually everybody but me; I failed to get the memo. I still haven't gotten it and I still love them both. Town was quite deserted when I got there so I went straight to the field. I planted myself on the bottom bench, took out the larger book, and pretended I knew what Alfie's pretty phrases meant for a while. I had my water beside me and sipped on it from time to time. I even gave a few lines a go myself as I wrote in my journal. I have that little book to this day and the scribbles and scratches on that particular page say I was no Chaucer. I still can't read that stuff, so I don't even know what that means; but it sounds smart, don't it.

At 4:30, I looked down at my trendy little Casio look-alike and realized that after the bicycle incident I ought not risk life and limb by crossing my mother twice in one day. I threw my kit into my little pack, whipped it from shoulder to shoulder onto my back, and started off toward the train tracks as fast as my dwarven frame and my size 10 seal flippers would take me. Now that doesn't sound like much of a footprint by adult standards, but if I was asked my height back then, I'd be lying if I uttered five-foot-two. I'd have been much less awkward barking, clapping, and balancing balls on my nose for treats. As I ran and slowly lost steam, I saw something, no, someone in the distance coming around the corner at Railroad Street. I could barely breathe and the kid on the bike was still too far away to see. I had to slow to a walk and speed my breathing to a wheezing pant as the bike came closer.

Now, something you may not have noticed yet is that up until this point in my life I considered all music recorded after about 1965 or so to be little more than filler for trash receptacles with few exceptions. My soundtrack of the time was a little out of season and my muse was about to have it spinning like a 24-hour broadcast from here on out so keep that in mind. Once I caught my breath I was able to focus in on the shiny new pink bike and the lanky brown-haired girl cruising on it. As I noted Amy Kathryn's pretty little face, the piano and doo-wop opening of 'Earth Angel' by The Penguins swelled up in my heart and everything went into slow motion. I could swear she was moving at such a stalling pace she should have fallen right over but for her grace and … and … symmetry! Then she flicked her brown shoulder-length locks around her little shoulders at me, or at least that's how I chose to chisel it. She had on a white tee and pink shorts and jelly sandals. While I was a fool in love humming along with that forty-five spinning in my head and dragging nerves up outta the asphalt, her attention was, in fact, elsewhere. When I finally realized her eyes were caught up in something across the street, it shook me outta my trance and I looked with her to see what was going on, oblivious to the collision that was about to ensue.

In the time it took to turn my head, that bike was on me; first into my right knee and then straight between my legs and into the stones. I grabbed what was left of my masculinity for protection but it was too late. The needle skipped right off the turntable, my eyes filled up, and I went down like a felled redwood, taking the pink bicycle and its unprepared rider with me. I writhed in pain for just one second, but one second too long. With that flash of opportunity, my big mouth offered up its wisdom.

"What kinda dummy rides a bike on the side-" and then I paused. I spent the last ten months hoping this belle would notice me and instead of showing her a gentleman like she deserved, I handed over the hindquarters of a jackass. I slowly lifted my mortified tomato head and there she was sitting on the ground nursing a scraped-up and bloodied right knee. She already had tears in her eyes and now her cheeks were beginning to rouge. I tried to speak but up went her hand. I held my breath as she slowly got to her feet and picked up her bike. I got up and dusted myself off as she turned her bike around and started back toward Railroad Street where I could now assume she lived. Still holding my breath, I attempted to utter an 'I'm sorry', but the words wouldn't come. Amy, however, found her line as she rode off.

"You'd think you'd see a girl on a bike when you have a pair of Bushnells strapped to your face!" With that, she turned the corner and as I finally released my breath I knew I'd have to take my shame right past her house on my slow trudge home.

That walk home took forever. By the time I got there, the only thing left sore was my ego. And my chance with Amy. She looked so gorgeous in the ticks before she ran me down. Now I didn't know that I had the grit to go within a thousand yards of her let alone look into her big blue eyes again. I moped through the door past six and my mother had it out with my ears for three rounds before she let me go to my room to punish myself. I sat on my bed with pad and pencil and tried my best to eke out an apology. It was no use. Fifteen balls of crumpled paper all over my floor and nothing more than a salutation on each, Miss Amy Kathryn was not going to be getting a letter from me any time soon. There were no words I could stick to that pulp that could make up for calling the girl of my dreams a dummy on the first go around the block. A smooth operator with a silver tongue indeed.

~~~

The next day I woke up early but got up late; 7:15 AM, which was two hours and fifteen later than usual for a Saturday. I was a weird kid. I wasn't keen to face the day but I couldn't stand my own thoughts any longer. I put on my cheaters, dragged myself into some semi-clean clothes from my floor, and had some cold cereal with too much milk and a glass of too much milk. I got my sneakers on and spent a good hour staring at grass in various parts of the yard. I couldn't get the tears I crudely pressed out of Amy's deep blues off of my mind. I ran scenario after scenario for a solution but ideas dried up pretty quick. I wanted to see her so much, but I wanted to miss her so much more. I was going to have to avoid her like she was carrying the Spanish Flu and licking cheeks. Now that I was bored of moping in my own yard I thought it best to mope around town instead. I went into the house and asked my mom if I packed a lunch and enough to drink could I spend the day away from the house.

She hesitated but then warned, "Be back by supper this time if you want to make it to thirteen." My birthday was the very next day. Oh the wit. "And put on a hat. We're already having barbecue for supper."

I dumped the books from my pack onto my bed; those old fogeys and their fancy phrases failed me the previous day as had my own harsh hamfisted hacks. I grabbed in their stead my 'portable cassette player' and a two-cassette compilation of hits from the early days of rock n' roll. I placed cassette one in the deck and clipped that heavy monstrosity to my shorts while I tossed cassette two into my pack. I put on a grubby trucker hat, grabbed the pair of PB and Js and the thermos from my mother, and headed back out and down the driveway, determined to get Amy K off my mind. I was dead focused on my mission as I marched and nothing was going to stop me - until I got to the road and turned right and remembered the tracks chugged clean past her house. Well that lasted long. I made an about-face and set off toward the main road. It would take another ten to fifteen minutes but it was a sacrifice I was willing to make, you know, for the greater good.

That morning I learned something about the boys of the fifties and sixties: they had about as much luck with the ladies as I did. I put on my earphones and pressed play. "Someday, some way, you'll realize that you've been blind," comes sobbing along through the little speakers. Stop. Fast forward. Play. "Now that you're gone ..." What fresh hell was this?! STOP! FAST FORWARD! PLAY! On come The Diamonds with 'Little Darlin''. I gave up. That cat was pleading too, but I couldn't relate. He had two gals on the go and I couldn't get even one. I sang along as I always did without even noticing I was doing it, much to the chagrin of the entire island I'm sure. Nearly half a tape later Del was asking himself what went wrong with his love. By this time I was so lost in it that I was practically down on one knee belting that chorus so loud I later got a cease and desist order from Del himself, and he died the year prior. When the tune ended, I straightened myself and realized I had made it to the beach already. I also noted that I had just held a free music festival the entire way so I took my phones off so as to not make further a scene. I was thirty seconds too late. There on the sidewalk coming straight at me with a smirk and some conviction was Amy Kathryn. My whole face went to flames, my heart started playing some panicked surf beat, and I knew I had no escape.

Since I was now walking myself to the chair for my last rights and a quick demise, I decided to fulfill the last wish of most any red-blooded boy of twelve. I checked out Amy Kathryn. She looked as pretty as ever, maybe prettier. She had on a pink tank, a pair of denim shorts, and these white strappy flat sandals on her feet. Her hair was pulled loosely back into a pink scrunchie. This was a top-notch sight for a late preteen in '91, seriously. Before I changed the record back to 'Earth Angel' though, I came to my senses and put my head down to continue toward my fate in silence. I stopped maybe five feet from her as soon as I caught her toes sticking out of the end of the sandals. We stood silent for a second. I contemplated walking past and pretending I didn't see her, running in any direction but toward her, or simply backing up if she came toward me.

Instead, Amy threw a curveball into the lobes.

"I'm sorry I ran you over yesterday. I wasn't looking."

I looked up, absolutely flabbergasted. I just looked into her blues in awe. After what was clearly a little too long she became impatient. "Do you have anything to say, or are you just going to use the coke bottles to focus sunlight on me? I burn easily you know." I shook myself into reality and said, "Oh, yeah, I'm really sorry too. I didn't mean to get in your way. And I'm sorry for what I said. I speak sometimes before I think."

She cracked a smile again, "I couldn't tell."

We each waited for the other to do something, anything. I walked up beside her and she turned to walk with me.

"I'm Frankie," I said as we sauntered into town.

"I know," she replied, "my name is Amy Kathryn. I'm named after my mom." She knew my name? Could this be a dream? Man, I didn't know girls at all. The Chords spun up on the table as we started.

I looked up at her and admitted, "I know your name too. I see you every day in class." I blushed a little and kept going, "I looked over every day when I walked in. Can't say why and maybe I shoulda just said hi." I looked up and Miss Amy's cheeks were glowing pink in the bright sun.

"Maybe you should have, but you have a bit of a mouth on ya," she said as she evened the score. We strolled all over town side by side, sometimes talking and sometimes not. The breaks didn't seem to matter and we just blithely drank in the company. When it was time for shut down, I walked her home.

From across the street she turned to me and yelled, "I hope you're coming back to town this evening. Take the tracks so I can meet you." My jaw bounced off the pavement before I rolled it up and nodded in agreement. Then from her front step, she turned and yelled a little louder, "and I was looking at the lilacs when I ran into you. Purple is the color of royalty you know." Royalty? Whatever! Amy Kathryn wanted to meet me again that evening!

~~~

I don't remember the walk home, but I assume I cartwheeled or floated the whole way. Supper probably would have resembled food had it been taken off the grill about seven minutes earlier, but I didn't care; I had more pressing matters to attend to. I ran from the table and knocked the chair over in my haste. I ran back and threw it wobbling on its legs and it dropped in the other direction. I made my way down the hallway to the bathroom and got in the shower. I blasted some ice-cold water down my back and followed that up with a rush of scalding hot. I near slipped out of the tub with the shock. I got the water all straightened out to a temperature hot enough to remove the top layer of my pasty hide. I grabbed the soap, started to wash up, looked down, and stripped off my drenched duds. I finished the job and dried off. Once I was spick and span, I got back in the shower and washed up. Yes, I got back in the shower. I got out, dried off, and bathed myself in this cheap old cologne my father had been given as a gift before I was a twinkle. I brushed my teeth, flossed, and grabbed the bottle of the cologne to rinse. To the toilet I went for some gagging. I almost expelled the charred remnants of my supper but I held it together. I grabbed the mouthwash and left it at that. I threw on a red plaid collared shirt, a pair of slacks, and my black dress shoes. My mom even had me figured so she gave me a sweet smile as she slicked my hair for me. If this dork to dapper do-over didn't draw that dazzling young dame, probably anything else would, but you weren't tellin' me. I was smelling like a buck twenty-five and feeling like a million.

My birthday money advanced a day early, I was off by seven o'clock to meet Amy Kathryn. I couldn't have asked for a better evening; warm with just a hint of a breeze. My step quicker than usual, I was near her house in about three blinks. Lucky for her, cheap cologne fades fast; I was going for breathtaking, but not of the ammonia variety. She must have been watching for me because as I made my approach her front door swung slow and out she stepped with all her elegance and poise. She had on a little light pink dress and her white strappy sandals. Her pretty brown hair was down now, stopping just above her bare shoulders and framing that perfect face. She turned to peer at me with her big blue eyes and smiled as she made her way across the street. And what do you know. 'You Send Me' comes on the juke in my old soul. Amy was radiant and I was glowing as we started toward the candy store.

"I'm glad you got back to town," Amy opened up, "I was a little nervous you weren't going to show up."

I looked up at her and replied, "I had to come back. I wanted to talk to you a long time ago but I get a bit nervous when I see you." She looked down at me puzzled. I looked forward and breathed in deep. It was time to just man up - or boy up, 'cause I'm pretty sure I'm still a boy. "I think you may be the prettiest girl in school. Maybe the prettiest girl I've ever seen. Every time I thought about talking to you I kinda choked on air." I knew I was blushing but man was I relieved to say it.

Her quieted voice returned, "I spent the whole year hoping you would but I blush easily and I didn't think you'd want to talk to me." So I could have been chatting her up for ten months but neither had the mettle to exhale the letters H and I past vocal cords to the other. Well hadn't we just mastered our grade primary social skills.

We got to the store and I asked Amy what she would like. She smiled and jabbed, "are you making a play?" I smiled back and adjusted my glasses.

"I just thought I could do something nice." She happily twirled around and took her pick. I could have taken a guess and there was no way I'd be missing this beat. She handed me the cream soda and I grabbed a pair of colas in the old-fashioned glass bottles. I hadn't had a drink in hours and I was parched. I downed the first bottle in one gulp. Amy came up from behind. "Thirsty?" My attempt at a reply was a carbonated emission that registered a 3.7 on the Richter scale. She giggled and though I was awful flush I had to laugh along. I tossed the bottle in the trash and we walked all over town sipping soda and playing twenty questions. It turned out we had a lot more in common than a bit of stage fright when it came to the respective apples of our eyes.

There were a lot of kids out that evening. They were either wandering around the park at the center of town waiting to get chewed out by badges every half hour or they were headed to the dam to try their hands at alcohol poisoning. My companion and I rarely noticed the goings on around us. We talked about authors we liked and made mental notes and verbal promises to check them out. I told her that her favourite colour was pink and she told me that I was turning thirteen the next day. Now I was the one with the puzzled look. She looked down and reminded me that the teacher always gave away the birthdays and he had noted every birthday coming up that summer.

"Do you remember mine?" she asked slyly. Well of course I did. It was, it was … ah damnit. "It's fine. I'm going to remind you anyway." We got to the fire hall, away from all the, ahem, hustle and bustle of downtown Dominion. The sign outside said 'FIFTIES NIGHT / 19 AND OVER". 'Runaround Sue' was booming through the open doors.

Amy Kathryn gave a little hop and exclaimed, "I love this song!" This song? Well, me too but I was hoping it wasn't a theme thing. I scoped the scene and noted a lack of bodies outside.

"You know, just because we can't get in doesn't mean we can't listen for a bit. C'mon." I took her by the hand and we sat down on the grass outside the open windows down the right of the hall.

I kept that little hand in mine while we sat and listened to another few tunes. Amy and I both grew up in homes where there was always music. I filled her in on how I got to play deejay when my folks had company. She talked about how her mom grew up in the fifties and said it was the greatest time to be young. She told me her dad liked to dance with her to a lot of these songs. One song into the next and an opportunity arose. The soft lull of 'In The Still Of The Night' started and I revved the engine before I ran out of gas.

"Do you want to dance?"

She paused and then said, "yeah, I mean yes I do." So I helped her up and we stood face to face. I never once in my young life danced with a girl but I watched a lot of old movies so how hard could it be? I placed my sweaty mitts on her tiny waist and she rested her digits gently on my shoulders. I took some initiative and stepped in a little closer with my left foot. With my other left foot I nearly took out three of her toes but I caught myself just in time. She wrapped her arms around my neck and we slowly spiraled and smiled bashfully at each other. I thought this had to be the top of the heap, that life couldn't get any better than those last two hours. But before you can say Anbesol, it turns out I was just cocky enough to prove myself oh so wrong. And man did I get it oh so right.

Now there's only one way to wrap this nifty narrative. It wouldn't be complete if a guy don't get his gal and there's only one thing a fella can do to seal that. As the ballad harmonized to a close, something came over me. Every nerve I had for almost a year disappeared and all I wanted was right there in front of me. I looked up into those two beautiful pools that were now staring anxiously back. I was right. This was without a doubt the most stunning creature I had ever laid my lookers upon. Before my head could high tail it, my heart took charge. I propped myself on the tips of my toes. Amy Kathryn swallowed and leaned in just a little. I stopped just shy of her lips. We both took a little breath. We closed our eyes. And then? And then I kissed her. Our lips locked for the next seven Mississippis and from that moment on all that mattered was the skipping of my heart and the beauty in my arms. With that, she was all mine. And you know what? The very next day we walked the beach and made out for eleven more Mississippis ... twice! Yeah I counted. What did ya think I was? Fourteen?

Departure

By Melanie Forrest

The reds and oranges of autumn blazed in the late October sun as Dustin crested the hill. He paused at the top, taking a few deep breaths to regain his composure before taking in the sights of the valley below. It was worth the climb. As far as he could see in all directions, trees. Nothing more. No signs of civilization. He was completely and utterly alone, and it felt invigorating.

He stooped to pick up a long, thin branch that would make a perfect walking stick for his descent. He admired the branch for a moment before pulling off the excess twigs that sprouted from the sides. He grasped it firmly, pressing it into the ground, putting his weight on it, to ensure that it would be strong enough. It bent slightly but did not break. Perfection.

After a few more minutes of soaking up the view and the warmth of the sun, Dustin started his descent into the forest. It was cooler under the canopy of the leaves, much closer to the temperature that he had been expecting this time of year. The sweat on his forehead from the arduous climb now chilled his skin and he shivered slightly. The straps of his heavy backpack dug uncomfortably into his shoulders, but he knew he wouldn't have to carry it much longer. He was almost there.

At the base of the hill, he finally stopped, dropping the backpack on the ground gratefully. He stretched out his shoulders, rolling them back and forth to work out the tension. He pulled a granola bar from his cargo pocket and ate it in two bites. Looking down at his pack, he sighed heavily at the dark spot on the canvas, then leaned down to detach the shovel that was strapped to the side.

Dustin started digging and didn't stop until he was waist deep in the hole. As he dug, he thought about the last time he'd been here; how happy he had been and he knew that he was in the perfect place. He paused to wipe his brow and take a swig of water and dug some more. Once it was mid chest, he figured he should stop, otherwise, he'd never be able to climb back out.

He stood over the hole for a long time, thinking. This was where he would have peace. This was where he would finally be safe. Eventually he resigned himself to the remainder of the task. He tossed the backpack into the hole and started filling it back in with the dirt he had shoveled out.

It was nearly dark when Dustin finally picked up his newfound walking stick and made his way back up the hillside. Halfway up, just before losing sight of the spot, he turned back one last time, said goodbye to his brother, and continued on his way.

Outcasts

By Melanie Forrest (*CONTENT WARNING: mention of self harm*)

He ran as fast as he could. He ran until his lungs ached and his legs burned but still didn't stop. If he paused for even a moment, the bigger boys would catch him and then he'd really hurt. He chanced one quick glance backwards and saw that they had stopped pursuing him. He still didn't stop, rounding the corner and heading straight towards St Edmund's.

It was the perfect hiding place; he scaled the short wall behind the abandoned church and slipped between the doors. They were chained shut, but he was small enough to fit in the crack when you pushed them open. Once inside, he was finally able to gasp in some much-needed air.

He plopped down onto one of the dusty pews and waited for his heartbeat to calm, his breathing to regulate. The punks weren't messing around this time. They had roughed him up a bit before he managed to break away and run. He wondered if it would ever get easier to be him but somehow knew deep down that it wouldn't. He'd always be an outsider, a weirdo, a loser. All he had done this time was look in Attwell's direction. He didn't want them to hate him but it seemed that everything he ever did around them was wrong.

After a few minutes, he rose from the pew and made his way to the altar. He liked to be in the dusty old church. He felt strangely like he belonged. It was one of the few places in the entire world that made him feel that way.

He didn't see her sitting in the front pew so when she let out a tiny cough, he turned around in shock.

"Faux? Is that you?" he asked. She was sitting cross legged, slouched down so far that her head wasn't above the back of the pew.

"Hey Farron," she said, pulling back her hood so he could see her properly. "I didn't know anyone else came here."

Farron shuffled his feet, "Yeah," he dragged out the word, trying to think of how to explain it, "Attwell and his gang were chasing me. It's... safe here."

Faux simply nodded, but her expression was as if she understood that it was more than safety that drew him here. She looked down at her hands, picking at a Band-aid on her right pointer finger.

"What are you doing here?" Farron asked, instantly regretting it.

"Thinking. It's quiet here."

It was Farron's turn to nod; she wasn't wrong. In fact, it was his favourite place to come to think. He was shocked he hadn't run into her before. She seemed quite comfortable in the church.

"I... uh... come here a lot," he said. "You?"

Faux looked up at him, surprised, "All the time, actually." She stared at him for a long time with a look he couldn't quite comprehend. So long that he felt as though she was staring into his very soul.

"Uh, anyway... I guess I'll go. Leave you to think," Farron said, pointing his thumb in the direction of the door.

"You can stay," Faux replied, shrugging slightly, "I don't mind."

So, he did. They sat for ages in companionable silence. They watched the sun glinting through the cracked stained-glass windows and watched as it faded away in the sunset.

Finally, Faux stood, stretched, and started towards the exit. Farron followed her out wordlessly.

When they squeezed through the crack in the doors and were back outside, the scent of spring apple blossoms was strong in the breeze. They both inhaled the scent deeply, refreshed after the stale air of the abandoned church. Faux reached across the space between them, grasping Farron's hand in hers. He looked down at their linked hands, confused, but this confusion was quickly erased when she pulled him closer, kissing him firmly on the lips.

Farron was completely astonished. He'd never kissed anyone before. Her lips were very soft and tasted minty. As quickly as she had advanced on him, she pulled away, but she didn't release his hand.

"Thank you," she said.

"For what?" he asked, still thoroughly baffled by what had happened.

"I was going to climb the bell tower. But then you showed up and sat with me. So... thank you."

"Oh," he said, stupidly. He didn't know what else to say, but he gripped her hand tighter and led her away from the church.

Boggle On The Train
By Lynn Lipinski

My nephew Ryder was the kind of plump, pink-skinned know-it-all I would have thrown in a garbage can had this been middle school. He had something to say on every topic. In the rare moments he refrained from speaking, his mouth hung half open, perpetually poised to start yapping again the minute you took a breath. He'd only gotten worse since landing his first software job out of college. My brother Powell told me how much money that firm offered him, and I knew right away that I was in the wrong business. Writing never paid that well and I've been doing it for two decades.

"This is a huge opportunity for me to learn product development at one of Chicago's top tech companies. Now, maybe doing scrum and pre-production code deployment isn't exactly saving the world right now, but with a few years under my belt, I'll be able to create my own destiny. Write my own ticket, you know, Uncle Drew?"

The kid spouted cliches so earnestly he must have thought they were original ideas. My brother hung on every word like they were undiscovered Lennon/McCartney lyrics. Christ. And was I supposed to know what scrum meant? I wasn't about to ask wannabe Steve Jobs.

I hadn't believed Powell when he told me the kid wanted to come on our annual train trip across the Rockies. The trip was one of the few things in this world that my brother and I agreed on. We disagreed on the merits of a Catholic school education, whether the stock market was going bearish, or on the significance of the television show Breaking Bad. But we both loved being on the move and the way traveling by train allowed us to savor the experience.

Growing up, Ryder had never shown desire to leave his Chicago suburb with his video games and his online friends and coding conferences. But somehow, here he sat on the Amtrak, shaking my vintage 1980s Boggle box much harder than he needed to mix up the letter cubes, and talking about the importance of "stretch assignments" at work. I hoped that meant they were making him do yoga because he certainly needed the exercise.

Playing Boggle was as much a ritual as the train trip itself. Powell and I were well-matched, though I did win slightly more often than he did. Ryder, I assumed, didn't know how to play anything without a joystick, just like the fresh-faced college grads they kept hiring for less and less money at the magazine where I worked - and who were nipping at my heels every day to take the best assignments. Since when was age forty-two obsolete?

Powell kept his eyes focused on the box, competitive and ready to win. The difference, I knew, was that Powell would throw the game like Jake LaMotta if he thought Ryder might get upset. After all, this boy was raised in the generation that got trophies for putting their soccer cleats on the right feet. Powell watched that high-strung boy's moods with the intensity of an abused woman waiting for her boyfriend's next violent outburst. Yes, I chose that metaphor on purpose. Ryder held his dad hostage to his every fleeting happiness. It was abusive, at least to watch.

I had no such inhibition about beating Ryder. He blew off my offer to explain the rules and set the box down with a bang. Powell flipped the tiny plastic hourglass and I ripped the plastic top off the box. Go time.

I focused on the jumble of letters in the five-by-five grid. The thin lead of the mechanical pencil broke the first three times I tried to write, and I punched the eraser to extend more. The splintered pieces of lead rolled around the table like tiny logs with each lurch and push of the train.

Ryder bit his fat bottom lip in concentration; I could hear him breathe with the wheeze of an out-of-shape middle-aged man.

Words piled in my head, and I rushed to get them onto paper. ATTENDS snaked through the grid, ALOUD was nearby, DENSE ran diagonally across the board. I listened for pauses in their writing, enjoying a sweet feeling of triumph when Ryder's pen faltered for ten seconds or more, then resumed but only for a few letters before stopping. Meanwhile, I found a new run of words with ENDUES. No way Ryder would even know that word; he would probably burn precious seconds trying to make ENDURES not realizing he had a word staring right at him without that pesky letter R.

Powell called time. Ryder, impatient and bouncing like a child on the upholstered seat, demanded to be first to read his list.

ENDUES, he said. I scratched it off my list, then another, and another and another. Damn. My mind immediately concluded he was cheating.

"Do you even know what 'endues' means, Ryder?" I asked.

He grinned at me. "Hey, this isn't the SATs. I don't have to know what the words mean."

"Ryder's good at seeing patterns," Powell said, almost apologetically. "It's what makes him good at computer code."

"And Boggle," the kid said.

"Rematch," I said.

Words were my thing. I paid the rent by stringing them together for America's last greatest sports print publication. I finished the New York Times Sunday crossword puzzle in thirteen minutes last week. And I've played Boggle for thirty years. Experience had to count for something, I thought. I got this.

I snatched the box out of Ryder's hands and shook it with a deafening rattle that made the several of the other passengers turn to look at us. I didn't care; all I wanted to do was to take the stupid childish pleasure of shaking the box out of his baby hands. Mine, I wanted to say.

"Play nice, now," Powell muttered under his breath at me, his eyes sliding between my face and Ryder's, like we were two toddlers gearing up for a tantrum showdown.

I put the box down on the table, popped the top off and turned the timer all in one fluid movement. See, I thought, I don't need any of you. It was a ridiculous gesture, but I was coiled tight now, nerves jangling and eyes scanning the board.

"Just a game, Uncle Drew," the kid said and I grunted at him.

He reminded me of every smart-ass kid who'd come into the magazine the past five years, talking about social media and click-through rates and info-graphics. They made shitty little videos on their phones to go with their ubiquitous blogs. They were like vacuum cleaners of information, sucking it in and churning it back out in this endless vortex of new, new, new. They laughed behind their backs about old-timers like me who refused to tweet and who took three days sometimes to turn in a thoughtful, well-written article. These kids didn't value quality, only quantity.

And it all came so easy to them. Just like my nephew, as smug as a middle-aged man, counting on his gift for pattern recognition and his ability to write robot language.

RAW. RAM. LOSIL? CHOMA? FAOS? The letters turned into nonsense. My mind went blank, worse than writer's block. Like I lost my language abilities. Nothing registered. My mind panicked.

"Time," Powell said, his eyes on my list of two words. He licked his lips like he did before delivering bad news. "Why don't I go first," he said.

"ARF. ALSO. FAR. JAMS." He continued reading while I watched Ryder looking through his list, marking some words out, still smiling, still expecting to win.

"RAW," Powell said. I marked it out.

Ryder read his list next. "LOAM. MAW. MISO. OVALS." I saw him pause, his lips just starting to form the word RAM. I raised my pencil to mark it off my list when he did the inexplicable. "RAMS," he said, "SIM, SOLAR."

"Give me that sheet of paper," I said, fury stacking in my gut like stones and forcing hot bursts of anger out of my mouth. I tried to snatch it from him but he pulled it tight to his man breasts.

"If you wrote down RAM you should say it," I spat at him. "You can't tell me you came up with RAMS and not RAM. That's Boggle 101, pattern-recognition boy. And isn't RAM even a computer term?"

"I missed it, Uncle Drew. I didn't write down RAM." His eyes were on his father's, not mine, and they were pleading. The kid didn't know what to do. He wanted his dad to bail him out, just like always.

"You look at me when I'm talking to you, Ryder," I shouted. Powell stood up and clamped his hand on my shoulder to keep me in my seat. Ryder stared at the table as though the veins of fake marble were the most fascinating pattern he'd ever seen.

"Drew, come on, man," Powell said. "Doesn't matter."

I made one last grab for the piece of paper and tore a small piece. Ryder shoved the rest of it into his mouth and started to chew.

My fist balled around the scrap of paper and shot across the table to hit him in the ear. The cartilage turned bright red on contact and Ryder stared at him with glassy eyes, stunned.

The carriage went silent. Powell pressed down on my shoulder, his fingers digging in painfully between tendons and muscles. I heard our collective breathing, rising and falling in an adrenaline-fueled concert.

After a few moments, Ryder started chewing again, then swallowed the paper with a loud gulp.

Powell must have figured I was no longer a threat to his boy and slumped into his seat.

"You all right, Ryder?"

The kid nodded. "Uncle Drew, I was only trying to..."

"I don't need your pity, kid," I said. I glanced at Powell who watched his son with shining approval. I could practically hear the pride bursting out of his heart. He couldn't wait to call his wife and tell her what a nice boy they'd raised. Ryder unsheathed his tablet and poked it to life. I stared out the window at the green and brown slopes of the Rockies, until the train entered a tunnel. In the blackness, I saw only my face looking back at me. I looked like an old man.

Black & Brown

By Luke Swanson (*CONTENT WARNING: violence, historical depiction of Nazism*)

23 December 1933

G ero?" A large soldier named Kiefer stood in the doorway and yelled into the crowded tavern. "Gero, are you here, you *sitzpinkler*?"

"About time, *angeber*." A loud, mischievous voice responded. Kiefer's friend was in here somewhere.

From his relatively secluded position in the doorway, he scanned the tavern, which was almost filled to capacity with soldiers and civilians alike. Every available space was packed with men who wanted to escape the cold night but still celebrate the holidays as any good German would: drinking without any signs of slowing.

Finally, Kiefer spotted his friend Gero, an impishly handsome soldier with bright eyes. The two of them had been inseparable as children growing up in Spandau, one of Berlin's nicer fringe cities. They had attended different universities and led separate lives ... until they both joined the German army and Nazi Party. Now, they were each members of one of Chancellor Hitler's special divisions: Gero was in the SA, Kiefer in the SS.

The smallish man waved to his friend from the bar, laughing, and then raised his half-empty stein so Kiefer could see his position, like a lighthouse above a sea of blond heads and raucous laughter.

Kiefer chuckled to himself—he wasn't exactly surprised that Gero had set up camp at the bar.

"Took your time, did you?" Gero called and beckoned his friend further into the tavern. "I thought I was going to have to drink this nectar alone." He unleashed a hearty chortle, which ricocheted around the room. Gero's animated laugh was distinctive enough to pick out during a full-scale battle, and it hadn't changed since their days in grammar school.

Kiefer squared his broad shoulders and began to navigate through the massive crowd. He saw several other men sitting at the bar, all dressed in crisp brown uniforms. Gero's fellow *Sturmabteilung* soldiers —members of Chancellor Hitler's SA paramilitary force. He sat, and all but Gero eyed his black uniform with weary glances.

In response, he glowered at the other men, which caused them to quickly avert their gazes. He tried not to feel a smug warmness in his chest, but he couldn't help it. He imagined a lion felt the same way anytime a gazelle or field mouse showed proper deference.

He cleared his throat and waggled his brows at Gero. "Aw, so you missed me?"

"Hell no! A bunch of the guys were betting on how many drinks I could finish before you showed up. Thanks to you ..." Gero put the stein to his mouth and threw his head back, draining the dark beer straight down his throat. He slammed the stein on the wooden bar, beaming like an Olympic champion. "... I just made 50 marks."

The half-dozen soldiers sitting at the bar cheered or clapped. Always the showman looking for admiration, Gero exaggerated his drunkenness by donning a dopey smile, saluting, and bellowing, "For the *Fuhrer!*" Gero's SA friends laughed, without needing to exaggerate their drunkenness, and staggered away, likely ready to move on to another tavern.

Kiefer smiled as he shook his head. "You can't go one evening without trying to make a profit." He took off his black military hat and dropped it onto the bar. Rubbing his slicked-back hair, he made eye contact with the barkeep, who nodded and poured Kiefer's usual poison.

Gero's smile was reckless, boyish, one of his most charming features. "And?"

"I'm just saying, *kumpel,* you need to pace yourself. Not every activity is a damn race. Even twenty years ago, I remember you running laps around the schoolhouse and weaseling other children out of their chocolates."

"Hey, if those pipsqueaks knew they couldn't beat me, they shouldn't have bet their candies. Not my fault."

Kiefer wagged a finger in mock discipline. "If I didn't know better, I would think you were one of those gambling addicts I see at the baccarat tables at Baden-Baden."

"Whatever you say," Gero laughed. He gestured to Kiefer's ink-colored uniform. "So, this is why you were late?"

"One moment." Kiefer grabbed the stein right out of the barkeep's hand, froth spilling over his fingers. "Long day." He gulped enough alcohol to sedate a small child, then turned back to Gero. "What were you asking?"

"You answered my question!" Gero adjusted his brown uniform's collar. "The *Fuhrer* has you clocking in more and more overtime. Running all over Berlin from sunrise to sunrise. I told you, *kumpel*—"

"Yes, yes, you told me." Kiefer donned a falsetto voice as he remembered what his friend had told him nearly a year earlier: "The SS is going to be one big headache. The new Chancellor will work you to death."

They both chuckled and took hearty swigs from their drinks.

"And I was right!" Gero slammed his fist on the bar, the tavern's low lights dancing in his eyes. "Your precious SS is Chancellor Hitler's private police squad. Chasing leads? Sniffing out corruption? Bah!" He tried to casually shove Kiefer's muscular forearm, but it was like pushing against a brick wall, and he ended up nearly falling off his stool. "The *Fuhrer* has you catching raindrops."

"Well, look who's talking!" Kiefer returned the favor, slapping his friend's shoulder. "You half-wit, you're in the SA! We're *both* in his army, lest you forget. Your compatriots are the *Fuhrer*'s original guard dogs, have been for years, even before he became Chancellor."

"But there's one key difference between the two of us, Kief."

"You mean besides the fact that I could snap you like a twig?"

"Yes, besides that." Gero stood and beckoned for his friend to do the same. He threw his arm around Kiefer's shoulders and turned him around so they faced the roiling crowd. "What do you see?"

The SS man took in the sight: dozens and dozens of patrons, many of them soldiers. Off-duty, of course—the *Fuhrer* did not partake in alcohol, and he certainly did not tolerate soldiers who did so while on the job. Some sang Christmas hymns, some told stories, some played cards, but all the soldiers had one thing in common. Kiefer could see Gero's point, but he did not want to give his smaller friend the satisfaction of hearing him admit it. He shrugged and finished his beer. "What are you getting at?"

"Look at your uniform, and look at theirs." Gero's face split in a wicked smirk. "Look at mine! Nice and brown. Practical, natural, a soldier of the earth. A man of the SA! But your uniform ..." He scoffed for comic effect. "Black. So dark and gloomy. And ..." He gestured grandly across the whole tavern. "Nearly alone!"

It was true. Kiefer was the only SS soldier in the entire establishment. His black uniform was as conspicuous as a beetle in the desert sand. In the vast crowd, over half of the men sported the tan attire of Ernst Roehn's SA.

"Acknowledged." The large SS man set his empty stein on the bar. "What's your point?"

"Well, our numbers reach nearly two million. *Million*! There are more SA soldiers than there are people in all of Czechoslovakia! We are a force of nature, my *kumpel*. We could overthrow the SS without taking a break for lunch. Hell, we could storm the Reichstag if we so desired." He cackled. "*And*, best of all, there are so many of us, I only work a three-hour day."

"You cannot be serious." Kiefer sighed. "Three-hour work days? I know for a fact *you're* lazy, but is the rest of the SA? There's no way Roehn is that lackadaisical."

"Now, now, big fellow, no need to use words with more than three syllables. Roehn is a fine leader, and he's a close ally of your man, the *Fuhrer*."

Kiefer gestured for two more beers. "You're right, there are key differences between your SA and the SS: We blend in with night, you camouflage in the Sahara. We number in the thousands, you in the millions. We," he flexed his mighty biceps and Gero cowered sarcastically, "are elite like foxes, you are innumerable like ants."

"Have you ever been swarmed by ants? Wouldn't recommend it."

Kiefer guffawed and sat back down, waiting for his second beer. "True. I suppose we both serve Germany. We are both in the *Fuhrer*'s army, just very different wings."

"Exactly!" Gero sat next to him. "It just so happens that we are far more fashionable. Brown uniforms stand out far more than black ones at galas and parties."

30 February 1934

It was a Monday evening, not yet night, so the tavern was lightly populated by the depressed and unemployed who craved an alcoholic buzz. Kiefer sat in a corner booth, attempting to avoid eye contact with the forlorn patrons—which was fairly easy, since they all stared into their steins as if the universe's secrets were hidden at the bottom.

He pushed away his untouched pint of beer, unsure why he had ordered it in the first place. His taste for alcohol had dwindled over the past few months—if the *Fuhrer* did not partake, why should one of his most elite soldiers? The SS was held to a higher standard than the regular army and the SA. Civilians whispered when he walked past them on the street, eyeing his black uniform with either awe or fear. Both filled him with pride.

Other soldiers tended to scowl at his uniform, which deflated Kiefer's spirits. Perhaps they were jealous of the SS's influential status. Chancellor Hitler praised the SS, calling them his "protective echelon," a title that made the regular army seethe. Sometimes, the brown-suited SA men went so far as to mock him or scoff.

But not Gero. They still met for drinks at this tavern, joking and laughing, swapping insults and tall tales. Kiefer loved being with his old friend—nothing had changed, except for his own drinking habits. But that was it, he told himself.

He checked his watch. Gero was twenty minutes late this time. Which was not necessarily alarming. Both had been tardy on several previous occasions.

Kiefer sighed, rubbing the day-long scruff on his chin, and began humming softly to himself. A lively march, upbeat like a circus tune. It took a moment before he realized he was unconsciously humming the Nazi Party's anthem. Everyone was singing it now, not just Party members—Chancellor Hitler had made it Germany's national anthem last year.

He began to sing under his breath: "The flag on high ... The ranks tightly closed ... Clear the streets for the—"

Before he could finish, Gero's vigorous laugh echoed through the nearly deserted tavern. "I love that song!" He placed both hands on his chest like an opera singer and bellowed the line: "Clear the streets for the brown battalions!" His vibrato shook the tables.

"Don't get too cocky, you *sitzpinkler*," Kiefer said, crossing his trunk-like arms.

"Hey, I'm not cocky." Gero slid into the booth. "I'm just singing our beloved anthem ... which just so happens to praise my brown uniform over your inky black garb."

"I don't recall those lyrics."

"That's the French translation, I think." Gero swiped the full stein from the middle of the table and took an emphatic gulp. He stifled a belch and unleashed one of his reckless smiles. "Thank you for lending me a sip. I'm sure you don't mind."

For the first time he could recall, Kiefer didn't return a grin. "Should you be drinking so much at this time of day? You're one of Hitler's warriors, even—" He quickly shut his mouth.

Gero's smile flickered. "Go ahead, *kumpel*. What were you saying?"

"Nothing." But they both knew it was a lie.

The silence hung like a thick fog. Gero cleared his throat and let out a ghost of a chuckle. "It's okay, Kief. I know what you were thinking." His posture became ramrod straight, like a cobra staring at an opponent. "You were going to say, 'Even though you're only SA.' Am I right?"

Kiefer clenched his jaw and did not avert his gaze. "I don't mean to insult you. Or the SA, for that matter. I stopped myself from saying it."

"But you *thought* it." Gero shrugged, feigning nonchalance. He adjusted his uniform's cufflinks and straightened the SA insignia on his breast. "You wanted to say it. I know there's ice between our divisions, but I never would've guessed there would be between us." Then he snatched the stein and finished the beer. After drinking, he wiped his chin with a brown sleeve.

"Gero, come on—"

"No, listen to me, you *angeber*," the smaller man snarled. "We aren't in the schoolyard anymore. Just because you're big and strong doesn't mean you're God's gift to the world. The SA is part of me. I am part of it. Your man Himmler may be the Chancellor's best friend, but my leader Roehn is far from weak or powerless. You were wrong before— we are not ants." He shot to his feet, rocking the table. "We're piranhas."

Kiefer, still sitting, looked up at his friend for the first time in his life. It must have been a sight: a small, wiry SA soldier roaring at a muscular SS man cowering in a booth.

"Don't be like that." Kiefer held up his hands as if in surrender. "Please, let's not fight. Let's ..." He wanted to say, *'Let's go back to the way it was before. As kids. Hell, before joining the Party.'* But he knew that was simply impossible. Nothing would ever be the same.

Gero proudly tapped his tan shirt. "The SA is the protector of this state, and the SS is a group of thugs pretending to be important. I don't want to fight either." He balled his fists. "But I do what I must."

Kiefer felt the weight of his uniform over his entire body. Instead of smothering him, it gave him strength, confidence, vindication. It gave him power.

"And guess what, *kumpel*?" Gero scoffed, grinning like a snake. "We number over three million strong now. We're larger than Germany's regular army. Even they wouldn't stand a chance against us. Your precious SS is nothing in comparison."

It was Kiefer's turn to stand. He towered over Gero, casting a dark shadow like an impending rain cloud.

"Watch your step, old friend." He marched past the SA soldier and left the tavern, jackboots beating the floor with the force of the entire Reich.

25 April 1934

Kiefer sat in a booth with his three best friends—Eckhardt, Killian, and Max. They sipped water and shared a basket of peanuts. And they all wore pitch-black SS uniforms, various decorations pinned to their chests.

"Dresdner is going to take the season, I can feel it," Killian said through a mouthful of chewed nuts.

"You can't be serious." Max rolled his eyes. "No one can touch Wacker Halle on the field. They're the best football club the world has ever seen."

"Wacker Halle? No way!" Killian threw his hands in the air. "I'm telling you, it's Dresdner this year."

"And by that," Kiefer cut in, "you mean you have money on Dresdner?"

"Well, yes!"

The four SS men laughed until the table shook.

It was late evening, the tavern almost full. The summer weather was beginning to show itself, but spring coolness still kept the soldiers from boiling in their uniforms. Kiefer smiled at his new friends, then crushed a peanut shell between his massive fingers.

Suddenly, the tavern doors flew open, crashing against the walls. In strolled a small group of seven soldiers, cackling and hollering like a flock of gulls. They wore the brown uniform. A smallish man with reckless eyes led the pack.

Kiefer snarled.

"Barkeep, the usual, if you please!" Gero bellowed, sounding as if this was not the first tavern he had frequented that evening. His posse staggered throughout the tavern, shoving civilians out of their way.

"Excuse us, *trottel*," one of them jeered, throwing his elbows as he lurched toward the bar. "The *Fuhrer's* right-hand man needs some liquid courage."

Eckhardt scoffed quietly, rocking in his seat. "Brownshirt bastards."

"Don't give them the benefit of your attention," Kiefer told everyone in the booth. "They'll tire themselves out in a few minutes, like toddlers."

"What moronic, drunken pigs," Eckhardt huffed, nearly bending a metal fork in his fist.

The SA man leaned on the bar, waited two seconds, and banged his palms against the wooden surface. "Hey, whiskers! I wanted a beer, if that's not too hard for you to manage." Spittle flew from his mouth, and his fellow tan-suited soldiers gathered around him, each yelling and catcalling.

A medium-build man in a civilian work uniform—perhaps a custodian or a cab-driver—stepped up behind the SA man. "Hey, *Blödmann*, pipe down!"

A hush blanketed the brownshirts, and they turned to face their opponent like a hydra: a single beast with multiple heads. The loud-mouthed soldier cocked a brow. "Excuse me? What did you say?"

The German gulped but didn't yield. "I-I … Show some respect, alright, you brownshirted goon, okay? And speak to the bartender like he's an actual person!"

"Oh?" The SA man nodded slowly. He turned to his compatriots, silently conferring with them. For a moment, he relaxed his shoulders and clasped his hands in front of him.

Then, like a heavyweight champion, he slugged the man in the jaw, knocking him to the floor. The rest of the crowd couldn't even react, it happened so fast. The brownshirt bounded on top of the fallen man and began pummeling him with gusto. Without fear of consequences.

"Goon?! You call me a goon, you plebe?! I'll kill you, I'll tear you to pieces!"

Kiefer's heart thudded and his blood began to boil. He couldn't sit and spectate while the brownshirts ran amok. One look at his comrades confirmed that their thoughts were in lockstep. As if a silent signal had been given, all four SS men leapt from the booth, running side-by-side into the fray.

"Trooper!" Max's oaky voice boomed. "On your feet, away from the civilian!"

The SA man whipped his head around to glare at the four SS soldiers who stood before him like an obsidian wall. "Who do you think you are—"

"You may be stupid," Max cut him off, shooting him down with dagger-like eyes, "but you're not blind. Look at my shoulders, *schattenparker*." He referred to the patch marking him as a senior storm unit leader. "Look at my collar." The silver lightning bolts—the emblem of the SS. "I outrank you, trooper," he growled.

The SA man scrambled off the sprawled civilian and rejoined his tan-attired peers, fuming and sputtering like a tea kettle. "You self-righteous slime!"

Killian coughed a sarcastic laugh. "Slime? At least the public respects us. The people are sick of your arrogant, gangster-like behavior. Extorting our businessmen, showing off your wealth, getting dead drunk and harassing innocent bystanders."

Eckhardt rumbled, "You SA scoundrels are worthless. Dirt on our shoes."

Kiefer nodded, standing shoulder-to-shoulder with his brothers in arms. He tried to look imposing, as if he didn't care a speck for the SA soldiers. But he noticed Gero glaring right at him, malice dripping from his stare.

Another SA soldier, tall and missing a tooth, shouted, "At least we aren't the lapdogs of that limp-wristed Himmler! Roehn is aggressive, ambitious, a street brawler. That's the kind of leader I want to stand behind. There are three million of us. We could—"

Kiefer interrupted, "Oh, I've heard this spiel before. '*Your precious SS is nothing in comparison to us.*'" He rolled his eyes. "You SA *sitzpinklers* may be innumerable like ants, but we are elite like foxes."

Gero let out a roar as if it had been building up in his gut for a millennium. "Shut up! You aren't better than us! We could overthrow the entire SS without taking a break for lunch. Hell, we could storm the Reichstag if we so desired. And we just might, *angeber*!"

Kiefer staggered backward, as if Gero's words had physically shoved him. He was stunned. Shocked. And furious. The air before his eyes shimmered as if a single spark would cause a deadly explosion.

Gero pounded his chest like a cocky gorilla, still in the middle of his tirade. "We have three million brothers—you're *nothing*."

"Stop flapping your jaw, Gero, or I'll rip it right off." Kiefer trembled from the rage flowing through his veins.

The entire tavern froze. Every single patron held their breath, eyes wide as saucers.

Kiefer looked down. Without realizing it, his hand had clasped the handgun on his belt, knuckles white from the intensity of his grip.

Silence. No one spoke, no one breathed. Kiefer's heart hammered like a war drum, sweat accumulated at his brow. His SS peers stood at his side, tense and still as statues. Braced for the explosion.

Kiefer eyed the seven SA men, his hand never leaving the gun. "Stay in line, troopers. Obey your superior. Or you'll deeply regret it." He moved toward the exit, his three friends at his heels.

As he shoved open the tavern doors, he heard Gero's voice, speaking in a boyish lilt: "Be careful what you wish for."

1 July 1934

It was five o'clock in the morning. Darkness ruled Berlin.

Gero burst into the empty tavern, a rifle slung over his shoulder, chest heaving, teeth clenched, sweat blurring his vision. His fellow brownshirt—a soldier from Düsseldorf named Ludwig—stumbled in behind him, limping and wincing with each step. Gero slammed the doors shut, grabbed a chair, and shoved it under the handles.

Ludwig crumpled and grasped his ankle. Fat tears rolled down his face and pooled on the scuffed floors. "Oh God oh God no oh God please ..."

Gero wrapped his hand under Ludwig's shoulder and dragged him further into the tavern. "C'mon, trooper, we need to take cover."

"Oh God no please ..."

Gero gritted his teeth and upended one of the tables. He set his fellow soldier behind the solid oak, grasped his rifle, and crouched.

Berlin had become a hellish hunting ground. SS blackshirts marched through the streets, searching for every brown uniform in the city. Chancellor Hitler had ordered his black-clad private army to terminate Ernst Roehn and the entire SA, and the whole world had immediately changed.

The long night was a blur in Gero's memory. Sprinting down roads ... stepping over bloody, tan-shirted bodies ... hiding in alleys and behind piles of garbage.

The resistance had begun as a team effort, just as every SA man had always envisioned—brownshirts banding together and fighting as one, a school of piranhas devouring anything in its path. But the SS was too strong, too organized. The situation quickly spiraled into an every-man-for-himself scramble. It was now a matter of survival, not victory.

Gero peeked out from behind the overturned table, rifle shaking in his grip. He had three bullets left. Three.

"Ludwig?"

"No please no … "

"Ludwig!" he snapped.

The other man looked at him, baffled, as if rousing from a coma. "Gero?"

"What's happening out there? What do you know?"

The man's eyes sunk into his face as he practically shriveled on the floor. "It's over, Gero. We're dead."

"I didn't drag you into this place for you to give up!" he bit, his deep-rooted composure cracking slightly. "What are you talking about?"

"They took Commander Roehn. The black uniforms beat him and hauled him away for treason."

Gero slumped to the ground, his legs sapped of all strength. "What? How do you know?"

"I saw. And I ran." He paused and clenched his jaw to keep it from trembling. "I saw."

Gunshots echoed from outside the tavern, making the two wary soldiers jolt and recoil behind their makeshift cover. They sat in the deafening silence for several moments, waiting, hoping their time wasn't up yet.

Dust motes drifted through the air. The wide, empty room was deathly still, as if conspiring to keep the SA soldiers hidden.

Ludwig laid his head on the grimy floor. "Why is this happening?"

Gero scavenged his mind for an answer, but he couldn't find one. "I don't know. Roehm is … *was* good friends with the *Fuhrer*. We're all a part of his army, just the same as the SS. I don't know why he turned on us."

Scrape …

Gero's ears twitched. An unseen entry opened, somewhere in the rear of the tavern. Someone slipped in through the back door. They were no longer alone.

"Set down your rifle, Gero. It's useless now."

The hearty baritone of a broad, powerful soldier. A man wholly in command. A former friend who had known precisely where Gero would hide.

Heavy, fearsome footsteps drew closer and closer.

Gero's heart galloped, and he almost started hyperventilating. The overturned table protected them from the front door, but this new voice advanced from the back. They were completely exposed. A lump of fear clogged his throat as he hoisted his firearm and aimed it at the approaching footfalls.

Kiefer appeared, a black phantom looming in the shadows of the empty tavern. His rigid face stared down at the two SA men who leaned pitifully against a toppled table. A table he and Gero had used on innumerable occasions.

"Put it down." His voice carried throughout the barren space, ricocheting and amplifying his command.

Gero's hands trembled, but he kept the gun trained on his SS enemy. His breathing intensified, making his aim waver all the more. But he did not dare drop his rifle. Not while Kiefer wore a pistol on his belt.

"Take that gun out of your holster and throw it behind the bar," Gero said, trying with all his might to sound bolder than he felt.

Kiefer simply answered, "No."

Gero nearly collapsed from that one word. Kiefer was in charge, they both knew it, and nothing could change that fact.

"You're finished, old friend," Kiefer said, ignoring the prostrate Ludwig entirely. "Shoot me or don't. But you will be dead within the next ten minutes."

Something in Gero's mind snapped. Tears formed on the rims of his eyes. "We're both German soldiers, you mindless cretin! We both serve the *Fuhrer*. We're Nazis, goddammit! What're you doing?!"

Kiefer's face didn't budge a centimeter. "Spineless. I remember you boasting just a few months ago that you could overthrow the very *Fuhrer* you claimed to serve. It was only a matter of time before that sort of talk reached the Chancellor's ears."

The trembling in Gero's hands morphed into total incapacity. He could hardly aim anymore.

"You called the SS *nothing*."

Finally, Gero relinquished. It was futile. "Fine, Kiefer." With a sob, he tossed his rifle across the room and slumped against the table, facing his former friend, utterly defenseless.

Instantly, like a bolt of lightning, Kiefer drew his handgun and fired. Ludwig jerked once and stopped moving. Blood flowed from his chest like a hellish geyser.

Gero cried out and clutched the sides of his head. He wanted to vomit, to weep like a frightened child. He refused to look at the dead brown-suited soldier beside him, instead staring straight into Kiefer's icy eyes. "We were friends, *kumpel*. Schoolmates. Inseparable. I know you better than I know my brothers! If I could take back every hateful word I've ever said toward you, I would in an instant. Please, Kief."

Tendrils of pale sunlight seeped through the windows and under the doors. Morning had arrived in Berlin.

Gero sobbed and held out his empty hands. "Please."

Kiefer stared at his friend for what felt like an eternity. "Ant," he scoffed as he raised his gun and fired.

Torn To Pieces

By Nicole Zelniker (CONTENT WARNING: *medical drama, death, mention of substance abuse*)

For the most part, Valeria loved her job. She loved her students and the look on their faces when they understood a new concept, or when she read particularly beautiful prose from an essay. She loved spending her days with young people, expanding their worlds. But she never enjoyed it when she had to rat on a student to their parent.

When Willow turned in assignments – the key word being when – they were some of the best in the class. The last few weeks, though, Willow had turned in her homework more and more sporadically, and then not at all. So after another student complained that Willow hadn't done anything for their group project, Valeria had no choice but to reach out to Willow's father.

Valeria invited him to sit at one of the desks. "Sorry. I know they're not built for actual people."

"It's fine." Jay took a seat, folding his long legs to the side. "I'm actually glad you called."

"Oh?"

"I spoke with Willow. She said she didn't want me to tell you this, but I think it's important. So, I'm Willow's dad, but not biologically. My cousin Eddie died when Willow was three and she came to me. For 12 years her mom has been AWOL and just ... showed up a few weeks ago demanding to see Willow. It's been ..." Jay trailed off, running a hand down his face. He had said all of this very quickly, like it was poison he needed to get out.

Valeria felt a swooping in her stomach, the same feeling she'd gotten last year, when she found out one of her former students had been in the hospital with colon cancer. It was a desire to protect them, even though she couldn't. "I'm sorry, Mr. Santiago," she said. Jay nodded, and Valeria added, "I can give her makeup assignments. She's really bright, Willow. I don't want to see her fall through the cracks because she's in a shitty situation."

Jay smiled at her. "Thank you," he whispered.

Later that evening, when Jay and Willow were clearing the table, Jay recounted his meeting with Willow's teacher. "I can't believe you told her!" Willow stomped her foot and stormed off to her room, slamming the door behind her.

Jay followed her and knocked. "You can't stay in there forever, Willow."

"That was my business, Dad. Now she's going to think I'm some freaking basket case."

"You were going to fail English if you kept this up."

Silence for a second, and then, "So?"

Jay inhaled sharply, then exhaled. "Look, when you want to talk, I'll be here. Ok?"

Willow didn't answer. It wasn't until several hours had passed and her need to pee forced her from her bedroom that she came into the living room, her hands behind her back. Jay had fallen asleep on the couch with the TV on, the blanket covering only one foot. She hesitated, considering whether to say something. He'd had late night classes the last two days in a row, plus work early in the morning. And Willow knew she didn't make anything easier.

Finally, she whispered, "Dad?"

Jay startled and sat up. "Are you ok?"

She nodded. "I'm sorry. I didn't mean to ... I'm just frustrated."

He knew that. It was hard to be mad at Willow, and even harder to stay mad. He rubbed his eyes and asked, "About your mom?"

Willow's face darkened, her brow furrowing and her mouth in a tight, thin line. "She's not my mom."

"Sorry," Jay said. "Nida."

Willow nodded. Then she burst into tears. Jay sprang up from the couch and wrapped his arms around her thin shoulders, holding her close to him.

~~~

Willow frowned at her mid-year report card as she walked alone to the bus, her backpack hanging off one shoulder. She'd managed to get Bs and Cs in chemistry and math and all that, but an A in English. Which didn't make sense. Even after Ms. Garcia had given her makeup assignments, Willow had forgotten them in her locker, or just stared at them until she decided to go to bed. At the highest, she expected a C. Willow tucked the card in her bag and looked up. She froze when she noticed the woman standing on the sidewalk in front of her.

Nida turned, spotting Willow and walking toward her. "Willow!"

Shit. The last time Willow saw her bio-mom was ... two years ago? More? "What are you doing here?"

"Can't I see my daughter?" Nida raised a hand to Willow's cheek. Willow took a step back.

"Willow!" They both whipped around. Ms. Garcia had snuck up on them unnoticed. "Could you come back to my classroom, please? I wanted to speak with you about your last assignment."

"Oh. Sure." Willow sped-walked back toward Ms. Garcia, leaving Nida frowning behind her. She wasn't sure how she'd get home – the bus would leave before she could walk to her English classroom and back – but she'd do anything to get away from Nida. As soon as Ms. Garcia shut the door, she turned back to Willow. "Are you ok?"

"Y-Yes?"

"Sorry, I didn't mean to pry. Your dad just told me what was going on with everything and ... you looked scared."

Willow stared at Ms. Garcia's shoes. "Oh. Yeah. I'm ok."

"I can drive you home if you want. You probably missed the bus."

"That ... That would be good." Ms. Garcia grabbed her keys and Willow followed her out to the staff parking lot and into Ms. Garcia's green Honda. "Thanks," Willow said.

"No problem." Valeria backed out of her spot and looked back at Willow in the rearview mirror. "Sorry if I was out of line."

"No, it's fine." Willow turned her gaze to the window. Her thoughts turned to the crumpled report card at the bottom of her bag. "Could I ask you a question?" Ms. Garcia nodded and Willow asked, "Why did you give me an A?"

Willow's teacher frowned, mulling over how exactly to answer. "I don't think you should have your life ruined because you failed to turn in a few assignments," she said. "You're really smart, Willow. I still think you can turn things around."

Willow nodded and quickly wiped under her eye with her sleeve. They rode the rest of the way in silence, until Willow thanked Ms. Garcia for the ride and dashed into her house, slamming the door shut behind her and locking it tight. Nida knew where she lived after all.

The following day, Valeria looked up from her desk during her free period to find Jay Santiago hovering at her door. "Oh. Hello."

"Hi. You're not teaching right now?"

Valeria shook her head. "Come in."

Jay did, leaning against the wall beside the door. "I just wanted to thank you for yesterday. Willow told me what you did. And that you gave her a ride home."

"It was no problem. Really."

"Well. Thanks anyway." He looked over at the door again. "I was just on my way to work. I thought I'd stop by but ... I'll just go now." He turned to do that and ran right into the doorframe, nearly knocking his glasses off.

Valeria stood, reaching for him, trying to keep her lips from twitching into a smile. "Are you ok?"

"Yes, yes." Jay shook his head. "Er ... Thanks again."

"Jay?" He paused and turned back to Valeria, who said, "She'll be ok. Willow."

"I know," he said. "She's a good kid."

~~~

Valeria and Jay had never met before Valeria called about Willow, but they seemed to be running into each other all the time now. He spotted her in the grocery store, at the deli, and, finally, at the bakery where Jay worked. "Fancy seeing you here," Valeria said as she got up to the front of the line.

Jay grinned. "Of course you'd come here."

"I'm secretly stalking you."

"You're the most pleasant stalker I've ever had, then."

Valeria laughed, and Jay's heart skipped a beat. "Have you had very many stalkers?" she asked.

"None," Jay admitted. "So the bar isn't very high."

During his Saturday morning shift at the bakery, Jay saw Valeria again, her hair pulled back into a tight ponytail, no makeup, and wearing a green sweater. When she smiled at him, Jay almost forgot how to speak.

He had been thinking about her all week. About her sharp eyes and her witty retorts. He thought about how she laughed at an unfunny joke he told in line at the deli and touched his arm lightly, sending shivers down his spine. He thought about what it might be like to hold her hand.

At last he managed, "Matcha latte again?"

"Yes, please." She handed him her debit card and their fingers brushed. He wiped away a nervous sweat as he prepared the latte and passed it over the counter.

"Valeria?"

"Hmm?" She met his eyes with hers, hazel and bright, and he actually flinched.

"I, er, I was wondering if you were doing anything this weekend?" Jay's stomach did a backflip and he immediately regretted his impulsiveness. She was way out of his league and his daughter's teacher besides.

"Seeing you, I suppose?"

She was probably busy and ... wait, she said yes? "Oh. Um. Yes! Tonight?"

"I'm free at seven," she said. "Anything you had in mind?"

"Have you ever been to Starlight? It's this diner that just opened up."

Valeria grinned. "That sounds great."

When Jay told Willow – almost apologetically – she flung her arms around his neck in a tight hug. "I'm so happy!"

"You are?"

Willow let him go and gripped his shoulders. "I want you to be happy, Dad. But please, please don't mess this up."

Jay laughed. "I'll do my best."

~~~

Valeria grabbed Jay's hand across the table, her dark eyes bright under the artificial light. "Stop being so nervous."

Jay flinched under her touch, but she held on. "Oh. Yes." The two of them had met at Starlight, an 80s-themed diner one town over. Valeria had ordered a sandwich. Jay had been so nervous he'd almost forgotten how to read the menu.

She was stunning tonight, though she was always beautiful. Her half-up hair cascaded over her shoulder and her crooked smile illuminated the whole table, or at least that was how it appeared to Jay. "I like you, Jay," she said. "You're sweet. And funny."

He smiled at her from across the table. "I like you, too."

They went back to her apartment after and sat on opposite ends of her couch drinking mimosas. "These are really good."

"I was a bartender in undergrad," Valeria admitted. "This isn't natural talent."

"Ah. I, er, never finished undergrad." He took another swig of his drink.

"What were you studying?"

"Biochemistry. I dropped out my sophomore year ... I don't know why I'm telling you this."

"No, go on."

So he did. Jay told her about his mom, who had died halfway through his second year. He told her about going home to take care of his sister, six years his junior. He told her how he was supposed to go back to school when his cousin died and Jay gained custody of Willow. "I'm taking night classes now," he said. "But I don't know how I'd go on to get a masters, let alone a doctorate." His eyes suddenly grew wide. "Willow doesn't know that she's the reason I never went back, though. Please don't say anything."

"Oh darn. I was really hoping to tell your daughter about your sordid past." Valeria gave him a half-smile. "I promise not to say anything."

"Thank you."

"You're a good dad. Willow's really lucky."

Jay shrugged. "I try. I really try."

"I can see that." Valeria fell quiet suddenly, contemplative. Finally, she said, "I was a foster kid. My homes weren't great so ... I'm really glad she has you."

"I didn't know that."

"Why would you? College was kind of my out."

"Well ... I'm glad you told me." Jay looked away and his eyes fell on the clock behind Valeria's head. "Oh! It's after midnight."

"You got a curfew, Cinderella?"

"No I just – I should go." He stood.

Valeria frowned. "Ok."

"But I'd love to do this again," Jay quickly added. "Next weekend?"

Valeria nodded. "Yes."

~~~

For the next three weeks, Jay saw Valeria every Saturday. He always came home before Willow went to bed until she confronted him one morning before school. "Don't you want to stay over?"

Jay, who was leaning up against the counter, choked on his coffee. "Willow!"

"What? You like her. She likes you. What's the deal?" Jay didn't say anything, so Willow crossed her arms and said, "I'm staying over at Alyssa's this weekend for her birthday. Do what you want."

"You shouldn't be so involved in my love life, you know."

"Well someone has to be invested," Willow said with an eye roll. "I might as well be your wing woman before Nida comes and takes me away."

Jay frowned. "She's not going to –"

"I know." She didn't, though. That was clear in her far-away gaze, in the way her shoulders had tensed.

"There won't be a legal battle, Willow. She was declared unfit. You're mine."

Willow frowned into her cereal. "Why do you never talk about how Eddie died?"

Jay blinked at the sudden change in topic. "What?"

"I know he was in a car wreck. But that's it. And if he was with someone like Nida ... I don't know. Was he a good person?"

"Your ... Eddie was my cousin and I loved him. He was also a mess." He sighed and sat diagonal from Willow. "Eddie met Nida at a party. They weren't together for a long time before she left but ... Eddie also had problems. When he got into the accident, he wasn't sober."

"I was in the back seat."

Jay nodded. "Do you remember that?"

"Not really." Willow bit her lip and didn't say anything else.

"He loved you, Willow. I know he loved you."

"Not like you do." She sprang up from her seat, wrapped her arms around Jay's shoulders, and squeezed. "Thank you, Dad."

Jay found her hand and squeezed back. "You don't have to thank me," he said.

As Willow got ready for school and kissed him on the cheek goodbye, Jay thought about what she'd said. He hated how she carried Nida and Eddie's mistakes with her. He hated that she thought about Nida coming to take her away. He hated that she worried about him. But he also wasn't sure how to make her burdens go away.

That wasn't true though, at least for that last one. He did like Valeria, and for some reason, Valeria seemed to like him, too. Unless he had already messed it up by not making a bolder move?

Jay frowned and pressed the palm of his hand to his forehead. He had to do something.

~~~

It was her own damn fault, really. If Valeria hadn't assigned these essays to begin with, she wouldn't be grading them in her classroom at – she checked her phone – almost nine o'clock at night. She was about to work on Jaime Tran's when a knock at the door made her jump.

Jay waved to her through the plexiglass and she waved him in. He slipped in and shut the door. "Hi."

"Hi." Valeria stood. "Is everything ok?"

"No, actually. You see, I really care about you. And I think I've been scared to take things further because of that. But I don't want to waste any more time." With that, he came to her and put his hands on her face, pulling her into a kiss.

They'd kissed before – a hello or a goodnight kiss, mostly – but nothing like this. Valeria wrapped her arms around his neck and pulled him closer. He fell forward a bit, pressing her up against her desk as she wrapped her leg around his.

Valeria had never had sex in her office before this. After, she decided she wouldn't mind doing it again.

By Willow's birthday, Valeria knew she was in deep. She had never trusted someone like she trusted Jay, or wanted to be around them as often, or said "I love you" so quickly. It didn't help that she adored Willow, who had invited Valeria to her birthday party. Which, Jay insisted, had to be a big deal. "You're turning 16!"

"Let's just do something here," Willow said. "Just me and Leigh and Alyssa."

"What about Jaime and Tiana?" Jay and Valeria were sitting on the couch, his hand on her leg. Willow sat in the chair adjacent to them, her arms crossed.

"Fine, Jaime and Tiana."

~~~

Jay spent Willow's birthday in the kitchen, reminiscing with Valeria and Leigh Price's parents while Willow and her four friends sat around the coffee table living room, opening presents.

"I feel like they were just kids," Gianna Price said. "They're so grown up." Gianna and Ryan had both known Willow since she was six years old, when Willow and Leigh became best friends in first grade.

"Willow asked me yesterday when she can get a driver's license," Jay said.

"Oof," Ryan said. "That's rough."

The four of them turned as the doorbell rang. Jay frowned. "We're not expecting anyone else." He got up then and answered the door.

Nida stood there, her pupils dilated and her hands shaking. "I want to see Willow."

Jay looked back at the kids, none of whom seemed to notice anything, and slipped out of the house, shutting the door behind him. "You can't."

"She's my daughter."

"Nida, stop."

"You can't keep her from me!" Nida raised her fist in Jay's face.

He took a step back, putting his hands up to block just in case. "You need to leave. Now."

"I want to see her."

Jay shook his head. His heart pounded and his own hands shook. "You're stoned."

Nida shrieked, banshee-like, and covered her face with her hands. "No, no, no –"

"We can talk about this later. But now you need to go."

Sobbing, Nida turned and walked down the driveway, swaying as she did so. She reached her car and got in. Jay hesitated for a moment. *Should I stop her from driving high, and probably drunk too? Is it worth putting Willow through that? Oh God, had she heard Nida's screams?* Paralyzed by his racing thoughts, he let Nida get in the car and drive away.

His own hands still trembling, Jay walked back into the house and took his seat beside Valeria. "Is everything ok?" she asked, putting a hand on his arm. "We heard screaming."

"Yes," he said. "Everything is fine." Willow came up behind them a moment later and asked when they would cut the cake. Jay's heart hammered as he told her they would do that in a moment, arranging his face in an expression he hoped passed as calm.

Valeria came up behind him as the others enjoyed dessert in the living room. "Are you sure everything is ok?" she asked, wrapping her arms around his waist. "You've been quiet."

Of course he had been quiet. He had about a million thoughts running through his head. Was Nida going to come back? How could he have let her drive off on her own? Would Willow ask him later what had happened when he stepped outside?

Was he being selfish, dating right now when Willow needed his protection?

He shook her off. "Fine," he said. They didn't bring up what happened for the rest of the day.

~~~

The following night, Valeria opened her bleary eyes in her dimly lit bedroom. She spotted Jay sitting at the edge of the bed and glanced at her phone. "It's six o'clock," she mumbled. "Come back to bed."

"I should go."

She sat up and frowned. "What? Why?"

"I should be with Willow."

"It's six o'clock," Valeria repeated. "In the morning. She's sleeping."

Jay turned his head so that she couldn't see his face in the dark. "I don't think I can do this anymore," he whispered.

Valeria's heart dropped into her stomach. "Do ... what?"

He waved a hand between them. "This. Us."

"Jay –"

"I'm sorry."

Valeria took a deep breath in an attempt to stop the tears. One slipped down her cheek anyway. "You said you'd stop this. You said you were going to do something about –"

"You don't make sense for me right now," he said, turning back to face her. His face was flushed and his eyes bright. "I can't –"

Valeria reached for him and he pulled away. "Jay."

"I'm sorry," he repeated, and then he stood.

"You can't just leave!"

He pulled his shirt on and walked out without another word. She sped after him, catching him by the shoulders before he could walk out. Then she spun him around and pulled him into a deep kiss.

In his initial shock, Jay leaned into her, kissing her back. The next moment he pulled away. "I ..." He trailed off, grabbed his coat from the rack, and walked out of her apartment. As the door shut behind him, Valeria took a step back, tears streaming now. Then she took a glass off the counter and threw it against the wall, where it shattered into a million pieces.

~~~

Willow wouldn't speak with her dad at all the week after he broke up with Valeria except that first night after he told her, when she screamed at him for self-sabotaging. "You really fucked up," she said before she said nothing else.

The following Friday, she waited outside the school, missing the bus on purpose and declining Alyssa's offer to drive her home now that she had a permit. She waited until Valeria walked out of the building and chased after her. "Ms. Garcia?"

Valeria turned. "Willow? Are you ok?"

"Yeah, I just, I missed the bus ..."

"Oh. Do you need a ride?" Willow nodded and Valeria motioned for Willow to follow her. As Willow strapped herself in she said, "I'm sorry. About my dad."

Valeria looked away. "It's ok. It won't affect me teaching you, Willow. But I understand if you want to switch –"

"I'm not worried about that." Willow took a breath. "He thinks I don't know that Nida came to the house. I heard her screaming at my birthday party. He's ... He thinks he needs to do all these things for me. He's a really good dad. I just want him to be happy, too. And you made him happy."

"Not happy enough."

"That's not true." They were driving downtown now, past the fast food sandwich places Willow frequented with her friends.

"Look, I appreciate it, but I'm ok. I don't think it's really appropriate for me to be discussing this with you."

A pause, and then Willow said, "Ok. But –"

BANG! The car flew forward and into a tree before Willow registered what happened. Valeria's body flew over hers. Glass exploded into her face. Her whole being felt disconnected from itself, still going a million miles per hour and zero all at once. Her ears buzzed and she saw white spots for a moment. Willow shook her head to clear it and winced at the pain in her head and neck.

"Shit," she hissed. Slowly and painfully, Willow turned to Valeria, lying across her lap. "Ms. Garcia?" Nothing. "Valeria?" Willow lifted a bloody, shaking hand to Valeria's neck, feeling for a pulse. It was there, rapid. Valeria blinked her eyes open and groaned. "Willow ..."

"Oh thank God." Behind them, Willow heard a siren.

"Can't ... breathe ..." Valeria took a short, painful breath in and winced. Her whole face had broken out in a cold sweat.

"It's ok. You're ok." Valeria's eyes rolled back and Willow's own heart sped up in her chest. "No, please!" she cried. "Stay with me. Please stay with me."

~~~

For a wild moment after Willow called him from the hospital, Jay imagined it was Nida who'd hit the car, still coming home from Willow's birthday party. It turned out to be a woman who'd had a seizure at the wheel and spun out of control. Jay didn't know what happened to her other than that she wasn't dead.

Jay ran into the emergency room and spotted Willow immediately. He ran to her and she reached for him, but she was stopped by a nurse. "Your injuries," the nurse scolded. Willow had a mild concussion, the doctor had told Jay over the phone, and whiplash. Other than that, she had short, vicious cuts on her face from the glass, one long one under her eye.

Still, Jay came up next to her and took her hand in lieu of a hug. "What happened? I thought you were taking the bus home."

"I missed it," she said, suppressing tears. "I asked Valeria to drive me home."

Jay froze. "Valeria?"

"She threw herself in front of me and ... She's in s-surgery." Willow was openly crying now, and Jay carefully wiped the tears from her face with his hands. She took a breath and said, "I'm sorry, Dad."

"It's not your fault –"

"We wouldn't have had to pass that way if I'd just taken the bus." Willow broke down sobbing and Jay gathered her in his arms, ignoring the grumbling nurse.

As soon as the doctor gave Willow a drug to knock her out, Jay asked her about Valeria. "The woman who came in with your daughter?" Jay nodded and the doctor grimaced. "She had a bad concussion, a fractured tibia, broken ribs, and a collapsed lung. She's out of surgery now, but we can't be sure of the prognosis until she wakes up."

"Ok. Ok ..."

"Do you want to see her?" Jay looked down at Willow and the doctor said, "Your daughter will be out for a while."

"Then yes, please."

The doctor led Jay to Valeria's room and left him there. An oxygen mask covered Valeria's pale face and the machine monitoring her heart beeped steadily. Jay sat on her right and took her hand. He took a breath and let the tears fall down his cheek. How long he stayed like that, crying quietly and holding her hand, he wasn't sure. But he was there when Valeria's eyes fluttered open.

She turned her head slightly and her hazy eyes met his. "Oh," he mumbled. "I'll leave. I'm sorry." Jay made to get up when he felt Valeria's hand tighten under his, a silent question. He answered just as silently, by sitting back down, agreeing to stay.

~~~

For the week Valeria was in the hospital, Jay came every day. He met her friend Wyatt this way, and her two brothers, though she said she'd have preferred if they hadn't come at all. "They're just so judgy."

Jay laughed. "They seem to care about you."

"Yeah, yeah." She waved her hand in the air and Jay took it in both of his, planting a kiss on the back.

Valeria turned away suddenly. "You don't have to do this if ... if you just feel bad. I don't want you to –"

"Hey, no." He lowered their hands but kept them intertwined. "I made a mistake. But I love you, Valeria. I want to be with you. If you can forgive me."

Valeria nodded. "I want that, too."

Another week after Valeria left the hospital, Jay walked past Willow in her room, studying herself in the mirror. "Sometimes I can't believe how beautiful you are, either," he teased.

"Ha. Funny." She turned away and prodded at the cut under her eye, the one that hadn't fully healed. "This ... is going to scar, isn't it?"

"I don't know."

Willow shrugged, her lower lip trembling. "It's fine. Whatever."

"Willow –"

"It's not a big deal."

"You're allowed to be upset," Jay said. "You don't have to be strong for me."

"Hypocrite."

Jay gave her a small half-smile. "I'm your dad. That's my job."

Willow shook her head. "Not like you've been doing. I don't want you to keep things from me, ok? I hate that."

He bent over and kissed the top of her head. "Deal," he said.

That evening, Valeria joined the two of them for dinner, where Jay presented her with flowers. "Oh, violets are my favorite," she said.

"I know," he said with a wink. "Your brother told me. The younger one. Alex."

"Huh. I never thought he paid much attention to anyone but himself."

Willow poked her head into the living room and said, "If you lovebirds are done, I set the table."

Jay laughed. "C'mon." He helped Valeria up off the couch and onto her crutches. As he pulled Valeria's chair out a sudden, terrifying and wonderful thought hit him like a freight train.

I want to be with her forever.

~~~

"Jay."

Jay flinched and opened his eyes. It was still pitch black in his room. "Valeria? What time is it?"

"Can't ... Breathe ..."

He sat up and flicked on the light. Valeria was lying next to him in his bed, her hand pressing on her chest. Her breathing was shallow and her lips were tinted blue.

"Shit," Jay mumbled. He grabbed his phone and dialed 911. The operator asked for his emergency and Jay said, "Hi, my girlfriend can't breathe. She was in a car wreck a few weeks ago and she had a punctured lung –"

Valeria heard Jay rambling to the person on the line, but she wasn't really listening. She focused all her energy into breathing in. Out. In –

She began to cough, hard, and couldn't stop. Then she felt Jay's hands on her back, gently rolling her over so she was on her stomach. She coughed until she didn't have any air left to do so and was left gasping. Her mouth formed Jay's name again, but no sound came out.

"Hang on, ok? The ambulance is coming. You're going to be ok."

"Can't –" she ran out of air again and squeezed her eyes shut tight.

"It's ok. You're ok. I love you."

Her mouth formed the word "love" and her eyes rolled back into her head. She fell forward onto the pillow.

"Valeria!" Jay flipped her over and felt for her pulse, willing it to strengthen under his fingers.

"Dad?" Jay turned and saw Willow in the doorway, her eyes wide.

"What's going on?"

"Valeria ..." Outside, the ambulance lights flashed through the window and turned the room blue and red. Willow ran downstairs to greet them, and then it was her arms pulling Jay back from Valeria's body, her voice telling him it was ok, it was going to be ok.

He believed her through the drive to the hospital, through his anguish in the waiting room. But with a shake of a doctor's head, it suddenly wasn't, and Jay fell to his knees and screamed.

~~~

A memory: Laying with her head on on Jay's chest and listening to his heart beat in time with hers. Thump. Thump. Thump.

"They really called you Her-o?" he asked in response to her story, grinning.

"We were kids, and I was the only girl! Honestly though, I was never big on playing Heroes. By the time I was eight I started to 'betray' them during the games and become a villain."

She felt the shake of Jay's laughter under her ear. "How devious of you."

"Hmm." She tilted her face up and went in for a kiss. Their eyes met and Valeria whispered, "I love you."

Jay leaned forward and kissed her again, soft and powerful all at once. "I love you, too," he murmured against her lips.

~~~

Willow had never been to a funeral before. Well, she supposed she had been at Eddie's, but she didn't remember that one. It seemed like half of their small town had come out to honor Valeria. Willow's friends from school stood in the back, huddled together for comfort. Willow stayed with her dad, holding his hand the whole time. They stood by Valeria's brothers, all clad in black. Willow had worn dark sunglasses to hide her bloodshot eyes, but Jay had done no such thing, letting tears run down his face the whole service. When they got home after, Jay sat on the couch, buried his head in his hands, and sobbed.

Willow sat next to him and put her head on his shoulder. He leaned his head into hers and they stayed like that for a moment, her silent tears slipping down her cheeks and Jay crying until he fell asleep.

In the following weeks, Ryan and Gianna Price came over often, probably to make sure Jay ate and slept. Willow sat on the stairwell and listened as Jay recounted the details of Valeria's death to Gianna. Jay never cried when they came over though. It seemed he had run out of his own tears after the first few days.

He was with Ryan Price one day when Willow joined them in the kitchen. "Hi."

"Hey, kiddo," Ryan said. "How are you doing?"

Willow shrugged. "Everything sucks. But I guess I'm doing ok." She grabbed a granola bar and made to leave when Jay asked, "Are you going out?"

"Meeting Tiana. Ok?" Jay nodded and Willow left, grabbing her bike on the way.

She was, in fact, riding by Tiana's neighborhood, even if she wasn't really going to Tiana's. Another three blocks and she reached the park, hopping off her bike and walking the last few feet to the bench beside the lake, where Nida was waiting. When Willow sat down beside her she said, "I didn't think you were going to come."

"I almost didn't," Willow admitted.

They stared out at the lake for a moment before Nida added, "I heard about your teacher. She was also Jay's girlfriend?" Willow nodded and Nida said, "I'm sorry."

Willow turned away and blinked back more tears. Would she ever run out? "Thank you," Willow said.

Another moment of silence, and then, "I just wanted to tell you I'm getting clean. I kept thinking about you in a second accident and ... I just wanted you to know."

"Ok." She met Nida's eyes and gave her a small smile. "I'm happy for you."

"If you ever wanted ... a relationship, I'd like that a lot."

"I know that." Willow stood. "I should get back. My dad –"

"Oh, yes, of course." Nida stood, too. "I ... Could I have a hug?"

Willow took a step back. "I don't think I can do that yet."

"Oh. Ok," Nida scratched the back of her neck and looked away. "Take care of yourself."

"I will." She cast a final nod at Nida and got back on her bike. She wasn't ready for that yet, that sort of intimacy. But maybe one day, she would be.

Willow detoured around by the cemetery, since her dad wouldn't expect her to be back so soon anyway. She rode up to Valeria's stone and sat on the sprinkler-damp grass. She hadn't brought flowers or anything to offer, but so many other people had. Violets and roses and daffodils spilled from Valeria's name and onto the surrounding graves.

"Hi." Willow took a deep breath. "I don't know what I believe, like, in terms of an afterlife. But I thought I'd talk to you just in case." She sat cross legged and continued, "Dad's having a really hard time. I think you had a really big impact on him, you know? And I think he regrets that you didn't get to be together for longer. He's had a lot holding him back. I think he's not doing that so much anymore though. Yeah. So thanks for that."

Deep breath. She continued, "I miss you, too. Mr. Song is taking over English for now. He's doing ok, but it's not the same. I dunno. You were everyone's favorite teacher, you know. And it meant a lot that you believed in me, even when I didn't give you a reason to. You were a really good person." Willow took another slow breath. "You made me feel like I mattered. And I'm lucky I knew you." She touched the headstone briefly – just above the 'a' in 'Valeria' – and got back on her bike. She looked back once as the wind blew through the grass, and then she rode away.

I Come To The Tree

By Amanda Fernandes (CONTENT WARNING: murder, blood, implied sexual assault)

I come to the tree. I come every day. I look for the one who took me away. He's not in the sea, the salt in the air, the rustle of leaves, or the breeze in my hair. He makes not a sound, no whistle or cry, no tears of regret or whimpers goodbye. Yet here I will find him, and though I do yearn to make myself scattered, I always return.

I come by the tree. I come by the sea.

I came to the tree. I came every day. I sat by the roots to read, laugh, and pray. I ate from its fruit, I rested in shade, I daydreamed of places, yet I never strayed. I stayed by the tree and I wouldn't dare to wander too far and end up nowhere. I tasted the fruit, the pears large and sweet. I climbed up the branches and dangled my feet.

I lived by the tree. I lived by the sea.

I came to the tree, just like every day. I picked all the pears that on the grass lay. I savored the fruit in cold autumn chill, then watched it in winter, when it was so still. I cried in the spring at the time of rebirth. In summer I rested, splayed down on the earth. I came to the tree and he saw from afar that I was alone and that help was too far.

I was by the tree. I was by the sea.

He came to the tree. He came every day. He said not a word but watched anyway. He licked his dry lips. He rubbed his wet palms. He heard me sing songs and recite all my psalms. He crept up the tree. He made not a sound. He smelled like a pig and he huffed like a hound. He came with a knife, the steal tainted red. He took all he could and he cut off my head.

I died by the tree. I died by the sea.

I saw first the tree. I saw the moon next. I felt my self grieve. I felt bruised and vexed. I saw the pears dangle and sway in the breeze, and though fall is over, I no longer freeze. With fingertips shaking, I found the wound wide. The green grass was tainted and in that, I lied (LIE as in LIE DOWN). I looked for the one who'd taken me away. I look for him still. I look every day.

I am by the tree. I am by the sea.

I come to the tree. I come every day. I rise with the sun and fade with midday. I float in the breeze, like a pear, sweet and green. I rest on the grass and stay there, unseen. I wait in the morning. I climb to the crown. I watch over fields as well as the town. I watch over maidens and those who're uncared. I look after children and those who're scared.

I stay by the tree. I stay by the sea.

I come to the tree. I come every day. And if you are careful, you might hear me pray. I whisper the words in the rustle of wind: somehow, fate will find him and bring me the fiend. I wait for the moment. I'll find him at last, make equal our ledger, and right what was past. I will drag him under. I'll trap him below. He'll rot in the summer and freeze in the snow.

I wait by the tree. I wait by the sea.

I come to the tree. I come every day. I look for the one who took me away. It's here I will find him, and though I do yearn to make myself scattered, I always return.

Abandoned

By Stephanie Houseal (CONTENT WARNING: *death*)

She placed her pale, translucent glowing hand upon the cloudy glass of the window, staring out at a neglected yard and overgrown red clay path leading away from her shelter. Her home stood abandoned and looming on a tiny plot of land set back from the road. Dark, gloomy clouds swelled overhead with the heaviness of a threatening storm, making her wonder if this would be the one to rock the Victorian structure to its foundation.

No one came anymore. The rumors faded over time of a "tormented teenager" haunting the rooms and hallways. She had sighed and longed to explain how the stories were false. She'd been ill, not murdered or scorned or taken her life. It was almost unfair how the living could pick and choose the stories regarding the dead. Once gone, one's truth didn't matter anymore.

Decades ago, she'd shut herself away in the room where she had died when visitors' curiosity turned to fear and they scrambled to leave. She'd close a door; she'd drop a doll or book. Their reactions to her tricks brought a form of entertainment to her little world. Unfortunately, misinformation and a sizable misunderstanding from those people labeled her as malevolent. Whispers abounded concerning the screams in the night. Truthfully, she cried out because the overwhelming loneliness of it all and the inaccurate rumors left a deepening scar on her heart.

Perhaps it would end today. The sky turned black as hail pelted against the windows and roof, sounding like the dull clatter of rocks against wood. The wind howled through the trees, the brief gusts stretching the branches and causing them to snap and groan as their leaves were carried into an unknown distance. Puddles formed in patches on the grounds as a torrential downpour came in intermittent waves. Lightning flashed, followed by the deafening BOOM of thunder.

The corner of her mouth turned upward at bittersweet childhood memories. She adored storms and the way everything seemed bolder against the stark gray of the clouds. Most were gentle and calming. But ... she would always wait in eager anticipation for a true thunderstorm. The walls of the house would shudder with the rumble of thunder. Branches and leaves littered the yard. It would take a team effort to clean the disarray.

Sometimes, upon inspection the following day, her father would note a few shingles were stripped from the roof. He'd gather his ladder and needed materials, getting to work promptly. He would replace or repair them while her mother watched and chatted away about the day before. He'd nod without a word to her, remaining focused on his task.

She was jarred from her reminiscence when tendrils of lightning snapped across the sky, illuminating the room around her with its brief appearance. She cast her gaze to the path below as movement caught her attention. Had he not been wearing a bright neon green shirt, she would have missed him. He was running toward her house to escape the downpour.

"What on earth ..." she whispered, a hint of a smile touching her lips. She wanted to giggle with glee, opting instead for a calmer demeanor. This was company out of a coincidence instead of an investigation. She didn't want to get her hopes up, but it seemed better when considering her previous encounters. Besides, he could still choose to take his chances in the rain if the creepiness of her abode became too much for him to handle.

She left her room; heading down the hallway to the staircase, she waited at the top landing for the sturdy cherry wood door to be thrown open. It hadn't been long as the boy barged in, almost with an air of theatrics. Slamming the door behind him, he rested his back against it, then slid to the floor for a respite. The only sound was his heavy breathing and the wind outside.

She lingered, avoiding any motion as she didn't want to frighten him away. From what she could tell, he was a teenager, sixteen or seventeen, probably no older than she was before she passed. She studied him as he gathered himself, allowing for a bit of happiness at having another presence close by, if only temporarily. It was intriguing the way he appeared to ignore the dangerous world outside once in the confines of the dilapidated walls.

Sitting on the landing with her legs tucked beneath her, she noted how the droplets fell from his short flaxen curls to the neon green clad shoulders. His eyes were closed for the moment, dark lashes stark above nearly red cheeks. He raked his fingers through his hair, pausing atop his scalp and shaking the excess water from the tips there. It would still be wet, just not as heavily.

He moved on to the bottom of his shirt twisting the water out of the fabric above the rotted wooden floor next to him. His demonstrations were very meticulous and she had the notion he may not be too fond of rain. After a few moments, he settled in his little spot. He finally raised his gaze to take in the less-than-elegant foyer, looking about without a single comment. Prior to him entering, others would make very obvious statements to their companions about the rotting condition of her home. He, however, remained quiet and observant.

She wondered what he was doing in the middle of nowhere. Was he hiking? Did he get separated from his family or friends? Was he a vagabond? She shook her head at that. Surely not. What then? There were so many questions running through her mind that she was unable to determine the answer for. It was vexing to say the least.

He brought his attention toward the stairs, his cobalt eyes intense and...curious? She'd hold her breath if she had any. It was very disconcerting how it gave the impression he was staring *at* her instead of *through* her. She backed away gradually, uncomfortable in the silent scrutiny. His lips spread into a wide grin. She wasn't certain what to do with that.

"So, the rumors are true," he said casually. He stood, keeping his movements as minimal as possible. "I always thought seeing your face in the window was my mind playing tricks on me. I guess I was mistaken."

She was speechless, having a hard time processing that this person was not only seeing her, but talking to her as easily as if her existence was natural. Instead of responding, she spun around and rushed back to her room. She heard him call out to her and the sound of his footsteps chasing after her.

Once in the confines of her room she hastily closed the door, bolting it. She listened carefully for his approach, expecting his frustration. He didn't pound on the door, demanding to be let in. He didn't try to force the handle to turn and yell for her to come out. He wasn't loud or abrasive at all.

To her surprise, he rapped gently and said, "I didn't mean to scare you. Will you please come out?" He quieted as the house trembled and groaned under the pressure of the wind. After the sounds passed, he said, "It would be nice to wait this out with company. Your home's a little intimidating with all the creaks and everything."

She shook her head, furrowing her brow in confusion. What was his deal? Still ... he was being polite despite the circumstances. She considered his words, looking out of the window as if an answer hovered beyond the glass. The sky appeared to be bathed in a thin shade of green, an eerie foreboding calm settling amongst the clouds. She marveled at a familiar funnel formation as it quickly touched down. Debris easily ripped from the ground, either whirled aimlessly at its base or shot some short distance away. She cursed the powers that be and wished to wait a little longer for that true thunderstorm, but it was here now creating a path of utter destruction.

The resounding roar of the tornado bearing down on them was the frightful nudge she needed to attempt to save her one chance at a possible friend. What she'd always hoped for was now a devastating reality. Why did the first person who treated her kindly have to arrive when hell was coming for them? It didn't matter. She had to take action. She materialized through the door in front of him. Had this not been a moment of desperation, the way he nearly fell back would have roused her slumbering amusement.

"Get to the basement!" she snapped. Clearly, the peril wasn't registering with him. Had he already forgotten why he entered her home to begin with? The boy who was so brave to speak to her a moment ago was now in shock that she'd just spoken to him! Maybe he wasn't any different than his predecessors. All the same, he needed to hurry.

"GO!" she shouted.

That did the trick. It finally clicked that his life was going to be forfeit if he didn't move. "Where is it?" he asked.

The air stirred around them from the suctioning force of the tornado. She motioned down the hall to the stairs, urging him to follow her lead. His head bobbed in acquiescence, and they both raced to the first floor. Something above them caved in with a tremendous crash, causing the floor beneath them to tremble. They weren't fazed, however. It couldn't be helped, whatever it was.

She saw the door to the basement, pointing it out to him. He grabbed the doorknob, twisting it. The moment froze, stagnant. The access to the basement held fast. Locked. He chuckled at the irony of it, and she wanted to weep. She couldn't save him. She didn't have a key for this door.

He let out a breath, taking a glimpse in the direction from whence they came. It was too late. "I guess," he began hesitantly, "we'll be keeping each other company a lot longer than I thought." She understood and she hated it.

The house crumbled around them and was swept away, taking the boy with it.

She remained in place, her spirit breaking. Her hope shattered. He was wrong. No one ever stayed.

Emilys' Revenge

By April Berry *(CONTENT WARNING: blood, murder)*

Of course, they wanted to come out here on a rainy night. "Guys, maybe we should do this another night? It looks muddy," I tried to reason.

"What? Are you scared, Ginger?" Lisa's tone was so snotty.

"No, it's just storming, but whatever. Let's go."

We piled out of John's truck and ran through the field. Lisa and John had gotten ahead of us, but Danny and I were still walking at a fast pace.

"Hey, I'm sorry we dragged you out here. But I won't leave your side, promise." Danny was so kind and considerate. I had the biggest crush on him since, well, as long as I can remember. So, when he invited me to come hang out, I accepted. I didn't know we were tagging along with Lisa and John.

John seemed nice enough, but he graduated two years ago so I didn't really know him. But Lisa, I knew. She tormented me in elementary school, and middle school wasn't much better. In high school, I finally blossomed and gained the attention of some of the popular boys. I was able to avoid them the last two years, but someone nominated me for Homecoming Queen this year. I wish I knew who so I could strangle them. But I ended up making it to Court and Danny asked me to be his date, which made sense seeing as how we would be walking the court together. The dance was just days away. Even though I had been trying to avoid dates and boys like the plague since freshman year, I was excited at the prospect of spending some time with Danny before we had to get dressed up and I was stuck in a corset for hours.

Danny was popular and could model for GQ Magazine, but he wasn't pretentious or obnoxious like most of the popular boys. I had noticed him before, okay, I stalked him since middle school, but I never imagined he would notice me. When they made the announcements at the pep rally and my name was called, I was frozen in the stands even though everyone around me was pushing me to stand up and go to the floor with the others. It wasn't until Danny broke away from the floor with the others that had already been announced and offered his hand up to me that I moved. He smiled up warmly, extended his hand to me, and mouthed something like, "c'mon, I got you," but I couldn't actually hear over the noise in the gym. Once I stepped down with him, he placed my arm in his and escorted me down. My heart nearly jumped from my chest at that moment. Ever since then it has been a whirlwind. Which leads us back to this *brilliant* idea Lisa had.

We trudged through the thick growth and mud but eventually made it to the porch of the old, abandoned house. Everyone called it the Shagging Shack, but it was also supposed to be haunted. Boys would bring dates to scare them then offer their safety and comfort. *Barf*. Lisa and John had been known to shag everywhere anyway, so John didn't have to come up with creative ways to get her in the shack. I had a sinking feeling Lisa decided to drag me out here to either scare the crap out of me or use the happenings of the night to drag my name through the mud later. The look on her face when my name was called at the assembly was almost worth the trouble it's been, but she suddenly started acting like we were besties ever since. I did my best to be cordial and play along without any real commitments to anything until tonight. Once I realized it was a double date, it was too late to back out. I didn't want to be seen as a chicken or goody-goody.

"They say the spirit that lives here is actually kind to the fairer sex," I said as we walked through the rickety door.

"Oh, so you know about this place?" John asked with disdain in his voice, flashing the light in my direction nearly blinding me.

"Why is she nice to girls?" Danny asked to change the tone, but also seemed genuinely curious.

Knowing Lisa likely wanted to scare me encouraged me to share my wealth of knowledge to see if I could turn the tables. I shared the story as we slowly investigated the small shack.

"Well, the legend is that a girl lived here with her father over a hundred and fifty years ago. It was the middle of nowhere, and if they needed food or water, the father would go fetch it, and she would be here alone to tend to the house and the garden. According to most variations of the story, the father had left to go fetch supplies, but when he returned just days later, he found her dead. She had obvious wounds implying she had been sexually assaulted but she was also beaten badly. In fact, it was so bad that there was a trail of blood from the small room she slept in all the way to the front door where he found her cold body."

I stopped and turned to see the three of them still as rocks with their mouths gaping open.

"Why would you tell us that? What's wrong with you?" Lisa squealed out.

I shrugged my shoulders and Danny just chuckled, then walked over to me and grabbed my hand. I could see from the moonlight pouring in the window behind me he was staring into my eyes.

"So, do you think you can keep me safe, since she likes girls?" Before I could say anything, I could practically hear Lisa roll her eyes as she started up the creaky stairs to the loft.

"Oh my God, get a room. C'mon John, let's checkout what's up here."

The shack was small and only had one separate room downstairs, which could have been a closet but there was a cot in there, then the main area served as a living area and kitchen. The house was over a hundred years old and definitely didn't belong to any family with wealth. Still, Danny and I walked slowly through and investigated the little piece of history with the flashlight function of his cellphone. To me it was charming, albeit with a sad story. When people thought of homes in the south during that time, they always thought of the huge plantation homes with slaves and great luxuries. The truth is, most didn't live that way, only the inherently wealthy landowners. Most lived the way these people did.

"So, do you know the names of the family who lived here, or did you make all that up to scare her?" Danny asked quietly as we kept investigating downstairs.

"It's a true story, but maybe I did want to scare her, just a little," I quietly said back. "The man was Thomas Charles and his daughter was Emily. Records were bad during that time, but she was only about 12 or 13 when it happened. So sad."

Danny turned to me, close but far enough back I didn't feel threatened. Honestly, I wished he were closer.

"That is sad. So young. Such a violent end. I have a little sister and the thought of anyone hurting her, I dunno." He shook like he was shaking the weight of the world off his shoulders.

"I'm sorry, I didn't mean to upset you. Honestly, I just wanted to get the upper hand on Lisa."

He finally stepped in closer and slowly lifted his hand to my face, taking an eternity to make contact with my skin.

"Ginger, I know Lisa isn't the best person. Don't worry about her. I really like you. If they make you uncomfortable, we won't hang out with them anymore."

My heart was racing as he spoke, gently stroking my face with his large but incredibly soft hand. I cracked a grin and he returned in kind as he leaned toward me. As his soft lips connected to mine, I closed my eyes and excitement rushed through me. I instinctively put my hands around his neck and he kissed me deeper, groaning through my mouth. I was getting lost in the glorious moment of my first real kiss when I could sense a flash through my closed eyes.

"Hey, cut it out!" Danny pulled away without removing his grip from my waist enough to yell up at Lisa. She had snapped at least one picture with her phone.

"So, you think you're funny with your little story? Let's see how funny this pic is when it goes viral!" Lisa was still on the loft, but the light of the moon was bright on her sneaky face with her wicked grin as she meddled with her phone.

Danny let go and my heart was still racing but no longer from excitement. I didn't tell my parents where I was going, nor that I would be with a boy. That picture could not go on social media.

Danny was angrily pleading with John to get his girlfriend to stop as he slowly walked to the stairs. John did make a few comments about how she had her fun now let it go but she had already done the damage, turning her phone to show us what she did.

Danny began to run up the stairs, but John met him halfway down and they were tussling. Lisa just kept looking down over the loft with that stupid satisfied grin. I wouldn't give her the satisfaction of begging so all I could muster was an angry glare back up at her. I finally managed to get a few words out.

"You'll be sorry you did that."

Lisa let out a cackle and shook her head, "Ha, sorry for what? You did this to yourself. You aren't one of us so maybe now you'll learn your place."

Danny and John were still pushing and shoving on the stairs as I felt a cold breeze pass through me, like it pushed through my body. It was storming out, but it was September in Georgia, no cold air to be found. I dropped my phone from the shock of the chill so I bent down to feel for it. I was still patting my hands gently on the floorboards when a terrifying shriek came from the loft.

Danny and John stopped. I looked up, still crouched on the floor. The sound made me practically jump from my skin , my heart nearly beating from out of my chest. Danny ran back down to me, and John took off back up the stairs, and we heard him utter something.

"Lisa, oh my God, Lisa," before he let out a blood curdling scream

"John, John, what is it?" Danny yelled up as he cradled me in his arms.

John stood up, and with the help of the flashlight, we could see through the slatted rail of the loft. Danny and I looked at each other horrified, hoping we didn't see what we thought we saw.

"She's dead. She's dead." John repeated over and over as he held his shaky bloody hands up, staring down at them.

I was shaking uncontrollably, and Danny and John were yelling at each other, but the words weren't registering with me. He was cradling me, and I could feel the tension in his grasp. Everything was in slow motion. I turned my head to the front door ready to leave this place when I saw her.

The young girl in her ratty dress stood by the door smiling at me and tipped her head in my direction. The door was visible behind her. Then in an instant, she faded away like smoke dissipating. Apparently, the legend wasn't all right. Emily didn't like mean girls.

Little Black Box

By Donna Taylor

The air's so thick Jack can barely breathe. Sweat trails down his forehead and stings his eyes. He swipes at his face with his wrist and knows he just smeared dirt across his skin. His shirt sticks to his chest and back. His armpits are saturated. He could be in the pool at his friend's house right now. Instead, he's boiling alive in Grandma's attic.

Jack slides boxes from one side of the musty attic to another, stacking them in size order. As he pushes a box large enough for him to fit in across the floor, a floorboard creaks. He stops pushing and stands up with a groan, feeling infinitely older than his fifteen years. Once he stretches, he listens.

The floor creaks again from a shadowed corner and he whips his head around to look.

It's an old house. Old houses settle. But when the floorboards creak again, Jack stops rationalizing because that does not sound like settling. It sounds like a step and he's the only one up here. Maybe there's a big rat or something. He shudders at the thought.

He leaves the body-sized box behind and makes his way to the corner. The closer he gets to the shadows, the cooler the air gets. More boxes are scattered across the floor. An old wooden rocking horse with most of its paint chipped off creaks as it rocks with nothing touching it. A plastic doll's head with tangled hair stares up at him with one painted eye. Jack cringes and gently nudges the disembodied head out of his way and toes the boxes to make room to walk. The bulb over his head is dark. He taps at the glass, but it doesn't even so much as flicker on.

Another creak draws his eyes back to the corner, but no furry little bodies scuttle away. It's just a black box, lacquered to a shine and untouched by the dust churning in the attic air. It's small, something that could fit in his lap. The floorboards creak again, this time sounding like it came from directly under him. He can almost feel the movement in the floor, like something pressing up against the boards. He takes a small step to the side and watches the floor, but nothing moves.

A shiver rolls over him and the damp of his shirt sends goosebumps prickling along his skin. He takes a step closer and swears he feels the floorboards pushing back, like it's not empty space under his feet.

He crouches down and, with a dirt-caked nail, flicks up the latch, releasing the lid. It stays closed, but cracked open. With the pad of a finger he lifts the lid up, bracing himself. For what, he has no idea, but when it's all the way open nothing happens. It appears to be just a box lined in black velvet. He creeps closer, leaning over the open box.

At first it's just black, and maybe his eyes are playing a trick on him, but there doesn't appear to be a bottom. He leans farther over it and sees a black so dark he loses sight of the edges. The blackness drops into a tunnel that draws Jack closer. When his head is over the box's opening there's a pinprick of light that grows. Nausea rolls through him, like the floor beneath his feet is wavering.

Staring back at him is his grandma's attic ceiling. A phantom breeze flicks cobwebs in the shadows of dark, old beams. It is like there's a mirror at the bottom of the box, only there is no bottom and he doesn't look back at himself. Jack doesn't understand what he's looking at. He reaches a couple fingers out and gently touches them to the side of the box. Velvet.

He slides his fingers down the wall of the box and stops when he's wrist-deep. The box itself is only maybe three inches high. What's going on?

As he keeps sliding his hand deeper into the box, the edge hits his elbow and his hand reaches for the mirror ceiling at the bottom. Another wave of nausea rolls through him, vertigo pulsing in his head, making everything hard to see yet impossibly clear at the same time.

Once the edge of the box hits his shoulder he knows this is a dream. Has to be. He would have broken through the floorboards by now. But his hand reaches into coolness, not the stuffy oven of a crawl space. He keeps his eyes over the box, watches his hand grope around in the upside down attic space, when a head comes into view and Jack gasps.

His own face looks back at him, the same deep brown eyes staring at him, the dimple in his left cheek growing deeper as his mirror self smiles. There's no dirt on this other Jack, no sweaty, matted hair. Mirror Jack sneers and lashes out, grabbing onto Jack's dirty hand. The dry, cool skin of mirror Jack settles into Jack's flesh, sending a rippling chill across his body. Mirror Jack's other hand reaches out and wraps around Jack's extended arm and pulls.

"Hey!" Jack yells and tries to yank himself back out of the box, but his mirror self has him firm.

The attic ceiling at the bottom of the box extends, grows higher, sways, and bile rises to Jack's throat. The world behind his mirror self's head pulses like something out of a funhouse, but mirror Jack stays constant, smiling Jack's own smile back at him as those mirror hands reach Jack's elbow.

He screams and tries to yank his arm back out of the box, but mirror Jack holds tight. With another yank Jack falls deeper into the box, but that's impossible. He can't possibly fit. Until his head is pulled through the box's opening with ease, like it's expanding just to fit him without expanding at all. Jack screams again, but it's only into the mirror world he's screaming now.

Jack's ragged sneaker snags on the edge of the box and he grinds it in, holding on for dear life. But with one more yank it lets go, and he is swallowed whole by something the size of a shoebox. Fingers dig into his armpit and, with one more yank, Jack is thrown onto the mirror attic's floor, a gray world surrounding him.

Cold and empty, there are no boxes in this attic and when he looks behind him, the attic extends farther than any attic has the right to extend, beams and wood and cobwebs reaching into infinity. His head swims and he nearly faints.

Jack turns back around to see the clean version of himself standing in front of him. The imposter gives Jack a little smile and dives into the box as if he were diving into a pool. The lid crashes down behind the disappearing feet and the latch flips closed.

Jack scrambles across the floor, back to the little black box, and none-too-gently throws the lid open. But instead of his grandma's heat-filled attic staring back at him, it's just a black box, the velvet worn at the corners and along the bottom. He throws his hand into the box and cries out when he punches the hard bottom. It is truly just a box.

In the stifling attic of Jack's grandma's house, a hand emerges from the little black box in the dark corner, followed by an elbow, a shoulder, a head. The box doesn't change its size, but somehow a boy who looks just like Jack still fits. If one were to look at the box as he pulls himself out of it, one would almost lose sight of it, as if it ceases to exist and re-exists again when the boy is free.

With a thud he lands on the floor, a cloud of dust poofing up around him. Footsteps on the ladder draw his attention to the hatch and Grandma pops her head up through the opening, her eyes scanning the attic until they land on the prone boy who looks like her grandson. He scrambles to his feet and sneers at the dust on his clothes, unsuccessfully swatting at the mess.

Grandma snorts. "It's about time."

The boy who calls himself Jack stops swatting at himself and smiles at his grandma. It's been so long since he's seen her. She's had to deal with that fake for so long. She disappears back through the attic door and Jack turns around to get one last look at the little black box. He bends down and closes the lid, firmly setting the latch and not bothering to look back inside. Then he stands up, brushes off more dirt, and walks to the attic door.

Bloom

By Donna Taylor

Trees crave the fresh pulse of blood when they're about to bloom. It's why parents warn us away from the woods, especially tonight. The Equinox. Tonight is when the trees are hungriest.

It's a silly superstition that refuses to die in my little town of Cornwall, where trees are more plentiful than people. The woods are scary enough without making demons out of nature. It's not ghosts or goblins that get people out here. It's a hunting accident or animals or exposure. Trees don't kill people. People kill people.

This is the kind of tale I'd expect those from hundreds of years ago to believe. Back when they didn't know any better and didn't have nearly as many answers as we do now. Now we don't believe in those things, except maybe at sleepovers when we're trying to scare each other. But everyone knows better.

I know better.

Which is why I'm going to touch a tree.

The story goes that settlers desperate for a bad winter to end made a deal with some fair folk. In exchange for a bloom to push the winter away, they had to make a sacrifice. Send someone into the woods. The purer the better. It's always virgins, isn't it? And they did. With every passing spring the bloom came fuller and sweeter until time ran out of people to remember, and tales of the blood-hungry woods turned into legends to scare kids straight.

No one gets booted into the trees anymore to appease any faeries. I can't help but wonder how many bones are in those woods from all those poor past fools feeding a superstition. It's a forest of the dead either way. Still, it doesn't keep people from talking. Like about how no one can seem to stay in the area, which is a lie. I was born and raised here and my family's from Cornwall. Maybe I've had more than a few friends come and go. Can you really blame them? There's nothing here and the commute is hell to anything civilized. I don't blame them for running away without saying goodbye. So only those of us with roots already here actually stay.

It's a dead dark out, a night so heavy it crushes sound. My window is open and a light breeze rustles my curtains and I pull my jacket tighter around me. It's still bitterly cold out and patches of snow dot the lawn as if they're leading me right to the woods. Like my decision to prove a silly superstition wrong is right.

With a leg up I slide out the window and onto the ground only a few feet below me. The hard-packed earth crunches under my boots, but I'm not worried about waking anyone up. It's the middle of the night. My parents are dead to the world, and all I'm doing is going to touch a tree.

With each step I take my draw to the woods grows stronger. Murmurs in my ears tell me to keep going. I'm tired, I tell myself. I'm hearing things. Still, I can't shake it. Even as the wind bites into my cheeks and stings my eyes awake, the voices remain. They get louder. I don't think I can pull away from the woods if I tried.

Trees loom tall over me, dense and crackling in the wind, leafless branches clawing into the sky. Depthless shadows carving against a blue-black veil like veins. They say that their bark is like razors, made to slice flesh quickly and feed the trees even quicker.

Stars twinkle like faery lights way up high and I see a shimmer on the trunks of those looming trees. I step closer but I still can't make it out. Voices are thunder in my head now, a familiar tone calling to me, and step after step brings the woods nearer. The trees shimmer so beautifully in the darkness, as if lit up from within.

When one is close enough I reach out, bark patterning its outside like mottled skin. There is no hesitation, like it's not me controlling my hand. I press my palm to the tree and it's not rough or dry or brittle, but stinging sharp. Blades of bark glitter in front of me and I pull my hand away, wincing as my skin snags on the edges, tearing flesh even more.

I watch as blood runs down my hand, jagged wounds open and offering. My head swims, the voices overwhelming. I know those voices. I remember them. I thought they moved away, but they're still here. They'll stay here. I need to run. From what? The world tilts. My eyes can't seem to focus on anything anymore, but I see my hand clearly. The blood running in thick drops down my wrist, plinking onto the hard ground. It doesn't even hurt.

My legs feel stiff and when I look down shadows are crawling up me, turning my two legs into one. I can't quite see what's happening, but I have no desire to fight it as I sink into the swimming sensation. Warmth wraps itself around me as the voices get clearer, a tinkling singing that makes me not mind the weight on my chest, how my heart is struggling to beat. How breathing is becoming a problem.

I brush my cheek against my shoulder but it's no longer my skin and razor-edged bark slices my face. Blood drips down my neck as I look up into such a dark sky. My hands reach toward the night, fingers spindly and thin, creaking in the wind. Hair spins into wood as branch after branch reaches, threading toward infinity. I'm not walking but swaying and a lone bud sprouts from the tip of my finger, opening into a beautiful flower.

The first bloom.

I'm so incredibly hungry.

Lady Of The Night

By Karen Ruhman (*CONTENT WARNING: murder, mention of sex & SA*)

If you were to ask me to describe a place I've called home, I would laugh. Girls like me, we don't have homes. We have places we stay, places we sleep. Girls like me count ourselves lucky for surviving, for fighting and biting and crawling our way through every damn day. Oh, but bless, you wouldn't want to hear that, now would you? You don't want to hear us fight to survive when you've already condemned us. Girls like me are the fallen ones, yes? We're the rotten core of the whole rotten fruit. So isn't it right that we're the ones who get the knobbed end of the stick?

I could tell you about more so-called gentlemen's knobs than your fine ears would care to hear, I'd wager. You're the ones who like hearing about old Jack, and the girls what he done in. So, well then, here's one tale the coppers don't know about the old Ripper. It's not one about who he killed. It's not even about what started him. It's about who ended him.

I never stood out on the street corners, mind you. All them poor corner girls ever had was some bastard of a pimp who'd cuff them as soon as look at them. I was lucky, all told. Missy Hayes ran a clean whorehouse, close as you can call. She was a bitch of a business, but she kept her girls fed and roofed. She kept a bouncer in the place, too. Fat old Dicky-boy, who would joke with us, and throw out anyone who tried to get more than he was paying for. The problem was, one night, a fancy-bloke decided it would be a good time to put his hands around a girl's throat while he was over her. Dear old Dicky-boy never heard the ruckus. Or if he did, he didn't realize it for what it was.

They buried me, old Dicky-boy and Missy Hayes. I heard the other girls whispering, and a few even cried. I didn't go in any holy ground, mind. I don't know why, maybe even a pauper's grave was too dear for tight-fisted Missy. There was a warehouse nearby with earthy floors. There it was they laid me, tucked up, neat as you like. It's cold beneath the earth, and it seemed the only thing keeping me warm was my anger. I should have been smarter, quicker, known something was wrong. My damn instincts kept me alive for so long. Maybe living in the softness of a steady roof had dulled them. Dulled them, and done me.

It was my whispering, what done him in at the end. We, all of us below the ground, whisper, I think. Priests talk of paradise, and they talk about men like old Jack. What they know of the one probably equals what they admit to knowing of the other. If there is a paradise somewhere, it would be feeling the warm sun on my skin, and quiet around me. The sounds that come from under the ground never stop, despite our promised paradise. Or maybe this is just hell. Maybe God's as much a bastard as any other man, condemning me for trying not to die, and being a woman in the meanwhiles.

I don't know who he was, old Jack. But he made the mistake of walking over my bones every day. Connected to the warehouse, somehow, I suppose. I reckon he was on the wrong side of crazy already. How else does anyone hear the girl six feet below their toes, if they aren't a bit touched in the head? All's I know is, I hear a lot more now than I ever did upright. I felt in my bones, what was left of them, that it was him, see. I knew then that it was old Jack who walked over my bones, every day.

Your footsteps are all different, all you who still walk.

The warehouse men above me started talking about this Ripper fellow, the one what was doing in the working girls. I heard his steps slow. I heard his heart, all the way up there in the air above me, how it got faster, more excited every time. The men wondered about the monster at the door, and old Jack's heart danced with each word.

So I started whispering to him in particular, see? Just whispered to him from inside my winding sheet. Dunno how much he could make out, but I started talking to him direct-like. Every day that he walked over my bones, every day, I told him what he was. No better than me, and quite a damn sight lower, for all that he was still in the sun. He was still doomed to whisper once he died, doomed just like me. Maybe he whipped out at the later poor girls because he heard me. Maybe he would have done it anyways. But the fact was and is, he done it, and who knows what else.

Us working girls, we help each other. No one else will. Whispering to him, telling him what he was, and what was waiting for him, was all I could do. It was the only way I could help the girls he already had made to whisper. It's the only way I could save whatever girls would be next.

Day after day rolled by that he walked over me. The men above, useless creatures, kept talking about the fearsome Ripper. They kept wondering, but he didn't slow to gloat anymore. I made it so he wouldn't even hear them. He couldn't hear at all when I filled his ears with a dead siren's song. His steps dragged as he neared me, and sped as he passed me by. That blackened heart of his danced no more, but thudded quick and hard. It was the same as the heart beats I would hear of rodents, the instant before they were crushed by snares in the walls of the warehouse above me.

Come to me. It's the only way I'll stop calling out to you. Come down, come under the ground.

His footsteps stopped sounding over my head. And no more Ripper-deaths happened. The men above me still talked and wondered, but eventually moved on to other things. I don't know whether he done himself in, or ran away, but I know this much. I filled his ears so loud, he could run for years and still hear me. Even if he didn't do himself in from madness, he wasn't killing no more. If he did live out his days, and die natural-like, my voice in his ear kept him tame. No-one with his broken footsteps could be anything past a shell of a person.

And that's the thing, see? Dead or alive, it don't matter. It was the ripping that let him be the Ripper. But I think he's down here, with the rest of us. Or maybe, just maybe, he went even deeper than I did, and I'm not the one in hell. Because if anyone deserved hell, by any promise any priest ever made, it's old Jack.

So now you know another piece of the Ripper's story. But ask this, dearie, as you stand there in the sun. What manner of person are you, to hear a dead girl whispering below your feet? Jack heard me whispering, too. Be wiser than he. Be better. Because if you hear me, you can hear all of us. Listen well.

Romance

Good Fish In The Sea 🌶

By April Berry

G ood morning ma'am. How long until your companion joins us?" the handsome, and younger than expected, captain asked. He reached his hand out to me as I crossed the plank to step onto the impressive boat.

"Turns out it'll just be me today," I answered as I placed my hand into his. I looked into his face to find a curious look amongst the sharp details of the face that could have been shaped from clay. Blue eyes but dark like the deep waters we were about to travel to and chiseled features against a broad and soft smile. His hair was dark but covered with a floppy fishing hat.

I was so taken aback by the sight of the bronze god reaching out to me that, when I stepped down onto the deck, my foot landed on a slick spot and slipped right out from under me. To add insult to injury, I tightened my grasp on his hand but also reached out to him with the other and wildly reached for something to grab onto, capturing the sleeve on his tank. I heard a loud ripping sound as a squeal escaped me.

I closed my eyes to brace for the fall that was sure to come on the hard deck below me, but instead felt an arm wrap tightly around my waist. I opened my eyes and was mere inches from the bronze god's magical face, which now had turned serious.

"I got you, ma'am. Are you alright?" he asked as I looked around to see I was also inches from landing. He was crouched over me, still tightly holding me up, which was impressive considering I had forty-two years of weight on me.

I found my footing and he slowly pulled me until we both were standing.

"I'm fine. Thank you. It's been quite some time since I've been deep sea fishing." I stared at the frayed and tattered tank that was barely hanging on him. "I'm so sorry about that. It was a reflex."

He looked down and laughed. "No problem, we don't wear our Sunday's finest out here for a reason. So just you today? I had two on the logbook," he said as he pulled the tank from his well sculpted body.

I couldn't help but ogle his beautiful form as he stood holding the balled-up shirt in his large, rugged hands. My mind began to wander as I admired the sunkissed forearms that could probably easily lift me up.

"Ma'am are you alright?" he asked, snapping me from the trance. I felt blood rush to my face as I came back to reality.

"Oh, yes, totally fine. I don't mind still paying the full amount, but it's just me. We can head out whenever you're ready."

He nodded and looked to the docks. "Are those your bags there, ma'am?"

"Oh damn, I almost forgot! They are," I said as I turned to go back and grab the cooler and my bag.

He put his hand up and quickly headed across the plank, grabbing my things off the dock before running back across. I instinctively put my arms out to help him climb to the deck after my own slip, but he smiled and jumped down.

"I spend most of my time here but thank you for your kindness. Follow me to the cabin," he said as he walked down the side of the fifteen-foot charter boat. He was taking long, quick strides accentuating every little muscle in his back, ones I didn't know existed. I didn't want to keep getting caught staring, so I tried to keep up, but he stopped and turned around.

"Watch your step, you probably don't want to go as fast as I do, ma'am," he said with a smile.

"Right," I said as we both entered the cabin, "and you can call me Frankie. Ma'am only makes my current situation more miserable."

"My apologies, ma'-I mean Frankie. I was just raised to address folks as sir and ma'am and say please and thank you. I didn't mean to offend," he said as he put the small cooler on the floor and my bag on the sofa lining the interior of the cabin. "You can sit in here while we ride out if it gets too hot, but you're welcome to sit out on the deck as well. We have a long ride ahead, though. If you sit outside, be sure to watch your step and be careful if you decide to come back in."

He sat down in the large chair in front of the controls and started turning things and flipping switches. The engine loudly roared so I looked around to find a good place to sit.

"Almost forgot," he said as he jumped up, "follow me." I hadn't sat yet, so I did as he instructed and followed him down a narrow stairwell.

Once we got to the bottom, he opened a small door to the right. "This is the bathroom if you need it and over there," he pointed to another door across the small corridor, "you'll find some bunks if you need to rest, or if you get seasick." I wanted to be polite, but it was almost hard with all this talking of restrooms and getting seasick. It was a clear picture of what he saw when he looked at me.

"Okay, thanks. I think I'm okay for now. I may go sit on the deck for a while." He nodded to me and motioned for me to head back up. I reluctantly went ahead, understanding he was being a gentleman, but felt insecure as he was getting a full look at my wide ass that I shoved into some cotton shorts. I figured a bikini under shorts and a tank would be a good idea since it was projected to be in the nineties today and I'd be fishing outside in the open sea. But the shorts were loose in the legs and fairly short, so I imagined he just got an eyeful that he may not have wanted.

I walked out of the cabin onto the deck and found the chair. The sun was beaming bright, and it was already hot. I wasn't sure I could sit comfortably with Captain Delicious inside.

"We are about to take off, so hold on Frankie," the captain called from the speaker that fed to the deck. Hearing my name reminded me of something so I jumped up and walked as fast as I could inside without falling again.

"Captain, what was your name? I know the boat said Captain Jack, but what's your name? Or do I just call you Captain?" that all sounded so idiotic as I heard myself say it.

He grinned a wicked grin as he replied, "Captain sounds nice off those lips, but my name really is Jack. I never was one for marketing tactics." I was almost certain he was being funny and friendly, but the first part of that created a tingling sensation in my lower abdomen. I nodded quickly and turned to go back outside before he could see the redness wash back over my face. He grinned then said, "Frankie, you can call me whatever you like." *What was that?* I was glad I was already walking away when he said that.

Once I was seated firmly, a man on the docks came to untie the rope holding us to it and tossed it in the boat. I felt the boat jerk and saw the docks slowly getting further away before finally the boat turned, and we began our 8-hour adventure out to sea.

It wasn't long until we were so far out that I couldn't see anything but open water. It was a strange feeling. A little unsettling since we were so far from anyone or anything else, but also nice. I was far, far away from reality. Literally out in the great abyss.

The last few years were trying to say the least. This week-long trip to the beach was supposed to be a second honeymoon to help my husband and I reconnect. But two short months ago I discovered the reason for the distance that he tried to tell me was all in my head. Her name was Julie. She worked at his office, but not as cliché as his assistant, just a woman in the building. She knew about me, and that's how I found out. When I confronted him, he didn't have anything to say.

The papers had been submitted but the final hearing wasn't until after this trip. Luckily, we had no children. I always wanted them, but it didn't happen. He wasn't interested in IVF or adoption. He insisted if it was meant to be it would happen. I couldn't believe it had taken someone else showing me proof to realize it was over. It had been for a long time.

Here I was, alone on vacation, a trip I had hoped would fix us. To top it off, I'm on a boat with a hot guy with all my cellulite hanging out, no makeup, and my basic brown hair in a messy bun. Forty-two and no man, no kids, and no close friends. I had a fantastic but demanding job, which may have led to my blindness about my marriage, but that was about all I had to show for it. Besides going on the day trip on a fishing boat, I wasn't sure what I would even do here alone the rest of the week.

I hoped taking the trip alone would prove I can be happy by myself and help me rediscover who I am. So far it only proved seating for one is often at the bar.

The boat was slowing after several hours, and tears had been running down my face causing my sunscreen to burn my eyes from rubbing and squinting. I didn't want to scare Captain Jack, so I made my way to the cabin and tried to discreetly get to the stairs facing away from him.

I made it to the tiny bathroom and shut the folding door. The mirror was about as good as the one from the makeup kit I gave my three year old niece for her birthday. I pulled some toilet paper from the roll and dabbed at my face to collect the remnants of tears and smooth out the sunblock I had applied before I left. I'd definitely need more before fishing for hours in the Florida sun, but my bag was on the sofa in the cabin.

I wet a ball of toilet paper to dab over my puffy eyes and as I did, there was a loud knock on the door that sent me flying, and I fell over onto the toilet. I barely caught myself on the seat when Jack yelled through the door.

"Ma-Frankie, are you alright? I was letting you know we stopped but it sounds like you fell." He knocked again when I didn't answer. I was still leaning on the seat of the toilet when I started laughing. I kept laughing, harder and louder, until new tears formed in my eyes.

"Frankie, is there anything I can do?" he asked through the door.

I finally stood, still laughing, and pulled the folding door open to find him standing there with a concerned look on his face, but still no shirt.

"I don't know, Captain. My life is a damn mess, and it keeps getting worse. I'm sorry you're stuck with me all day," I said through my laughter that now was turning more crazy than funny.

"Is this about your missing companion?" he asked as he reached his hand out to mine to coax me from the small bathroom. I nodded as I took his hand.

"Companion. That's what he was supposed to be. My life companion. But he found another companion that he liked more." New tears formed. "Seven years. I wasted seven years with him and for what? I have nothing to show for it." I stopped talking as the tears came faster and my shoulders began shaking.

Jack rubbed my shoulders and leaned down to look into my eyes. "He must be an idiot. If I had a lady as pretty as you, I wouldn't look elsewhere."

I looked up into those dark blue eyes but quickly wrote off his comment as just being kind. "Ha, thank you, you're sweet. Maybe I was pretty a few years ago. Now I'm just a middle-aged divorcee who spends too much time behind a desk."

He stepped in closer and put his hand under my chin. "I'm a lot of things, but sweet isn't one of them. He *is* an idiot. You're a goddess and deserve to be treated as such." His voice was gravelly and low, like he said, anything but sweet.

I felt my breath catch in my chest as my heart started pounding. I don't know if it was his kind words or his searing stare into my eyes, or maybe that I haven't been with a man other than my ex in over seven years and not for a year with him, but some animalistic urge filled me, and I placed my hand over his bare rock-hard chest and leaned toward him. When he grinned at my hand on his skin, I decided to not fight the urge and I stepped even closer and put my other hand in the waist of his shorts.

Jack leaned in and attacked my mouth, twirling his tongue around mine as he pulled me closer with his strong, callused hands under my ass. A sudden rush of wetness that I hadn't felt in ages collected between my thighs and a small moan escaped my mouth into his.

He pulled away just inches but enough to look down into my eyes. "Are you sure you want to do this"

"I don't want to do this, I *need* to do this, Jack," I said, breathing heavily as I stared back. I was desperate to have his mouth on mine again and leaned up to him.

Before my lips made contact with his again, he had reached under my ass and picked me up, pulling my legs around him. He took a couple of steps after a quick turn and I felt him reach for the door behind me. We entered the small room with two bunks, and he kissed me hard again. I expected to be put down on the bed, but he grunted.

"This won't do. I need room to do this correctly," he said in a low voice. Then he turned and we began kissing again as he carried me back up to the cabin.

He carefully placed me on the sofa in the cabin and was on his knees in front of me as we continued kissing aggressively. His lips were much softer than I imagined, and while his hands were callused, they still felt amazing on my exposed skin as they gently grazed every inch of me.

My animal urge had intensified, and I wanted every piece of fabric between us gone, so I pushed him back briefly to pull my tank over my head. He leaned to my neck and ran his tongue down to my shoulder and his finger was running along the edge of my bikini top. I put my hand over his and pulled the top down exposing my heaving breasts below.

With a guttural moan he leaned down and took my hard nipple into his mouth and rolled his tongue over it sending a loud moan from me.

He mumbled between licks, "Can I touch you, Frankie?"

I managed to moan out an emphatic, "Yes, please yes."

Jack sat up straight and put his hand on the waist of my shorts and slowly started pulling them off my legs. He ran his hands back up my legs, leaning down to plant small kisses on my thighs as he did.

His hands reached my bikini bottom and he looked into my eyes, like he was searching for my approval so I nodded. As he slowly pulled them down, I reached behind me to untie my top and pulled it off.

Suddenly, he grabbed my hips, yanking me to the edge of the sofa and leaned down between my thighs.

Static filled my eyes as I felt his warm tongue between my folds, gently stroking up and down before he put his mouth over the firm nub and gently sucked. The sofa cushions were firm so I couldn't grab anything but slammed my hands down at my side as the long-forgotten feeling of ecstasy began filling my body.

I looked down once my eyesight returned and his hat was gone, revealing luscious dark brown waves. I reached my hands down to run my fingers through them and when I did, he gained a ferocity to his work that sent my head flying back. His thick, long finger found my opening and slid inside as he continued licking and sucking until my legs shook around him.

After a squeak escaped my mouth and my legs stopped shaking, Jack kissed his way back up to me, stopping to pay extra attention to my breasts before finding my mouth again.

"You deserve that every day," he said before he leaned in and kissed the sense out of me, not that there was much left now anyway. "Frankie? Are you alright? Frankie? Frankie?"

I opened my eyes and looked around. I was in a beautiful room in a comfy bed and the shades were open.

"Frankie, are you alright? You had a lot of drinks last night, babe."

I looked up and found Jack staring back at me with a loving smile.

"Here, I brought you some breakfast and coffee. And of course, these," he said as he handed me some pills for my head. "I know I told you to have fun on our honeymoon but didn't know you were such a lightweight."

"I was just dreaming. I did have a few too many though I think. Maybe we can hang at the pool today," I said as I took the pills and almost drank the whole mug of coffee.

"What were you dreaming about? I was trying to get you up for a few minutes."

"I dreamt about the first time we met. And you woke me up in the middle of the good part, Captain," I joked.

"Well, I better make it up to you," he said as he pulled the covers away and went down for a reenactment. God, I loved this man.

Beloved 🌶

By Kata Cuic (CONTENT WARNING: *religious satire*)

I think I need therapy.

It's the little things, you know? Just tiny irritations that get beneath your skin and stay there. Now, I can guess what you must be thinking. It's all the wailing. It's the infants, the children, the violent murder victims.

It's really not.

I might be Death, but I am the bringer of peace. Or, at least, the end. I'm an INTP, an eight on the enneagram scale, predominantly a D on the DISC evaluation—whichever hippie mumbo jumbo personality test you're into this year. The fact of the matter is I'm a Closer. I've always preferred finishing a task rather than beginning it. Nothing brings me more satisfaction than ending a human's suffering.

Especially the children.

The wailing is usually loudest for them, but what humans fail to see is that dying young is the greatest boon the gods grant to a generally miserable species. People fear me, and I get that, but man. That Billy Joel guy? He's one of my favorites. I will truly enjoy removing him from this temporal existence. He gets it, so he shouldn't have to stew on that planet and suffer for any longer than necessary.

Only *the best* die young.

Their souls are blessed with a short existence in those cases when something upstairs gets mixed up, and they're not removed from the cycle of birth and death. To put it another way, dying young is the equivalent of a quick fix when a mistake is made in the soul cycle. I don't know what the heavenly bodies do up there, sometimes. Seriously. How hard is it for a bunch of celestial beings to push papers and organize files correctly?

I don't even have a whole team, and I do my job just fine.

Except when I don't.

Which brings me back to therapy. It's not like I'm having an existential crisis. I'm timeless. But there are times...

Adolf Hitler is a great example. That one pissed me off to no end. The dude mass murdered millions of people. Yes, yes. I know. I already stated death is a release, so it shouldn't be feared, blah, blah, blah, but hear me out. Then, he goes and kills himself as the authorities are closing in, so *he* won't have to suffer.

Fuck. That.

I left his soul trapped in his rotting corpse for way longer than necessary. Right up until fuckin' Gabriel showed up to chew my ass out as I was transporting some of the people good ole Adolf had murdered.

God, damn it. (Read that again. Pun absolutely intended.)

So, fine. I retrieved his putrid soul and threw it into the Styx without waiting for the ferry.

And then Beelzebub jumped into my shit. Dude thinks he's Hades' right-hand man, but he's not. Hades has a great sense of humor. I would too if I had a mate. Don't look at me like that. Persephone is with him half the year, which is a Hell of a lot more than I get.

Satan didn't think my Hitler disposal was as funny. Kali was super pissed when she was tasked with fishing his soul out of the river. She really doesn't like cleaning up.

In all fairness, I was rather petulant with that one. I can't quite put my finger on why. It's not like I haven't taken mass murderers and damned souls before.

I think I'm just tired.

It's been eons. I don't get a wife/consort/partner; no one helps me collect all these souls; most humans hate me; keeping all the latest names of the gods straight gets difficult the more humans branch out from their narrow religious views and/or embrace ancient ways.

And you thought being Death was the mind fuck, right?

Sorry to disappoint you.

There is one soul I've been keeping an eye on who never disappoints *me*. I'm not sure when they first landed on my radar. I'm not even sure if they started out as a Neanderthal or Homo Sapiens. During the Black Death, he was a lowly undertaker who welcomed me with open arms, digging graves cheerfully and blessing the corpses for passing out of that time of eternal suffering. But, Hell. There were thousands of grave diggers! People just couldn't stop dying!

That was the era when I developed my formula for Red Bull. Even for an immortal being, handling that many souls in such a manner was exhausting. I'm still pissed that *someone* leaked my recipe to the masses. What does a jinn need with money anyway?

The gods get their ambrosia. Why is it so hard to imagine I need a little extra kick in times of chaos?

But I digress.

This soul. This beautiful soul. I find no reason for them still to be chained to the earthly cycle. They should have gone to Heaven (or the Illysian fields or Nirvana or Samaawat or whatever the majority of humans are calling it these days) many lifetimes ago.

In this lifetime, this trapped soul has taken the form of a woman. She sings soft lullabies to the dying, washing their frail human bodies with the greatest respect and care. She still doesn't fear me. She welcomes me with open arms and even smiles when the candle she always lights at a deathbed snuffs out upon my arrival.

She's smiling now.

She knows I'm here.

She doesn't know how much I wish I was here for her.

~~~

"I think I need therapy."

Hades rolls his eyes as he lays his cards face down on the table. "Not this again."

"I'm serious!"

In response, a swarm of flies wraps around my body like a vile blanket. Beelzebub emerges from a dark corner, grinning and licking his lips.

Hades rolls his eyes again, and with a snap of his fingers, the horde disappears.

"You know I hate it when you do that," I grind out.

Beelzebub swallows an errant insect. "You know I hate it when you come home for a visit."

"Jesus Christ," Hades mutters, rubbing the bridge of his nose. "Do I have to separate you two again?"

"Hey! I heard that!" a disembodied voice echoes throughout the room.

"Get over yourself!" Hades yells toward the ceiling.

After a flash of blinding light, another form appears in the room. His blinding smile irritates me, too. "Deal me in. I wanna hear all about this."

Buddha scoffs from his seat at the table. "You can hear it from Heaven. We already started playing. No late comers."

Jesus points a finger, still with that same smile on his face. "I'll come whenever I want to."

Everyone in the room snickers.

"Children. I'm about to play poker with children." He takes a seat anyway.

"You love us. Admit it." Hades wears a Cheshire expression.

"I love everyone," Jesus sniffs. "Now, Death. What seems to be troubling you?"

Hades and I exchange a quick glance. Not that it'll go unnoticed, but still. It's true. Jesus *does* love everyone, but even for a benevolent deity his interest seems…suspicious.

I take a seat and heave a deep breath. You know what? Fuck it. I need to get out of this funk I'm in. "There's this soul…"

"This will not end well for you," Hades murmurs, shaking his head as he redeals the cards.

"I didn't say anything yet!"

"Doesn't matter. It still won't end well."

"It ended well for you!"

"Do you see my wife anywhere around here?"

We would not be sitting at this poker table if it was winter and Persephone was here.

"You get her for half the year and have for thousands of years. Quit complaining," I volley back.

Hades opens his mouth.

"Shush," Jesus admonishes. "I swear with you Greek Gods. You're all so self-centered. This is not about you; this is about Death. You're acting like…"

Everyone tenses and glances around the room, afraid of even whispering Zeus's name.

"…you know who," Jesus finishes.

We all wait a millennium for thunder and lightning that never appears.

Even Beelzebub sighs in relief. "He's probably busy banging another nymph."

"Thank God," I mutter.

And damn it all to Hell because God appears, too. He's in male form today. Sort of like a loftier Charlton Heston. I swear, I have never laughed so hard at a human movie. Dogma was far closer to the Truth.

"You rang?" God takes a seat at the table, and no one questions it. Even among the slew of old and new gods, there is a definitive hierarchy.

Well, this just gets weirder and weirder. "I did not. I did not ring."

Jesus and God exchange a look. It doesn't take a deity to translate their unspoken words.

"Don't you have a multi-verse to run?" Beelzebub prompts.

Weird doesn't begin to describe Beelzebub sticking up for me.

God waves off his concern. "The multi-verse is self-sustaining. You know this. The beings have been given free will. Nothing that requires action is going to happen in this instant."

I stifle a laugh as Beelzebub bristles. An instant to God is an eternity to humankind. He's not wrong. We all know the end of time isn't up to us at all. It's up to the beings.

"So, now. I hear you believe you need therapy, Death. Why is that?"

I really have to learn to stop thinking things, let alone saying them out loud. Although, when all I do is collect souls for forever, it's hard not to get lost in my own head.

Also, there is a question only *He* can answer.

"Why is this soul still trapped in the cycle? Why aren't they free yet?"

I don't specify which soul. There's no need. He knows.

God shrugs. It's hilarious, actually. "That soul was put on Creation for you. It will only be free when you no longer require it."

What the fuck?

"For *me*?"

God sighs. The sound reverberates through the Underworld. For a brief second of eternity, all the souls trapped here sigh along. "Yes, for you. You perform a thankless job, and you do it well. We all know you're lonely and think too much. This soul was created for you. To give you a respite from all the, well…death."

I'm not sure whether to thank him or hate him.

"That's not very fair to the soul. Aren't they all supposed to have the freedom to choose?"

"Yes." That's all He gives me.

"Wait." A sickening thought takes root. "Are you saying you gave me a Theotokos? You *made* me a Virgin Mary? Technically created with the gift of choice, but predestined to accept the fate for which she was made?"

God chuckles, and Hades gives him a side-eye for it. The residents of Hell are getting far too many reprieves. One more and Satan will be summoned. *No one* wants that.

"There were many potential Virgin Marys. Just as there were many souls for you. They each had the freedom to choose. The one you watch now is the one that chose you."

"So...she knows?"

God tips his head back and forth and again, it's funny as Hell. "Not the way we know, but she has more of an idea than any of the souls who came before her or who will ever come after her."

"There will be *more* after her?"

God smiles. The third time's the charm. In a ball of fire, Satan appears. He doesn't look pleased. So, you know, normal.

His beastly growl returns the Underworld to its appropriate misery. "For the love of God, Death, just give it a try. You're driving all of *us* crazy with your incessant thoughts of therapy."

"You're all in on this?" I don't care what God said. Surely, the end times are upon us. None of this makes any sense.

I'm only a lowly personification of the end of human existence. I'm not a divine being. People didn't create an anthropomorphism of Death that has omniscience. They gave their gods that lofty characteristic. They did *not* create the gods to sit around and play, well...god with other immortal beings.

This is a dangerous game. None of us can break the constraints of what we were created for.

"I can't believe I'm saying this." Beelzebub finally sits at my right. "But yes. We're all in on it. Your constant sulking is throwing off the balance of this world. People *want* to die now more than ever, and their belief in any of us is rapidly dwindling. Either pull a Zeus and bang her out of your system or get over it already. All of Creation hangs in the balance."

My gaze travels to God. That can't be true. I can't be the bringer of the End Times. I'm not important enough for Creation to hang on *my* balance.

God nods. "It's...more complicated than that, but true in a way as well. More and more, they don't even believe in the idea of me. They're slowly realizing their power even as they squander it. When they stop believing in *you*, however, it could change the very fabric of all existence. Not even gods are truly immortal, but humankind is rapidly approaching an age where they could be. Once that happens, well..."

He leaves the rest unsaid. So many gods have come and gone. God will always exist, but He's fond of his creations, and He misses the gods who have been forgotten. He loves everyone. Even those of us on the dark side of light.

"So…how am I supposed to do this thing?"

Hades gets a scary glint in his vacant, icy eyes. "I still think this won't end well, but wooing, I can definitely teach you."

Everyone groans. Not because Hades is the lone holdout in this chess game. It's because gods aren't particularly romantic.

~~~

He's here.

My heart picks up pace; the blood pumps through my veins a little harder, pulsing beneath my chilled skin. The breath from my lungs fogs in front of my face from the suddenly colder air.

I've been waiting.

This poor soul has suffered far longer than necessary, far more than any decent human should have to. She's been to the brink of death and back so many times, her family doesn't even come anymore when we call. They no longer believe us when we tell them she's in her final hours.

They think they'll have more time.

They're wrong.

"Took you long enough," I whisper. Not to her. Never to my beloved dying.

I don't normally pay such disrespect to Death. I welcome it with open arms, with a lighter heart for the end of human suffering. But not this time. This time, I'm angry.

"I know," a strange voice responds. "When is not my choice. I only come when it's time."

I strain my ears, then study the lifeless form on the bed.

"She's gone," the voice says as if to confirm what I already know.

"Who are you?" There's no one else in this room. I'm not afraid because the answer is obvious. I simply don't understand why now. Why after all this time.

"Death," the voice responds.

It's not even a voice. Not really. More like an indescribable sound that only vaguely resembles words I can understand.

"I have questions." So many questions. If I'm going to be afforded this opportunity, I'm not going to waste it.

"I know." The voice is clearer this time, with an almost melodic but deeply soothing tenor timbre. It also has a direction.

I glance to the corner of the darkened room, where a man now sits in the recliner for guests who haven't visited in months. He's tall, even seated with his hands clutched in front of his face, his index fingers pointed together and touching his mouth. For all appearances, he looks ready to attentively listen.

He's also strikingly handsome, no matter the shadows that seem to dance along his shoulders.

"You're not a skeleton draped in a black robe."

"That wasn't a question." The corner of his mouth lifts.

Huh. Death has a sense of humor. I suppose it's only fitting. "*Why* aren't you a skeleton draped in a black robe?"

"I'm exactly what you imagined me to be," he responds, that lift in his mouth gaining a twin at the other corner.

I squeeze my eyes shut and picture a duck.

"You don't really want me to be a duck," he chuckles.

Fine. I don't. "If you can read my mind, then why did I imagine you as a man and not a skeleton?"

"Others imagine me as a skeleton draped in black, and you're aware of this. You also know skeletons are frail. Even they return to dust in time. You know me as powerful, timeless, and ever-present. Your current human form is a beautiful young woman, so you desire a handsome human man, fitting for what you know me to be yet constrained by your humanity in this particular life."

His words don't shock me as much as they might someone else. "Have I imagined you differently before?"

"No."

"Why?"

"You've always known I exist, but in this life, I confirmed it for you. That enables your mind to free itself from some of its bonds."

"How many lives have I had?" Like I said before—not wasting this opportunity.

"I don't know."

And...back to the anger. "How can you not know? You're Death. You know everything!"

He tsks, and it's the strangest sound. One that echoes through the room, reverberates through my bones, and seems to make the very air shimmer with disappointment. Maybe. I don't know. I've never experienced anything like this before.

"I'm Death. Not God."

This gentle statement gives me the sensation of waking from a vivid dream. I can almost recall what happened, almost taste the emotion I felt while I slept, but I can't quite reach it. I can tell the events of the dream to someone else, but I can never fully recapture the truth of it. I know, yet I don't.

"You said the form I've imagined for you is a byproduct of the constraints of this current life?"

"Yes."

There are a million things someone might think when faced with Death. I'm not sure embarrassment is particularly high on the list. Most people worry about having clean underwear when the unthinkably unexpected happens. I'm concerned Death knows I have zero love life.

"You've had other lovers," he says, again as if to soothe me. "You may continue to do so. It doesn't bother me."

Strangely, of all the things he's revealed to me, this one is the most shocking. "Why would it bother you?"

"Because you are mine."

My temples throb with a headache. I don't understand.

He rises from the chair and slowly approaches me at the bedside. Not like he's afraid that *I'm* afraid, but more like his steps are weighted with intention. His hand is surprisingly warm and solid when it lands on my shoulder. An entire blanket of relief envelops me from only a small amount of contact.

"You have been—and still are—bound to a human form. If you had known you were mine all along, you would have kept yourself for me only. That isn't fair to you. A human has needs. Needs Death does not share."

"So, I'm yours, but you aren't mine? You probably prefer the morticians and medical examiners, huh? I have friends in those fields. They talk to dead people all day. That's probably a turn-on for you."

He barks out a laugh in spite of the petulance of my assumptions.

Every molecule of my body feels like the very fabric of existence shakes loose. It's so incongruent, so…unnatural. Death laughs.

"I am a man now because your soul longs for me. In this life, your soul is embodied in a heterosexual woman. You tried being a mortician once, hoping it would bring me to you. You were a hetrosexual man then. If I had known I was allowed to have you, I would have appeared to you as a woman."

Oh, yes. I have vague memories of owning a funeral home. I learned a long time ago not to share those memories with anyone. I think I ended up in an insane asylum once.

"You did," he assures me. "I would prefer that not happen again."

"Me, too."

"You have more questions."

"So many. Is it okay? You can obviously read my thoughts."

He smiles. It's so weird. Death smiling should be weird, but the weird part is how right it feels. "It is more than okay. You still need to voice your thoughts and hear my answers. I understand."

I'm bursting at the seams. Where to start?

"Work your way backwards," he suggests.

Oh, okay. Brilliant plan. "So, you don't prefer morticians?"

He laughs again, and I laugh, too.

Then, I immediately slap my hand over my mouth, glancing at the body on the bed.

"It's okay. You are not being disrespectful. She is already gone."

Even from Death, that doesn't relieve my guilt. "Don't you need to go, too? I've kept you for so long as it is."

He smiles again. This one makes my heart feel as though it's leaping from my chest. "Time is a constraint you bear, not me. If it makes you feel better, I've already carried her soul to where it belongs. I'm here with you, yet I'm not. I'm doing my job all over the planet. Perhaps I should allow you to continue to do yours. Alert the nurses' station. File your paperwork. Call for the funeral home. I will wait for you. When you are done, we will talk more."

I hate to press the issue, but... "Are there more inhabited planets than just this one? Aren't you Death in galaxies that my human mind can't even fathom?"

He touches the tip of his finger to the tip of my nose. Another strange thing for Death to do. "The other planets have other gods they believe in. I am not needed there."

No, I suppose not. I feel it in my bones. He's needed *here*. With me.

~~~

Death is eating a donut at 3am in New York City.

Throughout the memories I have of my former lives, I've never even thought about such a strange combination of events.

"So, you need food and drink just like us?" I stare at the very male form sitting across from me in the booth at an all-night café. His biceps bulge against his soft, worn-looking black t-shirt. His hair is black, his eyes ice blue, and there's just enough stubble on his strong jaw to suggest a delightful scraping sensation should he brush against my sensitive skin with it.

"No."

"Does this current human male form need it?"

"No. This form is an illusion. That's something the Hindus got right. Everything is *maya*." He licks the glaze from his masculine fingers.

How strange. He looks real enough. His hand on my shoulder at the hospice facility felt real. The waitress who took our order didn't think I was talking to myself, even though my fellow nurses at the hospice facility couldn't see the man waiting in the shadows for me to be done with my shift. "You mentioned you're not here with me even though it seems to me like you are."

"That is correct." He takes a swig of coffee.

Black. As expected. Maybe only because *I* expect it.

"Why are you eating if you don't need to? I might be human, but I've managed to wrap my head around everything you've told me so far."

He stretches on his side of the booth, extending his long legs beneath the table until his feet brush against my own. The contact sends an electric jolt of awareness through me that I must not have experienced in any life before. I would surely remember that.

"Humans bond over food and drink. I am giving you what you desire."

Hardly. All I desire right now is him in my bed. Naked. I don't care if it's an illusion.

My cheeks flame as he grins. "Not quite yet, Beloved. First you must choose. You can't do that until I've answered all your questions."

"Beloved?" That flame settles lower in my belly.

He nods, a softer smile replacing the wolfish grin. "It feels good to finally admit that. Your given name will change, but your soul never will. You are my Beloved, regardless of the form you take."

"Just as you are mine?"

"No. Not necessarily. You are actually freer than I will ever be. Now, ask your questions."

There's a pattern in his words I can't ignore. Beloved, freedom, choices, lovers. I go back to his original suggestion to work my way back. "Why don't you prefer morticians?"

He laughs. This time the entire cosmos seems to sigh in relief instead of jolt from shock. "Because I've already claimed the souls of the bodies they work with. I'm not around morticians much."

"Yet you knew I tried being one once to bring you to me. I've also been a medical examiner, a grave digger several times, a cemetery guardian many times. Why did you never reveal yourself to me then? Why now?"

He reaches out his hand to tentatively brush against my own. Almost like he fears me more than I fear him. Once again, my skin feels electrified yet also comforted. "I have been with you since the Middle Ages. There was something about your soul that pulled me, called to me. I couldn't explain it. It honestly concerned me. I am more timeless than you can imagine, and I had never noticed your soul before."

"How timeless are you?" The breath rushes from my lungs, tugged along with the words. I fear this answer and all the repercussions it may bring.

"Since shortly after Creation." He withdraws his hand, obviously sensing my dread.

"God created you, too?"

"No. You did."

"I did?"

"Humans," he clarifies. "Since the very first death, they needed an embodiment for the end of life. I am it."

"Only humans on this planet created you? Aliens on other worlds have other versions of Death?" I'm skirting what I'm afraid to ask, and he knows it.

He smirks and gives me the time I need to adjust. "Other beings have other needs and different existences. I fear I can't adequately explain that to you."

I nod, accepting some things aren't for me to know. "Why here? Why now? Why not before? You said you've been with me for centuries. You didn't reveal yourself to me when you first became aware of...my soul."

He frowns. The sounds of city life, even in the middle of the night, suddenly seem more violent, louder. "Humans have this vast impression that I reside amidst the dead and decaying, but really I am with the living as they are dying. Perhaps I didn't notice you before the Bubonic Plague because we simply didn't cross paths. There has never been more death in such a short span on this planet for humans.

Perhaps your soul did not exist before then. I suspect the latter."

"You suspect? I know you said you're not God, but you obviously know more than a mere human."

"That's true," he acknowledges. "I am not human, so I am not constrained by the limits of human understanding. I am also not God. I am constrained by Death's knowledge, which is greater than yours but less than God's."

I nod. That all makes sense, but it's still not an answer. "Why now?"

"How much am I allowed to tell her?" His illusive lips don't move, and the voice I've come to associate with his form changes to something greater. Yet I'm acutely aware that he's allowing me to hear his question to someone other than us. *Something* other than us.

"You may tell her what you know she can handle."

My heart stops for a split second. I don't breathe. I've been given a peek behind the veil, and it's terrifying yet validating. The essence of my being wars with the duality of it all.

"Was that...was that *God*?"

"No," he chuckles. "You definitely could not handle that."

"So, that's something the Jews got right," I guess.

"Yes. Every religion gets a bit of it right and a lot of it wrong."

This doesn't surprise me in the slightest.

He doesn't wait for me to repeat the question that he undoubtedly knows is playing on a loop in my head. "I didn't know you were mine before. I didn't know why I was drawn to your soul. I didn't know God created you for me."

"I never would have guessed Death needed companionship." As much as I felt like I knew Death before, it was nothing like this. Is it wrong that I'm a little bitter about being created solely for him? I feel the truth, but it doesn't necessarily bring me the relief his revealed presence does.

"I'm an anthropomorphism of the end of life for this world. I assume the form you believe me to be, whomever *you* is. I'm not a constant essential existence like God. I wasn't even fully aware of my own shortcomings until very recently. I suppose because I am a creation of humankind, I am also bound by some of the same needs."

He's told me secrets of the universe that people spend all their lives trying to prove, and yet I cannot wrap my head around the idea that Death isn't as all-powerful and omniscient as I once believed.

He smiles in response without me voicing these thoughts aloud.

"You're not offended?"

"Not at all," he reassures. "If anything, I'm offended it took this long."

"What did?"

"Being told about you, being allowed to speak to you. I wasn't even sure if I could touch you in any form." He frowns again at this.

"So..." Screw it. I'm saying it. "You're not like the stories of all the Ancient Greek Gods, just floating around Earth, knocking up any mortal woman who interests you?"

"Ah." He taps his index finger against the table. "Now, we are getting somewhere. This is what has really been troubling you all along."

"Yes," I admit. Aloud. "You said it doesn't bother you for me to take lovers in any life. Am I also supposed to be okay with you taking lovers whenever and wherever you are?"

A hint of flame appears to thaw his eyes. "You are jealous of something that has never happened. I'm surprised how much this pleases me."

Death feels emotion. Who knew?

"Not me," he admits as a response to my silent question. "To answer your previous question, no. You needn't worry about me taking other lovers. The Greek Gods are...well, they are what they are."

"I'm not sure I know what the Greek Gods are anymore. I know what I learned in school, what I read about them. Yet you're nothing like I imagined. Minus the hot guy part, obviously."

He cracks a smile at that. It doesn't last long. "Your mind is running away from you. This is too much. I apologize."

He says it with such finality that panic seizes me.

"No, no! Don't leave!"

"I never truly leave. I am always here and always in the Other Places. I am always collecting souls and always with your soul." His frown grows deeper. "No matter how much I tried to shake off this pull, to let you live your lives alone, I have been unable to sever our connection. Now, I know why."

"You know I've had other lovers," I muse out loud, trying to organize my rampant thoughts. "I've always known you, and yet I haven't. Not like this. Is that what you meant about me being freer than you? I can choose to sever our connection, but you cannot?"

"Yes."

That seems unfair, especially knowing other Gods actually exist and are apparently free to make decisions about their romantic interludes.

"We have both been placed in an unfair position, I'm afraid," Death murmurs.

"Because my soul was created just for you?" Bitterness creeps up my throat, mingling with the flavor of the coffee that I sip for no other reason than to calm myself.

"Yes. I have no soul. I was not created by God, and I was not created for you, specifically." He inches his finger across the table to touch my hand again. Just the barest contact. Once again, there's no denying the truth of what his touch makes me feel even if it is only an illusion.

I stare at our joined illusions. "You said Death does not share the needs of humans. Does that mean you don't feel this?"

~~~

"Not in the same way you do," I answer her honestly.

Hades warned me that full honesty wasn't necessarily the best policy, but I feel responsible for this soul. For the way it's been trapped in the cycle. All because of me.

I may not feel the same sensations she does, but ever since revealing myself to her I feel...peace.

Death needs peace, too.

The gods are laughing at me even now.

Except *the* God. He's just smiling benevolently like He always does.

I sort of hate that. I want to prove Him wrong.

Prove that I can be more than just Death.

But, I know I can't. He knows it, too. I am bound by the beliefs of the humans who created me. Just like I am bound to the soul that God created for me.

Her mind is desperately trying to break free of its own particular constraints. She's trying so hard to reconcile what her soul already knows with what her humanity can never understand.

This does not please me nearly as much as her jealousy. "Your body grows tired. It needs rest. Come. Let me take you home."

She physically jolts from her thoughts. "You...you want to come home with me? Didn't you say that I had to choose first?"

I don't want to tell her that she's already chosen. She doesn't accept it for herself yet, and I'm still not convinced it's true. "You don't have to choose rest and comfort. I can provide that for you anyway."

I provide the money for our food and drink to give her a tangible example of what I am able to do for her.

Her eyes widen. Her thoughts are so loud.

Do Gods use money? Do they need it? Is it even real? Is this like stealing? Is money an illusion, too?

I detest being the bringer of her suffering. Wrapping my arm around her shoulders to lead her out into the city at night eases her anxiety. "Money and wealth are the biggest illusions of all."

"Some humans know that," she mumbles into my shoulder as she shields her face from the wind.

"Some do, yes." Humans are so much more powerful than they realize. "The longer a soul stays in the cycle of birth and death, the wiser they become."

"If my soul has been around so long, then why do I still have so many questions?" She yawns. More and more I'm supporting her weight against me. She isn't concerned about the illusion of it all just now.

"Even the souls who have achieved the peak of this existence can never understand everything."

"What happens then? When a soul reaches the peak of this existence?"

"It's complicated." She's too tired to process more, and I don't want to answer in a way that will lead her to the inevitable conclusion. That she has already achieved the peak, and she can be free of this cycle—of me—anytime she chooses.

I can be selfish for a short amount of her time in this life. I'm not ready to part with this very finite peace in the near-infinity of my existence.

Her exhaustion allows her to surrender fully to the illusion of my presence. I unlock her door without the key, perform the domestic rituals that allow her to relax—mundane tasks like feeding the cat she never told me about, setting the coffee maker for in the morning, turning off the lights, and re-locking the door.

She watches me through it all with half-lidded eyes and a half-smirk of mirth.

I'm too tired to even get ready for bed.

It's clever, this soul of mine. She thinks exactly what she wants me to know already. She's testing the boundaries of my powers without specifically asking for a display of them.

I've brought her so much bad; I would like to be the harbinger of good.

She blinks at the feel of the cooler air of her apartment on her naked skin. Runs her tongue across her teeth that feel freshly brushed. Lifts a hand to her face that feels already washed and moisturized.

"I'm not all powerful, but I do have power."

What else can you do?

She already knows what else she wants me to do.

She sinks further into the illusion and into my embrace in her bed. Relishes for a few precious moments in the feel of my naked body against hers beneath the cool, clean sheets.

"How can this feel so right, so real, when it's all an illusion? You're not even really here."

I'm dreaming this. I'm dreaming all of this.

I kiss her forehead because she needs me to. Needs the reassurance that while I might not be real in her sense of the word, I am very real nonetheless.

I must be more real than even I ever realized because I have never experienced anything so fulfilling. In all the eons of carrying souls to their final place of existence, all the times I have brought an end to suffering, I have never felt.

I have never truly *felt*.

I have so much more empathy for humans than I ever have before. They really are the most blessed of God's creation. To feel anything at all.

I surrender as much as I'm able to the illusion, too. Wrap her more tightly in my arms, almost ask her to describe to me what she feels, wish I could feel even a fraction of it, too.

God smiles more benevolently than ever.

The bastard. He's been teaching me a *lesson*. He's been showing me instead of telling me how to understand these creatures better. He's given me exactly the therapy I need. I have never lacked sympathy for their suffering. My entire existence is based on bringing an end to it. I have never empathized with what makes them wail when the inevitable end comes. Could never understand why—like my soul enveloped in my illusion of earthly arms—they didn't rejoice at breaking the chains of this miserable existence.

It's because they become attached.

Attached to things that aren't ever really theirs to begin with.

Attached in the way I can never fully be to this wise, old soul that knows exactly that.

She looks up at me with more unasked questions and pleading in her eyes. She wants me to belong fully to her in the same way she knows in her very essence that her soul belongs to me.

"I can't give you that, Beloved." I stroke her cheek with my finger, all too aware most humans do not recognize this simple gesture as the most intimate of all.

She does. She knows.

"I am not only yours to claim. Not in the way that you are mine."

"It's so unfair," she whispers.

It is. She doesn't know the half of it.

"Life is both unfair and the greatest blessing. You know this," I remind her.

"I know."

Her thoughts run wild again as she fights her exhaustion. She wonders what it would be like to choose me purposefully because she still doesn't know her soul chose me ages ago. She thinks I will appear and disappear as my schedule allows because she is constrained by the human bonds of time and physical presence. She questions what it would be like to make love to Death because her body has physical needs and wants so long as she is trapped in this cycle of birth and death.

"Not yet. Not until you know everything. I can give you a taste to help better inform your decision."

She opens her mouth to give voice to the questions dancing in the existence between us, but I selfishly place my hand on her chest.

The beating of a human heart is no stranger to me. Hers is magnified like the sound of God even to my immortal ears. To a human man, her breasts would be considered desirable and among the best females have to offer.

I have been drawn to her in all her earthly forms. This is only a fraction of the pleasure I can give to her that I can never receive.

She should have some perks for being Death's soul after all. The risks far outweigh the benefits.

The breath rushes out of her chest as her nerves dance and sing in a way that she's never experienced before. No lover who came before me or who might come after me will ever be able to make her feel this way even though it is not by the method her human body is familiar with.

I'm careful not to give her too much, not to overload her frail body with shock. Her eyes are wide nonetheless as she stares at me, those perfect human breasts heaving with labored breath even as her muscles pool in complete relaxation like she's never felt before.

"That was a *taste*?"

My human form laughs because my very being does, too. "Choosing me has rewards, but it also has drawbacks."

"What are the rewards?" She's still breathless.

If I could feel pride, I would be proud. Maybe I am. Only God knows.

"My human form escorting you home through the city in the middle of the night was an illusion, yes, but your soul is protected so long as you are mine. You will never come to harm if you choose me. Never experience some of the suffering others will. Your every earthly need will be provided for and your wants as well, so long as they conform to the nature of your soul."

"What does that mean?" She cuddles her body closer to mine, recovering from the high of her earthly pleasure, desiring to be closer to another body as humans are created to do.

"It means that you will never have to worry about money or food or shelter, but you will still work because your soul will always care for and minister to the dying. Because you were created for me, to be attractive to me."

Her mind struggles to comprehend this. "What if I choose to be a teacher in my next life? You said I have the freedom to choose."

"This is true, but you're also an old enough soul to recognize that souls have callings. Your soul is not called to be a teacher. You have never been drawn to that profession. You have always cared for the dying, about making the transition from this life into the next easier."

"What are the...drawbacks?"

She's imagining such human things. The inability to have children, to have a normal, loving family, to hide me from her peers the way she's learned to hide her memories of her past lives. She fights to understand how I will appear to her if she lives her next life as a transgendered man. What I would mean to her as a mere infant. As a teenager with raging hormones.

I laugh again at her thought she could easily use me as a relief from said hormones.

"The teenage years memories have stuck with me through all my lives. They were never easy," she defends.

"No. They are not. Life is hard."

Therein lies the crux of the matter. No harm will befall her, true, but she will still be chained to her humanity.

I stroke her hair and am surprised to find it brings me comfort. Perhaps I am falling prisoner to this illusion more than I knew I was capable of.

That cannot be allowed. I've been given far more reprieve than ever. Surely, there are limitations even God cannot grant.

I position our bodies until she's at my eye-level, then wrap my hands around her shoulders. I kiss her with all the passion she's ever imagined is possible but has never experienced. She needs to smell, see, feel, taste, hear me, so that she can understand the full meaning of my words.

She's breathless again when I release her lips.

"If you choose me, you will be chained to this human existence. You will be a dependent babe, a hormonal teenager, a frail old human for all time. You will die and pass out of every life your soul inhabits according to the constraints of time and your physical body. You will watch friends and fellow humans suffer. You will always be called to care for the dying in all their misery." I take a deep breath which I can *feel* even through the illusion. "Your soul will be a prisoner here until the end of time."

She doesn't push me away. Not even her mind rebels against this revelation.

"What happens after the end of time?"

"I don't know."

She doesn't slap me for my insouciance. For my lack of all-powerful omniscience. She smiles. "I know, I know. You're Death, not God."

"I'm Death. Not God," I confirm again.

She tips her head to the side in contemplation but doesn't recoil from my embrace. "Why did you reveal this to my frail human mind? It seems a lot for a mere mortal to comprehend. Why not just entice me with all the benefits and leave off the risks? I would never have known any better on my own."

"Because I love you," I breathe.

I *breathe.*

"I want you to have this choice. I want what is best for you, and what is best for you is not necessarily best for me. I cannot even share in the pleasure I gave you."

She places her hand on my cheek which she understands is real to her but not real to me. "And yet you gave me that pleasure anyway. I can be your respite, Death. I can be your peace. I can serve my fellow human until the end of time."

"Why?" What a marvelous thing for a human to say. I can barely comprehend it. "Why would you do that for me when I have so little to offer you? Why would you chain yourself to humanity in service to people who are capable of locking you away in an insane asylum?"

She pats my cheek. Such a human gesture. "Maybe what the gods don't understand that some of us old souls do is that...God is love. Existence is love. That is our greatest choice. It may come with great cost, but there is no greater reward."

This soul is too good for me. "You were created *for me*. That bothers you. I know it does."

"It does," she admits. "In a way. What happens if I refuse? What happens if I don't choose you?"

I hate to admit this, but she's given me so much. "I'm not sure. Either another soul is created that has free will to choose me or refuse me, or...the end of time. Once humans no longer believe in souls, all time will cease to exist. Apparently, many souls were created who refused me before you. Maybe the cycle will simply repeat itself. Or maybe I will disappear like the gods of ancient times."

"So, I have power over Death?"

This is not an actual question. She understands the answer.

"Yes."

"Hmm." She's already made up her mind. "Then, I have power over Life."

"You have no idea how much power you have."

"Oh, I think I have an idea."

She kisses Death.

Requiem Of Sorrow

By Jocelyn Minton (CONTENT WARNING: *death, homophobia, grief, near death*)

I sat staring at the letter, one of many in the box of previous exchanges between Heather and me. The only thing different about this letter was the fact that it had never been opened. This letter was addressed to me for a specific moment. I was only to open it once she had passed, only then would I be able to read those words. Now. That moment had come, and the irony of it all is that I wish she were here with me. I took the letter opener, engraved with our initials H and W, and broke the seal that held the envelope closed.

The sound of the paper tearing against the blade was the loudest sound in the room, almost louder than the ringing in my ears. But no, that noise couldn't be heard by anyone but me, and there was no one else in the apartment to hear it anyway. Heather and I used to have a pet cat together, but things had gotten too expensive so he now lived with her mother a couple of hours away. With shaking hands, I took the note from the envelope and slowly unfolded the page.

When the time comes to say fare thee well, leave me among the wildflowers.

I held back a sob as her handwriting bore its way into my mind. She had spoken her last words to me weeks ago. Her body was thin, pale, and broken. Heather's arms had been bruised from the countless needles that poked and prodded her, either for tests or to administer medicine. The Heather that had spoken to me weeks ago was a completely different woman than the one I married. My love for her endured, but the hard truth about losing someone to chronic illness is that, sometimes, you lose them before you lose their body. Illness has a way of capturing the mind before anything else. In the end, the person you say goodbye to is completely different from the one before the diagnosis.

Lay me under a tiger-striped sky, surrounded by that wild mountain thyme.

During my final visit to the hospital, she hadn't been able to smile.

Neither had I, not genuinely that is. Every smile I had produced over the last two months had all been a guise, something to give her a bit more hope. Something to let her know that it was okay. I understood. I knew that she wouldn't be able to fight for much longer. She did too. Perhaps that was why she wrote this letter, she knew she could no longer provide me with the hope I needed.

There wasn't much left to be said, her family had stopped in a week ago to say their goodbyes. My family refused to see us on account of their old-fashioned views of the way the world should work. Something about the Bible distinctly saying that Adam and Eve had been created for each other, and two women could never share a love deep enough to survive a marriage. Everything that needed to be said from either family had been. All that was left was comforting her in her final hours.

We listened to music and laid in the hospital bed together. The nurses brought us pudding, but neither of us ate. We only wanted to spend time with each other. Besides, the chemotherapy often made it hard for Heather to keep food down. It was the early hours of morning when Heather woke me up from restless sleep. She looked exhausted, but there was something like contentment in her face. As if she knew something the rest of us were unaware of, as if she knew years from now I would heal and learn to love again. She knew then and there that she would leave me.

"Life isn't worth living without those you love Winnie," She rasped from her side of the bed.

I couldn't respond, I could feel that we only had a few minutes left, and I knew she understood everything I needed her to know. That's how it had always been between us. There was a silent connection, neither of us needed to talk to know what the other was feeling. I was thankful for that connection then. During the time when my tongue couldn't forge the words she needed to hear, she understood everything.

"You belong somewhere you feel free and loved. I know you can't be close to me for much longer, but go. Run away from your sorrow, don't let it consume you. Be free. Find love again, and know that part of me is always with you. Always will be."

Tears streamed down my face as I took in what she was telling me. She was giving me permission to live after all this. After years of fighting a battle we both knew would end this way, she still wanted me to continue on and live a life she knew she wouldn't be able to witness. She was so sure that everything would be fine. And she knew if she hadn't told me directly, I would have never moved on. I would be stuck in a pit of grief mourning her for eternity.

Sing me novels, and remember our time on your favorite Florida key.

The illness was a silent ghost. It perched on her shoulder and fed from her like a parasite. Once we figured out what it was, there wasn't much left to do but relieve the pain and let the sickness run its course. It's a shame that her particular brand of cancer was hard to detect until later stages when symptoms emerged. At first, all I could focus on were statistics. How unfair it was that she had been part of a small percentage. 'Til death do us part.

The vows we had spoken to one another on our wedding day were promises we kept. No matter how unfair it was that death had picked her soul from the billions of others, we held true to our word. Through therapy sessions at the local hospice center, and nights sitting by the toilet until four in the morning, and the grief of losing someone who had still been alive. We were there for each other the entirety of it all. I'm not sure if she knew how much she had been there for me, even in her weakest moments.

Our wedding had occurred on one of the smaller keys at the tip of the peninsula. Florida had always been our home. Even though neither of us had grown up in the state, we met one another there. Our relationship bloomed through everglades, and Disney World, and cups of café con leche. Even though neither of our families supported the decision to marry, the wedding was my fondest memory. Seeing her walk down the beach toward the podium where our mutual friend stood to marry us was a picture that would forever be etched in my memory.

I remember long nights on the beach, staring at the stars and wondering about the life we had ahead of us. Did the stars know when she would leave? Had the universe destined us to meet, only for it to decide to split us apart as some cruel joke? Perhaps they were in fact all-knowing, maybe that was the essence of their beauty. Those nights on the beach where we read each other passages from our favorite novels and ate strawberries and champagne were magical. Why would the universe choose to destroy that? In the end, did it even have a choice or was it too under fate's control?

When the time comes that my spirit cold is gone to rest, remember clementine, come away to the water, follow the rivers and roads, they'll lead you back to me.

My eyes looked over that sentence once more. How could she have known so much? She was only 30. It was as if her soul had lived ages before it entered her body. As if she chose a vessel that would allow her to do the work she needed, and once it was done, she was gone.

Heather had been a whirlwind of energy. Everything she did, she gave one hundred and ten percent. She left her mark on those around her, and since she died the chasm in my heart seemed to continue to crack and grow with grief in the fact I would never know her presence again. I would never be able to live up to her beauty, her elegance, her purpose.

Don't cry for me darling Winnie.

- Your Hopeless Wanderer.

My chest hurt. It was as if my heart was so full of emotion that it needed to be released to expel the pain it felt. A black stain of grief had splattered upon my soul, and I wasn't sure it would go away. Even though I had heard the phrase "time heals all wounds" I was unsure how time would heal a loss so deep. This wasn't a loss that affected only my emotions. No, this loss permeated the space around me. It suffocated my being until I couldn't stand pushing it away, until I needed to confront it.

~~~

She had told me to go to the water, that I would find her there. It had to mean something. It had to be a final way of communicating something to me. Heather never did anything that didn't have meaning. I had to believe in this. If I didn't believe in this, then nothing else in this life was going to be worth it. I had read the letter, and with it went the final words she would ever speak to me. Nothing new would come from her soul.

I checked my watch, 6:43 AM. It was wintertime so the sun hadn't yet emerged from the horizon. Frantically, I found my coat, a go-bag that contained the basic sailing gear I would need, and the letter. I closed my door to the apartment but didn't bother locking it, I wouldn't be gone for long, and anything that was in there only brought back painful memories anyway.

The drive to the marina wasn't long, and it was even shorter due to the fact that there was nobody else on the roads. A wandering soul alone in the dawn.

As I made my way onto the Catamaran I threw my bag toward the seat in the cabin below. I untied the lines from the cleats on the dock that kept the boat in place and motored my way toward the open water of the ocean.

It was probably, no definitely, idiotic to sail on the ocean water without checking the weather, but I needed to do this. I needed to make sure that I was still connected to her. She said to go to the water. I was frantic and caught up in a frenzy of emotions, nothing would get in the way of the small sliver of hope that I would feel connected to her again. One last time.

Once I had motored out of the Intercoastal Waterway and made it to the open ocean, I opened the sails and let the wind guide my boat where it wanted. I trusted that I would know when I was in the right spot.

The sky was now a muted green color. The sun still hadn't breached the line of the horizon, but as the sky lightened, the earth awoke. Birds began to sing, a pod of dolphins made their way toward the surface investigating the strange moving vessel next to them, and humans made their way to work, school, or play.

After about half an hour the color of the sky turned a deep blue. The sun had risen but wasn't visible behind the dense wall of clouds that blocked it. I moved from my place at the front of the deck toward the helm. The digital camera that allowed me to see the depth of the water also showed weather patterns. It looked like a storm was coming. I could feel my emotions swell along with it. Throughout the months of sailing courses we had taken, Heather and I still hadn't faced a storm without the presence of a licensed captain aboard.

I hadn't realized how far from land I had sailed until I looked around and saw nothing nearby. I was quite literally, in the middle of nowhere. Hurriedly, I grabbed my radio to try to contact the mainland, but the storm had messed with the signals. There was no way to communicate with anyone on land, and no one had been notified of my current whereabouts. I was alone, in the middle of the ocean, about to confront a storm that looked brutal.

I took a deep breath to gather my thoughts. Heather and I had sailed through a few storms together. We were each good at dividing and conquering our tasks, but this time it was going to be up to me to do everything. I decided that the best course of action would be to return from where I had traveled, but the direction of the wind had changed, so it would be difficult to navigate back home.

Rain began to pour and I cursed under my breath. Once the rain started, that would mean it would be more difficult to maintain the direction the sail needed to face since the deck would be slippery. Not to mention the rocking of the boat due to the swells and waves crashing against the hull. All that mattered at this point was that I made it back to land, even if I was miles away from the marina the boat was normally docked at. I knew how harsh the ocean could be, I respected it. During my time sailing with Heather, we both had learned how strong the waves could be. Part of our training was learning about boats that had capsized. Which is why I never intended to be caught in a storm alone.

As the winds grew stronger, I knew that I would need to take down the sail. The gusts were becoming too large, and any more force would cause the boat to be at a hazard for going off course or ruining my perfectly good sail. As I grabbed the line to bring the sail back in, a huge gust of wind made its way into the fabric. My gloveless hands became raw at the force of the line being pulled from my palms. The boat was old and didn't have the proper equipment to help hold the line in place, everything aboard this ship was done by hand. Wincing in pain, I looked at the damage. Skin had been ripped raw, and the throbbing sensation could be felt along with the heat and pain. I cried not knowing what I would be capable of accomplishing now.

This was bad. A storm like this could come and go extremely fast, but in its wake would be a trail of destruction. I didn't want to be a part of the statistics. I didn't want to be known as the stupid sailor who got caught up in their emotions. After retrieving the line once more, I tried my best to pack the sail into its bag and secure it once again to the mast. Since I wouldn't be able to travel by wind, I would need to use my motor to get back to safety.

The waves continued to grow larger. White water crashed into the deep blue and ocean debris could be seen getting washed onto the boat. Thunder rumbled throughout the clouded sky, and I could see bolts of lightning in the distance. As my nerves spread throughout my body, I went under to the cabin to grab a flotation device, it was the only measure of safety that I could take right now.

As I was in the cabin a wave crashed above me. The boat lurched to the side and I rammed my body into the bed that was in the cabin, luckily I wasn't hurt, but it was becoming more and more obvious that this was a stupid idea to have come out here alone and already in a state of distress. I cursed myself for being so stupid. Heather wouldn't have wanted to watch me die like this. She told me herself that she wanted to see me live, to be happy again.

Another gust of wind and a large wave hit the boat at the same time. I could feel the way the body tilted and tilted. Until it fully turned on its side and upside down. I held my breath as I began to accept what was happening. I was stranded at sea. No one knew where I was, and they wouldn't know to come looking for me until it was too late. My parents didn't care anymore, and they were too uninvolved in my life to be any help for emergency services.

Even though fear tugged at my mind, I finally realized what Heather had felt in her final moments. The clarity that entered my mind was peaceful. I still had so much to live for. As water began to flood the cabin I looked for things that would be useful once the storm had passed. I found the emergency flotation device we kept stored under one of the seats. It was bright orange, and had a sun cover so I wouldn't get burned. The color would help emergency services find me against the blue water. I also grabbed one of the bags that contained a small bit of rations and a first aid kit.

Wading through the water I made my way back toward the storm. I had to face this. My life would be worth nothing if I didn't continue to fight. It would be worth nothing if I didn't continue to live. I grabbed the line that was hooked around one of the cleats to secure the fenders. This would be able to help me grab onto anything that I might need later on. I could tie the emergency dinghy to the boat so I wouldn't go farther away from land.

My plan was set into motion as I pulled the tab that opened the dinghy. It quickly inflated and I threw my supplies into the seat. After securing the line to the boat, I climbed in and waited. All that was left now was to ride out the storm. Alone. With my thoughts. I reflected on my life, memories of my childhood and young adulthood. I remembered my relationship with Heather. The time we had spent together was short, but it had impacted me greatly. She had taught me how to live my life to the fullest. When she left, it was like she took a part of me with her, but now I realize that she had given me a part of herself to keep forever. I wanted to live. I wanted to be happy again. I wanted to make Heather happy.

When the storm had passed I unzipped the door to the dinghy. I could see that the damage done to my boat was irreparable, but it didn't matter. What mattered now was finding a way back to land. Because the boat was only partially submerged, I could see that the radio was still accessible above water. I pulled the bright orange floatation device toward the boat and boarded it.

"This is Wanderer reporting that assistance is needed. My boat got caught up in the storm and capsized. Coordinates are unknown, the map on the ship is broken. We sailed out from Conch Harbor Marina heading south at about 7 AM this morning. I repeat this is Wanderer reporting for assistance." I spoke through the mic.

Static was heard on the other side of the line for a few minutes. I repeated the call two more times before I heard someone respond.

"Wanderer, this is the United States Coast Guard. We are confirming your quest for assistance and have boats looking for you now. Do you have a flare available to use?"

"Yes sir, I can find one and set it out now. Thank you"

Relief flooded my body. I was going to be okay. Heading back to the dinghy I found a flare gun in the emergency first aid kit. It was standard practice for most boating kits. I took the gun and made sure that the flare wasn't damaged before firing it toward the sky. About thirty minutes passed before I was picked up. After making sure that I didn't need medical treatment we made our way back toward the mainland.

My experience through the storm left me a lot of time to think about Heather's death. I think I finally figured something out: the difference between grief and acceptance is peace. Both are painful. Both are exhausting expressions of emotion, and honestly neither ever end. But having peace to combat the grief makes things digestible. It allows us to realize that everything will be okay.

Once I returned to land I made sure to renew my captain's license. I went to therapy, reconnected with friends, and even went on a few dates. In honor of Heather, I now teach underprivileged children how to sail. Every day I spend working with kids who are struggling with their own battles. I hope that my work with them helps them just as much as their stories help me.

Three years passed after I first opened that letter. Every year I return to the harbor. I buy a bottle of rum, pour myself a glass, and pour a little bit into the ocean.

"Thank you. Thank you for challenging me and giving me a reason to live again. Tell Heather I said hi." I whisper.

Sometimes it feels like the breeze whispers back. Always a gentle, "You're welcome."

Make A Wish

By Carrie Godfrey

There were a lot of things about being an adult that Amelie wished she could unsubscribe from the same way she did newsletters in her inbox. Paying bills wasn't great. Working overtime to finish a project at work kind of sucked, too. But when that overtime was going to make her late for her own birthday party? Well, that's it. She wanted to be done with adulting. Thanks so much.

Except she couldn't just curl up in her bed with a glass of wine and watch bad made-for-tv movies with her cat because if she missed the birthday party her mother was throwing for her? Amelie would never hear the end of it. The last thing she wanted was to be subjected to the pitying stares from everyone when they asked about her love life (which was honestly none of their damn business anyway) and she said that, no, she was still single.

Dating was hard.

A lot harder now at forty-two than it had been when she was in her twenties and not because she was forty-two. It was just harder to meet people. Clubbing wasn't her scene anymore (waking up hungover with knees that hurt from dancing had lost its appeal for some reason) and who had time to play Nancy Drew at a bar to figure out if the woman seated at the other end with the Doc Martins and a flannel shirt was actually a lesbian or just trying to be trendy? Never mind the blind dates her friends set her up on. It was honestly exhausting, and she needed a break.

Reaching around to zip up her skirt, Amelie turned back toward the bed to grab her sweater and huffed when she saw Horatio, all twelve pounds of gray and white fur and attitude, plopped down in the middle of it. It was her own fault, she figured with an eye roll, ignoring the cat's protests when she nudged him aside. She might have broken him of the habit of jumping on the kitchen counter after she adopted him from a shelter four years ago, but anything on the bed was fair game. It meant most of her clothes ended up with a fine layer of fur all over them. With how much Amelie spent on lint rollers, she really needed to invest in 3M stock.

Amelie slipped the sweater on and examined herself in the mirror. The cream color of her sweater managed to camouflage most of the fur she couldn't brush off. She fixed a few dark curls that had fallen out of the quick up-do she threw her hair up in when she got home, moving a few other strands to uncover more of the gray peeking through near her left temple. It had freaked her out a little when she first noticed the changing color, but it was growing on her.

"Don't get old," her mom had lamented once when Amelie was sixteen. What was the alternative? she remembered wondering, taking the statement seriously. Her mom hadn't appreciated her suggested solution, which teenaged-her had thought was worth the look of horror. She understood the sentiment now, at least more than she had then, but she couldn't complain too much.

So, her back hurt sometimes when she woke up, and climbing the hill to her apartment when she couldn't find parking in front of her building was harder than it used to be but getting older wasn't too bad. She leaned forward to touch up her lipstick and examined herself more critically. There were some lines at the corners of her eye, but they were barely noticeable. And, she thought, straightening to slip on her shoes and take in the whole outfit, smoothing the skirt over the ample curves of her hips, her legs were still fan-fucking-tastic.

It might be a little petty, but Amelie thought about throwing those long-ago words back in her mom's face. Call her up and say, "You told me not to get old, so my birthday is officially canceled." But as much as she might resent it— No one had consulted her about it and Geoffrey would be so disappointed —she was an adult, and she didn't want to have dressed up like this for nothing. Amelie grabbed her purse from beside the door and headed for her car.

Today had been her lucky day. She found a spot right in front of her building when she got home from the office and ran inside to take a quick shower. The few extra minutes she took getting ready shouldn't have mattered.

Except they did matter, and it was not her lucky day because when she got outside a Honda Civic that had seen better days was blocking her in. Amelie bit off a few choice curses and glared back at the building. The good news was that she knew who the car belonged to. She didn't know them know them, but she knew what apartment they lived in. Amelie didn't make it a point to talk to her neighbors, settling for exchanging awkward smiles if they ran into each other at the mailbox, and this particular neighbor and she had never crossed paths. But she'd heard the door to the downstairs apartment close and that same Honda Civic be parked out front.

"They never seemed to have trouble finding a spot in front of the building," she grumbled to herself and started marching up the concrete steps, keeping the door marked 3B in her sights like it was going to disappear if she stopped looking at it. Her knock echoed in the empty stairwell.

"Just a second," a voice called from somewhere inside the apartment and a moment later, the door was pulled open, leaving Amelie blinking at the person on the other side of the security door. Amelie didn't know what she expected, but the woman standing in front of her wasn't it. She was—gorgeous seemed like too tame of a word. She was tall, brown eyes shining behind a pair of tortoiseshell glasses, long braids swept over one shoulder. The multicolored overalls she wore under a chunky cardigan complimented her dark skin and brought to mind her art professor from college, except Professor Rose had more of a grandma vibe and hadn't had this effect on nineteen-year-old Amelie. That would have made class awkward.

And her smile...

Damn, Amelie thought, realizing when 3B furrowed her brow that Amelie had spoken the word out loud. She winced.

"Can I help you?" 3B asked around a laugh, still smiling, and not slamming the door in Amelie's face. Her voice was smooth and accented— English maybe? Amelie had to work to untie her tongue, feeling all of her earlier annoyance melt away.

"Sorry, um, I'm Amelie. I live in 3D," she pointed up to the second floor like the other woman wouldn't know where that was, "I hate to bother you, but you're blocking me in."

"I'm—" She was cut off by the shrill whistle of a tea kettle. It was a sound Amelie hadn't heard since she was a kid, when her mom would make hot cocoa. "Oh, bollocks," 3B said, rushing away from the door. "Why don't you come in? I just have to grab that."

Their apartments had the same layout, just reversed, but that was where the similarities ended. Amelie liked mid-century modern, mixed with things she picked up at antique stores. 3B's apartment was color and kitsch. Artwork on the walls, fluffy pillows, soft throws. Amelie hesitated at the door when the tips of her heels sunk into a plush rug.

"I'm kind of in a rush."

"Oh." 3B rounded the corner from the kitchen holding an honest to God teapot and it might have been Amelie's imagination that she sounded disappointed. "I was going to ask if you wanted a cuppa, but I don't want to keep you."

The offer was tempting, very tempting. But if she came in, she would take her shoes off and she would stay. Curl up on that comfy-looking monstrosity of a couch, have a cup of tea, maybe two.

Then Amelie would have to call her mom and explain why she stood up the entire family for her own birthday party. They might understand, but Amelie would feel bad, and wouldn't that be a great way to look back on her birthday? Besides, this might be nothing more than wishful thinking. She couldn't help it if her smile was a little melancholy when she said, "I have a party to get to and I'm already late."

Her eyes widened behind her glasses. "Fuck. Right, let me get my keys." She set the teapot down on a white pedestal table in the corner by the kitchen, a vase of flowers in the center on top of a lace doily, and headed for the back hallway that led to the bedrooms. She kept talking, her voice muffled by the walls. "I'm so sorry. I've been a bit distracted lately. I can be a bit of a tit."

Amelie felt helpless laughter bubbling up and tried to smother it behind her hand when 3B walked back into the living room with a sheepish smile. "I still forget you Americans don't use that word that way. My students thought it was hilarious the one time I let it slip in class."

"You're a teacher?" Amelie asked, following the other woman out the door.

"Art," she answered over her shoulder, tossing Amelie what could only be described as a cheeky grin, before rounding the back bumper of her car to unlock the door, since there wasn't any room near the front with the Civic sandwiched against Amelie's Outback—the whole reason the two of them were standing out here in the first place.

And just that fast, Amelie was free to leave. The other woman climbed out of her car and met Amelie where she stood by the driver's side door of her vehicle. This close, Amelie could tell just how much taller the other woman was, even with Amelie being in heels.

"Nice car," 3B said, leaning in close like they were sharing a secret. "I almost got a Subaru, but the deal I got on Burt was too good."

"Burt?"

"I named my car," she answered with a light shrug. "I name everything really. The teapot is Myrtle."

Well, that was adorable. Amelie fidgeted with her keys, stretching the silence out for an uncomfortable length of time, enchanted by the way the other woman adjusted her glasses. "I guess I should go," Amelie started at the same moment the other woman said, "My tea is getting cold."

They shared a laugh and Amelie unlocked her door. Before Amelie could climb inside, 3B said, "I'll see you 'round."

"I know where you live," she said with a wink then wished the ground would swallow her up. "Oh God, please forget I said that." Amelie had successfully flirted with women before, she swore she had.

"It's alright. It was only mildly creepy because it's true." Amelie could listen to the sound of her laugh forever.

As Amelie drove off, she could see 3B standing on the curb in her rearview mirror. It wasn't until Amelie hit the freeway that she realized she had never asked 3B what her name was.

"Shit."

~~~

"Happy birthday!" Claps and cheers filled her parent's dining room. You would think Amelie did something more impressive than age another year.

She rolled her eyes with feigned annoyance and fixed the party hat on her head before she leaned forward to blow out the candles on her cake. At least they hadn't put forty-two individual candles on the thing, opting for a brightly colored four and a two, sandwiched together.

"What'd you wish for?" Josephine, her oldest cousin Dan's seven-year-old daughter asked, leaning across the table on her knobby elbows.

"You can't tell," Amelie's mom tutted, walking in from the kitchen with plates and forks. "It's bad luck. It means it won't come true."

At least once a year, one of the kids (Amelie had like fifteen cousins so there was always a new baby) asked what someone had wished for, and her mom always said the same thing. She was superstitious that way and Amelie couldn't hold back her snort. It earned her a poke and she stuck out her tongue.

The happy, bickering chatter of her family surrounded her while her mom cut slices of cake and passed them out. Amelie smiled and nodded and ate cake. When cake plates were replaced with coffee mugs, she took hers out on the back porch and watched her cousin's kids play tag in the setting sun.

She didn't know how long she was standing there when she heard the sliding door open and her mom wrapped her up in a tight hug. "Are you alright? You seem distracted. Is it work?"

"No, work is fine," she waved off. It was great actually. Maybe being a marketing director wasn't her dream job, but she was good at it and she didn't dread going into the office every day.

"Ah, it's a girl then," her mom said with an air of certainty.

"What?" Amelie turned her head so she could meet her mother's eyes, blue the same shade that Amelie saw in the mirror. "How could you possibly know that?"

Her mom scoffed. "I've known you your entire life. Think I can't tell when you have a crush on someone?"

"I don't have a crush. Crushes are for fourteen-year-olds," Amelie said, but even to her own ears, she sounded petulant. She thought back to her freshman year of high school and how she had been so sure she was in love with Bethany Peters and they were going to get married. And how heartbroken she had been when she found out Bethany was dating the quarterback. This wasn't quite that level of teenage angst, but it was... something.

"Oh, sweetie, you're never too old," her mom leaned in close and dropped her voice to a conspiratorial whisper, "I get a crush on your dad every day."

"Gross! I don't need to hear about that," Amelie complained. But she thought it was sweet how in love her parents still were after fifty years of marriage. It kind of gave her hope that it was even possible.

"Without that you wouldn't be here," Amelie's mom reminded her with a mock glare. "I was in labor for ten hours—"

"I've heard the story, I know, I know," she surrendered with a laugh, holding up the hand that was mug-free. Amelie was pulled back into her mother's strong arms, a kiss pressed to her temple.

They lapsed into a comfortable silence. For all they had butted heads when Amelie was younger, being so similar, another thing that growing older had brought her was closeness to her mother that she cherished. Even when her mother stage-whispered, "When do I get to meet her?"

"Mom," she gasped, aghast but not surprised because Beverly

269

Thompson always cut right to the point, and turned wide eyes on the older woman. "I haven't even asked her on a date yet."

"Then you better hurry up."

~~~

When Amelie got home, the only parking spot she could find was almost two blocks away. She switched her heels for a pair of flip-flops she found in the backseat and started the climb up the hill back to her building, trying not to grimace at how sore her legs already felt after chasing the kids around the backyard during a game of tag. Maybe she needed to start forking over the extra money for a space behind the building, she thought with a sigh.

It was a perfect San Diego night, the breeze cool with the coming winter and smelling like the ocean. She let the quiet of the night settle around her, heels dangling from her fingers, swinging with the motion of her arm. When she mounted the steps that led to the stairwell to her apartment, she almost headed right upstairs like she always did, but her eyes were drawn to the door marked 3B.

Light was visible through the living room window and it was barely nine o'clock, but Amelie hesitated before thinking 'Fuck it' and knocking. If the knock went unanswered, Amelie figured she'd take it as a sign. They would run into each other doing laundry or getting their mail and exchange banal pleasantries.

It would be fine. Really, it would be. She was a big girl and it wouldn't be the end of the world, after all, she told herself.

Amelie still found herself letting out a breath of relief when she heard the door lock click and then there was 3B standing right in front of her again. The gut-punch feeling hadn't been a fluke. She felt her stomach swoop, a spontaneous smile curving her lips at the other woman's soft, surprised, "Hi."

"Hi," she echoed, realizing she hadn't thought about what to say if the door was answered. She went with, "I realized I didn't get your name. Before."

The wariness left the other woman's face, her posture relaxing as she propped one shoulder against the door jamb, braids brushing her shoulder when she tilted her head. "It's Edith."

Edith. It suited her somehow. Pretty, a little old-fashioned but still edgy. Edith had changed into a soft-looking pair of sweatpants and a worn SDSU t-shirt, feet covered in fuzzy socks, the edged of a tattoo peeking out from the sleeve of her shirt, and Amelie found herself thinking; *This. I want this.* She also saw the edges of tattoos peeking out from the sleeve of her shirt.

And Edith, still standing there, when it would have been understandable for her to tell Amelie to piss off, gave her the courage to ask, "Is the offer of tea still good?"

Edith's eyes widened behind her glasses and then she was stepping back, making room for Amelie to come inside. "Sure. Yeah. I'll put the kettle on."

When she got back to her apartment five hours later, cheeks hurting from smiling and laughing, warm from the Scotch they switched to after the teapot was empty ("My dad's family is Scottish," Edith told her when she pulled it from a cabinet along with two glasses, "So it's the good stuff."), Amelie leaned back against her front door, a giddy feeling welling up inside of her that she hadn't felt in she didn't know how long.

Horatio came padding out of the bedroom, giving Amelie an inquisitive meow when she slapped a hand over her mouth to contain a helpless giggle.

"I think I might have a girlfriend," she told him and didn't even care when he walked off, clearly uninterested in his human's affairs.

It didn't matter because she had a date with Edith next Friday.

This might turn out to be the best birthday ever.

I Really Can't Stay

By Monica Misho-Grems

Maria sat on Lincoln's couch as she watched the snow fall outside the floor-to-ceiling windows that overlooked Lincoln's backyard. It really started coming down hard as it accumulated on the patio. He'd lived in the house since before she moved in a few blocks away, many years ago.

Maria chose the small gated community with her fiance at the time, thinking it would be a great place to raise a family after they married. As it turned out, behind the white picket fences lay some of the nosiest neighbors she'd ever met in her entire life. She'd kicked his cheating ass out, and the whole neighborhood knew exactly what had been happening behind her back. It didn't help that her mother was the queen of gossip and lived three doors down from her.

Three weeks after she kicked her fiance out, Maria met Lincoln while rage-jogging in the nearby park. He inadvertently saved her from being run over by a bicyclist, one she hadn't seen coming. They'd been friends ever since, jogging together at least once or twice a week and having dinners at each other's house at least twice a month. They flirted constantly but never progressed past that, much to Maria's dismay. She enjoyed every second she spent with Lincoln, but the guilt she felt over the fact that they met so soon after she broke up with her fiance stopped her each time there was a chance for their friendship to become more. She was worried about what the neighbors might think.

With time to kill before her family's early Christmas celebration, she walked to Lincoln's house while the sun had been shining, but the temperature dipped below freezing. She prayed for snowfall all day. Winter was her favorite season; and snow her favorite weather. The memories she held near and dear to her heart happened in the winter; it was also likely because she had a winter birthday. Her mother used to call Maria a "snow baby", citing how every time it snowed she would stare out the window before peacefully falling asleep, curled up on the couch.

They spent her time that evening talking about the local football team, hoping against hope that they'd make it to the Superbowl. Given the team's win-loss record it was unlikely, but Maria often argued that Lincoln just needed to put better vibes out into the universe for them. Maybe they'd win more if he stopped trash-talking his favorite team. Lincoln's general reply would be that he's only hard on them because he cares, and that they've needed to replace their offensive coordinator for far too long.

She sipped on the boozy apple cider Lincoln handed her once she arrived, and had kept refilling since.

As Lincoln was in the kitchen preparing his own drink, Maria moved around the familiar room. She grabbed the wood and a firestarter - dryer lint mixed with petroleum jelly all stuffed in a recycled egg carton - from the box next to the back door and the matches from the bookshelf next to the fireplace. She set a firestarter in the middle of the fireplace and stacked some kindling on top, then lit it all with a match. The small flames danced as they began burning the thin pieces of wood, growing and growing. She added a couple of thicker pieces and dropped back onto her favorite spot on the couch, the corner next to the fireplace.

When Lincoln came back with a mug of his own, he sat on the floor in front of the fire next to Maria's legs. His shoulder brushed her knee when she readjusted herself to give him more room to sit. He smiled at how cozy she was in her knitted sweater, leggings, and thick wool socks. She never failed to make his heart flutter when she looked him in the eye. It made him wonder why they hadn't ever tried to be more than friends. They got along so well, never ran out of things to talk about and enjoyed each other's company. "Thanks for starting a fire."

"Of course! I mean, you keep your house at like 10 degrees, I had to do something to warm up!" she joked with him as she laughed.

"Hey, 68 degrees is the most energy efficient," Lincoln chuckled. He took another sip of his drink, the burn of the alcohol distracting him from the fuzzy feeling in his chest he got as he thought about Maria being right next to him.

"Maybe for a corpse, but I need heat to survive this terrible blizzard!" She glanced outside. "It may have stopped snowing but it's freezing. I think my toes may fall off, they're so cold." She stuck her sock-covered feet out in front of them both and wiggled her toes.

"Here, let me warm them up." He set his mug on the coffee table, scooted closer to her, and began to take her socks off.

Maria giggled when he pretended her feet stank. She shoved his shoulder and wiggled her toes, holding her feet out to be rubbed. The last time he'd given her a foot rub was two months ago when she'd twisted her ankle on a jog with him; she'd been trying to get another ever since.

When he hesitated she batted her lashes and stuck her bottom lip out in a ridiculous pout. He laughed and started massaging her feet.

Maria's head lulled back as she enjoyed his strong, warm hands working the sore spots on her feet. She sighed, wishing it would never end, but she knew it would soon, as she had a family dinner. "That feels so good, Lincoln," she hummed, her eyes closed and head resting on the back of his couch.

Lincoln watched her mouth form a small circle as he rubbed the balls of her feet. Lincoln could imagine the face she made when she was pleasured looked similar to how she looked then. Her eyes were closed, her face relaxed and peaceful, a little twist of sultry sexiness thrown in with her lips parting. Lincoln felt his cheeks flush and his whole body become uncomfortably warm next to the fire.

Lincoln frowned as his heart filled with guilt as the inappropriate thoughts of Maria writhing under him in pleasure filled his mind. *If she'd wanted anything more than friendship, it would have happened already. You know that, dumbass.*

Maria hummed as she picked her head up off the back of the couch. "As amazing as your hands feel, I have to go soon. My brother is in town, but only until tomorrow, so my family is having Christmas dinner today instead of actually having it on Christmas."

"Are you sure? It's cold outside," Lincoln said matter of factly. He selfishly wished she would stay. He knew her brother lived on the West coast and hardly got the chance to visit, but he couldn't help wanting her to be next to him all the time.

"I'm sure, they're probably already waiting on me." She pulled her feet back and held her hand out, waiting for him to hand her the socks he'd removed. She watched as he looked at her, then to her socks, then back to her. If she didn't know any better, she thought he looked like he didn't want to give her the socks back.

As he set them in her hand, her fingers brushed his, sending a shock through his body. Almost electric. His eyes met hers, hoping she'd felt the same thing, but the warm brown depths revealed nothing. "If you try walking home now, you could freeze," he grumbled. If she stayed just a little longer maybe he could build up the courage to actually make his move, to tell her how he felt.

"I've had such a great time with you, and the foot massage was so very nice." Maria pulled her socks on as she replied. If only there were more time before her family dinner. She desperately wanted to stay with Lincoln next to the fire, sipping their wintery drinks as they talked about football and the snow and anything that meant she wouldn't have to leave his side.

Lincoln knelt in front of her on both knees, grabbed her hand and held it gently in his. His thumb brushed her knuckles before he spoke. "Your hands are ice cold. Stay. Warm them by the fire." He was careful to keep his voice warm and inviting, the last thing he wanted to do was scare her off by not letting her leave.

"My mom will start to worry ...you know what a worry wart she is." Maria didn't pull away. Lincoln's hands were so warm around her own, they were melting her resolve to leave more and more every second.

"Elena knows you're safe with me. What's the hurry?" he asked as he moved to sit on the couch, still holding her hand.

"Well, I do have about half my drink left ..." her voice trailed off into silence. *Damn his warm hands and gorgeous eyes*. The mesmerizing pair kept Maria firmly rooted in place on the couch.

"I could pour you some more, warm you up before you go?" he asked, leaning in a little closer to Maria.

"Depends on what you put in that drink," Maria joked. She didn't pull away or look elsewhere. Maria never noticed how icy blue his eyes were before, a complete contrast to the warmth they were spreading through her body. *Wish I knew how to break this spell*, she thought. "I ought to say no, although I do love your cider."

Lincoln scooted just a tiny bit closer as he brought her hand to his lips. He pressed a kiss to each of her knuckles as he held her gaze. He watched as her cheeks turned a rosy pink. He released her hand from his gentle grip and pressed a kiss to each cold finger tip.

"I really can't stay." Maria swallowed, suddenly finding it hard to remember why she had to leave. "You've been so sweet, as always," she said as he brushed a piece of hair away from her face, their eyes still locked together.

Lincoln couldn't stop himself from looking down at her plump, glossy lips. They were so close, if he just leaned in a little closer he could see for himself if she wore flavored gloss or not. "Your lips look

... delicious," he whispered. The words he hadn't meant to say out loud seemed to have the effect he wanted, though. Her lips parted, as if they were inviting him in. Lincoln tried to resist, unsure of exactly what Maria was thinking, if she wanted him to kiss her. But he couldn't pass up what could be his only burst of courage, alcohol-fueled or not. He had to see if her lips tasted as good as they looked. He closed the small space between their lips and kissed her. Time stopped as their lips moved together in harmony. It was Lincoln who pulled away first. He knew he had to stop when he tasted her lip gloss. "Mango?" he asked after running his tongue over his bottom lip. He clenched his jaw and squeezed his eyes shut as he rested his forehead against hers. He had to regain control over himself before he devoured her in the very spot she sat in. *Mango fucking lip gloss.* Who knew that would be his undoing?

Maria's eyes were wide when they met Lincoln's again. She was having a hard time figuring out how she should feel. She wanted to be shocked and upset with what he'd done. He'd just smashed through the guise of friendship they'd carefully crafted for years, but she wanted him to do it again and not stop. She could feel her lips beginning to tingle as she hoped beyond hope he would kiss her again. "My brother is vicious, he'll make up stories if I'm late," she said as she looked down at Lincoln's lips then back up to his beautiful blue eyes. Maria rested her hand on Lincoln's stubbled, chiseled jaw. If he didn't kiss her again, she thought she might implode. All the feelings she kept at bay over the years were bubbling up and over the wall she'd hidden them behind.

He snaked his hand into her silky, brunette hair. She looked like she might pounce on him. The thought made his jeans uncomfortably tight. They both leaned in and their lips met again in an Earth-shattering kiss. Lincoln had to fist his hand in her hair to keep himself from floating out into the stratosphere. She was stealing his breath away. He may as well be in space.

It was Maria who stopped the second kiss, her breathing heavy as she kept a hand firmly placed against his muscular chest. They'd self-destructed right out of friendship and into oblivion. She wanted to care, but Lincoln's lips made her brain hazy. "Maybe just one more kiss," she whispered. She pressed her tingling lips back on his, lightly sucking on his bottom lip. Lincoln groaned in response and pulled her into his lap, securing her in place with an arm around her waist. He tasted like a mix of chocolate and peppermint schnapps, an intoxicating combination by itself, but when it was mixed with his lips it was like a drug.

"There's never been a blizzard like that before," he said in between heated kisses. "You should probably just stay."

"You could lend me a coat?" Maria joked as she wrapped an arm around Lincoln's neck, pulling him closer to her and taking her fill of his lips. She had no intention of leaving.

"It's knee-deep out there. I don't think you have the right shoes for it," he told her as he slipped a warm hand up the back of her shirt.

"There's bound to be talk — family, neighbors ..." she said quietly as he started to kiss her jaw and down her neck. "But, I'm very likely to slip and fall, maybe twist another ankle."

Lincoln pulled away and looked in her eyes, concerned as he asked, "What if you got pneumonia and died?" *If something happened to her...* He didn't even want to think about the possibility. He knew they crossed the threshold from friendship into something more, he couldn't imagine what he'd do if she got sick or hurt.

"I was born in the Midwest. I'm pneumonia-proof," Maria whispered jokingly as she leaned back into him. "I've really gotta go, but..."

"It's cold outside," he said as their eyes met. Maria's dark brown eyes warmed his body all the way through. The magnetism between them was so much stronger than lust. He pulled her close as he nuzzled into the crook of her neck before peppering it with kisses and nips.

"My brother is going to be irritated if I'm late," she said before she let the last of her resolve crumble and kissed Lincoln again. He smiled as they kissed, glad he could finally hold her close to him the way he'd always wanted to. They ignored her phone as it rang on the coffee table.

Chlorine Kisses

By M. Williams

Hannah tried not to look too disappointed after getting off yet another water slide. Her grandparents had generously paid for this trip and she didn't want to miss out on the fun because she was too busy pining for a guy who wasn't interested. She'd gotten her Masters for goodness sake, she was supposed to be celebrating.

"What's wrong?" Abby, her favorite cousin, asked. Abby was two years younger than her and had graduated with her bachelor's degree.

In fact, all of the cousins on the trip recently graduated. Tiffany, Sydney, and Nathan from high school, Abby and Connor with a Bachelor's degree, and Hannah, Alex, and Alex's friend David with Masters. The only exception was their thirty-year-old "cool" aunt Liz who was acting as guardian to the younger set of graduates.

"She's still moping because David hasn't paid her any attention," Aunt Liz smirked.

Hannah bristled, "Is he fucking blind and stupid? Here I am practically naked and definitely willing and he just wants to bro out with Alex. It's like Christmas break all over again." Pouting, Hannah crossed her arms under her more than ample chest.

Alex started bringing David around as soon as they became roommates his first year of grad school. And Hannah had been doing her damnedest to get his attention since then. He was the most attractive man she'd ever seen. It wasn't just looks, either. David was smart, funny, and respectful. He made her whole body feel tingly and hot.

"Not naked enough," Abby told her. She grabbed the zipper on the front of Hannah's baby blue swimsuit top and pulled it down about halfway, showing off a considerable amount of cleavage.

Hannah looked down at her overflowing chest and started to protest. "I want to get David's attention, not every creep in the park!"

Nathan, who came up out of nowhere, nodded towards a trio of old guys watching them from a distance. "Hate to break it to you Hannah, but you've had their attention all day."

Hannah glanced over and sighed as the old guys waved at her. "Great. I attract old perverts but not hot young guys I want to attract."

"Incoming," Abby muttered.

Hannah glanced behind her and saw David and Alex emerging from the pool. Discreetly, Hannah fixed her boobs in her swimsuit so they looked perky and tempting, but didn't show every guy in the park her nipples.

Nathan ran off to join Sydney at the drink stand and the trio of women made their way to where their stuff was setting on some chairs. Hannah swayed her hips, trying to draw attention to her plump ass.

Hannah plopped down with a sigh and put her hands behind her head, knowing it made her chest stick out even more. She watched, eyes hidden behind her sunglasses, trying to hide her hungry look as Alex and David came up to where they were sitting. While Alex talked to Aunt Liz about dinner, she saw David sneak a look at her chest. Feeling bold, Hannah unzipped her top a bit more. His eyes darted back, lingering for a moment. He swallowed hard, his Adam's apple bobbing.

"Well I guess me and David will go see if we can't find Connor. Last I saw he was flirting with some lifeguards. Real hot. Nice asses. Right, David?" Alex was asking.

David didn't look away from Hannah's chest as he said "Real nice."

Then, with a shake of his head, the spell was broken and the two went away. Hannah sighed and rolled over onto her stomach so her back could tan. The sun was warm and she was still tired from all the late nights she'd stayed up working on her thesis defense the previous week. Before she knew it, she was starting to doze off.

A while later, Hannah felt herself being shaken by a hand. She muttered a bit and turned over to lay on her back.

She heard someone suck in a breath and mutter "fuck" before she felt a towel drop over her.

"Hannah, please wake up. Your entire tit is out and I'm trying to be a gentleman so Alex won't kill me," David said, his voice husky and close to Hannah's ear.

She blinked slowly and rolled onto her side, propping herself up on her elbow, forgetting entirely about the swimsuit she'd unzipped and the boob David just told her was out. She caught David's eye and he looked like he might have a heart attack.

"Hannah, I'm begging you. Please fix your top." David's eyes were wide and heated and it finally clicked in her fuzzy mind what he said.

"Oh!" She gasped and her hand flew to her chest. She quickly tucked everything in and zipped her top all the way up. David looked both relieved and disappointed.

"Everybody decided to go to a movie. Do you want to go?" David asked.

Hannah scrunched her nose. "What movie?"

"Some horror film." He shrugged.

"No thank you. I hate horror." A shiver raced down her spine.

David half-grinned sheepishly. "So do I. In that case I've been instructed to protect you from creepy weirdos and walk you back to the house when you are ready. Liz said the movie is two hours long and they'll probably get dinner after. She said not to expect them to be back until late tonight."

She blushed and hoped David didn't notice. She knew exactly what her aunt Liz was doing and hoped to God David did not. She probably picked a horror movie intentionally knowing Hannah hated them. Meaning she would either end up terrified and in David's arms at the theater if he liked horror films, or home alone with him if he didn't. She'd have to remember to thank her brilliant aunt later.

"I'm ready to go back to the house if you are," Hannah said, standing from her chair. She suddenly realized her swimsuit was all up in her ass and David was about to get another show when she turned around. *Good*, she thought. She wanted him to look at her. She heard David gulp when she leaned across the chair to grab her beach bag.

"Ready to go?" She asked, straightening.

He nodded, eyes dark. Hannah gladly led the way back to the house they were renting close by.

David was silent as they made their way back to the house while Hannah chattered away. She talked about how that was the nicest nap she'd taken in months, about spotting more than one creeper staring at her cousins, about the weather, about how great her grandparents were. On and on she went until they made it back to the house.

"After you," she said after unlocking the door. She smiled sweetly at David as if she hadn't flashed him her entire tit, by accident, or most of her ass, on purpose. He walked in without argument and Hannah followed. She quickly locked the door behind them and when she turned back around he was staring at her, his eyes intense.

"Must you make everything hard, Hannah?" David sighed and pinched the bridge of his nose.

Hannah smirked. "What exactly did I make hard, David?"

He huffed. "Don't think I don't know what you've been doing all day, all week. Ever since I started coming around with Alex, for that matter."

Hannah picked at her nails, feeling self-conscious all of a sudden. "What have I been doing?" She asked, her voice coming out less confident than she wanted.

"Teasing me." His voice sounded even deeper as he said the words and Hannah shrugged.

"Every man thinks I'm teasing them." she huffed. *If he didn't want her, fine.* She wasn't about to listen to his lecture. "Just because I have big tits doesn't mean I'm a tease."

"The mini skirt at the bar on Alex's birthday was to tease me, the Harley Quinn cosplay at Halloween was for me, and unzipping your top today was for me, too. Don't try to deny it. You make sure I see you, really see you, every time." He came closer, boxing her in by the door. "Every single sexy thing has been for me but your damn cousin made me swear I wouldn't mess with any of his innocent little cousins."

"Well, lucky for you, I'm not so innocent," the words came out in a sultry whisper and Hannah didn't know how she'd pulled it off.

David seemed to be fighting the urge to pull her over his knee. He clenched his hands at his sides and glared at her. "What's that supposed to mean?" he growled.

"I've had sex before," she whispered, suddenly intimidated. He gave off an experienced air. She wondered if she would be good enough to get him off.

David's eyes bore into her, making her nervous.

"It was one guy freshman year of college. I didn't even get off. We only did it like three times. He wasn't inter ..." Hannah rambled, but cut off suddenly at the look in David's eyes. She wasn't sure if it was anger or jealousy she was seeing, but whatever it was, it was hot.

"He was clearly an idiot," David muttered the words as he leaned even closer.

Hannah was breathless with nerves and excitement. "You think so?"

"Not only are you brilliantly smart, funny, and one of the nicest people I've ever met, you've got more curves than any woman I've ever seen. If I ever managed to get you in my bed, I guarantee you I would pull out every trick I know to keep you in it." David was inches away from her now and Hannah's breath was coming fast.

"Is that a promise?" She leaned toward him, waiting to see if he would close the gap.

"Alex will kill me," he muttered.

"Alex isn't here." Clearly, that was all the convincing he needed because his lips finally crashed into hers roughly, his tongue slipping into her mouth. The faint taste of pool water lingered on his lips. His tongue stroked against hers and sent heat straight to her core.

"Let's take this to my room," she said, pulling away.

"You sure? I don't want you to feel like I'm pressuring you." David's hands gripped her waist and she could feel his erection against her.

"I've been waiting two years for this." Hannah felt bold all of a sudden and moved against him. "Come on," she whispered, her voice starting to sound whiny and desperate. "Show me you aren't all talk."

Before she knew it, David picked her up and was carrying her to his room, not hers.

"Wait," she gasped as his lips attacked her neck. "I've got protection in my room."

"So do I," He mumbled, and kept walking.

"I thought you said ..."

"Hannah, a man can hope," he said. David's voice in her ear went straight to her already wet pussy. "I can only take so much teasing."

When they finally made it to his room, David dropped her on the bed. Hannah yelped in surprise. He made quick work of rummaging through his bag, pulling out a condom and walking confidently over to Hannah.

He looked at her seriously. "If you decide at any time you want me to stop you tell me. I don't want to do anything to make you uncomfortable or hurt you."

Hannah was surprised by how hot she found his little speech. Although consent was really the bare minimum a man could do, she was touched by how hard he was trying to be respectful when she desperately wanted him to have his wicked way with her.

"David," she said, her voice coming out husky and breathless. "I love that chivalry isn't dead, but my pussy is literally aching for you to pay her a little attention."

David's eyes darken again, "Did the dumbass ever go down on

you?"

Hannah's breath quickened, "Once. Halfheartedly."

"Unacceptable." David undid the ties on both sides of her swim bottoms and removed them before pulling her to the edge of the bed. Kneeling in front of her, he pressed a hot kiss to the inside of her thigh.

Hannah suddenly felt nervous. She'd only been intimate a handful of times. What if she wasn't any good? What if David didn't like her? What if?

David's tongue flicked over Hannah, lapping her up.

Hannah's mind could hardly keep up with what she was feeling, but her body didn't have any trouble reacting. The deeper his tongue stroked her the wetter she got. Heat pooled in her belly and her muscles tightened. She quivered and David gripped her thighs to keep her still. It didn't take long for an orgasm to rush through her like a freight train.

Next thing Hannah knew, David was on top of her. She didn't remember laying down but she wasn't about to complain about this arrangement. While the aftershocks of pleasure wracked her body, David latched on to one of her nipples and sucked. Hannah swore her soul left her completely.

"Fuck, David," she moaned loudly. She had never been worked like this before. When she glanced down to see he left a hickey on her boob, she about came again.

"David, fuck. Fuck." She wanted him inside her badly but couldn't manage a full sentence while he was sucking her tit like his life depended on it.

Then his hands touched her all over. He played with her boob, massaging it and rubbing her nipples with his palms until they turned into hard buds. He grabbed her ass roughly, squeezing it in his large hands. Then he slowly slid two long fingers inside her, his thumb pressing against her clit.

Hannah barely let out a little gasp before she was coming again. She could feel David's smirk against her neck as he continued to rub the special spot inside of her.

"What do you want, Hannah?" His voice was a husky whisper that nearly sent her over the age.

"Fu—," she tried to get the words out but then he rubbed her clit again and all she could do was moan.

"You have the most wonderful body. All it needs is the right touch," he said, his voice husky as he nibbled her ear.

"David," she responded in a breathy moan, "Ple-please."

She wasn't even sure how she managed to get the word out but she hoped he got the message. When his fingers stopped moving, she almost cried.

"Hannah, do you still want to do this? You can say no." David looked at her seriously.

"Yes," she moaned as she ground against him. Her heart hammered. Through his swim trunks she could tell he was big.

He stopped her hips with one hand and somehow managed to wiggle out of his shorts with the other. When Hannah saw how big he was she worried for a minute he wouldn't fit inside her, but she desperately wanted him to.

David leaned down close to her ear. "It's been a while since you've had sex and based off your expression, he wasn't this big." David smirked before getting serious again. "If something hurts you tell me."

She was so desperate for more of him that she nodded her head and waited.

Hannah hissed as her body stretched to accommodate his size. David whispered sweetly in her ear and planted little kisses on her jaw and neck. She was so distracted by how caring he was being, she almost didn't notice he'd slid all the way into her until his breathing hitched. Suddenly she realized how full she was. Her body clenched around him and she couldn't help but lift her hips to meet his.

They both groaned as he thrust even deeper. Hannah felt as if he was filling up her entire body. After a moment he started to pull out and Hannah's eyes rolled back.

"Fuck," David muttered. "So tight."

Hannah moaned. She trembled as he moved in and out, gripping the sheets tightly and wrapping her legs around his waist.

"Wanna try something else?" David whispered in her ear.

Hannah was so lost in her own pleasure and so close to coming again that she'd try anything to get there. She nodded absent-mindedly and clung to him.

"Roll over," he commanded.

He eased off of her so she could roll over to her stomach. Her body was shaking so much she could hardly manage the move, but he helped, pulling her ass up so she was on her knees with her face down in the sheets.

When he entered her again it was indescribable. Pleasure shot through her, making her moan. Her body didn't know what to do with all the sensations he was inspiring in her. She quivered and when he started to rub her clit again she knew it was game over. Her orgasm tore through her and she sobbed, it felt so good.

"Fuck, Hannah," David gritted out through his teeth as he continued to pump into her a few more times before pulling out.

Hannah felt him move away for a minute before he was back. He rolled her over and looked at her with concern in his eyes.

"Are you okay? Did I hurt you?"

Hannah suddenly realized she was crying. Her breathing was so labored that all she could do was shake her head.

"It's okay." David climbed into bed with her and pulled her close so her head rested on his chest.

"Too much?" he asked, stroking her hair.

"So good," she finally managed to stammer out. Her whole body was still convulsing and her mind was in a haze.

David didn't try to ask her anything else, he stroked her hair and quietly talked to her until she managed to come down from her high.

"You have such a beautiful and responsive body, Hannah. It's expressive just like you. Crying is okay as long as you aren't hurt. I admit I've never had that reaction before. If you hurt, let me know and I'll do my best to fix it. Once you calm down, I bet a hot bath would be good for you."

As Hannah came down, she started to feel drowsy. She'd never orgasmed like that before and it both exhausted and relaxed her. David's quiet voice and his hand rubbing her hair lulled her back to sleep.

When she woke later, the room was much darker. One of David's arms was around her still, holding her close. He was watching a movie on his phone, the volume so low she could hardly hear it.

She shifted in the bed and he glanced down at her with a smile.

"Hey, sleepy head. Have a good nap?" he asked as he brushed her hair out of her face.

"Yeah." She stretched her aching muscles. "What time is it?"

"Six. Alex texted me a little while ago and said they waited to see a later showing of the movie so they probably won't be back until about nine." David shifted so Hannah was on his lap.

"How are you feeling?" His hands rested on her bare waist, reminding her she was naked.

"A little achy," she admitted. "I could definitely go for a bubble bath."

David smiled. "One bubble bath coming right up."

Hannah climbed off David and wobbled as her feet hit the floor. Her legs felt like they were made of jello.

David smirked. "Did I give it to you that good?"

Hannah shook her head. "You have no idea."

He stood up and Hannah was a little disappointed to see he'd put shorts on at some point. He held her waist to steady her and kissed her lips gently.

"The tub in my bathroom is big enough for both of us," she whispered.

"Your bathroom it is then."

Hannah squealed in surprise as he scooped her up and carried her across the house to the bathroom she was sharing with Aunt Liz and Abby. The big jacuzzi tub looked heavenly in the middle of the room. Hannah couldn't wait to get in and turn the jets on.

David sat her down on the counter and she watched as he went around readying the bath. She took the time to check him out again, because lord he was beautiful. The muscles in his back rippled as he turned on the water and put down the stopper. He brushed his light brown hair out of his face and turned towards her, offering a small smile.

"This is an awful big tub. You sure you don't mind if I join you?" He asked.

Hannah smiled. "I would love for you to join me, although i'm not sure I can handle anymore sex at the moment."

He flushed. "Of course. I just meant—"

"I'm teasing, David." Hannah was intrigued by this bashful side of him. She'd never seen him like this before.

He came over to her and put his arms around her waist. "Have I mentioned I think you are beautiful?"

She blushed. "Really?"

He nodded and pressed a soft kiss to her nose. "Absolutely breathtaking."

Before she could pull him in for a real kiss, David turned back towards the tub. He tested the temperature, and tossed in one of her fizzy bath bombs.

"Ready for a dip?" he asked as he came back over to pick her up from the counter.

She nodded and wrapped her arms around his neck as he carried her over to the massive tub. The water was warm and felt great against her skin as she eased in. Her muscles began to relax immediately. David stripped out of his shorts and climbed in behind her. Hannah went to lean back against him but he stopped her. Before she could protest he started massaging her neck and shoulders.

Hannah sighed in contentment. "Have I mentioned you have the world's greatest hands?"

"I don't think you have," he answered with a smile in his voice. "Maybe you should tell me," he teased.

"You have the most amazing hands. The world's greatest. Like, I think they could be the eighth wonder of the world." Hannah's eyes drifted shut as he worked out all the tension in her shoulders. Between the twelve hour drive, the water slides, and the sex, she was definitely in need of this.

"I didn't go too hard on you today, did I?" David asked.

"Definitely not."

They sat quietly for a few minutes while he massaged her shoulders before he finally pulled her back against his chest. He took one of her hands and started to massage it.

"Can I ask you a question?" Hannah's voice came out much more timid than she wanted.

"Sure."

"Why did you ask so many times for consent?" she asked, quickly adding, "I'm not complaining! It seemed like you thought I might change my mind and be afraid you wouldn't stop."

His hands continued to rub slow circles up her arm. "I've seen first hand how shitty guys can be. Alex liked going to frat parties even though we weren't in a frat. I tried my best to help any girl I could from a guy who didn't understand the word 'no' but I'm only one guy."

Hannah thought about it for a minute. She pictured David coming to the rescue of more than one drunk or desperate college girl. She decided she liked that idea.

"So you're like a real life Superman?" she said as she looked back at him over her shoulder.

David smiled and kissed her forehead, "Can I make a confession?"

Hannah nodded, wondering what he could possibly have to confess.

"When I first met you, you terrified me. I'd never met a woman like you before. You were powerful, and smart, and demanding, and you practically oozed sex appeal," he told her. "You seemed like a sex godess, like some type of dominatrix who could bring a man to his knees with nothing but a look. It was intimidating."

Hannah laughed, "Sorry to disappoint, but I'm about as scary as a kitten."

He hugged her tighter. "I'm so glad your cousins went to see a horror film today."

Hannah blushed. "That may or may not be because Aunt Liz knew I, uh—"

"Wanted a little action?" David teased.

Hannah's blush deepend. "Her and Abby unzipped my top."

David lifted her chin so they were looking eye-to-eye and said in a gravelly voice, "Thank them for me."

Then his mouth enveloped hers and before she knew it she was straddling his lap. They fooled around for a bit in the tub before finally getting out. After dressing, they met back in the main area to scrounge up some dinner.

"How about we order a pizza?" Hannah suggested. "We passed a Papa Johns on the way into the resort."

"Sounds good." David pulled out his phone. "I'll call it in."

Hannah smiled and went to the kitchen to find something to drink. She found a bottle of rosé in the fridge with a note from Aunt Liz. It read: "Try not to make any babies. I'm not ready to be a great aunt! -Aunt Liz"

Hannah shook her head and pulled the bottle out of the fridge. She had no clue how her aunt managed to go get wine without anyone noticing. Her cousins weren't alcoholics but when it was available, they drank wine like it was water.

After popping the cork, Hannah grabbed two plastic cups and headed back to the living room. David was still trying to order their dinner but he smiled when he saw her.

If there was one thing Hannah loved, it was David's smile. It was always so genuine. She loved that it was a little crooked and revealed dimples on each cheek. Combined with his full lips and scruffy face, he was swoon-worthy.

"Pizza should be here in about fifteen minutes," David said, taking the bottle of wine from her. He read the note she'd forgotten to remove and blushed. "Your aunt Liz never ceases to surprise me."

Hannah laughed. "She comes by it honestly. The stories I've heard from grandma's youth are startlingly similar to the stuff I've witnessed Aunt Liz do."

"I don't even want to know," he said as he shook his head, a wry grin on his lips.

"So, fifteen minutes, huh?" Hannah asked, sliding her hand down his chest.

He smirked and backed her towards the counter. In one swift move he placed her on the cool countertop, her legs around his waist.

His lips crashed down on hers in a kiss that made her toes curl. Soon they were both topless and panting as David's hand found its way into her panties.

They got so caught up in each other they didn't hear the door open. They did, however, hear a voice loudly exclaim:

"What the fuck are you doing?"

They broke apart quickly. Alex stood in the doorway, Aunt Liz and her cousins behind him. The younger cousins gaped. Aunt Liz and Abby grinned. Alex looked like he could kill. Boy were they in trouble.

Persephone Jayne's writes for the child inside herself and the adult who never forgot what magic childhood was. You can find her military kids series, Base Brats, at all online retailers.

~ In 2013 Neil Gaiman embarked on his Calendar of Tales project. I didn't learn about it until 2019. I looked up his old tweets, made a ton of notes and embarked on my own calendar of tales. *Leap Day* was my very own *February Tale*, inspired by answers to his original tweets.

Juniper Lea has just begun her publishing journey. *Unknown Caller* is her debut publication.

~ As a preschool teacher by trade, I often felt like being called into a war zone when I was asked to cover a shift. I often felt as if I was preparing for battle, donning my armor, for any given day. Once my own kids were born, I 'retired', passing on my knowledge to the next generation of fighters.

Zain Patton is a natural storyteller even though he refuses to write. He resides in Connecticut where he has just started high school and majored in languaging hence his amazing writing skills.

~A few years ago we went to the Balloon Festival in New Mexico. We read about the first passengers on a hot air ballon, they were in fact a duck, a rooster, and a sheep. My Mom wondered what that looked like so I started to tell the story. Then she ruined my life by making me write it down. Now, here we are.

B.A. McRae is a radically optimistic author who has been pursuing her passion for writing since 2008, she resides in the tundra of Wisconsin, where she spends her time being groovy and drinking coffee.

~ I'm not entirely sure what sparked the exact inspiration for this story, but quite honestly after I wrote that first sentence the essence of that main character and her story completely flooded me and took over. Writing this story felt like such a rush, I couldn't be happier with the doors it has opened.

Donna Taylor saw way too many scary movies when she was far too little to see them and now is a little obsessed with all things horror. She's the Watty Award-winning author of BLOOD ON THE BOARDWALK, a young adult horror comedy novel that's the first in a series, and enjoys finding ways to creep out her readers. Find her on TikTok, Instagram, and Wattpad @dtaylorbooks, on Twitter at @dmtaylorbooks, and at her website, www.imaginewrite.net.

~ *Little Black Box* is the result of a story prompt on Wattpad and my need to write something spooky for a slightly younger crowd. I have a deep love for Alvin Schwartz's Scary Stories and Jonathan Maberry's Don't Turn Out the Lights, an homage to the same. Consider this story a tip of the hat.

~ *Bloom* takes my not-so-irrational fear of the woods and turns it up to an eleven. Set in my home state of Connecticut and drawing from the creepy history of Cornwall, I twisted it into my own urban legend with far bloodier results.

Erica Jackson creates scenes of glorious chaos and snarky love interests in worlds both fantastical and familiar from her hometown of Summerville, South Carolina, when she isn't binging anime, obsessing over fictional men, or making tiktoks, that is. Although she's been a published author since she was fifteen, releasing her works of fiction into the wilds of voracious readers is relatively new.

~ My hyperactive imagination made quarantine a writer's wonderland. Being bored during the pandemic, thinking of my late grandmother, and my apparent addiction to mischievous fae love interests gave birth to my short story. Being a part of this project has been a fairytale come true.

Melanie Forrest is an independent author from Nova Scotia, Canada. After a long hiatus filled with having young children and a demanding job, she rediscovered her love of writing in late 2020 and has since penned six novels. The first book in her YA dystopian trilogy will be published in early 2022. When not writing, Melanie enjoys reading and music.

~ Both *Departure* and *Outcasts* were born from a TikTok short story challenge (a name, a season, a place, a random object) to bust out of a writer's block and flex my creative muscles in different genres. *Departure* is free standing, but *Outcasts* is destined to be a middle grade fantasy novel or even perhaps a series!

Carmilla Voiez was born in Bristol but lives in Scotland. She was weaned on a diet of horror, and early influences include Graham Masterton, Brian Lumley, Clive Barker, the romance of Hammer

Horror and the visceral violence of the first wave of video nasties. Combined with the threnodies of eighties post-punk, these influences created a creature of darkness: a lifelong Goth who is pansexual and passionate about intersectional feminism and human rights, and an autistic introvert who expresses herself best through the written word. Her books are both extraordinarily personal and universally challenging. As Jef Rouner of Houston Press once said - "You do not read her books, you survive them." Carmilla's bibliography includes the Starblood four novel series, The Venus Virus, the Starblood and Psychonaut graphic novels, The Ballerina and the Revolutionary, Broken Mirror and Other Morbid Tales, and she co-wrote Our Fearful Roots with Faith Marlow. Her short stories have been included in Zombie Punks Fuck Off (Clash Books), Slice Girls (Mocha Memoirs Press), Elements of Horror: Water (Red Cape), and Sirens Call Magazine. Her website and blog can be found at www.carmillavoiez.com

~ Both *Good News* and *The Magpie* were written as assignments and submitted as part of my creative writing degree. The stories share the theme of womanhood and mother/daughter relationships but diverge in style. *Good News* was written around the idea of a stranger at the door. We all dread the unexpected caller, afraid that a slick salesperson will sell us something we don't need. It was written during a recent Covid Lockdown when I was trying to figure out what made people take unnecessary risks. I explored this idea and added a slice of Cosmic Horror. *The Magpie* was inspired by my ex, who I continued to love despite continual betrayals. I considered that relationship through the gaze of an adult daughter and how my submissive naivety might affect her future relationships with men.

Melanie Sovran Wolfe was born in Kansas City, MO in 1971, and began writing fiction at the age of 38 while living in Oklahoma. Her frustrations with her culture unconsciously bled into her novels and set the tone and uniqueness for all her books. After 13 years of writing fiction, she wrote her last story The TikTok Angel and transitioned to screenwriting. Her screenplays have received Honorable Mentions and were selected for eight film festivals. Melanie lives in the magical Coastal Mountains of Maine with her BFF, two teens (she has two adult children as well), and four crazy cats. Learn more at www.melanieswolfe.com.

~ I came up with the idea for *The TikTok Angel* story when I was making TikTok videos and thinking about how this could be a place where my kids could find me long after I was gone; a virtual memorial, if you will, for them and for those who come after them. I wrote the story in less than a day and didn't really plan on publishing it at the time. But, alas, as fate would have it, my last short story would make it into an anthology. A lovely goodbye to a hard and long writing career.

Luke Swanson is a fiction writer who was raised on a steady diet of stories. He's a member of the Oklahoma Writers' Federation, and he lives with his wife in Oklahoma City. He has published three novels: one mystery, one action, and one tragi-comedy.

~ I love history. It's full of great beauty and triumph…as well as unspeakable pain and tragedy. *Black and Brown* is based on the true event known as the Night of the long Knives, and I hope it demonstrates that hatred takes no prisoners. There are no winners on the side of prejudice.

Jocelyn Minton is first and foremost a poet. Her love for literature and writing in general has led her to her first formal publication in Mood Reader. Jocelyn lives in Dayton, Ohio and is studying Creative Writing and German at Miami University. When she is not writing, she can be found reading, singing along to her favorite music, playing video games, and drinking coffee. You can connect with Jocelyn on TikTok at: @jocelyn.reading or on Instagram at: @jocelyn.minton.

~A poem I had written struck inspiration for a longer narrative. I wanted to discover who was behind the letter I had come up with, and why they were no longer there.

Francis Alex Cooke is a multi-genre author living in Cape Breton, Nova Scotia, Canada. Within his vividly descriptive worlds, he pens stories with contemplative characters one can't help but laugh at, love with, or mourn for. A proud dad to his son Ayden, when not writing fiction, Francis can be found at his day job or writing poetry or music.

~At the beginning of a global pandemic and tethered only to a voice on a telephone, I was challenged to write a story about a pair of awkward kids that never really were.

Sonya Lawson (she/her/they) is a recovering academic currently writing fantasy, light and dark, in a variety of subgenres. Some might say she switches it up too much, but her stories have at least one common characteristic — sassy, intelligent, articulate women trying to do the best they can in whatever world they inhabit. While she remains a rural Kentuckian at heart, she currently lives in the Pacific Northwest where she fills her days with writing, editing, reading, walking old forests, and watching sitcoms or horror films. You can find more information about current projects and upcoming releases at www.sonyalawson.com.

~*Illuminating Manuscripts* takes some influence from the idea of the tree of knowledge and Lovecraft mythos. My years of driving through the flat and barren farmlands of Ohio while working as an academic at OSU also had a hand in this. Mainly, though, I wrote it as an experiment, an early test in how to blend midwestern sensibilities, Lovecraftian images, and academic snark for a future urban fantasy novel project.

Monica Misho-Grems is a young and budding author from Portland, Oregon. As a child, she split her time between many hobbies, including dance, reading, and writing. At a young age she showed a deep passion for literature - both reading it and writing it - but it wasn't until her teen years that she began to dream of doing it professionally. She got her start writing more serious content by writing fanfictions on various message boards late in her teen years and early twenties. Once she became more comfortable, with herself and her writing, she began dabbling in more erotic literature, and eventually found the style that we see. Nowadays, she lives in Southeast Portland with her husband, John, their three daughters, and her father. She is a full-time mother, wife, daughter, friend, and Clinical Trainer for a local OB/GYN company; she hopes to add "writer" to the full-time mix.

Karen Ruhman is involved in physical therapy and research, by day. By night, she enthusiastically brings the beauty of the horror aesthetic to life through crafting and cooking. This is her first published fiction, and second authorship.

~ I remember being eight and watching the sunset over my elementary school, and thinking there must be another version of the world in front of me, hidden somewhere in the long shadows. That little girl grew up to keep asking questions, and sometimes, write down the answers that I found.

Veronique Manfredini was born and raised in Bedonia, Italy. Now she calls New Jersey home, though she returns to the B&B her parents run in the mountains of Parma as often as she can. She graduated from Brookdale Community College with degrees in English and Business Administration. She is currently pursuing an undergraduate degree in Creative Writing at Columbia University's School of General Studies. As a writer, she is a three-time NaNoWriMo winner and is working on five projects. Her preferred genres to write in are fantasy and romance. You can find her online at veroniquemanfredini.com and on Instagram, @VeroniqueManfredini and TikTok, @TheBookishGodmother.

~ During the summer of 2021, I wrote *Holy Ransom Demands!* as an in-class assignment for a How to Write Funny class. It was a timed exercise shared with the class, but it's probably my favorite piece by far and it was the most fun I'd had writing in a while.

Carrie Godfrey is a queer romance author living in southern Arizona with their partner, two kids, and six cats. When not writing or working on their bachelor's degree, they enjoy watching everything Star Wars, playing board games, and spending time with friends and family.

Monroe Wildrose has been stuck between the pages of books since the fifth grade when her father bought her a copy of Eragon by Christopher Paloni. She makes her home at the base of the Sierra Nevada Mountains where she and the loves of her life, her husband and two rowdy toddlers, are fortunate enough to have Lake Tahoe at their fingertips.

Stephanie Houseal is a fiction author, currently residing in Georgia with her husband, two children, and mother-in-law. Apart from writing, she enjoys deep conversations with her husband, going to the park with her kids, reading, singing in the bathroom, listening to music for story inspiration, and being involved in community theater.

~ Whether it's a prompt, picture, song, or dream, my imagination flows like a river through my mind. *Imaginary* and *Abandoned* are both examples of the challenge of conveying what I was given by visualizing the story and then spilling it on the page. It's messy, but there is always some beauty in the chaos.

Jeni Lee had already lived in Arizona and West Virginia before she was nine, but was fortunate enough to arrive in St. Louis, Missouri just in time to see Star Wars at the theater the week it was released. Her love for Sci-Fi, Fantasy, and the supernatural was born in that moment. With Philip K. Dick, Edgar Rice Burroughs, Sir Arthur Conan Doyle, Diana Gabaldon, and Jane Austen among her favorite authors, she has never been lacking for amazing inspiration on a variety of topics. She has been writing for the last 25 years, but she has always looked for the next "what if?" Jeni lives in St. Louis with her two cats and one parrot.

~ My purpose with this story is to bring stroke awareness. Here are some things to remember:

F-A-S-T. Facial drooping, arm weakness, slurred speech, and time. This acronym is a fantastic way to quickly assess what may be happening to you or your loved ones. Time is crucial to getting the appropriate treatment as quickly as possible. Don't hesitate!

Call 9-1-1 instead of taking someone to the hospital is critical. When EMTs know they are responding to a potential stroke, certain steps can be taken on-site and on the way to the hospital to help stem the tide of damage. They also can call ahead and have stroke response teams prepped and ready to take over, making more effective use of a limited window for most successful treatments.

Physical Therapy Techniques are constantly evolving and even becoming more intense, in some instances, affecting drastic recovery times and rate of responsiveness in patients.

Strokes can be preventable. Nearly 80% of strokes are preventable with regular doctor visits, healthy eating, lifestyle change, and increased physical fitness, you may be able to prevent stroke

For more information about ischemic and hemorrhagic strokes, you can visit www.stroke.org.

Anne Marie Brown is a children's book author and lyrical poet based in Denver, Colorado. She spends her time hiking, skiing, and chasing after two small children.

Lucas William Barnes born in Texas and raised in southern Illinois. He is a happily married father of 3, Navy Veteran, and currently work in the department of corrections. He has several side hustles from selling candy to performing media transfers from old tapes to a thumb drive. He has always wanted to write a book and this is the closest he had ever come to having any of his work published. he is hoping this is his first step in the right direction to one day publishing a book of his own.

Kai Mathis started their writing journey 7 years ago when they made their son do a writing project and he convinced them to do one too.

~ I am unsure where exactly *Julia* came from, one day half the story just came tumbling out when doing a writing exercise. Instead of turning it into a novel, this short story was the outcome.

April Berry is a romance author born and raised in Georgia. She still resides there with her husband, son, and daughter. When she's not creating fun stories with happy endings, she loves to bake, read, and sneak off to her favorite winery with her friends! She also loves snuggles with her various fur babies and binge watching series!

Amanda Fernandes writes horror and queer stories in Toronto. She immigrated there from Brazil, where she was born.

Christina E. Patrick is a fantasy author living in Arkansas with her cat and writing companion Rogue. When not writing or reading, she enjoys playing open world video games or running Dungeons and Dragons games as both a Dungeon Master and player.

Elizabeth Willsea is an explorative author living in Kalamazoo, Michigan. She currently lives with her family and cuddly cat, Aere Berry Banana Boat. When she's not writing emotional poems or intense worlds of magic, she's creating journals or playing with two-year-old's at the day care where she works.

Erin Slegaitis-Smith is a fantasy author from Upstate New York in the Adirondack mountains. When she's not teaching, drinking far too much tea, or writing, she enjoys attending Ren Faires and playing D&D.

Javier Garay is passionate about unleashing the natural curiosity children possess. He left a 12-year career on Wall Street to start a business that taught STEM-focused programs and now writes children's books. When he's not exploring the world, he is in

Philadelphia conducting experiments and making a mess in the kitchen with his wife and three children.

~ *Make a Grown Up Read This* is the first story I ever wrote. I like to say that it was inspired by The Book With No Pictures, but in reality I just got tired of reading that book. I started making up bedtime stories for my kids, which ultimately led to the creation of The Blocks Books series. My books are STEM-filled adventures that also promote cultural awareness and you can find them at all online retailers.

Jiya Kaye is a Fantasy/Sci-fi author currently living in Boston, MA. She started making up story ideas whenever she couldn't sleep, thanks to her insomnia from college. Eventually the stories were too much for her to handle by herself; so, she's making it everyone's problem. Now, you get to read her musings of Fae in battle, dragons, space exploration, and taking down corrupt dystopian governments. When she's not writing, or on social media, you can find Jiya obsessing over MCU, Supernatural, and Doctor Who. Yes, this is her introverted way of saying, 'Yes! Please come talk to me about these topics!'

Kata Čuić lives in Pittsburgh, PA with her husband and three teens. No one told her life was gonna be this way. She writes everything from angst-filled YA series to standalone rom-coms and has been known to dabble in a bit of paranormal on the side.

Lynn Lipinski is a writer who channels an overactive imagination into fictional worlds where justice rules, karma is real and the good person comes out on top. Her second book, "God of the Internet," was named to Kirkus Reviews Best Indie Books of 2016 list. She's "TikTok famous" for throwing her three thriller books at Disney Studios and Warner Bros, but is still waiting for that movie deal.

M. Williams has been a writer her whole life but is only just now venturing out into the publishing world. Chlorine Kisses is her first published piece and she is thrilled to see her work in writing! In the future she hopes to publish spicy New Adult romance novels. In the meantime, you can find her curled up with a good book doing lots of "research" for her own books.

Nicole Zelniker (she/her) is a writer, activist, and managing editor at The Nasiona. She is the author of several books, including *Letters I'll Never Send* and *Until We Fall*.

Rethley Gil Chiru is a Panamanian American writer and artist currently dwelling in San Antonio. They studied film and literature at Western Carolina University and they create stories about what it's like to be a human being living on a random rock spinning in the ether.

Shanti Leonard grew up in a tiny town in the mountains of Northern California, riding bikes and sleds, and playing in the forest surrounding his house. Many people who live in his hometown claim some sort of experience with the supernatural. He remains skeptical... with unexplained experiences of his own.

~Amanda Palmer posted a picture on social media of her son, Ash, and her husband, Neil Gaiman. She wrote, "Caption this" above it. The picture was of a boy and his father on, what looked like, a rocky beach surrounded by natural stone walls. Neil is looking at something that Ash has in his hands, but we can't quite see what it is. And Neil is saying...something. So I commented: "So this is where you get all your ideas, Daddy? This one seems so small...", "Ah, yes, but the secret is... they're all like that in the beginning." Then I stopped...and in a brief, but vivid, flash of inspiration opened Word. It came quickly, and I had trouble keeping up with it, but after about 20 minutes it was finished. I wasn't sure what it was or where it would fit in the world. It was so short and didn't follow any storytelling conventions. No conflict really. No plot. No antagonist. Just a moment. But I liked it. It was weird and sweet. And it floated just beyond what we recognize as our reality. When I saw the call for entries I went to my computer. I was going to submit a different story for this collection, but when I turned on my computer this one was giving me puppy dog eyes from my desktop. So I gave it a chance to live. I'm glad I did and I hope you like it. But if you don't, at least it won't take up too much of your time.

Lightning Source UK Ltd.
Milton Keynes UK
UKHW012205140322
400052UK00004B/979